"I DON'T THINK I CAN LET YOU GO SO EASILY . . ."

When Jacelyn glanced down to where the pistols lay on the top of the basket she held in her hand, he smiled, teeth white in the moonlight. "Terrorized by highwaymen, threatened within an inch of my life, deprived of my dinner. Yes, I think I'm owed some restitution, wouldn't you say so, Miss Trevaine?"

"Yes, my lord," was Jacelyn's whispered response.

"What's that my girl, not used to paying for your crimes?"

"No, my lord," meekly.

"Ah, in that case, I won't demand too high a price. Perhaps just a kiss?" And he stood there, his arm negligently across her shoulder, waiting expectantly.

After a moment's indecision, Jacelyn stood on tiptoe and darted forward, quickly brushing the side of his mouth with hers.

"No, no, you'll have to do better than that. That was not even dustman's wages, much less an officer's. Come, little sparrow, let me show you."

He pulled her to him and bent his head to hers, his lips very soft and gentle on her mouth . . .

D0054588

THE BEST OF REGENCY ROMANCES

AN IMPROPER COMPANION   (2691, $3.95)
by Karla Hocker
At the closing of Miss Venable's Seminary for Young
Ladies school, mistress Kate Elliott welcomed the invitation to be Liza Ashcroft's chaperone for the Season at
Bath. Little did she know that Miss Ashcroft's father, the
handsome widower Damien Ashcroft would also enter her
life. And not as a passive bystander or dutiful dad.

WAGER ON LOVE   (2693, $2.95)
by Prudence Martin
Only a rogue like Nicholas Ruxart would choose a bride on
the basis of a careless wager. And only a rakehell like Nicholas would then fall in love with his betrothed's grey-eyed
sister! The cynical viscount had always thought one blushing miss would suit as well as another, but the unattainable
Jane Sommers soon proved him wrong.

LOVE AND FOLLY   (2715, $3.95)
by Sheila Simonson
To the dismay of her more sensible twin Margaret, Lady
Jean proceeded to fall hopelessly in love with the silver-
tongued, seditious poet, Owen Davies—and catapult her
entire family into social ruin . . . Margaret was used to
gentlemen falling in love with vivacious Jean rather than
with her—even the handsome Johnny Dyott whom she se-
cretly adored. And when Jean's foolishness led her into the
arms of the notorious Owen Davies, Margaret knew she
could count on Dyott to avert scandal. What she didn't
know, however was that her sweet sensibility was exerting a
charm all its own.

*Available wherever paperbacks are sold, or order direct from the
Publisher. Send cover price plus 50¢ per copy for mailing and
handling to Zebra Books, Dept. 2850, 475 Park Avenue South,
New York, N.Y. 10016. Residents of New York, New Jersey and
Pennsylvania must include sales tax. DO NOT SEND CASH.*

Rake's Ransom

BARBARA METZGER

ZEBRA BOOKS
KENSINGTON PUBLISHING CORP.

All the characters and events portrayed in this story are
fictitious.

ZEBRA BOOKS

are published by

Kensington Publishing Corp.
475 Park Avenue South
New York, NY 10016

First Zebra Books printing: December 1989.

Printed in the United States of America

*To Stacy and Jeri,
my two favorite nieces,
with love*

1

"By all that is holy, Trevaine, you've got to do something about that daughter of yours!" If complexion were a barometer of feelings, Squire George Bottwick was in a raging gale of a mood. His round face as red as the scarlet hunt jacket he wore, he stomped into the library of Treverly Hall and pounded on his friend's desk. "It's unlawful, unlady-like, and . . . and unEnglish," he sputtered, the last being the worst, in his view.

Lord Trevaine carefully placed a marker in the book he was reading, laid it gently on the side of the desk farthest from the Squire and, looking up, settled the spectacles on his nose. "Good day, George. I didn't hear you come in."

"Didn't hear me? Didn't hear me?" roared his guest. "And I suppose you didn't hear the riot and ruckus outside your front door, not an hour past?"

"Why no, I was studying this passage here. . . ." He waved a thin hand in the book's general direction. "Quite interesting. You see—"

"No, blast it, Elliot, it's your daughter you should

be seeing to, not some demned book. I know I ain't bookish, but anyone can tell you the chit can't keep haring around the countryside, riding astride like a boy—"

"She is only seventeen, and it's safer that way."

"That's what you said at fourteen, and fifteen, and sixteen. Man, she's not a child anymore, to be out with nary a groom."

"Come, George, nothing is going to happen to her in our own neighbourhood, and she does have her dog for companion."

"It's not *her* safety I'm concerned with! And you call that monster a dog! Hellhound more like. Misbegotten whelp of a—"

"Irish wolfhound, actually, for the most part."

"Aye, part Irish revenge on the English, and part devil. It's a pretty pair you've set loose on us, Trevaine, a ragtag hoyden and a barn-sized bristle brush with fangs. Do you know what they've done now? Do you even care? Look at me, Trevaine, just look!"

Squire was still storming around the small room, brandishing his riding whip at a bust of poor blind Homer and challenging the neat stacks of books. His face was still red and his waistcoat, already straining to meet across his more than ample girth, was in danger of surrendering the cause, with all his huffing and puffing. The whole ensemble, in fact, was mudspattered and wet, with spots, stains and scuff marks. Fox one, locals zero? No, there had to be more to it, Lord Trevaine ruefully acknowledged. There always was, when his daughter Jacelyn was involved. He gestured Squire to the leather seat facing his, while he reached for the cut-glass decanter of

8

fine French brandy he kept on the side table. This was not the first time he had entertained his friend in such a fashion, and he well knew the delaying tactics to let the storm of Squire's anger blow itself out. While his friend sipped and mopped at his damp brow with a handkerchief, Lord Trevaine steepled his fingers and considered how times like this made him miss his wife more than ever. She had been dead almost ten years now, leaving him the sole raising of their daughter, a sunbeam in his darkened life. Jacelyn was bright and happy and lively and loving, everything her mother would have approved. Perhaps she was a trifle high-spirited, her father admitted, but that was to be expected in a girl surrounded only by doting servants. The rough edges would smooth out in time, he was sure. After all, she was ever kind and tenderhearted. The last thought brought Lord Trevaine back to the present, and his present company.

He cleared his throat. "I take it this has something to do with, er, fox hunting?"

Squire Bottwick sputtered, choking on his swallow. "Were you even aware there was to be a hunt this morning, then?"

"Actually, no. But by your dress . . . and discomposure . . ." Lord Trevaine hurriedly refilled the squire's glass.

He sympathised with the Squire, truly he did, for he knew that what books were to him, fox hunting was to George Bottwick. Squire did not read much more than farming journals, and Lord Trevaine's uncertain health kept him from the saddle, yet they each respected the other's ways. Miss Jacelyn Trevaine, however, in the plainest of unvarnished truths, did not approve of fox hunting. Oh, she listened to the arguments of chicken farmers and gameskeepers, but countered with the foxes' depredations of the far more destructive rodent populations. If, in a rare moment of conciliation, Jacelyn was willing to concede the possible necessity of controlling the foxes' numbers, she would never, with her last breath if need be, agree to such a brutal, bloody, barbaric method as the hunt. So, with the single-minded dedication of youth and righteous morality, she set out to eradicate the gory sport, or at least make it dashed uncomfortable for the local Master of the Hunt, Squire Bottwick.

One of Jacelyn's earliest efforts employed a vast quantity of pepper, primitive but effective. Another involved most of the village lads and all the dead fish they could accumulate. Jacelyn strewed the latter over the deer paths and forest tracks, covering whatever scent a fox may have left. That cost many a stand-up supper for the boys, and lost Miss Trevaine her last of many governesses. Whether Miss Polk resigned due to the stench, or well-bred dismay at the deed, or simple acknowledgement that the task of making her charge into a lady was beyond her, her departure freed Jacelyn, at age fifteen, from whatever constraints society was wont to impose on young females. The following season someone managed to keep overfeeding Squire's hounds with good beef and mutton until they grew too fat and lazy to chase anything more than dream foxes. Bottwick had suspicions, of course, but could never prove them. Lord Trevaine quietly grew fond of omelettes.

10

Even her loving father felt that Jacelyn had used unfair tactics last year, bringing two orphaned fox kits over to Bottwick's where Squire's three little girls, still in the schoolroom, could help care for the "innocent victims" of their father's bloodlust and butchery. Such whining and weeping had to reach even the hardest heart; Squire discovered business in London.

For all that, Jacelyn never injured the dogs or the horses or their riders, which she could have, setting out traps or deadfalls or draglines across the ridings. No, it was only Squire's pride—and pleasure—which got hurt. Bottwick seemed relaxed by now, warmed by the fire in the grate and the good brandy, so, taking care to top the glass first, Lord Trevaine cautiously suggested, "I take it you and my daughter had another, ah, confrontation this morning?"

"Confrontation? No, I never saw her but, your daughter or not, if I'd had my hands on her—"

Trevaine cleared his throat.

"—what you should have seen to years ago." He stomped over to the window, pointed with his wine-glass. "Look at it out. Cool, crisp, no rain for the first day this week. Everyone came out for the hunt—not the London crowd; they'll get here week's end—but all the local gentry. There we were, assembled in my drive for a stirrup cup to get the blood flowing. Horses pawing, the kennelmen barely holding the dogs, they're so eager. The trumpet sounds *Away*. Ah, Trevaine, there's no sweeter sight nor sound than the pack in voice on the trail, gorgeous horseflesh, fine riders. Then my Jasper, the best pack leader I've ever seen, starts belling. I can hear it now:

11

A-roo, A-roo. And we all follow, through the home wood, across the spinney, over the stream, then cut back through Granders' and over the bridge at Treverly. We lost the vicar at Four Corners. What a ride! No *View Halloo* though, just the dogs running like the wind . . . right up to your front door."

"Hold, George. I know Jacelyn's got no fox cubs here now, and she could not get your dogs to follow a dead pelt. So what—"

"It wasn't any damned fox! It was that infernal dog of hers, in season. Anyone with a ha'penny's worth of sense knows to keep a bitch like that inside, but is that what your daughter does? Oh, no. Miss Trevaine takes the dog, and its bedding, and marks every blasted trail in the neighbourhood, leading every jack dog in the county right to your doorstep and the biggest dogfight you've ever read a damned book through. It took all your people and all mine, and buckets of water, just to separate them. Now my Jasper is back in the kennels, howling like some curst Romeo. And there's nary hide nor hair of missy and the dog, of course." Squire realised his last bellows were rattling the windowpanes. He wiped his face again, turned and in a quieter voice asked, "What do you think of your sweet, tender-hearted girl now?"

Lord Trevaine coughed to hide his laugh, but he answered, "A trifle indelicate, but ingenious all the same. I'll make good on any damages, of course." He refilled the glass.

"You always do. When the dog steals a ham curing in the sun, or attacks some villager's washline as if it were a row of advancing Frenchies, or when missy talks the tenants' sons into letting her plough the

12

fields. You've got to stop laughing, Elliot. It is different now. Oh, I'll recover m'dignity, and the dogs will be fit by the house party, and old Reynard can have a rest till then, but it is high time you took your nose out of your books and had a better look around. The tabbies are talking about Jacelyn, and it ain't good. This morning's escapade alone will keep them meowing for days."

"You know better than that, George. I don't care what the local matrons say, and neither does my daughter."

"That's just it, you don't care. But what's to become of your daughter, eh? She's not a little girl anymore. She cannot just stay in Cambridgeshire, sitting at your feet, making Maygames of the locals."

"Why not, if it suits her? You are just concerned with your own peace of mind," Trevaine said with a smile.

Squire was thoroughly at ease now—after four brandies anyone else would be comatose—and earnestly tried to make his friend see clear. "Nay, it's not my comfort, Elliot, but yours. Think on it. You won't be here to make good for her forever. What then?"

"Then she will be a wealthy young woman, free to make whatever decisions she wants."

"Free to fall prey to every loose screw with a sad story. You know she's got no more sense about men than a kitten."

"So what are you saying, that I should teach her not to trust anyone?"

"I'm suggesting that you try—try, mind you—to get her shaped up like a lady instead of a harum-scarum chit, get her launched into Society before she's blotted her copybook for good and all, and get her a good man to hold the reins when you're gone. Then we can all rest easy."

"A husband? But she's only—"

"Seventeen, I know. And how old was your Elizabeth when you met, hm? Remember, you are not going to make her into a butterfly overnight. Men don't want a gal with Greek and Latin; they want one with blushes and fluttery eyelashes. I bet my ten-year-old Amanda knows more about it than Jacelyn. And men *don't* want a wife their mothers won't invite to tea."

Lord Trevaine nodded. "You've given me a lot to think about, George, and I will this time, truly. Perhaps if I ask my sister again. . . . Yes, and I'll speak to Jacelyn too."

"And what about the hunt party for my house guests?"

Lord Trevaine pulled the bell cord near his desk.

If the adage about beauty being in the eye of the beholder needed any reinforcing, proof entered the library ten minutes later, along with Miss Jacelyn Trevaine and a footman carrying the tea tray. While the tea was being placed, Jacelyn gave the Squire her most demure curtsey, then dimpled at her father when she kissed his cheek and straightened a shawl around his shoulders.

What her adoring sire saw was a graceful sprite of a girl, not quite five foot three, with heavy brown hair falling in graceful waves halfway down her back,

14

held off her face by a yellow ribbon to match the cheerful colour of her dress. Her moves were all that was gentle and gracious, and her face exquisite, with her mother's dark brown eyes, now twinkling at him in shared humour. He saw a laughing, generous mouth, a serious, straight nose, and a healthy, sun-touched complexion that was all the more beautiful to him after his own indoor pallor.

What the Squire saw, on the other hand, was a skinny little dab of a chit in an outmoded gown, and way past the age not to put her hair up. Thank goodness his own little dumplings fit the mould of blonde, blue-eyed, rounded beauty. Oh, Jacelyn Trevaine was passable enough, he supposed, in an unfashionable way, but his eldest, Samantha, would have cried for weeks over the freckles, and even his youngest knew better than such public displays of affection. Why, if any of his girls gave him such a saucy look, he'd take a birch rod to her. If any of his girls, in fact, ever so much as hinted at causing him as much upset as this one, he'd drown the passel of them, see if he wouldn't. No amount of brandy was going to improve his opinion of Miss Trevaine. Squire was a firm believer in that other old saying: Pretty is as pretty does.

"Jacey, my dear, Squire and I have been talking," Lord Trevaine began.

"I'm sure you have," she agreed with an impish smile.

"Seriously, my dear, I begin to see his point. What would you think if I wrote to my sister in London about arranging a comeout for you?"

"Lady Parkhurst? I'd think you were wasting good

paper, Papa. You know she washed her hands of me the last time I visited when I—"

"Yes, yes, but that was two years ago. You are quite the young lady now, and perhaps it is time to consider your future."

"Do you mean marriage, Papa?" When he muttered something about that being what all girls dreamt of, he supposed, she saluted the Squire with her teacup, but said, "Oh no, Father, it's just the favoured method of ridding the neighbourhood of plaguey females. I'm quite content right here." Miss Trevaine then made a very pretty though incomplete apology to the Squire, with no prompting from her father. She apologised, that is, for causing him distress and for any injuries the dogs may have sustained, which she sincerely regretted, not having considered such a possibility. She did not, however, apologise for her behaviour or for disrupting the hunt. "I'll say the words if you think I should, Papa, but we all know I won't mean them."

What a good, honest child she is, thought her father. What a devious minx, thought George Bottwick.

"What about my hunt this Saturday, then? I've got a whole house party arriving, m'sister and her family. You remember m'nephew Arthur, don't you, Elliot? Fine boy, just back from Belgium now that the war's over. Mentioned in the despatches, don't you know. He's bringing some tonish friends, and my niece Priscilla is also. I've invited some other London acquaintances up too. Promised them fine sport, and I intend them to have it. Can I have your word on that, missy? If things go well, perhaps we could get up a

16

small dancing party so you could come meet all the young bucks. You'd like that, wouldn't you, puss, *if all goes well?*"

Jacelyn considered the nature of the offer, bribe actually, and the nature of the implied threat, and her own nature.

"Squire, what you like best about the hunt is the chase, the ride, the jumps, all the noise and excitement, true?" At his nod and the dreamy look that came over his face at the thought, she went on to ask, "Then why, after your glorious chase, don't you let the poor fox go?"

Bottwick chuckled at Jacelyn's naïveté. He did not usually have discussions with females, but perhaps he could humour her this time. "What, just tell the dogs good sport, let's go home? There is no calling them back once they've got their fox cornered, my dear."

"Then, sir, why don't you shoot the fox, to kill it cleanly and quickly, before the dogs get to it?" Jacelyn asked in what she thought was a reasonable tone of voice.

All the brandy, the tea and macaroons, the quiet talk and apologies, all went for naught as Bottwick thundered to his feet and roared: "Because that bloody well ain't the sporting way!"

It might have been a moral dilemma for Jacelyn, the hunt versus the ball which, she thought wistfully, would have been her first, even if she had no desire to dance with a bunch of London dandies, or to be held up as a rural frump by their feminine counterparts, including Squire's niece Priscilla, whom she had

17

known—and disliked—for years. Whatever decisions Jacelyn might have made were scrapped when Squire took action of his own.

Failing to secure Miss Trevaine's cooperation, needless to say, Bottwick rode home in high dudgeon. His temper was not improved when he found his dog Jasper trying to dig a hole under the kennel fence, nor was his digestion aided by his daughters' prattle about the London guests, over luncheon. He left the table in mid-meal and retired to his study with his port, a cigar, and a grudge. He told himself no little chit was going to make a fool of him—again. Especially not in front of his uppity sister, the Town swells, and soldier-heroes he had coming. After all, he was the Squire; he was the Master of the Hunt; he was the magistrate.

Perhaps it was his solid body filled only with liquid nourishment that day, or perhaps all that fluid had washed away the cobwebs of his mind, but Squire had an idea, a strategy to deal with the troublesome Miss Trevaine and her pet. He was the local magistrate, wasn't he? He had the authority, the right, nay, the duty, to uphold the law and preserve the peace. The key to his peace of mind was simple: He would arrest the dog as a public nuisance, and hold it in gaol as surety for the girl's good behaviour. Simple!

"It's simple extortion, Papa," Miss Trevaine fumed. "Bribery didn't work, his efforts to get me shipped off would take too long, so he is resorting to blackmail! How could you let him take poor Pen?"

"I am not entirely certain Bottwick isn't within his

rights, my dear, and it is only for three days, after all. You know Penelope is being well cared for; Squire even said you could visit. Just think of her namesake, Ulysses' wife, waiting patiently all those years. You'll get through, both of you." He patted her hand. "Perhaps it is a good time to consider Squire's suggestion of a London Season, though."

"You know I would rather stay here with you, Papa, and it won't fadge anyway. Aunt Amabel vowed she would never have me back. . . . I wonder whatever happened to the monkey." Father and daughter both laughed. Jacelyn had been fifteen when she was last invited to visit her aunt in London, a good opportunity to widen her horizons, according to Lady Parkhurst, lest she think the whole world was made of Cambridge farmland. All had gone well, shopping, sedate teas with her aunt's cronies and other girls not yet "out," and carriage rides in the park. It was at the start of one of these drives, however, that disaster struck. Jacelyn and her aunt were seated in Lady Parkhurst's pink-satin-lined open coach for the afternoon "strut," when all the Beau Monde paraded down Hyde Park's Rotten Row for the daily spectacle. They were right at the entrance to the park when Jacelyn "rescued" an organ-grinder's monkey from its master's mistreatment. What a spectacle it turned out to be: grooms, guards, gypsies, high-strung horses and higher-strung ladies — and a monkey who did not like carriage rides! Aunt Amabel retired to Bath for the restorative waters, Jacelyn was banished home, the coach had to be sold.

Now it was time for another rescue, Jacelyn decided as she dressed for bed. It wasn't only the injustice of innocent Pen's capture, it was the whole idea of Squire's trying to dictate her behaviour, when he was the one who was so obviously wrong. Besides, Miss Trevaine simply did not like having her will crossed. As far as she was concerned, the gauntlet had been cast.

The plan she evolved by the next evening had all the derringdo appeal of the Minerva Press romances she read as avidly as the Greek and Latin she studied with her father. It had been an easy matter to find out from the servants that Squire's precious nephew Arthur was expected long after dinner. She would, therefore, waylay Arthur after her father's bedtime, stash him away in the old gardener's cottage with her friend Shoop, who would not be quite as easy to convince, then negotiate for a trade of hostages — and be home before her father missed her at breakfast! The plan wasn't a perfect drama, of course, for if Squire were the villain, and Penelope the damsel in distress, where did that leave her and Arthur? She remembered Squire's nephew from a visit at least ten years ago as a pouty, fleshy rudesby who had disdained the company of a mere girl on his country rambles, even though she knew all the fish holes and climbing trees. Since defeating Napoleon single-handedly, if one listened to Squire's boasts, Lord Arthur Ponsonby must be even more puffed up with his own conceit than ever. No, no tragic figure there. She would just have to portray the avenging hero herself. Jacey giggled as she drew on the old boots, breeches, and coat from the back of her closet, crammed her hair under a widebrimmed, low-crowned hat, and crept down the stairs, shielding her

20

candle. She looked more like a skulking stableboy than any kind of hero, which wasn't surprising, considering that her outfit's source was Lem, the apprentice groom. The lingering odour was less than epic too, and she wrinkled her nose as she tiptoed to her father's desk. His old pistols, even unloaded, made her feel more the part. The cold metal as she tucked them in her waistband sent a delicious shiver down her backbone. Maria Edgeworth and Mrs. Radcliffe would have been proud.

2

The beat of the horse's hooves was as steady as a clock, that and the creak of saddle leather the only sounds intruding on the night. The moon was reflected off the hard-packed dirt road, and the hedgerows shut out the rest of the world. The horse was sure-footed and tireless, the road was straight. Riding in the country after dark was a perfect time for thinking, if one's thoughts were good company. The thoughts of Leigh Merrill, Earl of Claibourne, were not.

Things were not universally gloomy, of course. At age thirty-two the earl still had his health, though the French had done their damnedest to change that during the last seven years. He still had his lands, mortgaged and marginally profitable that they were; he had rugged, fair-haired good looks enough for success in the petticoat line, and luck enough, combined with his army pay, to keep himself in a style his title and acreage could not. He had his brave charger, Baron, under him, and good friends like Arthur Ponsonby, for whose uncle's house party the earl was already late. What he didn't have was a future worth a groat.

Born to the land, coming to the title at a tragically early age, he should have been seeing to his estates, but he had managers far more capable than he, and what the land needed was not another mouth to feed, but money, for repairs, equipment, modernisation. Trained for war, rising to the well-decorated rank of major on Wellington's own staff, Claibourne could have stayed in uniform, but the battles were all fought, and he had lost his taste for vagabond army life. The war years had been hellish, costing him so many good friends, but at least they were full, and the command staff lived every day as if it were their last, which it well could have been. The victory was celebrated in Paris, Vienna, London, with almost enough hell-raising to deaden the pain of memories, or at least satisfy any hunger a soldier could name. Even that palled after a time.

And now? Now he was accepting invitations to provincial parties at strangers' houses for want of anything better to do. At least he and Baron would get some healthy exercise out of the visit. The earl had kept fit by sparring at Gentleman Jackson's, but the stallion was restricted to a few tame canters in the park. That was why the earl had come on alone, bringing his horse along in easy stages instead of driving up with Arthur and their baggage as they had originally planned. This way Arthur had not had to kick his heels while the earl kept his appointment with his man of business, which was all to the good, since after hearing Pettigrew's latest news of the cur-

23

rent price of corn, Claibourne did not feel much like company.

Company. There would be plenty of that, besides exercise, at the gathering. The men were no problem; they would accept anyone who could ride hard, drink long, and gamble deep. The women were another . . . proposition. There would be the young widow or the married cousin whose husband was off in the diplomatic corps, or some such convenient errand. These ladies had an altogether different form of exercise in mind when they invited the tanned, well-muscled, elegantly dressed earl on a private chase. Even the younger ladies made much of a handsome war hero, giggling into their fans and blushing at his compliments, until they were warned off by their mamas.

The gabblemongers always had a picnic when Leigh Claibourne, as he was now called, so much as danced with a debutante. That he held a title supported by ancient tradition instead of wealth was no novelty among the ton, and no cause to strike his name from the invitation lists to come-out balls, even if the female's family was too hard pressed to consider an impecunious suitor. No, what kept him from being wholeheartedly welcome in these circles was a family closet so full of skeletons it was surprising the Claibourne crest still fit in.

What father of a wealthy girl — Claibourne's solicitor had just spent an hour impressing the earl that no other type of female would do — would give her hand, and dowry, in exchange for a name tainted with dishonourable duels, divorce, and the filthy blot of slave trading? Gads, they had it all, even near

24

imbecility, in his cousin Percival. The scandals had been well aired ages ago, in Claibourne's childhood, and only the highest sticklers held his Uncle Fenton and Percy against him. Still, all of Society read the Claibourne wildness in his own richly deserved reputation as a rake. As Leigh had ruefully commented to his solicitor, if he could afford a wife or mistress of his own, perhaps other men's wouldn't have so much appeal.

Mr. Pettigrew's next suggestion for refilling the Claibourne coffers, if not reroofing Claibourne Abbey, was a marriage of convenience—dashed inconvenient, according to every tender feeling the earl still harboured—and to a cit, besides. Wealthy merchants were willing to overlook a lot in a son-in-law, Pettigrew explained, in order to see their daughters' names in Debrett's Peerage. Damme, that was how the family got landed with Fenton!

They were in Dun Territory even before Leigh's father Jonathan ran through most of his inheritance and then married a French noblewoman. The lady's family lost their lives and fortunes, including her *dot*, in the Terror. Jonathan rashly agreed to an arranged marriage between his sister Sydelle and Josiah Fenton, a man with no title but with considerable wealth and ambition. It was perfectly acceptable for a gentleman to make investments on 'Change or abroad, even gamble on trading ventures, as long as the gentleman refrained from soiling his own hands. Slave trade, however, soiled everyone connected with it. Fenton was no gentleman. The knowledge became public and Fenton was no longer accepted into tonish

25

circles — or into Sydelle's bed. When he grew abusive, possibly due to another unsavoury product of his merchant trade, the opium pipe, Sydelle moved home. Furious, Fenton pressed for a divorce, claiming her unborn child was not his. Vowing he'd see Sydelle a widow before he'd let Fenton call her wanton, Leigh's father withdrew all of her marriage settlement from Claibourne holdings, mortgaging the property to establish a fund for her coming child. Then he challenged his brother-in-law to a duel. Duels were not outlawed yet, just discouraged.

Fenton shot early, making Leigh, at age five, the sixth Earl of Claibourne, with a French-speaking mother and an impoverished estate. Jonathan got off his own shot before he died, leaving Fenton crippled for life, although some said Fenton used the injury as an excuse for staying in his house instead of facing society's cuts and ridicule. Sydelle was forced to return to her despised husband, where she died shortly, and perhaps gladly, after bringing forth Percival, Leigh's cousin and heir.

If it weren't for that drunken fool Percy and his blackguard of a father, Leigh would have emigrated to America or journeyed to India to seek his fortune. He could even remain a carefree bachelor. But leave Claibourne Abbey to those two? Not on his life — or death!

Blast, if he stayed lost in his dreary thoughts, he'd soon be lost in Cambridgeshire. Where was that third Ryefield marker?

* * *

A light bobbed up ahead. The earl reined Baron in while still a way off, loosening the pistol from his saddle pack. Another gun rested in his greatcoat's inner pocket, and a very thin, very sharp pearl-handled stiletto reposed in a sheath carefully sewn into the seam of Claibourne's right high-top riding boot. He'd been a soldier too long and too recently to be easy game.

Baron took exception to the delay and the flickering light, sideskipping and snorting until Claibourne clucked him forward again. Soon the source of the light was discernible: a small man, no, a boy, from his high voice, dressed in rough, rustic garb and waving a lantern.

"Mister, hey mister," the boy was calling. "Please stop, sir. Please, sir, m'granfer's hurt somethin' awful, 'n needs help. Please, mister, won'tcha help me?"

"Aye, lad," the earl answered, "give me directions, and I'll ride for the doctor."

"No, no sir," came the desperate reply, hastily amended to "m'lord" when Leigh was close enough for the boy to see the obvious quality of the large grey horse, if not the elegance of the rider's clothing. "It'd be too late. He's took real bad, and . . . and I ain't knowin' what to do. Can't you follow me, please?" the youngster pleaded, wringing every drop of melodrama from the scene. Jacelyn was having a marvelous time.

Claibourne heard the near-tears tremour in the voice and instantly responded with an offer to take the boy up behind him, to make faster time. Jacelyn knew her disguise would never pass that kind of close, tactile inspection, not when Lem's outgrown jacket already barely concealed her very feminine charms. She mumbled, "Faster'f I lead the way. Hurry," and took off down a side path before her quarry could change his mind.

As they turned off the main road, the taller trees blocked what moonlight fell, so Leigh was forced to slow Baron's pace, carefully picking his way on the turnings, the wavering light staying too far ahead for him to ask any more questions, like how much farther did they have to go, what would the lad have done if horse and rider had not chanced along, and what was the nature of the grandfather's illness? The earl hadn't seen any lights indicating habitation for ages, so why would the boy come *this* way, instead of ahead, which had to be getting closer to Ponsonby's uncle's place, or set off himself for the doctor? It occurred to Leigh that the old man might have been shot while out poaching, on Bottwick's land, perhaps, eliminating the Manor as a source of aid, as well as the doctor, since he would be bound to report a bullet wound. That would account for the boy's nervousness and reticence. He'd also said "hurt," not sick or ailing. Ah, well, Claibourne had seen enough of gunshots to know what to do as well as any surgeon, if it wasn't already too late. He hoped not, for the boy's sake.

After so many twistings that the earl knew he'd never find his way back to the main road by himself—at least not till morning—the lantern finally came to a standstill outside a small stone cottage. There was a fire's glow in the one facing window but the door was shut.

"Please, yer lordship, g'wan. I'll tie yer horse," the boy offered, stepping from the darkness of the clearing beyond the circle of light from the lantern, which he had hung by the door. He touched the floppy brim of his hat as an afterthought.

"There's no need, Baron will wait here. What's your name, lad?" the earl asked, quickly dismounting and looping the grey's reins back over the saddle so the horse couldn't trip on them. With a "Stay, Baron," Leigh followed the boy toward the door.

"Jace—Jason, m'lord," the youngster answered, scurrying on. At the doorway he stopped, as though adjusting the lantern, but urged the other in. "G 'wan, sir. It be unlatched."

A soldier is used to gathering impressions quickly; his life so often depends on assessing a situation in mere seconds. Ex-Major Merrill had the time between heartbeats to note a warm, tidy cottage scented with herbs hanging to dry; a cot, a table, a few log-hewn chairs and benches, some rough-fashioned shelves; a skinny old man with weathered skin crouched at the table, pointing a gun at him—and no back door. The next heartbeat added still another relevant impression: the unmistakable sensation of a gun being pressed into his back.

Lord Claibourne raised his hands slowly, not making any sudden moves which might jar unsteady fingers. The greybeard peered at him closely, as though he had difficulty seeing even the short distance, a fact the earl mentally filed, as well as the distance to either window.

29

"Please have a seat, m'lord," the boy said, coming around from behind. The hat still shielded most of the lad's face so Leigh could not read the intentions in his eyes, but the gun stayed firm. Leigh sat. He took the seat facing the old man, careful to place his hands in plain sight on the table. The grandfather nodded and, picking up some rags, started to clean the gun, his eyes still on the captive's. Any fool knows not to clean a loaded gun, Claibourne noted. What was going on here? The fine pair of bridle culls hadn't even searched him. Claibourne raised one eyebrow but the ancient only grunted, shrugged his boney shoulders and bent to his task. The earl relaxed, biding his time. Whatever huggery-muggery this was, it didn't seem to require drastic measures, like gunning down a smooth-faced youth or overpowering a wizened septuagenarian. The situation was beginning to appeal to his lordship's sense of humour, far more than dinner at the squire's would have. And here he'd thought civilian life was going to be dull!

Jacelyn was undergoing a few surprises herself. She'd never expected pudgy Arthur to turn out so . . . masculine, for one thing. Of course she'd not seen him for ten years, since he was just fifteen, and after all, what did she know about how boys developed into men? Still, he looked much older than his years — maybe that's what wars did, and living in tents — and so much more formidable than she could have dreamt of Arthur becoming. The boy she remembered was pudding-faced, sulky at being sent to visit relatives in the country when he'd rather have stayed in London with his own chums. He was a soft city child, singularly inept at the simple country pursuits which were the only available entertainment, and he had snidely refused to take advice from a mere moppet. The grown-up Arthur, however, looked to be all muscle, and all in command, all polite good humour as he sat there in captivity. She'd feared Arthur would throw a fit, just as he'd thrown rocks, fishing poles, and tantrums when frustrated. This man looked as though he could give a setdown with one golden eyebrow, never needing to raise his voice at all. If this was what the army did for young men's characters, Jacelyn heartily approved. As for his appearance, well, his hair was a lighter blond than she recalled—from the same sun that gave him such a bronzed look, she supposed—but neither the sun nor military discipline could explain the glow she felt just looking at him. Arthur was beautiful! With his wide brow, square chin, and strong, straight nose, he was positively the most attractive man she'd ever seen, and he didn't even recognize the know-it-all tomboy who'd followed him around, laughing at his mistakes. Goodness, she had to stop staring and get on with this.

"My lord, I am dreadfully sorry for any inconvenience you may have suffered," she began, too absorbed still in his lordship's features to remember her rustic accent. "It is just a small matter, really."

Shoop cleared his throat. "Methinks we'd best reconsider, Miss—"

"Missed his dinner?" Jacelyn broke in hastily. "Of course he did. I brought some wine and cheese,

31

remember? We have to take care of business first, though." She dropped the pistol on the table when she jumped up to fetch something, to Shoop's grumbled "Aargh." His lordship's lips quivered as the old man disgustedly reached over and switched guns, starting to dismantle the lad's for cleaning while the youngster set a bottle of ink and some paper on the table. The delicate white hand that offered the earl a pen certainly didn't match the oldster's workgnarled, knobby mitts, no more than that cultured accent matched this rough dwelling. The earl wished he could see the lad's face, but the hat's low brim still obscured all but a pointed chin and a full mouth which seemed on the verge of laughter.

The boy picked up the pistol, quite obviously unloaded, and determinedly pointed it at the prisoner. "Will you do as I request, write what I say?"

"You see me trembling with fear, ready to obey your every command," the earl drawled, which earned him a "Bah," from Shoop and a chuckle from Jacelyn.

"You're really being a good sport, Arthur. I should say Lord Ponsonby, shouldn't I?"

She began to pace, planning the words to use, so she missed his lordship's start of surprise. What would staid Arthur have to do with such a havey-cavey pair? Unless . . . no, the boy was too old to be a by-blow. Perhaps a young cousin, then. This was getting more and more amusing.

" 'Dear Squire,' " the boy dictated. "No, 'Dear Uncle.' No, 'My Dearest Uncle.' That's it."

That did sound more like Arthur, Claibourne ac-

32

knowledged, writing, but how could the boy know Arthur's style and not recognise—

" 'I am being held hostage, my life is in dire peril, and I require your immediate assistance.' The earl had to laugh out loud at this. Not just at the threats as empty as the guns, but at the thought of his own uncle's reception of such a message. Fenton would be in such high gig he'd dance, crippled legs or no. And if, as Claibourne suspected, this missive was to be a ransom note, why, Fenton would rather see his nephew rot in hell than spend a brass farthing in his behalf.

"Please, my lord, this is serious. Continue: 'I will be freed as soon as you release the prisoner you now hold in . . . in durance vile. Your instant compliance is urgently requested!' Sign it, 'Your affectionate nephew, Arthur.'

"There," Jacelyn said triumphantly, sealing the note with a flourish and handing it to Shoop. "Remember to hand it to one of the grooms, as we discussed. Say some stranger gave it to you, a big, nasty looking brute with a scar down his face. Then you'd better play least-in-sight for a bit, in case Squire has questions."

Shoop made a last try at dissent, but gave it up when Jacelyn handed him a shilling for the local pub and herded him out the door. He shook his head resignedly and left, muttering about, " 'adn't oughta be 'ere atall, divil a bit alone. Niver could talk reason . . ."

Jacelyn called after, by way of reassuring her friend, "Don't worry, it's only Arthur." Then she

33

busied herself emptying a hamper onto the table. Bread, wine, cheese, mugs appeared, no utensils. Her "oh dear" changed to an "oh" of admiration as the gentleman withdrew a knife from his boot top. Wasn't Arthur complete to a shade?

Claibourne sliced off a wedge of cheese, pushed it toward the boy and said, "That's it? No names, no places, no times for exchange of prisoners? A most peculiar kidnapping, cawker. I take it the Squire, Uncle, that is, knows both you and your intentions?"

Jacelyn giggled around a mouthful. "You might say so."

"Then what's to keep him from coming after you, young Jason? Even if you succeed in obtaining your friend's release, you've still committed a crime. One cannot go around kidnapping people, you know, especially not a peer of the realm. You are obviously well-born, though, and young, so Squire might consider it a boyish prank. He mightn't send you up for hanging after all." Claibourne pensively sipped his wine, which, he noted incidentally, was excellent. "No, my guess is that he'll take a birch rod to your backside."

"I don't think so, my lord," Jacelyn answered as she removed the droopy hat, letting a heavy shower of dark brown waves cascade down past her shoulders. "I don't think so."

"Do you remember me now, Arthur? It's Jacey, Jacelyn Trevaine."

Remember her? The gentleman barely remembered

34

to breathe! No, if he'd seen this girl, he'd never have forgotten her. No girl, though, definitely a young woman, he could see now, especially as the shirt strained across her chest as she reached in a pocket for a ribbon to tie back her hair. He watched as she gathered the chestnut mass into a haphazard pony's tail, the rich brown colour catching the fire's light and reflecting its gold. Some of the waves strayed loose to frame her face delightfully.

"Don't ever cut it." He surprised himself by speaking his thoughts.

"No? Papa likes it too, but it's very unfashionable, you know."

"It's perfect." And it was, in a way, even trailing wisps, just as the girl herself was enchanting, in a warm, softly smiling way that was far from Society's standards. No china-blue eyes or rosebud mouth or porcelain complexion, or affectations. Miss Trevaine had pansy-brown eyes which sparkled with her enjoyment and a full, laughing mouth just made to be kissed! Claibourne cleared his throat and redirected his thoughts, with great effort. He carefully wiped the knife on a napkin and said, "Well, Miss Trevaine, I'd be mightily obliged to know just what rig you are running."

Jacelyn was a bit disappointed at the formal address; she much preferred "Arthur" to the sober "Lord Ponsonby," which did not seem to fit the gentleman now grinning as if ready to share her triumph. She compromised with, "Of course, my lord, you have every right. And I'd like to say that you're a regular Trojan, letting me play my game. I know I couldn't have kept you here against your will, even without the knife."

"You mean you wouldn't have pulled the trigger?"

The chit even had dimples—unfair! "But you didn't know the guns were empty, not at first, did you?"

"No, but I knew mine weren't. Come now, an explanation. And if it's not a good one, my girl, and honour-true, then I *shall* leave, and you'll really be in the suds." It was a silly threat; he could no more leave now than he could fly. He was already thinking ahead to what difficulties such a madcap might be in, to resort to kidnapping, and what strings he could pull to extricate her. First, however, what was such a little charmer doing in britches—he was trying not to stare—in a workman's cottage? "Now, ma'am, if you please," he ordered, severe with concern.

That voice had commanded whole battalions. Jacey started. "You see, my lord, Squire, your uncle, that is—and I'm sorry for that, not that he's your uncle, of course, else you'd not be here, but that it's your uncle that I'm referring to. Does that make sense?" Jacelyn was unaccountably flustered by her companion's look of disapproval. "Squire arrested Pen, and I kidnapped you in exchange," she hurried on, not choosing to discuss the reasons behind Squire's actions. "He will release Pen, I will, ah, let you go. You'll go on to the house party, I'll return home. Simple."

Her explanation wasn't simple, it was simple-minded, telling him nothing he didn't previously know except the other prisoner's name. If this friend were a man, if this were all to free her lover . . . "Who is Pen, and what are the charges?" he demanded.

Jacey shrank back in her seat. "There *were* no charges, Arthur. Squire arrested Pen so I wouldn't interfere with his fox hunt and . . . and Pen is my dog, Penelope."

"A dog? Squire, er, Uncle, arrested your dog?" Leigh had to laugh, partly at the idea, but mostly in relief that a convict lover didn't wait in gaol for her. He poured another glass of wine, then it struck him as even funnier. "You are actually holding me hostage to ransom a dog? My dear, what a blow to my pride! I'll have you know I was once traded for three French prisoners of war, two officers and a spy; our esteemed government thought I was that valuable. Three Frenchmen, one dog. How the mighty are fallen."

Jacelyn laughed with him. "But she's a very special dog, my lord. She's named for Ulysses' wife, you know, and she is every bit as faithful and wise."

"Wasn't Ulysses' dog named Argos? Why didn't you name your dog after him?"

"Argos died when his master finally came home. It was too sad."

"What a curious mix you are, Miss Trevaine. Swaggering highwayman one moment, sentimental schoolgirl the next. I don't even want to go into the fox-hunting reference. I'm not quite ready for that yet. Tell me about your grandfather."

"Oh, he's our gardener, Shoop. I thought you would remember him for sure. He shouted at you for practicing your cricket in the formal gardens."

"Did he? Will he find himself up on charges over this nonsense, or dismissed from his position?"

"Oh no. Squire only blames Papa. He'll turn all red and rage at my poor father to do something about me."

"And will he? Your father, I mean. You'd ought to be spanked, girl, for what I'm beginning to suspect is a long history of thoroughly disreputable behaviour. It's too much to hope, I'm sure, at this late date."

Jacelyn laughed at the idea of her dear sweet father even raising his voice in anger, much less his hand. "Papa is a scholar, remember?"

"Well, someone had ought to tan your sweet britches over this escapade, pet, for you've landed us both in the briars this time."

"You haven't changed so much, after all, Arthur. You always were a spoilsport. Too bad, I was beginning to like you. What, are you afraid of what Squire will say?"

"Aye, girl, Squire and the whole countryside, likely. Here you are in the middle of the night, in an isolated little cottage, improperly attired, alone with a man. Didn't you even think of your reputation?"

Jacelyn threw back her head and laughed, a sound which nearly melted the earl's heart for good and all. "But I don't have any reputation to speak of!" At his sudden scowl she hastily added, "Not for being a lightskirt, Arthur, just a hoyden, you know. And if you think Squire is going to storm in here, demanding you do the honourable thing by me, you're more paper-skulled than you used to be. Never fear, the last thing in the world Squire would want is to have me as part of the family."

She giggled at the very thought of it, till her companion quietly announced, "The only problem, sweetheart, is that I am not Arthur."

3

"George," Squire Bottwick told himself, hands crossed over his full belly, "life is sweet." Good wine, good food, good friends, and, for once, good riddance to the aggravating Miss Trevaine. He patted his inside pocket where reposed the most satisfying correspondence he'd had in years. He had received the note before dinner, and was still tickled pink at the idea of letting the interfering little wench cook in her own stewpot while he enjoyed his meal.

It was good English fare, none of those Frenchified dishes drowning in sauces that curdled Squire's digestive juices. It was good enough for the fine London folks, too, judging from all they ate and drank, even his sister Clothilda Ponsonby, who'd put on enough airs for a duchess after snabbling herself a title. In her widowhood she had grown positively stiff-rumped with pride. Plain missus was good enough for Mrs. Bottwick, Squire thought, glancing at his wife at the opposite end of the table. She had done him proud, just as though she set ten places with five courses and six removes every evening. Even his daughter Samantha, invited to leave the nursery party when they found themselves an odd number at table, was behaving just as she ought. The gal was young, but she could take a few lessons from her cousin Priscilla, who had been Out for two years and was considered last Season's Toast. Too bad Priscilla seemed to share her mama's top-lofty consequence. Still, she was a taking miss, judging from her part-ners' attentiveness. Colonel Highet, was it, and Lord Humboldt, or Captain Humboldt and Mr. Highet? Ah well, friends of Arthur's.

Arthur sat between Samantha and Priscilla's pretty friend Miss Marcella Chadwick, here at Squire's table, unthreatened, unfettered, uncaptured! Squire beamed. Top of the trees, young Arthur was, too, his shirtpoints nearly reaching his ears, his neckcloth done up in some pattern so intricate that it must have a name of its own. Personally, Bottwick thought it all a little overdone for a country dinner, but what did he know about fashion? He looked down regretfully at his own figured waistcoat, just a trifle redecorated with his dinner's spatters, and wished he could undo a few of the buttons. Ah well, a man couldn't have everything, he decided. It might spoil him.

By the time dinner was over and the men had shared port, cigars, and lies of their prowess on various hunting fields, Squire was fit to burst more than the seams of his jacket. A few more brandies, and the joke was just too good not to share.

"Arthur," he said when the tea tray was brought in, "do you recall Jacelyn Trevaine, m'neighbour's daughter?"

"You mean the nasty little tomboy with freckles? How could I forget? She pushed me in the lake once when I was searching for birds' nests."

"She's not changed much, I'll warrant. Oh, she's filled out some, but she still gets up to her mad starts. You'll never guess what she's done now!" He slapped his beefy hand down on his thigh, the sound drawing the attention of everyone except Lord Smedley, Clothilda's cisisbeo, who was snoring in the corner, a handkerchief over his face.

"I was just telling Arthur here about my neighbour," Bottwick informed his listeners. "The father's a good man. Not the sporting type, you understand, but good, for all that. The daughter, though, is an unprincipled baggage. Always was, always will be."

"You don't mean Jacey, do you, Father? You know she is the dearest, most good-natured girl. I —"

"You've said enough, girl. Past your bedtime anyway."

"Yes, Father." Aghast that she had disagreed with her father in front of all the fine London company and been reprimanded, Samantha made an awkward curtsey and fled the room, nearly in tears.

"That was unkind, George." His wife took Squire to task. "Jacelyn has been a good friend to Samantha, even though she is older." This last may have been quietly directed at Priscilla who, after a perfunctory kiss in the vicinity of Samantha's ear, had totally ignored her young cousin in favour of the gentlemen's company. "Miss Trevaine may be somewhat high-spirited, but even you, George, have admitted that she is pluck to the backbone, as you

42

would say."

"Aye, the gel's got bottom, I'll grant you that. Just listen to the scheme she's concocted now." Squire read the note aloud, then guffawed so hard tears streamed down his red cheeks.

When he was able to speak again, Captain Highet pressed him for an explanation. "I do not understand, sir. Arthur's right here, and there is no mention in the letter of any Miss Trevaine. I say, could you let us in on the joke?"

So Squire sketched a background to the scenario, using such phrases as "like a boil on m'butt," and "a bitch in heat," to his wife's frown, his sister's pursed lips, and his niece's twitters. "And now she thinks to diddle me with this farrago of nonsense," Squire finished, "with Arthur right here!"

The young men up for the fox hunt were all sympathetic and now shared Squire's amusement. The lines of displeasure on Lady Ponsonby's face, though, deepened, until she recalled they might become permanent if held too long. "This is highly unseemly, George. I hope we are not to be subjected to more of this indignity. Kidnapping my Arthur, indeed."

"George," Mrs. Bottwick asked thoughtfully, "if Arthur is here, who do you think penned the note? Whatever Jacelyn might be, and I'll acknowledge that this does sound somewhat irregular, she is not foolish."

"Quite right, Uncle George. She always was a little hellion, but a downy one. She must have thought you'd go for it, but why?"

Squire was off in a laughing fit again when the

43

captain made the obvious deduction: "You mean the chit's held up some poor chap she thinks is Arthur here, and is holding him to ransom a dog?" He and Lord Humboldt pounded each other on the back, saying it served the pushy female right. Priscilla and Miss Chadwick, side by side on the sofa, shared haughty looks of feigned disinterest. *They'd* never be caught doing anything so ill-bred or vulgar, much less anything as silly as getting between a man and his sporting instincts. Mrs. Bottwick was murmuring about the "poor, motherless child" while Clothilda Ponsonby simply looked disgusted.

"Arthur," she addressed her son in an effort to change the topic, "I've told you not to wear that shade. It makes you look liverish. Or was it the food?"

Indeed, Arthur had paled to a greenish tint. He ran a finger under his suddenly too-tight collar. "Yes, Mother. That is, no, Mother. I'm quite the thing. A trifle weary. Um, Uncle, perhaps I might—"

"Dang," interrupted Squire, "I'd give my best mare to know who the chit's snagged."

Arthur choked. There was no hope of getting his uncle alone, not with everyone looking at him. "Do you remember when I arrived early I said there was another fellow who might come this evening, or else tomorrow, if it got too dark to ride? Another army friend?"

Mrs. Bottwick was relieved. "That's all right then, an officer friend of Arthur's. I'm sure he'll see that Jacelyn's just an impulsive child."

"Aunt Rosalie, ma'am." Arthur kept twisting his neckcloth. "It's not that I'd ever invite a here-andthereian to your home. Leigh is a fine gentleman and officer, one of the best. Even Wellington's said so, hasn't he, Highet?" Highet's mouth was now hanging open, so Arthur got no support there. "It's just that, well, he's got a name with the ladies. I mean, I'd trust Claibourne with my life, Uncle George, ma'am, but I wouldn't leave him alone with my sister, and you know she's up to snuff. As for some unschooled country chit—"

"Claibourne?" Clothilda Ponsonby screamed, along with horrified gasps and exclamations from Priscilla and Miss Chadwick, a chorus of doom that would have done Macbeth's three witches proud. "You left a young woman alone for four hours with Rake Claibournc? George, how could you?"

Mrs. Bottwick dropped the teapot.

By the time Jacelyn heard the dog's woofs and whines, and then frantic scrapings on the door, she was beginning to doubt her wisdom. Not in the matter of Squire and his hounds, of course. Not even in the absurdity of capturing the wrong man, a natural error under the circumstances. No, Miss Trevaine was wondering if her own good sense could ever win over the new sensations shuddering through her. Perhaps Squire was right after all, that she did need some Town Bronze before facing such a nonpareil. Maybe then, when a tall, handsome gentleman gazed at her so warmly she would know where to look, instead of staring dreamily back into his blue eyes, mesmerised like some poor terrified mousekin waiting for the cat to pounce. Of course she wasn't precisely frightened, only trembly and breathless and, oh dear, what did one do with one's hands? Ah, she realised with a shock of clarity, that must be why ladies carry fans!

It was with a great deal of relief that Miss Trevaine opened the door and welcomed her pet, hiding her uncertainties in a fierce hug and having her burning face slobbered on.

"My lord, this is Penelope. Pen, meet your . . . your benefactor."

"Yes, hardly a rescuer," said Claibourne, coming forward with the heel of the bread loaf, which he offered to the big dog, making an instant friend. "She certainly is large," he said, looking for something good to say about an animal that stood as tall as his waist, with a miscellaneous assemblage of gangly parts covered with grizzled whiskers going every which way. The bread gone in a gulp, Pen looked up at him mournfully from under an overhanging shag-rug brow. "And marvelously expressive eyes. You are certainly worth a king's ransom, old girl. Sorry you had to make do with a mere earl."

Blushing, Jacelyn began gathering things into her hamper. "We'd best be going, my lord. Squire will be looking for you, I'm sure, and I'd rather he not find me at all! Besides, if you keep petting Pen behind the ears like that, her tail will destroy Shoop's cottage, as if I weren't in bad enough straits with him already." She carefully wrapped the pistols in linen napkins before placing them in the hamper. Opening the door, she remembered to tell the earl, "Your direction is just to the rear of the cottage. You cannot miss the break in the hedge. The path there leads straight back to the main road, and Squire's gatehouse is only minutes ahead. I brought you 'round Robin's barn lest you—Arthur, that is—recognise Shoop's cottage too soon. My way cuts right across this clearing, my lord, so . . . so I wish to . . . to thank you and—"

"Not so fast, sweetings," drawled the earl, still looking perfectly at ease in Shoop's high-backed chair. He slipped his knife back into the boot, then slowly rose and came toward her. Jacelyn backed away until she was half in, half out of the doorway, feeling the cool night's breeze on her cheek. Then she was stopped by his hand at her neck, his thumb caressing that same cheek.

"No, I don't think I can let you go so easily." Leigh spoke almost regretfully. When Jacelyn glanced down to where her pistols lay on the top of the basket she held in her hand, he smiled, teeth white in the moonlight. "No more of your games, love, now it's my play. Or don't you think I deserve a reward for all I've been through, hm? Terrorised by highwaymen, threatened within an inch of my life, deprived of my dinner. Yes, I think I'm owed some restitution, wouldn't you say so, Miss Trevaine?"

"Yes, my lord," was Jacelyn's whispered response.

"What's that, my girl, not used to paying for your crimes?"

"No, my lord," meekly.

"Ah, in that case I won't demand too high a price. Perhaps just a kiss?" And he stood there, his arm negligently across her shoulder, waiting expectantly.

After a moment's indecision, Jacelyn stood on tiptoe and darted forward, quickly brushing the side of his mouth with hers. When she moved as if to

47

leave, that strong hand firmed at the back of her neck.

"No, no, you'll have to do better than that. That was not even dustman's wages, much less an officer's. Come, little sparrow, let me show you."

He pulled her to him, his other arm pressing at her back, and bent his head to hers, his lips very soft and gentle on her mouth. She almost thought she was floating, till his hands started to move, to knead and caress. He raised his head briefly, to see a wondering look in her eyes, her mouth formed in a bemused "Oh." With a groan he covered her mouth again, this time with his lips opened, his tongue running over hers until she could taste the wine and his breath and his very soul, she supposed, as he must hers. Then she gave up what little rational thought was left to her. She had no frame of reference, nothing to compare these fiery new feelings to, to understand them better, so she stopped trying and joined wholeheartedly in her first real kiss. She raised her arms and held him as close as she was able, wanting to stir him the way his hands were rousing her, straying down her back to where a lady would have skirts and petticoats, so a gentleman couldn't take such liberties. Then his hand pushed aside Lem's jacket and stroked the side of her breast until she felt she'd faint if this went on much longer, and die if it ever ended.

It's one of those interesting observations that, whenever the cards are stacked against you, there are so very many jokers in the deck. Take now, for instance. Miss Trevaine had not only abducted the

48

wrong gentleman, but she'd spent four hours alone with him. Furthermore, he'd turned out to be, by his own confession, one of the worst womanisers on two continents. And now, just when she was enthusiastically, devastatingly, definitively helping him prove that claim, who should come thundering into the clearing but Squire and half his house party.

It was Lord Arthur Ponsonby who, first spying the couple silhouetted in the open doorway, locked in a passionate embrace, gave the evening's most superfluous statement by shouting, "There she is!"

Jacelyn was right. Arthur always was a spoilsport.

4

She'd done it again. Squire Bottwick had no idea
how the she-devil'd managed to bring off such a
complicated, convoluted plot, but she'd done it. Here
it was, a perfect Saturday morning in autumn. You
could almost taste the crispness in the air as the
thoroughbred trampled leaves under its hooves. Was
Squire out riding neck-or-nothing on the heels of his
hounds? Was he feeling the wind in his face as he
took the jumps along with his friends, ridding England of one more vermin? No, he was plodding
along, riding as slowly as the purebred under him
would tolerate, on his way to Treverly Hall. Miss
Trevaine had done it again, ruined another day's
hunt. It was enough to make a grown man cry.

Bad enough he'd miss today's sport, Squire
mourned; sure as hellfire his wife and sister would
have him in church tomorrow, for all his sins. Monday morning the guests would be leaving, and he'd
have to see them off. No hunting then either, but at
least now there was something worth praying for. If
his puffed-up sister sniffed down her nose at him one
more time, he'd wipe it for her, see if he didn't.

Cloth-head Clothilda she'd always been. Cloth-head Clothilda she'd always be, complaining about country morals corrupting her precious Priscilla. As if Squire didn't have enough in his budget, that skitterwit had decided to faint in his sitting room, as though she'd been in any danger. More likely she resented not being the centre of attention. As for Arthur, the twiddlepoop, they might have squeaked through this if the nodcock hadn't rushed back to his mama with the news of Jacelyn's fall from grace. Squire could have hushed the servants, and Claibourne's fellow officers could have been trusted to hold their tongues, but Priscilla and that milk-and-water friend of hers, Miss Chadwick? They'd have the news broadcast throughout Cambridgeshire faster'n a cat could lick cream. As for Clothilda, she was most likely writing to her friends in London this very minute. She'd announced her connexion, via Ponsonby, to Sally Jersey often enough, and everyone knew Sally Jersey was the biggest gossip in London. Devil take it! Besides, fumed the Squire, feeling thoroughly put-upon, that blasted dog had nigh ruined his wine cellar before they'd freed it, excavating an escape route through some of Bottwick's best duty-free bottles.

This was all beside the point, and Squire well knew it. What was really gnawing at him was the look on Jacelyn's face, so pale there in the moonlight, when, without more than an "I'll see Miss Trevaine home," Claibourne had lifted her onto the back of a huge grey charger. He'd walked beside it out of the clearing, the dog on the other side. Squire'd silently dismissed the other men—he cursed himself again for not seeing they'd keep mum—and followed. Nothing else was said until they reached Treverly, when Jacelyn announced she would use the back door. She'd looked Squire straight in the eye, chin up, and told him there was no need to disturb her father until morning; he needed his rest. She'd slid off that great hulk of a horse before Claibourne could lift her down and, turning without another word, walked toward the house. No tears, no vapours, no recriminations, all of which Squire found waiting for him at home.

Dang, the chit had backbone. Yes, and class, he'd give her that too. Too bad she wasn't a boy. She wasn't though, and now Squire had to face his old friend and tell him—what? That he, George Bottwick, had found Trevaine's daughter the perfect husband? A nobleman of impeccable background and repute, with fortune to treat his only chick better than she was accustomed, who could be trusted to love and honour her for all of her days?

The truth was enough to break a father's heart.

At precisely eleven o'clock the Earl of Claibourne rode up to Treverly Hall, to the front door this time. It was a stately mansion of warm brickwork, not the rambling hodgepodge of Squire's manorhouse, where each generation had added its own style, whether it matched or not. Treverly was elegant and understated, bespeaking good taste and the wherewithal to maintain it. Evidence of Shoop's skill bloomed in perfect harmony, although the earl's knowing eye guessed Shoop must command a whole platoon of clippers, mowers, and pruners.

The boy who ran up to take Baron's reins before Claibourne could dismount smiled when Leigh warned him not to pull on the horse. "He'll walk with you if I tell him, but he'll raise Cain if he thinks you're making off with him. Cavalry horse, you know."

"Yessir," the groom said, grinning. "I'll stand right here with'm, if'n that's what he chooses."

The door was opened by a liveried footman who also took the earl's hat, gloves, and riding crop. Only then did the whitehaired butler step forward. "How may I help you, my lord?"

"Would you please tell Lord Trevaine that Leigh Claibourne wishes to see him."

"Certainly. I believe his lordship is expecting you, my lord."

You can bet your shiny brass buttons he's expecting me, Leigh thought, and likely the whole staff of servants knows it, from milkmaid to *monsieur* in the kitchen. Only his twitching lips betrayed Claibourne's urge to laugh at the butler, who had more dignity than the Prince Regent. Before he followed that stately personage down a hall hung with priceless masterpieces, however, he couldn't resist winking at the footman who, grinning, made a mock salute. Leigh also gave one last look to the riding crop. It had been a gift from Squire Bottwick, with the words, "You'll need it."

"I have to admit it's not what I wanted for my daughter," Lord Trevaine told his caller, although he liked what he saw well enough. Not the external trappings of a finely turned-out gentleman, in fawn knee breeches and muscle-moulded jacket of dark blue Bath superfine, but the firm handshake and the way this young nobleman sat at his ease in a stranger's library. The earl showed no nervous sense of guilt, nor yet any cocky self-assurance as he looked the older man straight in the eyes. Trevaine saw much to admire. It wasn't the earl's lack of capital which disturbed him, either; he himself had fortune enough to rebuild three abbeys, and no use for it beyond his books—and his daughter. He didn't worry that Claibourne would squander away Jacelyn's monies: from the earl's own account of his less than formidable prospects, his lands were of primary concern, and that was always a good investment.

Furthermore, Trevaine would make sure part of Jacelyn's wealth was held secure for her, no matter whom she married. Not even the young man's dicey reputation bothered Trevaine overmuch. Old family scandals could be instantly forgotten. Trevaine hoped he had more sense than to hold a boy responsible for his parents' misdeeds, much less those of an uncle by marriage, all carefully enumerated by George Bottwick. Claibourne's own tarnished name could be nearly as casually dismissed: restless youth, the brutal scars of war, and the fact that if people are predisposed to think the worst, it is often in the nature of spirited young men to live up—or down—

to their expectations. Even Squire, so determined to give an honest reckoning, had found no fault with the earl's personal integrity. All in all, this prospective son-in-law would have satisfied Jacelyn's father. And yet . . .

"She is so young. Not in years, as Bottwick keeps reminding me, but in spirit, so free and innocent. She always reminds me of a spring breeze, as sweet and pure, and in such a hurry to smell every budding flower, touch every newborn lamb." Trevaine's voice broke a little, and he removed his spectacles, wiping them with a handkerchief. "I would do anything to keep her that way. I don't care aught for gossip, my lord, but I'd not see her hurt." He blew his nose. "Mostly I'd hoped to have her here with me for a few more years."

What could Leigh say to this fine old gentleman in his library, surrounded by precious volumes and works of art when he, Claibourne, was stealing the most cherished treasure of all? The man was far from well, obviously, his blue-veined hands trembling. Was Trevaine's anguish to be laid in Claibourne's dish too? He had so little to offer in trade. . . .

"My lord, I swear to you on my mother's grave that I'll make Jacelyn a good husband, and have as much care for her happiness as you do. You have my word and my hand on it, if you'll accept."

Trevaine did, and shook the younger man's hand with a measure of relief. "I'll not force her, you know," he cautioned the earl, lest Claibourne think the deed was done. "If she won't have it, we'll weather through, no matter what the tabbies say.

Some new scandal will come along to set their tongues wagging."

"Aye, sir, but your daughter's just as apt to cause that one, too, from all I hear."

They smiled in shared understanding, removing the last tension from the room.

"I wonder what they'll find to natter on about when Jacelyn's in London?" Trevaine mused, only to be caught up by the earl's laugh.

"Do you think they won't find her name in the newspapers' gossip columns? Your daughter, sir, will likely set London on its ear. Rake Claibourne's betrothed?" At Trevaine's look of consternation, he held up his hands. "No need to worry, my lord, I'll keep her safe from overstepping the line, but I'll not bridle her," he said, finishing with a doubt-tinged "if any man could."

It was Trevaine's turn to be amused. "Not any easy task you've set yourself, my boy, but you'll do, you'll do. Tell me," he asked in a more thoughtful tone of voice, "do you think my girl is pretty?"

Claibourne considered for a moment, straightening the cuff of his shirtsleeve. "Pretty? No, I wouldn't call Miss Trevaine that. I've only seen her in boys' clothes, recall, with her hair undone, nothing anyone could label pretty. Yet there was a glow about her, a vibrant, entrancing appeal. A man would never grow tired of watching her face change with her thoughts. No, I think she'll be beautiful in time."

"Good," Trevaine said, rising slowly from his chair. "You've still got your wits about you. Hang on to them, lad. I'll be sending Jacelyn in to you."

After Trevaine left, the earl wiped his forehead. Gads, he'd rather face Boney's whole army than another such interview—and the battle hadn't even begun!

"I shan't marry you, my lord, and that's the end of it. All this fuss over one silly little kiss." When he cleared his throat she paused in her angry pacing, but he seemed merely to be examining his gold signet ring. Jacelyn had the grace to blush. "Well, one kiss, at any rate. It's not as though we were caught out at some inn, having an assignation or something. I see no reason why I should have to wed anybody."

"Will you stop moving about, sweetheart, you're looking like a disgruntled chicken."

"I look like a *what?*" This was too much! To be likened to some idiotic poultry after a harrowing morning watching her father grow paler and weaker. Even Mrs. Phipps, the housekeeper, had added her tuppence, practically scalping Miss Trevaine under the excuse of putting miss's hair up, as befitted a young lady "who wouldn't want to embarrass her poor, sweet mother's memory." The look on Mrs. Phipps's face added the unnecessary "more than you already have."

Jacelyn even had to change out of her plain round gown and into a sprigged muslin, "like a young lady receiving a gentleman caller," according to Mrs. Phipps. To Jacelyn it was more like dressing the sacrificial lamb! The whole thing was beyond reason, and she wasn't having any of it, nor any of his fine lordship, leaning so nonchalantly against the edge of her father's desk, looking superbly elegant and supremely relaxed for a condemned man.

"You should be gratified then, my lord, that this . . . this chicken refuses to marry you."

"More like a hornet now, poppet, but that's irrelevant," he told her, delighting in the sparks in her eyes, "for I haven't asked you to marry me."

Jacelyn's hand flew to her mouth. What a fool she must look now! "But Papa said, and Squire said, and—"

"Squire says a great deal too much and your father has rightfully left it to us to work out." He held up his hand. "No, that does not mean you can forget all about last night's ah, events, and go onto your next hey-go-mad scheme. I do have some honour, you know. I don't go around strewing the countryside with soiled doves." Her innocent confusion made him amend that: "I don't ruin a young lady's reputation and then leave her to face the censure of her friends and neighbours. So what I *am* proposing is that you come to London with me and my greataunt, if I can arrange it. You'll like her, I know. Very much of the *Ancien Regime,* but a complete hand for all that, if you don't let her intimidate you. You cannot stay in my bachelor's quarters, of course, but your father spoke of an aunt of yours? . . ."

"Papa knows Aunt Amabel won't have me."

"He thought he could bring her 'round if she only had to give you house-room and an occasional introduction, if my great-aunt and I could act as chaperone and escort. Think of all the wonderful times we

58

could have, just for a few months. You'd be home before Christmas. The theaters and bookstores, the parties and balls, all the sights and all the shops. *Belle-tante's* been longing to visit her old friends in London, fellow *emigrés*, you know, so she'll be thrilled to look after you. And it would get you away from Treverly, which might be uncomfortable right now, and out of Squire's sight, before he throttles you."

Jacelyn had to laugh at that, before reminding the earl that Lady Ponsonby and Priscilla would be in London, and Lady Ponsonby and Aunt Amabel were bosom bows. "If I am ruined here in Cambridgeshire, where everyone knows I'm always in some scrape or other, it will be a hundred times worse in London, where no one knows me. I won't be invited anywhere, and poor Aunt Amabel will have to go to Bath again."

Claibourne smiled at the girl's candour, and at all the shifting thoughts he could read on her so expressive face. You'd make a terrible cardplayer, Miss Trevaine, he thought. Right now he was pleased to see disappointment mixed with the restored good humour. "That's the other half of my proposal," he told her. "I'm suggesting we put it about that we have an understanding, a prebetrothal agreement, if you will. That way we can travel together, and no one can comment that I am too much in your company. Most important, your good name will be preserved."

Jacelyn shook her head. "I don't understand, Lord Claibourne. Squire said I was compromised and had to marry. How can a mere 'understanding' uncompromise me?"

"Ah, that's the glory of idle gossip. As I see it, the reason for protecting a maiden's name so well is that no man wants a wife who will, ah, kiss other men. And the wives don't want a woman in their midst who might kiss their husbands. So they have decided that a girl who kisses two men is no better than she should be and not acceptable. But if she kisses *one* man and appears to be close to marrying him, then that is love, and safe."

"What a bag of moonshine, my lord."

"Leigh."

"Leigh?"

"Or Claibourne, or Merrill, if you'd rather. Anything but Arthur. Then I can call you . . . Jacelyn?"

"Or Jacey. Anything but chicken!"

And they both laughed, the earl feeling they'd gotten over the heaviest ground, Jacelyn in delight that she seemed to have made a friend of this paragon.

"But, my lo—Leigh, if it is just a private, unannounced engagement, who is to know? I mean, how will that stop all the rumours?"

"Oh, I might drop a hint or two to Lady Ponsonby, *entre nous* of course. That should take care of Cambridgeshire, London, and all of the counties in between, if not the Outer Hebrides."

Jacelyn's dimples appeared. "What happens then? We can't just keep on having an understanding, can we?"

"Not forever, no. But we can say it's for your first Little Season. That way if young Lochinvar rides up and sweeps you off your feet, I can bow out gracefully, a wounded but wiser man. If there is no one you'd rather have who will put up with you, brat, and you still don't want me, well then, I'll parade a few opera dancers in front of your aunt's house, so you can throw me over because of my rakehell ways. No one will blame you, I'm sure."

"And if . . . if . . . ," she began shyly.

"If we should decide we'd suit after we get to know each other better? Then I will get down on one knee and ask if you would do me the great honour, and you, you minx, will reply that the honour and pleasure are all yours."

"Yes, my lord," she replied with a chuckle.

"Unless, of course, you've reconsidered and wish to marry me now," he teased. "Then if we didn't suit, I could always find a war somewhere."

"That is not funny, Leigh." Nor was the idea of marrying a man — albeit he was everything she'd ever dreamed of in a husband — who offered simply to save her reputation.

He touched her suddenly serious mouth with one finger. "No, sweetheart, it isn't funny. Besides, it would just give the scandal brewers more broth if we married now, as if we were rushing to consecrate the union before the confinement. So shall we agree on our 'gentlemen's agreement'?"

Jacelyn knew she'd gone too far this time, abducting a gentleman, and she knew how upset her father was. She also knew how her heart yearned for her to say yes, because her body knew he would kiss her, to seal the bargain. How she wished to be held in his arms again! For once, however, possibly because her last calamity was so recent, Miss Trevaine was determined to think before she acted. Her father would be pleased to see her reputation intact, and Squire of course would be delighted to see her gone, even if just for the fall hunt season. And there was an undeniable, unnameable something within her that was dancing right now, at the thought of even those few months with this man. But what about Leigh?

If he didn't see to her name, his own reputation would be tarnished, yet from what Squire'd told her father, a rake did not worry overmuch about honour or what others thought. So why should this hero, this Nonesuch, wish to be saddled with a ragmannered brat like herself? Self-confidence? Jacelyn didn't even have enough self-*awareness* to think for a moment that his lordship could find her attractive. So, "Why, my lord? Why would you do all this for me?" she asked.

Now it was Leigh's turn for self-doubts. Would she believe him that it was because he found her adorable? That it was the only way he could think of not to frighten her or put her back up like an angry kitten's? Would she laugh if he proposed love-in-a-cottage to her, all he had to offer? He picked one of Baron's grey hairs from his jacket's sleeve, not looking at her face, at the hurt he might see there. "There is the money, you know," he drawled.

"Oh, that's all right, then." Jacelyn was surprisingly content. This made sense, and satisfied her own sense of honour. After all, the whole escapade was entirely her fault—except for the kiss she tried not to remember—so why should the earl have to suffer? It was only fair he gain something in exchange for his freedom. Besides, the story Bottwick had told of Leigh's struggles to bring his estates back from ruin had touched her with the same instinct that made her heart go out to motherless kittens. If her dowry could ease his way, it should be his, unless . . .

"Leigh, you didn't kiss me to ensure I'd be compromised, did you?"

He raised one thick golden eyebrow. "Do you mean did I know Squire and his house party were coming, or do you mean did I know you were wealthy? The former was obvious, I suppose, that sooner or later someone would come after you. As for the latter, an easy deduction. Any fool could recognise you for an heiress by your elegant dress, your fine manners, the table you set. On the other hand, perhaps I just kiss every pretty girl who holds me at pistol-point. You'll never know." He raised one of her hands to his mouth and gently kissed the palm. "Poppet, you'll just have to trust me. You'll hear many stories about me—some of them will be true—but I swear I won't do anything to shame you, or cause you upset. Do you believe that?" At her nod he softly kissed each finger before saying, "Good, because if this doesn't look like a love match, we'll never pull it off. Settled, then?" he asked, ready to pull her into his arms for the kiss he'd been long awaiting and felt he richly deserved for not simply throwing the chit over his shoulder and riding off to Gretna Green with her.

Jacelyn still had some reservations, despite the tingle in the hand he was nuzzling. She withdrew it and stood looking down, fiddling with the folds of her dress. "My lord," she said awkwardly, "I need a . . . a promise from you."

Claibourne groaned inwardly. Here it comes, he thought. She'll ask me to swear off ladybirds. He'd do it, of course, but it would be a dashed short engagement, no matter what he'd said before. "Anything, my love."

"Please, Leigh, swear you won't ever go hunting with Squire Bottwick? I couldn't bear him thinking he won, after all."

Claibourne laughed out loud and agreed, "But only if you promise to have a care for your reputation in return, if not for my sake, then at least for my poor aunt's, and your unborn children."

"My children?"

"Of course. You wouldn't want all those freckle-faced darlings to come crying home because Priscilla Ponsonby wouldn't let them play with her brats, would you?"

How wonderful a kiss felt, when you were already smiling!

Lord Trevaine invited Leigh to stay for dinner, but the earl refused, citing all he had to accomplish in the fortnight he'd be gone. He mentioned seeing Lady Parkhurst and fetching his great-aunt; he didn't mention trying to regain his sanity. He wished to be on the road to London well before dark, if Trevaine's letter to his sister was ready, since he was sure that Lady Ponsonby would not approve of travel on the morrow, a Sunday.

"And I am sure the good Lord sleeps better at night, knowing Clothilda Ponsonby is doing His work," Lord Trevaine added. "Godspeed, son."

Jacelyn only whispered: " 'Ware of highwaymen."

5

What a difference a few hours made in a man's life! Just the night before, Claibourne had been on this same road, his good horse under him, and not much ahead of him. Now his future looked interesting, at least, if not bright, and he rode a chestnut gelding from Squire's stable. His honour wouldn't let him touch a groat of Jacelyn's money before they were wed, although her father had trustingly and touchingly offered. The earl was not nearly so under the hatches as to be tempted to accept, nor to take Arthur's guilt-ridden suggestion of a loan for travelling expenses. Squire's offer, however, was harder to refuse: a tidy sum of money and the use of a mount, in exchange for Baron's service with the broodmares for the two weeks Claibourne would be gone. The brute would be hell to ride after, but he'd only be eating his head off in a London stable while Claibourne went north to fetch his aunt. Besides, they all had to make some sacrifices for the cause.

If his horse was back there in Cambridgeshire, so were a great many of my lord's thoughts. Gads, what had he gotten himself into? She was so young and so appealing, so honest in her nature, and so deliciously devious in her methods. She had the innocence of a loving child, yet her kisses were those of a seductive woman. What a conundrum, and what a delight! The high-born debutantes he'd known, admittedly few and those only slightly, had exactly three public facial expressions: smirk when they were being complimented, sneer when they weren't, and simper when they couldn't tell which. Each expression used the minimum of effort, as if they feared any movement of their lips might ruin the perfect china-doll look they struggled to achieve. His Jacelyn, though—already he thought of her with the possessive—held her emotions right in the eyes, in her full mouth, in the straight little nose which crinkled adorably. He was certain he'd not seen half the combinations the changeable little creature possessed. He only hoped London didn't teach her to cloak all her thoughts and feelings with the mask of ennui that Society deemed necessary.

His first chore, though, was to see that Jacelyn got to London. He had the letter to her Aunt Amabel, along with Lord Trevaine's hints toward obtaining her compliance. Trevaine had told Leigh that his letter appealed to Lady Parkhurst's strong familial instincts as well as her mercenary ones, the latter fed by the extremely generous sum put aside for incidental expenses beyond Jacelyn's clothes, servants, horses, and come-out ball. That and the fact of Claibourne and his great-aunt undertaking the day-to-day responsibilities for a debutante ought to convince his flighty, lazy, but generally agreeable sister, confided Trevaine. As for Lord Parkhurst, his seat in the

House, his dinner, and a good game of whist were the only things he considered worthwhile, and he disliked having any of them disturbed. Therefore, cautioned Jacelyn's own loving father, revealing whence she'd derived some of her circuitous logic, Claibourne was to play the trump card as a last resort only. Unwritten in the letter, but to be implied by the earl in person, was the precarious nature of both Trevaine's health and the proposed betrothal. If the engagement and Trevaine's heart both failed, the Parkhursts would have the sole responsibility for their impetuous, unconventional, problematic niece. Yes, the threat ought to clinch the invitation.

Lady Parkhurst's letter arrived at Treverly three days later, along with Leigh's note that he was now en route to Littleton at Stockton-on-Tees in Durham, to convey Lady Parkhurst's invitation to his own great-aunt. Lord Claibourne saw no difficulties there. He was finally offering *Tante* Simone a sojourn in London near many of her friends, along with the chance of a great-grandbaby to spoil. She had been after him to wed for years now, and a wife whose dowry would help restore the Abbey could only thrill her. Leigh could see no reason to mention any irregularities about the betrothal — or the bride!

Miss Trevaine, meanwhile, was finally acting in anything but an unusual manner for a seventeen-year-old girl. She was thinking about her future, clothes, and men.

It took all of one day for Jacelyn to discover the changes Claibourne had made in her life, outwardly, at any rate. At church that Sunday, she was no longer Miss Jacey to the villagers she'd known all her years, nor that wild Trevaine girl to the matrons who had barely given her a nod previously. Now her old friends bowed and tugged their forelocks, and even the gentrywomen graciously bent their heads in her direction, smiling. Of course now she was a few steps down the aisle and two short words away from being a countess, no matter how she'd done it. She, Jacelyn Trevaine, a countess! Even Priscilla Ponsonby and her mother would have to curtsey to her. That was a heady notion for a young girl, so she practiced her best *grande dame* looks, sitting in the Treverly pew between her father and Mrs. Phipps. She even tried raising one eyebrow as she'd seen his lordship do, to such majestic effect, until Mrs. Phipps pinched her arm.

Looking around, she caught Samantha's wink, across the aisle in Squire's pew. Her air dreams came back to earth with a painful thump. For there, next to Arthur in his high collar and nipped-in waist, sat Priscilla, in high-waisted primrose muslin, with matching ribbons holding silk roses to her bonnet. Her friend Miss Chadwick wore a sky-blue jaconet gown with an ermine tippet, and a white satin bonnet with blue ruching and a large blue bow tied off to one side of her heart-shaped face. Even Squire's daughters, dressed alike in pale pink pinafores, were better attired than the countess-to-be.

Jacelyn wore the shapeless navy kerseymere with the white fichu she'd worn to church every Sunday.

That was what Mrs. Phipps thought suitable, and since Mrs. Phipps made most of Jacelyn's clothes, cleaned them, pressed them, and laid them out for her, Jacey had never given it another thought. Her chipstraw bonnet was nearly new, but the ribbons were tangled, and Jacelyn had been in a hurry, late as usual, so they hung in a bedraggled knot somewhere under her chin. She had also been too late, exercising Pen, on a lead, at her father's insistence, to change her heavy wool tartan for a paisley shawl, and she'd only pinned it with a tin brooch from the last fair, lopsided besides. Why, she looked more like a rag-picker than an heiress! They'd all laugh at her in London. Worse, they would laugh at Lord Claibourne, with his reputation for beautiful women, being saddled with such a fright. No one would believe for an instant that he was attracted to her. Why should they, when she didn't?

After the service, when the congregation clustered in the churchyard, Jacelyn impatiently stood by her father, accepting best wishes and ignoring innuendoes as best she could, until Squire's party came near.

Lady Ponsonby wouldn't offer her hand to shake, sniffing that "it's a long way 'twixt St. David's and Dover," which Jacelyn took to mean my lady wouldn't acknowledge her till she had a ring on her finger. Priscilla took her cue from her mother: "Congratulations are in order, I suppose, Miss Trevaine, though I wish you well of your bargain. Heaven knows, *I* wouldn't have him.

"Oh," Jacelyn inquired sweetly, "has he asked you?"

Priscilla flounced off, leaving Miss Chadwick to titter, "I think you are very brave, Miss Trevaine. I couldn't even think of being alone with such a rake."

To which Jacelyn replied, "And I, Miss Chadwick, would never think of wearing some poor dead animal around my neck." It was the little beady glass eyes on the other girl's fur wrap that did it. Jacelyn excused herself to her father when she finally saw Mrs. Bottwick leaving the vicar's side.

"Ma'am, could I please ask a favour of you? It's terribly important, you see, and there's no one else."

"Of course, Jacelyn dear. I know you must miss your mother at times like this. I thought Mrs. Phipps would explain to you . . ."

"Explain? Oh no, Mrs. Bottwick, I know all about that." At the look of horror on Mrs. Bottwick's round face, Jacelyn hurriedly added, "The farm animals, you know. This is more important! I . . . I can't go to London like such a frump. I'd die. Mrs. Phipps can only make one kind of dress, short sleeves for summer, long sleeves for winter. And if Aunt Amabel has the dressing of me, I'll end up looking like a . . . silly debutante."

"But you are a debutante, Jacelyn. I'm sure your aunt knows what's best."

"No, Mrs. Bottwick. She only sees a hobbledehoy little girl she has to hide in ruffles and frills so no one will notice I'm different. And I'm not just a girl in her first Season, I'm nearly engaged, and to a top-of-the-trees Corinthian besides!"

Mrs. Bottwick was beginning to see Jacelyn's problem, more perhaps than Jacelyn did, and her natural motherly feelings were stirring, but it wasn't for her to interfere.

"How can I make you see?" Jacelyn wondered, desperate to be understood. Her eye caught Samantha Bottwick, standing next to Arthur. "There. Look at Sam." She didn't notice Mrs. Bottwick's wince, which changed to a proud smile with Jacelyn's next words: "She'll always look beautiful, just standing still, no matter what she wears. She's tall and blonde; she'll be exquisite in all the pastels and white lace. I'll get lost in them! A poor little brown dab of a thing!"

"What do you want then, my dear? You cannot dress in red satin like some opera dancer, and you cannot damp your petticoats like Caro Lamb. I won't hear of it, and I'm sure your aunt won't either."

"Is Jacey going to damp her petticoats then, Mama?"

"Samantha!"

"Hello, Sam," Jacey said, grinning at her friend. "I am trying to convince your mother to help me find some *style*. I need to cut a dash, as Arthur would say. You know you have *La Belle Assemblée* the same week it's out in London."

Samantha looked at her consideringly. "She's right, Mama. Everyone is going to stare at her anyway, you know. And it's not like there's ever been anything exactly ordinary about Jacey either, so maybe she does need a look of her own. Besides, if we don't go shopping with her, she's liable to go off to London looking like Cambridgeshire girls make their clothes from horse blankets."

"Now, Samantha. Jacelyn, if your father gives his permission, we'll all go into Ryefield. Perhaps I could have my aunt in Kensington send some fabrics. I

72

recall some dark green shot-silk at the Emporium Arcade. . . ."

So Jacelyn's next few weeks, and most of her thoughts, were taken up with clothes. There were trips to Ryefield and even an excursion to Royston, consultations with the *Ladies' Journal* and Mrs. Bottwick's aunt. And fitting after fitting. Jacelyn had never stood still for so long in her whole life.

She had an evening gown made of the emerald silk, with gold braid and gold slippers to match, and gold ribbons to thread through her newly styled hair, brushed back smooth except for a few curls at either temple, then piled on her head in twisted coils. Also for evening there was a cream satin embroidered with gold butterflies, and a gold tissue with a lace overskirt. Her day dresses were of peach and apricot and amber, with simple lines to grace her figure, and only simple trims, nothing fussy to overwhelm her.

This was only the start of her wardrobe. The rest would be selected in London by a much more knowledgeable Jacelyn, but it was all the local seamstresses could accomplish in the time. Amazing how "young miss" would have had to wait for weeks, after being served by the lowest apprentice. Miss Trevaine, after a few words from Mrs. Bottwick, could have her gowns fashioned in days, assured Madame d'Journet (née Nellie Jones) herself, nearly forgetting her French accent in calculating her income from this windfall. With the chance of dressing Squire's three daughters if she pleased the ladies now, Madame would sew the seams herself, if she had to.

There were two items of disagreement in the new wardrobe. The first was a deep rose velvet gown with a décolletage Mrs. Bottwick thought far too daring. Jacelyn adored it, and Samantha labelled it regal. They compromised with a lace insert, which Jacelyn determined wouldn't reach London.

There was no compromise on the other outfit Squire's wife considered in dubious taste. Jacelyn saw the fashion plate in *La Belle Assemblée* and couldn't rest until she had one made: a riding habit with a scarlet Hussar-style jacket with black buttons, and a black split skirt.

"But, dearest, you cannot mean to ride astride in London!" Mrs. Bottwick was aghast.

"Of course not," Jacelyn assured her, wondering if she could find a way. "But think about my present habit!"

Jacelyn's bombazine riding outfit was serviceable, Mrs. Bottwick had to give it that. Otherwise it was a mud-coloured brown that was always dirt-streaked. The girl never seemed to remember to pick up the extra width so the train either dragged behind her or tripped her up. It was remarkable how such a graceful rider looked like such a clumsy waif on the ground. Mrs. Bottwick relented. They even found a tiny scarlet cap to match, with a white feather to curl down the side of Jacelyn's cheek, highlighting the white lace she'd have at collar and cuffs.

All in all, Jacelyn was satisfied that her clothes were out of the ordinary without being outlandish. If she looked special, maybe, just maybe, Lord Claibourne would think she was special. Mrs. Bottwick, on the other hand, acknowledged that the new styles gave Jacelyn a more dignified, mature air, which should, the good Lord willing, make her act that way!

Luckily for Jacey, the new concern for her clothes took up a lot of time, time she'd otherwise have spent wondering about that other new discovery she'd made: men. Not men as in her father or Squire or Shoop or even Arthur. Men as in Lord Claibourne, as in all she didn't know about farm animals despite what she'd told Mrs. Bottwick, and all her father's books didn't tell her. These wonderings she hugged closely to herself at night, and dreamt of blue eyes and lazy smiles.

"But what if his aunt is a dragon, Papa?"

"Then tell Antoine not to overcook the beef," Lord Trevaine answered wearily, having lost his place in the Suetonius again. "Jacelyn, it's just a small dinner party for a few of our closest friends, stop fretting so. After three days in a carriage, Madame Aubonier won't wish anything more. Now go help Mrs. Phipps set the table, and leave me in peace!"

Miss Trevaine could face Squire's wrath and think nothing of taking hedges higher than her horse, but tonight's dinner had her quaking: her new gown, her new hair style, her new role—and to be putting them on for the first time at such a gathering! Most of the guests had known her forever. What if they laughed? No, as her father said, they were all friends. These people, her father had insisted, were the ones he wished to share his pride with, so the county would see this was no hole-in-corner affair. The alternative was worse, the evening alone with Claibourne and his aunt, so Jacelyn hurried to get ready.

Squire was fidgety too, ruining his second cravat. " 'Can't see what your daughter needed a new dress for. She's too young to be dining out in company anyway."

"Jacelyn particularly asked that Samantha attend. I'm sure she'll feel easier having another young lady there. Besides, it will be good for our Samantha to get out more before her own presentation. Those young girls pitchforked into Society all at once often make a mull of it."

"Well, I won't have a gal of mine picking up any froward behaviour from that Trevaine chit. Deuce take this linen!"

"Hush, George, let me. Though why your valet has to be in the stables is beyond me."

"He knows a lot more about physicking, humans and animals, than any stableman I've ever had, that's why, and that new gelding Raindancer's a deuced sight more important than all this dandification."

"Anyway, dear, think of how nice it will be for Samantha in her own Season next year, if one of her best friends is a countess. I'm considering bringing Samantha to London for Jacelyn's come-out ball next month. There, your neckcloth is tied. Don't tug at it so."

"What, another dress for the chit? Next you'll be expecting me to leave the country to go to London and do the pretty. No, madam, I tell you the girl is too young.

"Just as Jacelyn Trevaine is too young to face all of this without her friends nearby."

"Gammon. If you mean by that what I've heard all week, that the chit's too young to deal with a man of Claibourne's stamp, why, I say it again, he could be the making of her."

"He could break her heart. If it weren't for you and your—"

Samantha was going to London.

Bien. Everything seemed to be going *bien*. Mme. Aubonier had arrived on schedule, a tall, rigidly erect, thin-faced woman dressed all in black. She had raised her lorgnette to survey the house and its occupants, and declared them all *"Bien, bien."*

"How was your journey, Madame?"

"Bien, bien."

"May I show you to your room? Would you care to rest before dinner? Shall I have tea sent to you?" All received the same answer, till Jacelyn wondered if perhaps Madame didn't speak English. Hesitant to practice her schoolgirl French, she was relieved when Madame surveyed her chintz-papered room, fire well lit, fall asters in a Meissen pitcher, and declared it all "Lovely, lovely." What a peculiar chaperone this would be!

At least her presence saved Jacelyn from the awkwardness she'd been dreading, that first meeting with Claibourne who was, incredibly, as handsome as she'd remembered. She curtseyed, he bowed, a few polite words were exchanged between the *biens*. Then she'd gone off to see to his aunt's comfort, her own

77

toilette, the rest of the guests, and finally the dinner, all without having to face that first private moment. Madame, seated between Jacelyn's father and Vicar Shankman, seemed to have found her vocabulary, English or French, Jacey could not tell from her place at the opposite end of the table. Claibourne's scarecrow of an aunt also seemed to have found her appetite; she appeared to be a trencherwoman of Squire's caliber. And for all his grumbling, Squire seemed to enjoy the turbot in oyster sauce and the veal *marselaisse* as well as he did the plain rack of lamb Jacelyn had Antoine include for his benefit. Even Samantha was managing well, between the vicar and Admiral Hopkinton, who was an old dear, even if he was nearly deaf and persisted in refighting the Peninsular Campaign across the table to Claibourne, in a voice booming enough to stir the autumn leaves Jacelyn had arranged for a center-piece.

Claibourne was all poise and polish, making his replies to the admiral through Jacelyn, so she was the one forced to shout out Wellington's strategy, while Leigh conversed quietly with Mrs. Bottwick on his other side. Claibourne looked even more elegant in evening clothes, Jacelyn noted during a lull in the admiral's wargames, and she was quite sure his shoulders weren't padded, as Arthur's undoubtedly were.

All in all, she thought, the evening was going quite well, with only one adverse comment about her new looks. When Samantha had exclaimed over the green gown, Squire had commented to the admiral, in a necessarily carrying voice, "Well, I suppose it's an improvement, but I wouldn't let any daughter of

mine go out in public without her stays."
Claibourne's lips twitched, but he didn't miss a word
in his description of the road conditions to the vicar's
wife. Thank goodness no one mentioned the episode
behind this whole celebration, not even Squire, who
was still feeling guilty over his part in it, according to
Sam. *Bien*.

Dinner was finally over; the men had their port.
Madame retired to her bedchamber to rest for the
next day's journey, and the vicar, Squire, and Admiral Hopkinton joined Jacelyn's father for a round of
whist while the vicar's wife and Mrs. Bottwick discussed winter floral arrangements for the church and
Samantha softly played the pianoforte.

"Do you play?" he asked—the only *he* in the room,
as far as Jacelyn was concerned. He sat beside her on
the sofa.

"About as well as I do watercolours," she said,
laughing.

"Ah, that's the first time in two weeks I've heard
that sound. I thought you must have packed it away
with your britches."

Jacelyn was fingering the silk of her gown. "Do
you . . . do you like it, my lord?"

"Fishing for compliments, are you, dewdrop?
'Well, I suppose it's an improvement,' he teased,
quoting Squire and looking where Squire hadn't
found any corset. He smiled at Jacelyn's furious
blush, then let his hand between them softly brush
her thigh. "And here I was looking forward to stroll-
ing down Rotten Row with you in Lem's castoffs.
N'importe, you'll make just as big a stir now, poppet.
You look quite beautiful."

She laughed again. "Stuff! It's only the dress! I just didn't want your friends to think I was a shabrag. I didn't need the whole butterboat poured on me!"

He gave her a quizzical look. "Then you are the first woman I've ever met who didn't love flattery. How do you feel about diamonds?" he asked, taking a little box from his pocket. The ring he held out for her inspection was gold with a round diamond set in a circlet of tiny rubies.

"It's beautiful, Leigh, but —"

"But what, rosebud?" he asked, trying to see which of her fingers it fit best, while she sat benumbed.

"But I thought we didn't have to have a real engagement. You said we could just put it about that we had some kind of understanding."

"And so we do, don't we? Never fear, that's not the Claibourne diamond, just a little piece from the family collection. We'll have to fatten you considerably in London if you're to wear the real thing, else you'd not have strength to hold up your arm. There's a tiara and a bracelet, besides the wedding set. I simply thought you might like this."

"Oh, I do, Leigh. It's just that, well, if we're not really engaged, is it proper for me to accept such a gift?" Regretful, she looked over to the facing sofa, where the older ladies sat, pretending they weren't watching her every move.

"What, are you going all prunes and prisms on me? Fancy gowns, elegant hairdos, the perfect hostess, and now the picture of respectability! You must be a changeling; I'll wager you're some other brat Lord Trevaine's trying to foist off on me so he can keep the real thing to himself." He drew out his eyepiece and surveyed her slowly through it with all the affectation of a Bond Street Beau. From her side, of course, his eye looked like a distorted blue billiard ball.

"Silly, I suppose you'd prefer it if I still set frogs loose in the dining room."

" 'Still'?"

"Only once. I put some frogs under the covers of the serving dishes so when Phipps opened them to serve . . ."

"No wonder the man has white hair! And no, pet, I don't mean to encourage you to such pranks. Just know that I like the bandit as well as the belle, so you don't have to playact for me."

"Since you are being so agreeable, Leigh, there is something we should discuss."

"Oh-oh, I'm beginning to recognise a particular golden flicker in your eyes that betokens some deviltry or other, and I misdoubt that tone of voice. What horrible scheme are you concocting?"

"I want to take Pen to London with us. She'll be unhappy here without me and won't get enough exercise, so I've decided she has to come along. Either she comes or I don't," Jacey ended militantly.

Smiling, Claibourne raised Jacelyn's hand, the one with the ring, to his mouth for a sweet salute. "Of course, Jay-bird, it's all part of the deal."

"What deal?" suspiciously.

"Why, the deal I made with your father and Bottwick, of course. Your father agreed not to call me out if I took you off his hands, and Squire agreed not to challenge me if I agreed to take the dog out of

81

the county."

"Do be serious," she told him, meanwhile very aware that he had not released her hand.

"Serious? Then listen, Jacelyn, I'm not your father, nor even the squire, to call you to account for your actions. I want us to be friends, not keep coming to cuffs over foolish things. Agreed?"

Jacelyn nodded, though she couldn't help wonder if he meant she should be as complacent about his behaviour as he seemed prepared to be over hers. What if he meant he'd overlook a huge dog in the drawing room, in exchange for her turning a blind eye to . . . to a fancy piece in his flat! They didn't have a real engagement, of course, but even the idea sat like a lead weight in her chest. Many men had mistresses, she knew, yet how could she bear the earl's ever touching another woman's hand the way his thumb was stroking hers? Or smile that warm, slightly lopsided grin at someone else? She'd toss her in the Thames, decided Jacelyn, and see how easygoing his lordship was at *that* foolishness!

"About the ring." Jacelyn thought it best to change the subject lest she blurt out her intentions. "I don't understand why you've kept all these beautiful pieces in a vault somewhere gathering dust, when you needed money so badly. You could have sold them long ago and reinvested the money in the estates, or whatever, couldn't you?"

"The diamonds were handed down from countess to countess for centuries, part of the Merrill clan's history. They weren't mine to sell."

"But you can give this one away?"

"Yes," he told her, squeezing her hand but gestur-

82

ing around the room with his other. "You see your home, your friends, your father? I wanted to bring you a bit of my heritage, to have you meet the family, so to speak. I wanted the pleasure of making you smile, and I wanted something of mine to be special to you. Do you understand?"

Bien. Bien.

6

The heavy old coach had new black paint and the Claibourne family crest. It had four hired horses and two hired postillions with weapons. On the box it had Clive, Madame's old coachman from the Abbey in Durham, and a huge, scraggly dog sitting beside him, to Clive's disgust. His first trip to London in twelve years, and to arrive looking like a travelling road show. *Pah*. Enough to throw a man off his feed, it was, especially when the beast had enough of feeling the wind in its face and stretched out across the box seat — all across it, so those big cow eyes looked up from Clive's own lap, and hairs were clinging all over his new uniform. "I wouldna do this for nobbut the young master," Clive told the animal as he watched the road ahead, where Claibourne led the way on his grey stallion. Clive spat tobacco juice over the side of the coach. "You're my paying off a debt, belikes, for all them easy years a-driving madam to the village 'n church on Sundays while Master Leigh was off to war. 'Sides, if gettin' you and young miss to London is going to settle 'is lordship down 'n right things at the Abbey, guess I'd tote a

84

bear up here."

The situation inside the coach was very similar. Mme. Simone would rather have stayed in Stockton-on-Tees than spend another day being jostled across the length of England, but she also dearly wished to see Claibourne happy and the Abbey restored to a semblance of grandeur, if not glory. The little heiress seemed to suit on both counts. In her day the deed would have been done: a scandal, a wedding. Simple, no? Names and funds would already be transferred, and the bride and groom would be left to find love and affection later, inside the marriage, it was to be hoped. But these young English, they wanted it all. Leigh wanted to woo the *fille* and show her a good time in London. His Aunt Simone would do her part.

"So," she said to her charge when they were finally on their way and silence had lasted long enough. "We go to make you a success, no?"

Jacelyn laughed. "Oh no, Madame, we're not attempting the impossible, only the improbable, getting the ton to accept me."

"Why should it not? You have the birth, the breeding, I see. My nephew gives his ring. What is to interfere? You have manners, no?"

"Well, not always, Madame." Jacelyn was looking self-conscious in her new navy wool spenser and light blue travelling dress. She'd placed her new bonnet on the seat opposite almost reverently, to protect the blue silk flowers which peeped from under the brim. His lordship had called it a lovely cross between innocence and allure. Just like Jacelyn, he'd said, giving her a great deal to think about, beyond how she was going to miss her father and all she held dear. What a confused muddle her emotions were in altogether!

She was sad to leave Treverly, of course, but eager to explore London's attractions, including the exclusive shops, now that she had a taste of fashion. She was excited over Claibourne's company, yet anxious that she wouldn't please him. Mostly Jacelyn was uncertain she *could* remain a lady under such conditions as Mrs. Bottwick and Mrs. Phipps tried to drum into her up to the last minute: A lady never goes anywhere alone, a lady never walks on Bond Street in the morning. A lady may not waltz until approved, may not speak to a man unless introduced, may not — not — not! So many senseless and stupid restrictions, yet the slightest breach of this etiquette would see her sent home in disgrace. His lordship certainly wouldn't want a wife who was laughed at, no matter what he claimed.

"Its more than just my manners and breeding, Madame. Samantha says that Priscilla says that it will take a great push to get me into Almack's — it's this exclusive club attended by everyone who is anyone. My aunt, Lady Parkhurst, won't make the effort to get me vouchers. She doesn't quite approve of me, you see, and doesn't wish to jeopardise her own good standing. And Samantha says that Priscilla says I'll be ignored totally if I'm not accepted at Almack's. You know, not invited to balls and parties, not recognised by other young ladies."

"This Samantha I met, but who is this Priscilla who has so much to say?"

"She's Squire's niece Priscilla Ponsonby, and she's an Incomparable. That's what they call the most admired women. She had five offers in her first Season, but no one was good enough for her. Besides, she's tall and pretty and never has stains on her gloves or a single hair out of its pins."

"Ah, so we shall steal all of her beaux, yes?"

"Oh, Madame, I wouldn't want any of them, just . . . just . . ."

"Just to show this *chat* that Mademoiselle Trevaine can shine in the first circles also?"

"Yes, but I don't see how."

"Didn't my grand-nephew ask me to see about your debut? Today is what, Friday, and this Almack's meets when?"

"Wednesday."

"*Oui,* plenty of time. Don't worry, *petite.* I'll see it done."

Jacelyn did not want to offend the older woman, though she couldn't see how Mme. Aubonier could have any influence whatsoever in London, having been isolated in Durham for so long. She hesitantly mentioned, "Vouchers are extremely hard to come by, ma'am. Samantha says one must know the patronesses who run Almack's. Priscilla's mother is close with Lady Jersey, which means we couldn't ask her."

"Enough of this Priscilla, child. I am tired of her already. And that Jersey *chien* is a scandal unto herself, *l'affaire* with your prince. No, I would not let her invite us. Princess Esterhazy is still a patroness, no? She is a connexion of Claibourne's grandfather, my father *le Duc*. And Lady Drummond-Burrell, her husband brought her to *la maison* on their wedding trip, many years ago. *Il fait*. It is done."

"I am sorry, Mme. Aubonier, for doubting you. I did not realise you had such connexions in London."

"Call me *tante, petite,* as Leigh does. I like you. And *non,* how could you know I would still have good friends and good correspondents, so long since I have seen them?"

"But, *tante,* if you have all these friends, why did you stay alone all those years while Leigh was away? Weren't you lonely?"

"Child, I had lost my home, my husband, my son. The last of my family was Mignon-Marie, Leigh's mother. Then she too was taken, and the boy went off to fight to save my country, too late. How could I be anything but lonely, wherever I went?"

"I understood there were many other French men and women in London. Perhaps you could have stayed with them?"

"Ah, I could have stayed French, and stayed lost in memories, *n'est-ce pas?* But Claibourne Abbey had no mistress, and the boy had no one else to come home to. So I stayed and made a new life and new friends. It was still sad, *triste*. But listen, Jacelyn, and remember, you can be lonely among the largest crowds, without your own loved ones. They are who matter, not people like this Priscilla, whose opinions are worth cabbage, yes?"

"Yes, *belle-tante,*" Jacelyn said, impulsively reaching over to kiss the other woman. "Thank you."

88

After a relaxed luncheon at the Crowned Drake, about halfway to London, Leigh handed Baron's reins to one of the outriders and settled in the coach with the women. He took the corner opposite Jacey, his back to the horses, his long legs in tight buckskins and now-dusty Hessians resting on the other side of hers.

"So, ladies, time for a council of war. What plans have you made?"

"Clothes first," his aunt proclaimed. "The dressmakers can be working while we see to introductions."

"But I have plenty of clothes. They were sent ahead to Aunt Amabel's."

"A lady never has enough clothes. *Tiens,* styles change overnight in London. Now you two make your arrangements. I rest."

Jacelyn looked at the figure of Claibourne's aunt in her corner, all in black again, a high-necked stuff gown, and was dubious about the lady's taste, much less her knowledge of the current fashions. Aunt Amabel, however, would have the vapours over the styles and colours Jacelyn chose. She wasn't even in London, and already there were difficulties.

As if reading her thoughts, Mme. Aubonier opened her eyes briefly and fixed Jacey in her glance. "Not to fear, *petite.* I go to visit these *grande dames* of your English ton. They talk more frankly without a *jeune fille* present. *He* goes with you to the shops," she decreed, nodding in Claibourne's direction before shutting her eyes again.

"You, my lord, trailing after me in the dress shops?"

"And the milliners and booteries; I'll wait outside the corsetière, of course." He caught Jacelyn's look in his aunt's direction. "All very proper: an open carriage, your maid for chaperone."

"I haven't got a maid," Jacelyn contradicted. "I don't want one, fussing about me and telling me what to wear, like a child."

The earl inspected his sleeve for lint. "I'd be your abigail myself, pet, doing up all those little buttons and combing out your hair, but I draw the line at mending and pressing."

"Mrs. Phipps always did that for me. I see that I cannot expect Aunt Amabel's London housekeeper to sew new ribbons on my gowns. How does one arrange to hire a lady's maid in Town? At home Mrs. Phipps would have promoted the second housemaid, or found a cousin who was good with a needle."

"I'm certain your aunt has already seen to it, once your clothes arrived." He held his hand up when he saw her brow start to lower. "You needn't keep her, whoever your aunt selects, if she doesn't suit you. Remember, your father sent funds of your own, so you can hire any amount of fancy dressers, or second housemaids, if you'd rather."

That satisfied her but, curious, she asked, "Do you have a valet?"

"Arthur and I share a man-of-all-trades. Haggerty was my batman in the army. He can remove stains from a cravat and poultice a horse's hock and cook a fine rabbit stew, if need be. Mostly he makes certain I'm tricked out *à la mode*."

"Do you know a lot about ladies' fashions?" Jacelyn wanted to know, getting back to the subject at hand, though she was fairly sure of the answer.

That speck of lint seemed most tenacious. Claibourne cleared his throat. "I have had a, er, deal of experience in such matters."

"I'm sure you have, if half the rumours are correct!"

"Hold your claws, little kitten. I never said I was a monk. One mustn't listen to rumours, anyway."

"Sometimes one cannot help it. People think they should tell you, for your own good. One story has it that you have an uncle"—she lowered her voice to a near whisper—"who is a slave trader."

"Didn't your father explain about all that? I was sure he would."

"No. He said you had an unfortunate family history which had no reflexion on you. Is it true?"

"Yes, Fenton did own ships in the black trade; I don't believe he does any longer. You needn't worry about seeing him, however, he never goes out and I certainly never visit him. You won't meet up with my cousin Percival either. He is not received in polite circles, thank goodness. A greater nodcock you'll never see."

Then, under Jacelyn's interested questioning, he explained how his family tree got so infested, how his Aunt Sydelle was pushed into a hastily arranged marriage when a crop failure threatened the family with bankruptcy. The talk of divorce, the duel, Leigh

91

covered it all. "So now you'll know the whole of it, instead of the half-truths people will dredge up for your benefit. Now you'll also see why I'm not top-drawer elite. Will it bother you?"

In one sense it bothered her very much: what if she obtained those prized vouchers for Almack's and he couldn't go? Suddenly her desire to attend that pinnacle of snobbery evaporated.

"What is it, Jacelyn? Does my background upset you so much?" Leigh was concerned at the look on her face.

"Not at all, you gudgeon. It's just that your aunt is seeing to invitations to Almack's, and I wasn't sure if you . . ."

"Were granted permission to enter the sacred portals? Lord, yes, I've never been blackballed anywhere. Why in heaven's name do you want to go there, though? It's dull as ditchwater. It's hot and crowded, and the cakes are stale. The dowagers sit around like gargoyles making hideous faces at anyone requesting a dance with one of their charges, when everyone knows they only bring the chits there to get rid of them. The Marriage Mart, they call it. Dreadful place." He shuddered, making Jacey laugh.

"Well, you are going to have to attend, my lord, because I'm to be all the crack!"

"Are you now, my fancy lady? Then *avaunt,* let's go. Besides, if I'm to be seen with you, perhaps I won't get those gimlet stares. See how much good you are doing me already?"

"Don't be goosish. I have nothing to do with your ancient history."

92

"History, no, but there is, ah, a more recent past"—one eyebrow raised—"which we shall not discuss, save that it makes it impolitic for me to be judging your behaviour. Suffice it to say I was not an eligible *parti,* nor even a particularly desirable dancing partner for a young lady."

"What, did they think you would ravish them, right there on the dance floor?"

"You'd best watch your tongue, my girl, if Almack's is your goal," he teased. "One such remark and your next invitation will be when Satan goes sleigh riding. And no, I never stayed long enough among the debutante set to find out what their mamas feared worst: a flirt or a fortune hunter. Now, pet, thanks to you, they won't have to worry about the big bad wolf turning their daughters' heads. As long as you are on my arm, I'll be as safe as a lamb."

"You better be," Jacelyn muttered under her breath.

"What was that, my love?"

The next miles passed quickly, with a deck of cards. The earl played leisurely, relaxed as always, yet seeming to know where every card was in the pack. Jacelyn would begin a hand with great determination, vowing to concentrate on the discards, until she was distracted by a passing wagon loaded with baskets, or the need to know what dramas were showing at Drury Lane. After two hours Leigh put the cards away and consulted the tally sheet.

"You owe me five hairpins, two feathers and—

what was this last stake? The button from your gloves. I think I'll defer collecting, as it wouldn't do to arrive at your aunt's doorstep all undone. Don't ever consider making a career of the pasteboards, dear heart, you'd starve."

"Perhaps I'll go on the stage, then. I can't sing but I can handle the breeches parts well enough. Can you see me as Portia?"

"As well as I can picture you in hoops and head-dress for the Queen's drawing-room presentation. By the bye, have you considered at all what you'll do after Christmas, pet, if no one else catches your fancy and you decide not to have me?" Over my dead body, he vowed to himself, but his noncommittal, jesting attitude stilled any assurance Jacelyn might have given. How could she speak of her newborn feelings when he still considered this a temporary liaison at best, a bothersome debt of honour at worst?

Her pride answered for her: "Oh, I'll simply return home to Treverly. I never wanted a husband, or thought to need one. Most girls see marriage as a means to independence, a home of their own without chaperones and all the restrictions. I already have that, at home."

"What about children?" he asked.

"Oh, puppies are more appealing," she replied, "and a great deal easier to come by, from what I hear. Now that you mention it, however," she added, with that look of mischief which set off sirens in Leigh's head, "there are some things considered unsuitable for a maiden's ears, which I wish to understand.

94

Since we are nearly engaged, and this might be my only opportunity in life, perhaps you could explain them to me when we're in London."

The earl pulled his hat down over his eyes, crossed his arms over his chest, and pretended to go to sleep.

7

It's strange how spiders have such a bad name, even among the insect groups. Go outside on an early spring morning when the dew is still on the grass, or a late summer afternoon when fog settles down, and there, by the trellis or under the eave, you'll see one of the world's priceless treasures, gleaming with diamonds. The spider is not remembered as the master craftsman, however, only as the villainous nighttime schemer. Perhaps the spider's poisonous bite adds to such ill repute, coupled with the creature's methods. Not for the spider honourable face-to-face combat; he spins art into artful, then lurks in shadows by his trap, waiting for unwary victims.

Now picture Josiah Fenton, hook-nosed, shrunken of frame, huddled in his spoke-wheeled Bath chair, spewing his hatred like venom into a dank, ill-lit, cluttered room. With apologies to arachnids, he resembled nothing so much as an evil spider, weaving treachery.

"Wars," he muttered, tapping his long fingernails

on the *London Gazette* in his lap. "Years of wars. Countless dead. Why couldn't he be one of them? Hare-brained heroics ought to have done for him long ago. Blast his curst luck!"

The last exclamation did not manage to stir the dreary room's other occupant, who was sprawled on the loveseat: Fenton's son Percival, if son he was. Fenton was the only one to disparage Percy's lineage because, at twenty-five, tall, skinny, and stoop-shouldered, with an enormous, boney, bobbing Adam's apple presently unconcealed by the soiled neckcloth draped across his knobby shoulders, and that same hook nose, Percy was his father's image — and despair. The only feature Percy didn't share with Fenton was his hair; the younger man's dank dishwater blond was proof enough for Fenton of Sydelle's infidelity. Ignoring the memory of his wife's shining gold curls, he swore she'd played him false. She had to have; Josiah Fenton could not have sired such an infernally stupid son! Percy was so stupid she must have mated with a tailor's dummy. Percy was so stupid that he halfway, or hopefully, believed Fenton's claims himself.

"Wake up, you comatose clunch-head, you inebriated imbecile," Fenton raged. "Your lickspit life is being ruined. Get up and do something about it!"

Bloodshot eyes opened in their pouches. Stringy fingers groped among the debris on a nearby table for a glass, a bottle, anything liquid to irrigate the desert in his throat. "Aargh. It's water."

Fenton threw the folded newspaper at Percy's head. "Read this, you wantwit, if you can. Lord knows if you stayed at any school long enough to

97

learn how."

Percy bent to pick up the paper. A monocle, a fob watch, two keys, and assorted seals fell out of his pockets, all dangling by gold chains and ribands, now hopelessly tangled across his puce waistcoat, which was embroidered with green and red cabbage roses. Percy managed to gather up the paper and read: " 'The Upper House voted today in favour of—' "

"Not that, you feebleminded fribble. The *on dits* column."

"Oh. 'During last night's rout at Lady E.B.'s, a certain Miss G. W. was seen returning from the garden with a Spanish dignitary. Could it be—' "

"Lower."

" 'It is rumoured that a certain hero of the past campaigns, known to love 'em and Leigh-ve 'em, will shortly be escorting to Town for the Season an unknown deb, announcement to follow.' That was what has you in such a taking?"

"Are your attics to let, boy? Do you know what this means?"

"M'cousin Leigh's getting leg-shackled after all this time, right? It is about Leigh, ain't it, Da?"

"It means that damned Claibourne cub made it through the bloodbath, and now he's looking to marry and fill his nursery."

"Well, he is thirty-something, ain't he? Time he saw about his posterior."

"His posterity, you gap-toothed gudgeon! You're his heir!"

" 'Druther be yours, gov, more money, don't you know."

Fenton grasped his head in his hands and moaned. "Whatever I may have done in my life, I never deserved this." He took a deep breath. "Listen, Percy. Shut your mouth if it will help. With my money and his title, you could be anything, go anywhere. Parliament, Carlton House, you name it. Any woman, any government post, whatever you want. Don't you see? That's what they promised me, those Claibournes. They promised me, and then they stole it away and put me here in this chair. But it's yours, boy, yours. They owe you. Don't let some unbreeched bastard rob you of it!"

"He won't be a bastard, Da, if Leigh marries the girl."

"Then see that he doesn't, you addle-pated ass!" With a final roar, Fenton shouted "Jensen!" and a small-sized mountain lumbered into the room. Little-headed, beef-broad, and as mad as his master, Jensen picked up Fenton, wheelchair and all, and carried him from the room.

Alone, Percy gathered all his chains, fobs, and ribbon pendants back into their more or less appropriate places, and stumbled over his boots on his way to a bottle and a glass. He poured himself a generous portion while he tried to set the problem in perspective.

There was his cousin, Leigh Merrill, Earl of Claibourne. Handsome, heroic, handy with sword, pistols, fists. A devil with the ladies and accepted everywhere.

Then there was himself, Percival possibly-Fenton. Handy with nothing, accepted nowhere. But a fine dresser, if he had to say so. According to the governor, somehow it was Percy's job to prevent Claibourne's marriage.

No one was *that* stupid. Percy had another drink.

Meanwhile, across town in her Portman Square mansion, Lady Amabel Parkhurst was sipping a glass of ratafia to settle *her* nerves. Two weeks to prepare and she was still not easy about her niece's coming. She'd had plenty of notice: her brother's letter, Claibourne's visit, the arrival of Mme. Aubonier's baggage via post chaise. The baggage was attended by a homely shrew of a maid named Hammersmith who'd set Parkhurst House at sixes and sevens, ordering everyone about, redecorating Madame's room, informing the chef of her mistress's tastes. Then a carriage had arrived from Treverly with trunks full of Jacelyn's belongings, whose unpacking Hammersmith insisted on overseeing, while a newly hired, very pricey lady's maid had tea in the housekeeper's pantry. The Treverly chaise was accompanied by an impudent boy by name of Lem, in charge of two riding horses. According to Trevaine's message, Lem was to act as groom to Jacelyn, see to her mounts, etc. The *et cetera* had Lady Parkhurst trembling with memories of apes in little red jackets. How bad could it be? Lady Parkhurst wondered. The girl had a groom, a chaperone, a maid, a chaperone's maid, and a near-fiancé. Surely her aunt had nothing to worry about.

The butler, Marcus, opened the front door when the carriage pulled up. Through the entryway proceeded her niece, certainly looking much more presentable than Amabel had hoped. On one side of her, however, stalked a veritable vulture of a black-clad crone, and on the other side, smiling wolfishly down at the girl as if she were a tender game pullet, strode one of the most notorious womanisers in all of London. Worst of all—she'd strangle that brother of hers—was a creature so immense its wagging tail threatened the Chinese vase on the hall table. The outrageous girl was still trying to turn Parkhurst House into a menagerie!

The butler's lapsed "My stars" was shortly followed by Amabel's "My salts! My vinaigrette!"

Vapours cannot be hurried, but eventually matters sorted themselves out. Lem was called to take Penelope for a walk in the park and an introduction to the stables. Hammersmith was summoned to escort her elderly mistress to her rooms, after a few mindless "lovely's" and "*bien*'s." The earl forfeited his reputation for bravery by hastily bowing his way out of Lady Parkhurst's baleful stare. On his exit he reminded Jacelyn of their early morning ride, assuring her aunt he was at her service, if she required his presence sooner. She didn't, not even for the quiet dinner *en famille*, which would have been courteous, so he left the ladies to become reacquainted. It did not take long.

"Why isn't it a formal announcement, Jacelyn? Your father wrote that Claibourne offered. Let me tell you what a feather that is in your cap. But you cannot dangle a man like him forever, you know. He'll not stay still for your shilly-shallying. Or do you think you'll do better, and that's why you're holding off?"

"Oh no, Aunt Amabel. Leigh is everything that a girl could want. It's just that . . ."

"Just what, for heaven's sake?"

Jacelyn looked away. "He doesn't love me."

"Hogwash! What's that to the point? He offered for you, didn't he? You like him, it seems from that foolish grin on your face whenever you mention him, and he looks at you as if you are some bon-bon to be snapped up. So what's the difficulty? You'll lose him, girl!"

"He'd marry me for his honour, and be pleased with the money. Oh yes, I know all about that, and his reputation, too. That's just it: we'd be wed, and I'd lose him anyway, if he didn't love me. Oh, he'd show me respect, Aunt Amabel, but it's not enough, so I have to wait, and try."

"Jacey, you and your crusades and hopeless causes! Why do you always take the long way 'round? This fox-hunt business, that absurd chaper-one no one's ever heard of, now trying to win the heart of a man who may not even have one! Ridicu-lous, child. Do you remember that visit some years ago when Cook promised you one of her tabby's kittens to take home?"

"I was only ten, Aunt Amabel. You can't com-pare—"

"And she let you choose. There was a fluffy white one I admired, I remember that. But you couldn't pick the pretty one, or the biggest one, not you. You had to choose the one that wouldn't nurse, the puny one that kept getting stepped on by

102

the others."

"He needed the most love."

"Yes, and you cried for days when he died. You even climbed down the tree outside your bedroom, to sit by his grave so he wouldn't be alone at night. Thank goodness you're too old for that, my dear. You wouldn't listen then, though, and I'm sure you won't listen now, but I'm afraid you'll still cry over this new foolishness of yours."

Before going to her own room after dinner, Jacelyn scratched on Mme. Aubonier's door. It was opened by the hatchet-faced Hammersmith.

"*Belle-tante*, I just wished to see if you were comfortable."

The old woman was reclining among a flotilla of pillows, a glass of warm milk by her side, a book in her hand. "Fine, *petite*, lovely."

"*Tante* Simone, I don't wish to be impertinent, but why do you just say things are fine, even when my aunt was too busy having the vapours to offer us tea, and Pen tried to get the butler to play with her by stealing his gloves?"

Blue eyes twinkled back at her. "Why should I waste my breath, child, with useless chatter? This way I tell people what they want to hear, I smile and nod, and *alors*, I am free to read my book, see?"

Jacelyn laughed. "I see I am dismissed, Aunt." She went over to the bed and kissed the elderly woman's cheek. "Good night. Thank you."

Her own room was the neatest a room of hers had ever been. No clothes lying about, no stack of unfinished books, no dog hairs, only a very proper lady's maid in dark grey with a black apron and a black lace cap. Not a wrinkle, not a smile, not a first name. Just "Vincent, miss." Jacelyn dismissed her as soon as her gown was unbuttoned. She wanted to be alone with her thoughts, especially those that Aunt Amabel had termed her fool's missions.

She pulled her lawn nightgown over her head and unpinned her hair before she realised how silly she'd been to send the maid away. There was no Mrs. Phipps to put her long hair into a braid, and she'd only make her usual rats' nest of it, leaving it in knots by morning. Besides, she hadn't told anyone to call her early for her ride. This was only her first night in London. How many more mistakes would she make?

Maybe the whole trip was a mistake, maybe Aunt Amabel was right. Her father would know, but he was very far away. The bed was warmed by a brick; still, it was big and strange. The night sounds were different too, all carriage wheels and clatter instead of crickets and bird calls. It was her first night in London, and she could not sleep. Worries gnawed at her like gnats. There was only one thing to do. She opened her window—yes, the plane tree still almost touched the sill—and climbed down. Stopping a moment to locate the kitten's grave, she picked her way across the rear courtyard's gardens to the stable. She whistled softly and soon had Pen smuggled back up to her room via the back door, setting a great many worry bugs to buzz around the second footman Eugene and the under cook, enjoying an illicit after-hours cuddle.

Jacelyn's bed was a lot smaller now, and a lot more like home.

Jacelyn needn't have worried over waking at her usual early hour. If the sun didn't do it, the baker's boy would. Or the egg man, knife sharpener, or herb vendour. Milk didn't even arrive in its usual fashion, from beast to bucket. This was London; milk came in great clanking tins aboard creaking drays.

Jacey washed hurriedly and scrambled into her new habit. There wasn't much time to fuss with her hair, so she left it in the ragged braid she'd managed for bed, just pinning the whole into a crown on her head, and setting the red cap atop it. She and Pen went out by the kitchen door, winking at that same cook, whose job it was to serve breakfast, a chore considered beneath the French chef's dignity. The cook grinned back and offered a pan of still-warm, crusty rolls. Jacey helped Pen to two, then wrapped more in a napkin, to share later.

At least Claibourne had thought to notify the stables, for Lem was waiting with both the chestnut gelding and the little bay mare from Treverly, neither saddled.

"Didn't know which you'd prefer this mornin', Miss Jacey. Both be rested from the trip, but the gelding's not used to city traffic yet."

"Why don't you put the sidesaddle on the mare then," advised Claibourne, riding up on Baron, "since Miss Trevaine isn't familiar with Town congestion either." Just as she was about to bristle at his high-handedness, Leigh dismounted and disarmed her with: "Good morning, my love. I hope you don't mind my fretting over you. That outfit is much too grand to land in the gutters." With a smile he added, "You *were* intending to ride sidesaddle, weren't you?"

"Wretch. Only if I must."

"Almack's?"

"I must."

Hyde Park was blanketed by fog. The only figures to be seen were exercise grooms trotting horses up and down the paths. After a few such tame canters, the earl led his little party down a different path, headed farther into the park where there were more trees, less people. Pen took off after some geese, then seemed to decide that London squirrels could be gotten down from trees to chase, by barking at them. Jacelyn handed out the rolls.

Claibourne looked at Jacey, sparkling with animation and humour, and knew that, no matter what else, keeping her happy was all that mattered to him. "Lem," he called out, dismounting, "I think Miss Trevaine's horse picked up a pebble." When the groom came near, holding the gelding's reins, they both bent over the mare's hind leg.

"Nothin' there, sir."

"Sure there is, Lem. The gelding just won't hold

106

still enough for you to look properly. Why don't you make sure the mare is all right while we, ah, keep the chestnut from getting nerved up by the traffic?"

"Pardon me, m'lord, there ain't no traffic."

Jacelyn was already sliding off the mare, a delighted smile on her face. "May I really, my lord?"

"I won't tell if you won't, pet," Claibourne told her, giving her a leg up onto the gelding, her split skirts to either side. Before the earl could remount she was off at a gallop, her silvery laughter floating back to him.

Lem pointedly turned his back. "I don't see no traffic, I don't see no pebble, 'n I don't see whatever's goin' on back there."

"What will your maid think?" Claibourne teased as they rode home in perfect decorum. "Your hair is all undone, and you look decidedly windblown. Quite different from the lady she sent out."

"She won't think anything, because I dressed myself. I couldn't think of waking her at daybreak."

"But you are the mistress, poppet."

"Yes, but I'm sure it takes her longer to dress. She's so starchy she only needs one name!"

Later that morning Lord Claibourne was to see how seriously my lady's maid took her position. When they reached Madame Bertin's, the premier modiste of London, Vincent examined every bolt of fabric and scrutinised every design modelled.

"If I may be permitted, Miss Trevaine, knowing London ways as I do, the pink sarcenet, *not* the emerald lutestring," and, "With your pardon, miss, all debutantes must wear white for their come-outs."

The earl, lounging in one of the showroom's comfortable seats, wondered how long it would take for the fireworks. He wasn't in the fitting room, of course, when the superior dresser felt it was her duty, in accordance with Lady Parkhurst's wishes, to adjust upward the neckline of an azure blue crêpe. Vincent had to step over the little fitter's apprentice, making the girl drop all her pins, which earned her a scolding from Madame Bertin herself, coming into the draped cubicle to make sure all was going smoothly with this new, favoured customer.

Madame had had her doubts, at first, that the girl in the chic orange muslin mightn't just be Claibourne's latest convenient, a proper maid — and one mustn't discount all the rumours. Madame was always happy to have the dressing of a future countess, and this one would only add to her already high standing, if Miss Trevaine didn't fold under the maid's pressure to dress as demurely as any other debutante.

In her haste to take Miss Trevaine's side, figuratively and literally, the dressmaker also tripped over the apprentice, who was kneeling to gather up the pins she'd lost. There followed a lot of French words that would have made *Tante* Simone blush. Although none of the audience understood entirely, the gist of the modiste's angry speech was obvious: the little red- headed Marguerite was ham-handed

108

and hen-witted, more suitable for milking cows than for serving in a fine shop.

"Forgive me, Mademoiselle, I only took on such a one as a favour to my coachman. Farm girls, *pah*. This one shall bother us no more. About the neckline . . ."

The 'prentice sobbed quietly, still trying to collect the pins into her apron, and the fitter scowled, and the dressmaker gave Jacelyn a toadeater's smile, and Vincent gave the neckline another tug.

"With all due respect, Miss Trevaine, please recall that my previous employer was the Duchess of Richmond's daughter, so I know whereof I speak. That amount of cleavage is quite, quite common-looking. Not at all the thing for—"

"Mademoiselle sets her own fashion. Any imbecile can see she is not of the usual mould."

Jacelyn had had enough. She stamped her foot. "I shall ask Claibourne." At the cluckings, she added, "I'm sure he knows more about ladies' bosoms than any of us," scandalising two avidly listening dowagers in the next cubicle.

Trailing yards of blue crêpe and a shower of silver pins, along with the fitting room entourage and the interested matrons, Jacelyn stomped out to the showroom and demanded of Claibourne, "My lord, will you tell these peahens where a lady's gown must start and end."

Fireworks indeed. Not twelve hours in Town and she was putting on a show for Lady Rivington. Leigh recrossed his legs and raised that one expressive eyebrow.

Flushing, Jacelyn amended her request: "Forgive

me, my lord. Would you please give us your opinion of this gown? Is the décolletage suitable?"

Leigh almost ached to show her just what that creamy expanse now tinged with pink was suitable *for.* Instead he told her, "You'll have to decide, Miss Trevaine. You'll be the one drawing attention. I can tell you that many ladies"—he emphasised the last word—"wear theirs even lower, though not usually such young ladies. Then again, many young women wouldn't look as attractive. You have to consider whether you wish to be approved or admired."

That was all very noncommittal, Jacelyn felt, when what she really wanted was *his* approval and *his* admiration, without having to ask. "As you will be the one escorting me, my lord, I thought my choice would affect you."

"Quite right, my dear. Tell me when you are going to wear it so I can buckle on my sabre to fight off all the smitten mooncalves. Proud to be of service, ma'am."

"Gudgeon. Well, I can always wear a shawl. Thank you, Lord Claibourne, ladies." She turned to go back to the fitting room when the abigail tried one last time.

"Lady Parkhurst is sure to object, miss, and I regret that I must agree."

"Lady Parkhurst isn't paying your wages, Vincent, and I regret that I am. As a matter of fact, I don't think we will suit at all, so if you will return to Portman Square and pack your things, I'm certain Lady Parkhurst will write you a glowing reference. Lord Parkhurst's secretary is handling my accounts, so you may discuss your wages with him.

That will be all."

Scarlet-faced, Vincent rushed out the door. When it closed on a stunned silence, Claibourne softly applauded. "To the manner born, my lady. What a countess you'll make! Why, Princess Caroline couldn't have done it better."

Grinning, Jacelyn lifted her straight little nose in the air, pronounced "Quite," and glided regally out of the room.

Mme. Bertin was not amused. Such a scene in her showroom was bad for business. Still, she smiled at Jacelyn, guaranteeing that, yes, the gown could be hemmed by the next day, the others made up within the week. She expressed her annoyance again on her way out by berating the apprentice.

When she was gone and Jacelyn was being helped out of the pinned gown, she asked the red-eyed girl why she stayed in such a place.

"It's m'mum, m'lady. I send her the wages, so my little brothers won't have to go to the mills. I was happy to get this position, ma'am."

Jacelyn took a good look at the girl, a little younger than herself, and liked what she saw: curly red hair and wide, honest green eyes, and many more freckles than Jacey had. She appeared country-clean, healthy, and unhappy. Impulsively, Jacey asked, "Tell me, um, Marguerite—"

"Margaret, ma'am," the girl said, bobbing a curtsey as she fastened Jacelyn's buttons, "but my brothers call me Pinkie."

"Pinkie, tell me, what did you think of me in the blue dress?"

"I thought you looked a treat, ma'am, 'n the way

111

you held your head, why, no one would mistake you for anything but a real lady. I been working here a month, nearly, and seen all the young ladies and their mums. Not a one could hold a candle to you."

Jacelyn hired herself a maid.

It took a very short time, while Pinkie gathered her few belongings, to settle the girl's contract. Jacelyn had only to voice her doubts over the almond-coloured cambric for Madame to lower her outrageous demands. Claibourne's reminder that Miss Trevaine still had to consider a presentation gown, while Jacelyn herself fingered the lace of a bridal doll, had madame toss in the girl's grey and white uniform, and good riddance!

A very well-satisfied threesome, four if you counted Lem in his fine new livery on the footman's ledge at the back of the carriage, proceeded to every fashionable shop on Bond Street, and a few not so well known down side streets. As is often the case, Jacelyn found more courtesy and cooperation in the smaller shops, so she was able to ignore the fact that Claibourne seemed known by name in each establishment. Busy with cottage bonnets and kid slippers, she didn't need to disturb herself over his knowledge of women's fashions or his remarkable patience. She simply accepted, and enjoyed, both.

When the carriage was nearly filled with boxes and tissue-wrapped parcels, they proceeded to Gunther's, for ices, then drove around some, showing Jacelyn the sights.

112

"There is so much I want to do and see, like the Tower and Hatchard's bookstore and the Pantheon Bazaar and—"

"Hold, my dear. Enough for one day! I promised your aunt to have you returned in time for tea. We have months to do the town, unless you were planning on becoming a couch-kitten, sitting at home looking pretty, entertaining all the beaux."

Miss Trevaine just gurgled delightedly.

8

Fashionable London was like a sharp-beaked dowager in a purple turban: nosey. Miss Trevaine's appearance in Hyde Park that afternoon in Claibourne's curricle made the ton twitch with curiosity.

"There's that girl Claibourne escorted to the shops. Sophrina Rivington saw them at Bertin's. Said she bought out the place."

"They say it's a match; she'd better be rich."

"But who *is* she?"

Or, "Merrill's been driving around all day with that chit. Never known him to be so obvious before. Milbrooke told me they were laughing together at Gunther's. Handsome girl, but who *is* she?"

Speculation continued whenever two riders stopped for conversation, and in nearly every carriage. In one satin-lined brougham, however, a little girl, dressed as a precious miniature of her mother, was heard to ask: "Mama, why may that lady have her dog in the carriage and I cannot take Tippy?"

London also had a long memory. When Claibourne's curricle pulled up next to Amabel

Parkhurst's, enough people recalled she was expecting her niece; others could identify Lady Parkhurst's black-clad companion as Claibourne's great-aunt, so they made the same deduction. Either way, the question now was: "Wasn't that the chit with the monkey?"

If the *belle monde* had caught a glimpse of Miss Trevaine in the afternoon, that night they were to get an eyeful. Since Jacelyn wasn't officially Out, she couldn't attend large parties until her presentation at court, a formal come-out ball or, at the very least, an appearance at Almack's. Of course, without the last, she'd still not receive many invitations. In any event, Lady Parkhurst had chosen the Royal Opera House for the evening's entertainment, and had invited some young people to share their box.

"How kind of you, Aunt Amabel. What is the programme?"

"I'm sure I don't know. No one goes to listen, at any rate."

"Oh. And who else is coming?"

"Claibourne of course, though his aunt would rather stay home, and his friend Ponsonby, and Ponsonby's sister. She's all the crack, you know. You can take some pointers from how she goes on."

"But Aunt Amabel, I don't like Priscilla Ponsonby."

"What's that to the point? It will do you good to be seen with her."

"Is Priscilla's mother coming too?"

"Yes, so see that you do nothing exceptional. She

115

has agreed to forget the Treverly incident, for my sake."

"Has the blue dress been delivered, Pinkie? Yes, it should be perfect for this evening. . . ." The azure was not a hide-in-the-woodwork colour, even if the gown's low cut didn't cry for attention. It had silver ribbons at the high waist, and Pinkie threaded a silver ribbon through the curls she'd arranged atop Jacelyn's head, and wove another into the one long ringlet allowed to trail down across Jacelyn's shoulder. Nothing exceptional, indeed.

"Better take a shawl, ma'am, in case it gets chilly," the maid advised, draping a Norwich silk with silver fringe around Jacey's bare shoulders.

Contrarily, the theatre box grew more chilly after she removed the shawl. Lady Parkhurst's mouth hung open like a flounder on ice, while Lady Ponsonby sniffed her frigid disdain. Priscilla turned her back entirely, to survey the rest of the audience. It was Arthur, though, who thought he'd give Miss Trevaine a set-down by staring at her exposed parts through his monocle. She cured him of that with one raised eyebrow so much in Claibourne's manner that the earl applauded.

"How long have you been practicing, brat?" he asked, smiling and very casually placing his arm across the back of her seat where his hand could just touch the top of her neck. If that didn't put the seal of approval—and possession—on her, nothing would. Lady Parkhurst started chattering to Priscilla and her mother, while Leigh directed Arthur to point

116

out the notables to Jacelyn. Lord Parkhurst, who arrived late with his young aide, Mr. Carter Sprague, kissed his wife's hand absently, but told Jacelyn, twice, that she looked fine as fivepence. Ignoring the other ladies, he and Mr. Sprague took the rearmost seats and began discussing the day's Parliamentary debates.

A soprano seemed intent on shattering the prisms of the huge crystal chandelier with her piercing notes, yet no one except Jacelyn gave her a moment's notice. Jacey gave up trying to decipher the warbled Italian over the din in the boxes, and gave in to enjoying the spectacle. All the women were in their finest, many trying to fit much larger girths into much less material than made up her own gown, to Miss Trevaine's satisfaction. What they lacked in fabric, they made up in jewels, rivalling the same chandelier for glitter. The men were only slightly less gaudy, with their diamond stickpins and striped waistcoats. Many, like Claibourne, wore the dark evening shades decreed by Brummel, their intricately tied white neckcloths more gleaming by contrast. The Tulips in the pits were another matter. Wearing every hue imaginable, every ring or ruffle they could manage, they made a kaleidoscope of colour, especially since they never sat still. Despite the ongoing performance, the fops and bucks in the pit constantly moved around, calling to friends, teasing the orange girls, making arrangements with the women who plied their trade at other entertainment, and ogling the ladies in the boxes. Jacelyn drew her fair share of their attention, even laughing back when one of the blades bowed in her direction, blowing kisses.

117

Intermission brought even more noise and movement, as though the audience needed a break from their concentration. Leigh and Arthur left to fetch lemonade, and the older women joined Lord Parkhurst for a brief turn about the corridors. Priscilla preened. She smoothed her cornsilk curls and adjusted the folds of her shell-pink skirts, ignored the hungry-pup gaze of Mr. Sprague, and smirked at Jacelyn. Now I'll show you, Miss Nobody, her expression clearly read, what it means to be an Incomparable.

Gentleman after gentleman entered the box, as Priscilla knew they would. Lord This and Sir That, here was her devoted court. For the first time in Miss Ponsonby's reign as an accredited beauty, however, the callers had not come to worship at her throne. Instead of poetic tributes to her face and form, instead of invitations to late suppers and carriage rides, instead of pleas for a dance at the next ball, the gentlemen all wanted introductions to that underbred, overblown Jacey Trevaine! It was too much for a delicate — and not so generously endowed — female to bear.

"It's so very close in here, I fear I might faint," she lisped to the only gentleman who was paying her any attention, Lord Malcolm Anton-Fredricks. "Do you think you could accompany me to the hall for some fresh air?"

"My very heart's desire." The well-oiled nobleman's reply fairly oozed.

Priscilla departed, making a great to-do over her incipient swoon, which no one noticed, shamefully leaving Jacelyn alone with a box full of strangers and

118

only a mortified Mr. Sprague to play chaperone.

The situation didn't faze Miss Trevaine an iota. Goodness, if she could deal with the worldly earl, what were a few boys, more or less? Laughing, showing her dimples, she treated them all alike, even a Spanish count and the son of a duke, all the same way she treated Lem or her neighbours' schoolboy sons—like friends. Soon they were all laughing over some of Pen's exploits, for the big dog had certainly not gone unnoticed in Hyde Park, and dogs were such an easy, comfortable topic of conversation. No one had to think up flowery compliments or discuss the weather when an item like Pen was around.

Talk soon flowed from the subject of one four-footed creature to another, the major interest of the sporting gentlemen.

"I say, Miss Trevaine, do you ride?"

"You forget I'm a country cousin, Lord Milbrooke. Of course I ride, if you call your Hyde Park trails much of a course."

"My groom mentioned a lady riding with Claibourne this morning. That must have been you, then. He said you were a real goer, your pardon, ma'am."

Jacelyn chuckled. "No apologies needed, and thank him for the compliment. I like riding above all things."

There followed suggestions for day rides to Richmond and Surrey, so many conflicting invitations that Jacelyn had to smile and mention that her aunt may have plans. Then Viscount Farthingale had such a splendid idea he had to raise his voice to make sure that Jacelyn heard: "What about a fox hunt, Miss

119

Trevaine? I know Ponsonby's uncle keeps a pack. We could—"

"My lord." Jacelyn's voice rang out in the quiet following the viscount's shout. "I do not hunt. My friends do not hunt. If you choose to pursue such a grisly hobby—note I do not say sport—then I think you should consider something less gruesome, like bashing each other's heads in at your Gentleman Jackson's. Either way, I must request that you not discuss this topic with me, as it distresses me greatly."

The shocked silence was broken by Arthur's gagging. He and Claibourne had returned with the lemonade, which Arthur swilled at the first mention of a fox. Claibourne was about to come forward when the *Conde* de Silva, a polished fellow more interested in his clothes than his horses, put in, "No one would think of distressing such a charming *señorita, si?* Not when your laughter has more music than the *periquitas* on the stage. Who needs such exertion anyway, when just seeing you in your magnificent blue gown is enough for mortal man?"

Jacelyn's dimples returned. "*Gracias, señor,*" she said, "but I am sure you exerted more effort on your costume than any of us!" bringing the laughter back.

Priscilla was not taking chances with the second intermission. She commandeered Arthur to escort her to the vestibule. Since a mere brother added nothing to her consequence, she lowered herself to invite the secretary, Sprague, along too. Aunt Amabel stayed put, having been unpleasantly reminded of her duties by Lady Ponsonby's: "I see the chit's behaviour is still as common as her dress. My sympathy, of course."

120

In this *entr'acte,* however, curiosity overcame diffidence, as many of the mothers of the previous visitors called at Lady Parkhurst's box. This time Aunt Amabel performed the introductions, and Jacelyn answered prettily, not even bristling when quizzed about her pedigree by the Duchess of Hockney.

"Ah, Trevaine's daughter. I'm sorry to hear of his ill health. Yes, you have your mother's look. What a cheerful girl she was; we all miss her. Glad to see you've got her liveliness too, instead of your father's bookish ways. Not to say a girl should have more hair than wit, but we can use a little lightheartedness. This place has gotten so proper"—with an eye on Clothilda Ponsonby—"a lady dasn't belch. Why, in my day . . ."

Jacelyn and Claibourne were still chuckling when Her Grace and the others left and Priscilla returned to the box.

"I suppose that old dragon warned you away from her son, Farthingale," Miss Ponsonby hissed as she took her seat next to Jacelyn.

"Why no, she invited me to tea."

The Ponsonbys did not stay for the third act.

The next day being Sunday, everyone went to church, St. George's in Hanover Square, naturally, where everyone who mattered could be seen at prayers. Everyone except Mme. Aubonier, that is, who announced she would rather attend St. Francis d'Assisi, a Roman church popular with the French emigrés.

"I have been a loyal and devoted member of the

121

Anglican church at Littleton in Durham, the *only* church in Littleton, *n'est-ce-pas?* for nearly thirty years. Today, when I have the chance, I would like to visit a church of my younger days. Perhaps I shall renew some old acquaintances, who knows?"

"Of course, Aunt Simone," Jacelyn agreed, immediately calling for another carriage to be brought 'round. "But doesn't it matter? I mean, I thought one was either a Catholic or an Anglican or a Methodist or whatever."

"It is the same God, no? *Le bon Dieu* can find me when He wants me, I am sure."

Lady Parkhurst was still fussing about it on the carriage ride home from church. "A Papist, Jacelyn, of all things! She barely speaks English, she dresses as if she's in mourning for the whole French aristocracy, and now this. How your father thought she'd lend you countenance, much less make a respectable lady out of you, I'll never understand. Your behaviour last night was so bold, and that dress! Where was your chaperone then, miss? I don't know what I'm to tell your father."

Jacelyn was nodding and saying, "Yes, Aunt," having learned a great deal from Mme. Aubonier, and wondering what she should wear for the afternoon's carriage ride with Leigh.

Her aunt's tune changed abruptly when they entered the house. Resting on a silver platter, on the Sheraton table, in the marbled hall, was a thick cream envelope addressed to Miss Trevaine. Hand-delivered, according to the butler, who was grinning almost as widely as Lady Parkhurst. Marcus had won two shillings; Aunt Amabel would be able to show her face. Miss Trevaine was invited to Almack's.

Then it was "Perhaps you should take dear Mrs. Aubonier for a drive in the park, or maybe she would like to invite some of her friends for tea. I did mention the yellow parlour was at her disposal, didn't I? I'll have to write to your father immediately after luncheon; so proud, my dear. I knew you'd be a success. We'd better make plans for your come-out ball before all the dates are booked. I hadn't wanted to make anything definite until . . . that is, in case . . . you know."

"Yes, Aunt." Jacelyn went off to tell Madame the happy news. The old lady had her shoes off, her feet up, and a book in her hand. "This is what you wanted, yes? Now it is up to you."

Pinkie more than made up for Madame's lack of enthusiasm, dancing around with Jacelyn's pelisse in her excitement, then tearing open the clothespress for a hasty inspection. "We'll show them us country girls know a thing or two. My own lady goin' to Almack's! Won't mum be proud."

"If you want to write and tell her, I'll ask Uncle Parkhurst to frank the letter for you."

"Thank you, ma'am, but my writing's not so good, and mum's got no reading at all."

"Would you like me to help you with some lessons? Maybe your mother could find a neighbour or a curate to read her your letters, so she'll feel easier about you being so far from home. I taught Lem to read and write, you know."

Pinkie's face was scarlet as she stammered her gratitude. Jacey didn't think the girl could be embarrassed over her poor education, since most servants had even less. "Lem? Has he been teasing you, Pinkie? You tell me if he has, and I'll talk to him. He's a great one for pranks, but he means no harm."

"No, ma'am, he's been real kind." The girl's eyes still didn't meet Jacelyn's.

"I see. Well, just stay away from that second footman Eugene. He's a real flirt."

Pinkie giggled. "Yes'm. I already put him in his place. But Miss Jacey, about Almack's, if it's all right with you, maybe I could ask Hammersmith for some suggestions about your hair, since you won't hear of cutting it."

"Hammersmith, Mme. Aubonier's maid?" Jacelyn was mystified. Aunt Simone certainly did not show off her dresser's skill, and besides, everyone in the household seemed intimidated by the sharp-featured maid. "Why not Lady Parkhurst's abigail?'

"Your pardon, ma'am, but Miss Hammersmith's been teachin' me all manner of things. She knows all about what's proper for when, and she takes a real interest in your success, she does. Lady Parkhurst's abigail only worries that we won't do the house proud. We'll show her, won't we, miss?"

Jacelyn just shook her head. It seemed she still had a lot to learn about London ways, front stairs and back.

Arthur Ponsonby rode up to the landau where it was positioned near a tree. Mme. Aubonier was speaking French with an elderly gentleman on foot who wore his hair powdered in the old style; Jacelyn was talking to Claibourne, alongside on Baron.

"Miss Trevaine, Leigh, just the people I wished to see. My mother's getting up a party for this evening. No cards or dancing; Sunday, don't you know. A musicale, she calls it. I think that means Marcella Chadwick is going to play the harp and m'sister the pianoforte. Will you help a fellow out and attend?"

"It sounds dreadfully dull, Arthur. Why don't you just beg off?" Jacelyn couldn't bring herself to call him Lord Ponsonby, not when he looked so much like a squat old bulldog, bow-legged and testy.

He gave her the look he'd always given her: contempt mixed with conceit. You are impertinent, it seemed to say, but I am older and wiser, so I will ignore it, and you. He leaned past an amused Jacelyn to extend the invitation to Claibourne's aunt, who had finished her own conversation.

"Nothing very deep, ma'am, family commitment, don't you know," he added for Jacey's benefit.

Madame flatly refused. Jacelyn might go, she said, if Lady Parkhurst would attend with her, though why anyone would inflict such an evening on their friends was beyond her comprehension.

Jacelyn read the message in Claibourne's slight nod and told Arthur she would ask her aunt. Then she warned Arthur to get down and check his saddle's girth; she'd heard a strange creaking noise when he bent near. His bottom jaw shot out, and his brows lowered, reminding her even more of a bulldog—and of the pouty child he used to be, though she couldn't understand why the nodcock would be in such a swivet, nor why his face was turning the colour of his waistcoat, a bilious purple. She said she'd go, didn't she? Then Claibourne leaned over and whispered, "He's wearing stays."

Instead of looking contrite and apologising for drawing attention to such a personal matter, Jacey went into the whoops. Claibourne joined her, and even his aunt smiled, until Arthur had to grin too.

"Oh Arthur," Jacelyn said when she could talk again, "wouldn't it be easier just to leave the second cream puff? I know, you'll have to come riding with us in the morning."

Lady Parkhurst did not really want to attend—no one did; Parkhurst claimed a speech to memorise—until she recalled the invitation to Almack's. What was one more boring evening against the chance to gloat?

As the audience of twenty or so sufferers politely applauded the final duet, both Miss Chadwick and Miss Ponsonby having done solo turns previously, Jacelyn turned to Claibourne. "There, that wasn't as bad as I thought."

"That was only the first half, puss. We get to find some nourishment to sustain us through the second half."

Aunt Amabel's groan confirmed it, but encouraged Jacelyn to enquire, hopefully, if her aunt had a headache. "I am sure La Ponsonby would understand if we had to take our leave early.

"No, she wouldn't. Clothilda is one of my closest friends, but she can be somewhat overbearing. Claibourne, take my niece and find her some refreshment."

126

The supper room was crowded; the table was not. Lady Ponsonby was heard to comment that since it was such an informal gathering, and Sunday besides, they must all have had their fill at dinner. Fruit punch and little honey cakes were the only offerings.

"Get used to it, Jay-bird, the Almack's patronesses are just as nipcheese."

"What, are you going to Almack's?" Arthur asked, coming toward them with a plate full of the thin slices. "Lord, they must have relaxed their standards. Don't let the patronesses catch you in britches!"

Jacey looked around quickly to make sure no one else heard. "At least my britches don't need a tent's worth of fabric!"

"Children, children." Claibourne held a cup to Jacelyn's mouth, effectively blocking her next comments, and reminding Arthur that they were here only as a favour to him. "By the bye," he added, changing the subject, "your sister's over there with that Anton-Fredricks fellow again. He turned her pages for her too. Do you look for a match in that direction?"

"Dashed if I know. I thought m'mother was looking toward Farthingale, Hockney's heir, you know. I hope they don't choose Anton-Fredricks, at any rate; chap's all flash, no bottom, if you get my drift. I don't know if he's dropped the handkerchief yet, nor if m'sister would have him. Not my place to pry, you know, until he comes asking me if he can pay his addresses."

Jacelyn didn't agree with him, as usual. "How can you say that, Arthur, when she's your own—Why, good evening again, Priscilla. I must congratulate you on your performance. It was, um, edifying. Your interpretation of Vivaldi would certainly have delighted the composer." If he could have recognised it, she wanted to say, but didn't.

Claibourne and Arthur added their praise to Jacey's and the others' who were now gathered around. Very well satisfied with herself, Priscilla decided to appear gracious, offering to share the limelight with Miss Trevaine, especially since she was very well aware that Jacelyn had no drawing-room accomplishments whatsoever.

"Surely you'll oblige my guests," Miss Ponsonby pressed after Jacey's first, laughing, refusal to sing or play. "Everyone has some talent."

"I'm afraid mine remains undiscovered then," Jacey said, still smiling, until Priscilla smugly informed the group, "How odd. I thought all young ladies of breeding could entertain company."

"Now that you mention it," Jacelyn heard herself saying, "I do have one small talent. I can imitate frog calls."

Arthur was looking as pop-eyed as any lilypad dweller, and Miss Chadwick was tee-heeing. There was no backing down. She didn't dare look at Claibourne. She just shut her eyes and gave her best bullfrog croak, throwing in a few peepers for good measure.

Priscilla's mouth could have caught flies, but some of the young gentlemen, laughing merrily, took up Jacey's dare to do better, Lord Farthingale challenging anyone to best his chuckwillow. A whole stream of boisterous birdcalls and guffaws followed.

"That niece of yours is turning my parlour into a

128

barnyard, Amabel. Do something!" Lady Ponsonby ordered. Lady Parkhurst searched her reticule for her smelling salts.

Jacelyn, however, was no longer participating in the romp. This was *not* how she'd planned on behaving, not in front of Claibourne's friends. Now he'd never see her as other than a headstrong, rag-mannered child. Fancy clothes and elegant hairstyles weren't enough to show him that she was a mature, sophisticated woman, worthy of his attention — and his love.

Embarrassed, upset, not wanting to face the earl, she slipped back into the nearly deserted music room. A few older gentlemen were dozing in the back row, and a few young matrons boasted of their children in one of the sofas along the side wall. A single young lady, looking as dejected as Jacey felt, sat by herself at the pianoforte, her hands folded in her lap, her lower lip trembling.

"Do you mind if I sit by you for a few minutes?" Jacelyn asked. "If I sit by myself my aunt will find me, or Lady Ponsonby, and there will be the devil to pay."

Silently the other girl pulled the billows of her white tulle dress closer around her, making room on the bench.

"Are you to play next?" It wasn't a hard guess. "You *can* play, can't you?"

"And sing. A little."

"Well, a little would be a great deal more than we've heard. At least you have some talent," she added ruefully, thinking of her own shortcomings. "What could be the problem? Do forgive me, I know it's none of my affair. Here I was just scolding myself for my last indiscretion. My tongue seems to have a mind of its own."

"No, no, don't apologise. I wish I had some of your . . . your . . ."

"Brass? I'd gladly lend it, Miss . . .?"

"Endicott. I already know you as Miss Trevaine."

Jacelyn grinned. "Fame travels fast. I'd be pleased if you'd call me Jacelyn, or Jacey, if you wish."

The other girl finally smiled back. "Rhodine." She let her fingers trail over the keys; the smile faded.

"Are you nervous? You could say your throat is scratchy or something?"

"No, it's just that — Oh, listen to all the fun they're having out there. And . . . and they'll come back and take their seats and put on polite smiles. Their eyes will go all glassy, like mannequins'! They'll be bored again. Then they'll clap and tell me how charming my voice is. It isn't! My music instructor said my voice was pleasant, no more."

"*My* music instructor said the barn door needed oiling, and left!"

Both girls were laughing when the rest of the company drifted in and took their places. Catching sight of Leigh and Arthur coming their way, Jacelyn said, "I have an idea. Do you know 'I Met Him in Spring'? Why don't you do the opening and then ask everyone to join in for the chorus. Everyone knows it, and they'll be happy to participate, rather than sitting like logs."

"Oh, but I couldn't ask them—"

"Arthur could! They're his guests, after all. Besides, I think he'd like nothing better than to sit

130

turning your pages and directing us all. I promise to mouth the words! Then you could do some rounds or whatever. Arthur will know."

Everyone complimented Lady Ponsonby on the evening's entertainment. Most enjoyable night they'd had in ages, they told her, wondering why more hostesses didn't follow her lead. Of course, the departing guests sympathised, it was too bad Priscilla had developed the headache and couldn't enjoy the lively half of the party.

Jacelyn was pleased also, and not just with her new friend. Claibourne had a lovely rich baritone voice—and he held her hand during the entire second half.

9

"I've been hearing things, Percy."

"I told you to cut down on the pipe, Da."

"You blithering bacon-brain, I've been hearing things from my man Jensen."

It was after noon, but you'd never know it by the darkened room nor Percy's attire, his skin-and-bones, six-foot-plus frame covered by a dragon-embellished silk dressing gown and stubble.

He poured his breakfast. His shaking hand only spilled a little down the glass's side. "And here I thought he could only grunt, not speak."

"You have all the humour of a hangman, fool. I've been hearing from Jensen what they're saying in the taverns; I've been hearing from Cook what they're saying at the market. I've been reading what they're saying in the blasted papers." He brushed the *Gazette* off the table with one angry arm-sweep. "All about Claibourne's chit. How she dresses, where she goes, who her people are, how he's in her pocket. What I don't hear"—he smashed his fist down on the mahogany—"is what you've done about it."

As proud as an old man with a young bride, Percy announced that he was dealing with the situation. "I have a plan."

Silence.

"Oh, do you want to hear it, then?"

"You misbegotten mutton-head, why do you think I called you here?"

"You didn't call. I live here, remember? You really better watch the —"

"Your plan!"

An even more idiotic grin than usual swept over Percy's face. His Adam's apple convulsed in excitement as he solemnly intoned: "La Fleur, the Flower. Remember her? She's the high flyer Claibourne used to keep. Actually, talk was someone else always paid the rent and he sublet, so to speak. Then Fortenham bought her a place of her own out in Islington, so she's fairly independent about who she entertains. They say Claibourne stayed there to recuperate on one medical leave."

"So? She was in the Ballet Corps over fifteen years ago. What's some faded demirep got to do with anything?"

"That's my plan. I've been going out to Islington waiting for cousin Leigh to show. He will. He never stayed away from a willing woman yet, that I heard of. Then I've got him! No green girl's going to like seeing her beau with such a dasher."

"You've got him? What did you think, you stilt-legged sapskull, that he'd trot out his middle-aged mistress to impress his bride?"

Trimphantly: "I thought of that! I figure to write

133

a note to the girl telling her all about it. She'll turn tail back to Cambridgeshire 'fore the ink's dry."

"Percy, you have all the wit of three men: two fools and a lunatic! Why should she believe you? Claibourne would only deny it, of course. Besides, the chit may be an innocent, but even two days in London will show her that most *real* men have a bit of muslin in keeping."

The stress on "real," needless to say, was for Percy's benefit. He started working on his lunch. "Got another part to my plan. A good general has more than one strategy. Didn't Wellington always say that?"

"Yes, when he was in retreat. I'm almost afraid to ask, what's the rest of the brainstorm?"

Percy's face wore its usual nobody-home look, only more so. "I talk to La Fleur. Get her to see the girl in person. You know, by chance in the park or at some fancy shop. Then Claibourne can't weasel out of it."

"Ah, I begin to see a glimmer of hope for you. The old mare confronts the filly, for a price, naturally. Well worth it, if Miss Trevaine was hoping for a love match. Maybe there is some Fenton blood in you after all. What did La Fleur say? How much does she want?"

Red splotches spread out on Percy's cheeks. "I, ah, haven't asked her yet. Sent m'card up, but the maid came back, said her mistress wasn't taking on any new 'callers.' But I'm working on it."

" 'Working on it'?" Fenton sputtered. "What are you doing, passing out in front of her house so her carriage has to run over you? I cannot believe it!

134

She's a paid doxy, for heaven's sake, and she won't even *talk* to you!" He looked upward. "Are you happy now, wife? Are you enjoying your revenge?"

Wearily, he reached down for the newspaper on the floor. "Listen, you lobcock. The *Gazette* says Miss Trevaine's an animal lover, a real fanatic, she sounds. All the gossip about her says the same. Must be one of those do-gooders who preach about kindness to dumb creatures, meanwhile sitting down to their mutton and capon and turtle soup, wearing their fur hats. Where do they think their kid gloves and egret plumes come from, some beast that died of old age? No, they don't mind the killing as long as they don't have to see it. I know the type. Your mother, blast her soul, was one of them. Wept over the slaves while stirring sugar into her tea, as though that sugar hadn't taken African sweat to make. Soft-hearted and cloth-headed. London's a rough place for such a one, and you're about to make it rougher for Miss Trevaine."

"I am? I don't—"

"You are going to do two things: One, you'll wait outside the aunt's house and follow the chit so you know what she looks like. Don't let Claibourne see you; I don't want him to get suspicious. Two, you'll make certain she sees London's harsher side: starving cats, mangy dogs, you know, what would upset a vapourish female. Enough of that and either she'll go home, as your mother did, or Claibourne will have his fill of caterwauling watering pots. Again, don't let Claibourne see you. Don't tip our hand."

Percy wouldn't let Claibourne see him, not if his life depended on it, which it most likely did.

Jacelyn had a new plan for that day, too, which she put into effect early that Monday morning. No more fripperies, no more hoydenish behaviour. (She would start right after the mad gallop that had her cheeks flushed and her eyes sparkling.) Today she would show Leigh her love of learning, her aesthetic sensitivity, her cultured poise. When he asked what she wanted to do that day, she reeled off a list of attractions that would have impressed Marco Polo. She needed to take out her subscription to the lending library. She had promised her father a first-hand description of the Parthenon exhibit at the British Museum, and Lord Parkhurst had recommended a visit to the Royal Academy. There were also Westminster Abbey, Pall Mall, the Royal Exchange, and the Tower of London, for a start.

"What, all in one day, pet?" Leigh asked, flecks in his blue eyes dancing as he took in the picture she made, slightly tousled and out of breath from the ride. He knew what *he'd* rather do that day. All he could manage properly, though, was to hold her longer than necessary when he lifted her down from her horse. "Besides, you're doing it much too brown. You've already got the vouchers, and the dragons won't take them away until you have been there once at least. Wouldn't you rather visit the Arcade or Ranelagh Gardens?"

It was hard enough being a bluestocking for one day. He didn't have to test her resolve before breakfast!

"Another day? I told Papa I'd search out a new

copy of Longinus for him, and I promised Pinkie we'd go sightseeing. Can you believe, she's been in London a whole month and hasn't even seen London Bridge?"

Arthur, incidentally, was not with them in the park, having mumbled, "Good idea. I'll get to it right after breakfast," before rolling over and pulling the covers around his ears.

Pinkie got to see the famous bridge, which wasn't anything she'd have to write her mum about, when her penmanship improved. Westminster Cathedral echoed as if all the saints knew her mind was on Lem, not on the sacred. Things got better after that, when Jacey told her she could wait in the carriage outside the bookshop. Lem was up as footman.

Jacelyn found the Longinus with no trouble, and a primer for instructing Pinkie. She was having difficulty selecting a book for herself though, since buying the Minerva Press novels would have been like framing a Rembrandt with kindling wood. They didn't match the picture she was trying to paint today. Besides, Aunt Amabel was sure to have the latest purple-jacketed volumes, and Jacelyn was, in fact, a voracious reader with wide tastes. Unlike the tiny library in Ryefield or even the bookseller in Royston, one could get lost in these London bookstores, with shelf after shelf of titles to explore. While the earl was involved in a conversation with a man in a brown stuff jacket, near what seemed to be tracts on farming methods, Jacelyn wandered to the rear of the building. She thought she'd seek out that new author everyone was talking about. The Prince himself had requested the author to dedicate her next volume to him, it was said. A Miss Austen, Jacelyn believed.

A stunning auburn-haired lady a little older than Jacelyn recommended her favourite of the author's works and, smiling, some other titles she thought Jacey might like.

"The strangest thing," Jacelyn told Claibourne later, after she'd paid for her purchases and he'd handed her back into the carriage. "That lady told me not to worry, the game was worth the candle. What do you think she meant?"

"I am not sure, my sweet, but that was Lady Cheyne, one of the premier younger hostesses. Her husband, incidentally, was one of the greatest scapegraces I've ever known, until the army and then Lady Cheyne tamed him down."

"I wonder if—Oh, there was another odd thing at the bookstore. While I was looking over the shelves, I kept thinking someone else was there, only I didn't see anyone. I smelled something peculiar, like peach flambe, only with horse liniment mixed in. Then I took a book from the top shelf, and a man *was* looking at me through the empty space! He ducked away but kept popping out from behind stacks and around the corners of the aisles. I was quite relieved to see Lady Cheyne come toward me."

Leigh frowned. "You should have come for me."

"I was going to, if no one had come along. The creature seemed harmless enough."

"Still. What did he look like?"

138

"I never saw much of him, but he was very tall, with spindly legs. And he had a large nose."

"Sounds like my cousin Percival, but it couldn't have been. Not in Hatchard's. He's allergic to the printed word. No, must have been some lovesick suitor, rosebud."

The Royal Academy was not meant to be seen in an hour, or even two, although most of the well-dressed connoisseurs had no trouble ambling through the major exhibit halls deep in conversation, occasionally pausing in front of a Lawrence portrait to discuss the subject, not the art. For Jacelyn, the place was overwhelming. So many paintings and sculptures in such a small space, and displayed so poorly! Why, one of Claude Lorrain's landscapes in his new style was hung so high, on top of a cavalry-charge scene distinguished only by its immense size, that Jacelyn had to crane her neck nearly backward. Even then, she could only make out the wavery haze. The noisy, jostling crowds disturbed her, too.

"Why do they come, if not to see the art?" she asked. "They aren't paying any attention to the paintings at all, only to each other."

"That's why they come, my dear," Claibourne said, hurrying her past an undraped statue to which she was giving more than enough attention. "It's the same as Hyde Park and the Opera and the endless teas. They wish to be seen in the right places, with the right people."

"Is that what you want, Leigh?"

He turned her toward him, away from yet another full-length Apollo on a pedestal, and straightened the bow tied against her left cheek. "Today I only want what pleases you, pet, and the rest of the world can go hang."

"Well, it might please me to study those Greek sculptures, but I won't embarrass you, Leigh, so shall we admire the Gainsborough over there? Did you notice the portrait of my mother at Treverly? It's very similar in style. . . ."

Still, Jacelyn glanced over her shoulder. Yes, it was the same tall, gawky man from the bookstore, acting just as peculiarly. Now he seemed to disappear in back of one of the Greek gods, beakish nose emerging seconds later from a marble armpit.

"Leigh, do you see that strange person behind us?"

When Claibourne turned, there was no sign of anyone following, of course, just the naked statue in its full glory, without even the decency of a fig leaf. He shrugged. "Odd lot, those Greeks. Didn't care much for clothes."

Jacey shook her head and walked on. She couldn't resist one final look backward, though, so she just glimpsed boney fingers clutched around Apollo's derrière, as if for support. The Greeks weren't the only odd lot, it seemed.

"Why didn't Lord Elgin just leave them in Greece? Papa says they really belong there." They were in the vast exhibition hall, in a group of twelve, following a bald-headed guide. The lurker didn't seem to be on the premises, so Jacey could relax, sharing her impressions with Claibourne.

The guide, overhearing, frowned in her direction. He interrupted his discourse on frieze-work bas-relief and impedimental statuary to announce that Lord Elgin had shipped the pieces of sculpture from the previously destroyed Parthenon temple to protect them from further vandalism, with the approval of the Greek government. Souvenir hunters, he said, thought nothing of bringing home a bust or a horsehead to put in a stairwell niche or in their gardens. In addition, he declaimed, the political climate was such that the ancient buildings had frequently been used as battlegrounds, and could be again. Finally, with an especially hostile look at Jacelyn, daring her to refute him, the guide cited Lord Elgin's nobility, bringing these treasures home at great expense, "for the enrichment of the British peoples."

"I believe he made a bit of profit, too," the earl said in an undertone.

Without taking a moral stand, Jacelyn was free to absorb the grandeur of the pieces themselves, ignoring the guide's lecture about Pericles and the Phidean style. Her first impression was depressing: all those noses gone, hands, feet, even heads missing, like a rose browning on the edges, a reminder of mortality. Seeing beyond that, especially in the larger-than-life piece of the three headless women, she could feel the grace and flow of their draperies, their perfect composition for the triangular cornice. They and the large reclining male figure were supposed to be gods and goddesses watching the birth

141

of Venus from the head of Zeus, the guide was droning. They seemed fairly casual about such a remarkable event, a small portion of Jacelyn's mind irreverently noted, while the rest stared in awe at the sheer majesty. Together with the less three-dimensional horsemen from the frieze and smaller pieces displayed on tables and in cabinets, the statues created a sense of the wondrous artistry achieved. One could not look on such masterpieces without wanting to touch an edge. They were cold, hard marble, not clay, which could be shaped, moulded, *moved*. There was no adding to stone, no repairing errors. Each fold of the gowns, each sinew of the god, had to be chiselled and hammered and honed.

"I'm sorry, but I'm selfishly glad these pieces are in London, right or wrong. At least until I get to Greece."

Claibourne was holding her pelisse out for her. "Would you like to go to Greece someday, pet?" he asked, thinking bridal trip, warm beaches, long boat rides.

"Only if the men wear breeches," she answered, grinning.

Her heart smiled too, at the sound of their shared laughter.

Next stop was the Tower of London: shuddering past the dungeons and torture chambers, eyes turned from the room where the young princes died, a quick peek at the Crown Jewels in their dusty closet.

"Don't they ever polish them?" Jacelyn wanted to

142

know.

Then they moved on to view the Royal Menagerie. Claibourne tried to warn Jacelyn beforehand, that the animals were in small, dirty enclosures, and the air was nigh unbreathable. She had to see them anyway, naturally.

Now here was a moral dilemma a lot worse than the Elgin Marbles represented. After all, the Greeks hadn't been taking such wonderful care of their treasures, while the British were building a whole museum around them, for an admiring public. The Menagerie, however, had captured animals content where they'd been, she supposed, bringing them to live in deplorable conditions, for public amusement. She'd get to Greece sooner than she'd see India or Africa, most likely, and heaven knew when she'd see another giraffe, but oh, its big eyes looked so sad. Her first elephant, reaching that fire-hose appendage in her direction—

"Best step back, ma'am, the elephant be mean," a uniformed guard warned her.

"You'd be mean too, standing in your own filth! Why aren't these poor creatures given bigger areas and fresh air to breathe? We paid out admission; why isn't the money used for the animals' upkeep?" she demanded.

The attendant grimaced. Another bloomin' do-gooder. "We do the best we can, ma'am. There ain't enough money collected, 'n what there is goes for food. Prodigal eater, a elephant."

Claibourne was trying his best to soothe her. His best wasn't good enough, especially since it seemed to consist of reminders that he'd tried to warn her, which had nothing whatsoever to do with remedying the situation, as she told him.

"Do you mean to tell me the British government cannot afford to feed and house these unfortunate beasts, when there is a fortune in diamonds turning back into coal up there? When the Prince can fill Carlton House with every gilded geegaw that catches his eye? When the poor, mad king—"

"Watch the seditious talk, love," Claibourne teased. "Remember the dungeons." He was enjoying this hugely. Not her upset, of course, nor the gawping crowds, but Miss Trevaine on her uppers was better than Kemble doing King Lear.

"I doesn't make those decisions, ma'am," the guard was saying. "Its not in me wage contract. You want to take it up with His Highness, be my guest."

"If he'll be at Almack's Wednesday night I just may." Ignoring Claibourne's muffled snort and the guard's bulging eyes, she turned away and marched out of the room.

She was still ruffled when the earl's long strides brought him to her side. "Tell me now," he said in the slow tones he used for play, "if I should join the Royal Navy tomorrow. Save Prinny the trouble of transporting me on Wednesday."

She spared him a ha'penny's worth of dimple, called him a gudgeon, and resumed her angry monologue. "It's a disgrace, that's what it is. I'll bet the Prince spends more on one jacket than those animals get in care. Not enough money to go around, hah! I've a good mind to—"

She rushed off, back the way they'd just come.

The earl took his time following, having a good laugh, which was not entirely *at* Jacelyn, but couldn't be *with* her since she wasn't laughing. He doubted she'd appreciate his humour this time.

Surprisingly, however, Jacey was all smiles when she returned. "There," she announced.

"There? In two minutes you have paid off the war debt so the government can afford muckers for the Menagerie?"

"No, silly. I gave that man — his name is Lewis, incidentally — a crown to see to improving the conditions here. And I told him I would be back shortly with another, and so on."

"Well at least Lewis's family will eat better, my little innocent."

"Not on my crown, they won't," Jacey said, giggling. "I told him that if the pens weren't clean when we get here the next time, I'll have you use him for a mop."

"Its growing late, your aunt will worry. Perhaps we should ride home through the park so she'll see I haven't ridden off to Gretna Green with you."

"If she weren't afraid of the scandal, I'm sure she'd be relieved if you did!" At Leigh's questioning glance, she explained: "She's positively quaking that I'll do something outrageous and give you a disgust of me. Then she'd have me on her hands forever. She'd rather be boiled in oil."

Leigh vowed to tell Lady Parkhurst what a perfect lady her niece had been all day. Exemplary, in fact, if one omitted only a few minor details. "Indeed, you played propriety so well, I think you deserve a treat. I know I do. Would you like to go to Astley's Amphitheatre this evening? There is an early performance, so your aunt won't have to send the Bow Street Runners after us."

Brown eyes shining, Jacey nearly danced in her seat. "To see the fancy riding? I'd like it better than anything!" Then she remembered her dignity. "That is, how kind of you, my lord. I would be delighted to attend if you feel it won't be too, um, common."

"Come down from your ropes, poppet. You look like you smell something bad. Astley's isn't too plebeian for my taste. There will be a lot of cits there, and youngsters, of course, but I've always enjoyed it. Perhaps I'll ask Arthur to accompany us if you don't mind."

"Of course not. Do you think I might invite Miss Endicott? You know, the young lady who led the singing so prettily last night. She didn't appear to be friends with the other girls there, or to be having a good time. I promised her I would call soon."

"Invite whomever you wish, sweetheart, but you ought to be aware that your shy little Miss Endicott is properly called Lady Rhodine. She's Spenborough's granddaughter."

"The Golden Duke?" His nod affirmed it. "But Rhodine—Lady Rhodine—is not at all high in the instep. She never even mentioned a title. She didn't put on airs like some of the other girls, either."

"Her father's the third son, so there's no hope of the succession. Not much money there either, they say. Endicott gambles."

"But her gown last night—"

146

"A fortune in fabric, a groat in glamour, right? Lady Tina Endicott is bringing the chit out this Season. That's Endicott's second wife. She's less than ten years older than the daughter, and doesn't want any comparisons, so she overdresses the girl in frills like an infant. The girl is too quiet to complain, or doesn't have the sense to realise she's done up like a wedding cake to make Lady Tina look better. Endicott only sees that the bills are high."

"But if there is no wealth, why should they spend so much on her clothes?"

"First off, no one said Endicott's actually been paying the bills. Second, it's called baiting the trap. Your Miss Endicott is to be married off this year, no matter what it takes. They say she is to go to the highest bidder. Her father's debts, you know."

"How terrible! Won't her grandfather help?"

"That's the icing on the cake: Spenborough won't tow his son out of River Rick, but he's let drop hints that the girl is named in his will. No amounts mentioned, of course. The betting book at White's is full of speculation. Anyway, that's why the other young ladies stay away from Lady Rhodine. The competition."

"It can't be that awful, Leigh, so . . . so cold-blooded and conniving."

"Wake up, dewdrop, that's what the debutante Season is all about: finding the richest husband or the highest title. At least now the girls have some choice, and the fellow gets to see what he's buying before he steps into parson's mousetrap. Not so long ago these things were arranged from the cradle."

"Poor, poor Rhodine. It will have to be Arthur, after all."

"Arthur and Rhodine? What notion are you hatching in that pretty little brainbox of yours?"

"At first I thought Mr. Sprague would do. He's so very polite and refined, you know."

"Carter Sprague, Lord Parkhurst's aide? He's a good man, serious type. They say he has a fine future in the government. What has he to do with anything?"

"Well, Mr. Sprague is infatuated with Priscilla Ponsonby. It cannot be anything more, for she doesn't even notice he's around. So I thought to wean him away from such a hopeless *amour* and point him in Rhodine's direction. Now I see it won't fadge. He isn't wealthy enough for her family, is he?"

"No, but Arthur is. Is that what you're aiming at, vixen?"

"Its only a possibility, mind," she admitted happily. "But think of how proud Arthur would be with a titled wife. Especially one so sweet and unassuming. As for Rhodine, she needs someone to look out for her, to give her confidence. Arthur is so sure of himself, some of his pride would be bound to rub off on her. And consider how pleased he'd be to have someone to be important *for.*"

"But Jacelyn, Arthur's not anxious for leg shackles. Besides, you can't move people around like some giant chess set."

"Can't I, even if it's for their own good? Just watch me!"

The park was thinning of coaches and riders, but they did spot Arthur on horseback near a stopped chaise, which, to Jacelyn's irritation, contained his sister Priscilla and what Jacey was dubbing the shadow twins, Miss Chadwick and Captain Highet. Why was the man still in uniform, she wondered, if all he did was peacock around Town in Marcella's wake? No wonder the country was in financial difficulty!

Surrounding the carriage were a few pedestrians and a knot of riders, from which Lord Farthingale's voice called out: "There they are now. Miss Trevaine, Lord Claibourne, good day. We've been planning a picnic ride out to Richmond tomorrow, while the weather still holds. I know you might have previous plans for the evening, and you ladies need time to make yourselves even more beautiful" — Miss Ponsonby simpered — "but if we leave at ten we'll be home by four or five. My mother's going along, and she particularly asked that I extend the invitation to you. Would have done so myself anyway," he told Jacey, somewhat flustered. "Be pleased if you'd accept."

Judging from her scowl, Miss Ponsonby wasn't pleased at all. She had assumed the excursion was devised for her amusement, not the farouche Miss Trevaine's. Viscount Farthingale had been the biggest fish on Priscilla's line since her come-out. Just because she hadn't decided whether to keep him or not didn't mean she was ready to toss him back.

"I'm sure Miss Trevaine would find it much too tame," she advised Farthingale and the rest of the company. "We *ladies* do have to ride sidesaddle of course. Oh." She put her hand up to her mouth in mock dismay. "I wasn't supposed to say anything about that, was I?"

Arthur hissed, "Bad ton, old girl," at his sister, but Claibourne cleared his throat, deflecting the daggers in Jacey's eyes and the sharp words on her tongue.

"Quite all right, Miss Ponsonby." He addressed Priscilla but made sure they all heard: "Everyone knows Miss Trevaine rode astride on the privacy of her father's estates. It's the only way to break and train your own yearlings. From what I gather, riding astride is something all younger ladies of spirit try. When they are among family and friends, of course, who wouldn't betray them to censure. Miss Jacelyn, further, is a superb rider in either mode."

Bravo. Jacey wanted to clap! All she'd been able to think of, for wiping that smirk off Priscilla's face, was hurling her reticule at it. Instead, Claibourne had smoothly, gently, implied that Priss was old, dull, bad-mannered, and had a seat like a sack of turnips. Jacelyn rewarded him with her most brilliant smile.

" 'Faith, did you really train your own mounts?" Lord Farthingale was excited. He'd never understood women—just look at how Priscilla Ponsonby was turning from a purring housecat into a clawing tiger—but horses he knew. "Are they in London with you? Do you race them? Please do come tomorrow."

With just a quick glance at the earl, Jacelyn accepted, pending her aunt's approval, naturally.

150

"No need to worry about that, with m'mother along for chaperone," Farthingale reminded.

"Right, Priscilla," Arthur goaded his sister, "if Miss Trevaine sets too bruising a pace for you, sidesaddle, of course, you can always ride in the carriage with Her Grace."

Arthur rode alongside their coach on the way out of the park, still apologising for the odious Priscilla. "Bacon-brained thing to do anyway. Made her look no-account in front of her friends."

"Why don't you mention that fact to her, Arthur," Claibourne said, "in case she's tempted to make any more fuss about the Treverly happenings. No one else seems to care about the gossip at all."

"Wait until tomorrow night before you bet your watch on it," Jacelyn told him. "*Tante* Simone says the chaperones' corner at Almack's is the cruellest battlefield of any war."

The earl patted her hand reassuringly. "You'll do fine. You'll be so busy dancing, you won't have time to go near the dragon's den."

Even Arthur forgot himself into promising to stand up with her for the maximum two dances allowed, when he saw Jacey's big-eyed, woebegone look. A moment later he recollected. Gads, he'd offered to dance with little Jacey Trevaine! He better go home and physick himself.

Instead he agreed to go to Astley's with them after an early dinner. He always enjoyed the riding, especially the ladies in sequined tights. The last time he took his young cousins, there was a redhead

151

. . . He looked at Pinkie, sitting demurely with her back to the horses, studying her primer.

Claibourne coughed, almost as if he could read his friend's thought. Colouring, Arthur agreed that Miss Endicott just might appreciate the simple pleasures of roasted chestnuts and sliced oranges. She seemed like a quiet kind of girl, from what he remembered. "She didn't have a lot to say, which isn't bad, mind you." He glared at Jacelyn. Two dances! "In fact, I may as well toddle off there now to invite her in person. Quicker than waiting for you to get home to send a message. It may be too late anyway; I'll let you know."

Jacelyn gave Leigh a look of triumph, but he wasn't ready to concede. "Early days, my girl. I don't think your Lady Rhodine can hold a candle to silver sequins. I heard about *that* dasher for a month. By the way, my sweet, if Lady Rhodine does accept for tonight, we'll have to do something about a chaperone."

"Pinkie would love to see the horses too, I'm sure."

"Then Pinkie shall go on her afternoon off. No, my dear, she did admirably all day, trailing behind you like a grey-striped duckling, or sitting prim as can be on a bench studying her lessons. She'd be ample dogsberry if it were daytime, or just the two of us, since we have the supposed blessing of your father. But it will be night, and a closed carriage, and two gentlemen. Think of Lady Rhodine's reputation, if she comes along. You wouldn't want her to be called fast, would you?"

"Who would ever believe Rhodine capable of anything untoward, in her angelic white dress?"

"Still, those tabbies can talk, and I think she'd find it painful."

"Heavens yes, but are you positive Pinkie wouldn't be adequate? Lem could come too."

"Pinkie is just sixteen. She's much too young. Besides, she has no control over your behaviour, as a proper chaperone should. It's obvious she believes you can walk on water. As for Lem, he'd stand on the riverbank cheering. And that's supposing the two of them had eyes for anything but each other. Lady Endicott would never lower herself to anything so unstylish, so we'll just have to ask the aunts."

Mme. Aubonier acted like they'd asked her to go to China on a camel. She'd agreed to escort Jacelyn to social events, she said, not harum-scarum nursery parties. Lady Parkhurst, on the other hand, was too distracted to pay attention to Jacelyn's problem. The dowager Lady Parkhurst had sent a message that she would be arriving tomorrow, to attend Almack's with them. Her mother-in-law, according to Aunt Amabel, was the fussiest, snoopiest, sharpest-tongued woman she knew. On top of that, if that wasn't enough, besides worrying over Jacclyn's debut, some Bedlamite kept tossing cats over the courtyard wall and tying half-starved dogs to the front gates. The whole house was in an uproar, not at all aided by Jacey's dog. Pen, it seemed, disapproved of scruffy cats landing inches from her nose, to say nothing of the cats' thoughts on the matter.

As for the dogs, Marcus the butler was nearly in

153

tears. Not for their sad, undernourished, insect-populated conditions, but for the calling cards they left. Each had been untied and presented with a lamb chop, as Marcus saw his Christian duty, then sent on its way. Any fool could have told him that a hungry dog is less likely to depart such an hospitable neighbourhood than a pig is to fly. Finally the watch was called to bring a cart and fetch the whole barking, whining, growling herd of mutts away. Where to, Lady Parkhurst neither knew nor cared.

One silver lining shone out through this whole day of clouds, as far as Aunt Amabel was concerned: Jacelyn wasn't home. Otherwise, Lady Parkhurst was certain, every one of the mangy beasts would be sitting down to dinner with them and sleeping in the guest chambers—leaving fleas to bedevil her persnickety mother-in-law!

Such palpitations she had, and Jacey wanted her to play duenna at a circus! Devil a bit!

Aunt Simone finally unbent a little when Rhodine's note of acceptance arrived, delegating Hammersmith as chaperone. No one could remotely imagine anything havey-cavey going on in her austere presence. They wouldn't dare.

Before going upstairs to change for dinner and the evening, Jacelyn went to the stables to retrieve Pen. She went out through the kitchen door, hurriedly. Chef was throwing saucepans and skillets and Gallic curses, furious at having to replan his menu, without lamb chops.

Pen was exhausted, but content. Lem and a stableboy were trying to splint a pigeon's broken wing with a shaved stick and some string.

"What in the world has been going on here, Zack?" she asked the groom. "My aunt is nearly incoherent, and Marcus has locked himself in the butler's pantry."

"Coo, ma'am, you sure missed a rare sight. 'Twere rainin' cats 'n dogs in Portman Square. Sick pigeons too. Your dog took care o' the cats, all right n' tight, though she don't bother with the stable tom none. Then that Clive what drives for 'is lordship's aunt 'n Henesley, the head groom, they sent us out on patrol. A regular militia, we was, miss, only we had pitchforks 'n broom handles 'stead of pistols. We didn't see nothin' either, more's the pity, but what a peculiar day!"

10

"What a peculiar day," Jacelyn told Pinkie later, after her bath.

"Yes'm, it sure was. To think I've been in London all this time 'n never knew there were so many big buildings. 'N all those statues. Some were older nor London itself, his lordship says. I can't think of years in all those thousands, not when I'm used to hearin' about m'granfer's times. Those Greeks were dead 'fore even St. George was slayin' dragons. Bet m'mum won't never believe it."

"We did see a lot today, didn't we?"

Pinkie was towelling Jacey's hair. "Yes, miss. But if I'd had my druthers, I'd have seen the ruckus here. Or was that what you meant by peculiar?"

Jacelyn hadn't been thinking of the day's marvels at all, actually. She'd been considering his lordship, and not comprehending him any better than Pinkie did Greek history. He'd been so kind and attentive, laughing and teasing, even coming to her defense when needed, almost like an older brother—too much like an older brother! Then he'd carefully listened to her opinions, as though they were worth tuppence. Yet tonight they were going to Astley's, at his suggestion. Half the time he treated her like a real lady, as with the chaperone nonsense; the other half he encouraged the tomboy in her.

"Drat, what does the man want of me?" she said out loud, used to confiding her thoughts to the dog. Pen, lying near the open fireplace grate, perked her ears and wagged her tail, sending a cloud of soot into the room. Pinkie, though, was more helpful, correctly interpreting her mistress's question, if not all the uncertainty behind it.

"You know that second footman Eugene?" she asked, grinning. " 'N you know what he wants?"

Tossing a damp towel at the impish carrot-top, Jacelyn said, "That's all you know, Miss Margaret, with all your years of experience! Why, his lordship hasn't even tried to see me alone since we've been in London." She wondered, to herself this time, if maybe that's what had her so suddenly blue-devilled. Maybe if she wore that new peach muslin, with the brown velvet ribbons crisscrossed under her breasts . . .

"Pinkie, what gown have you laid out?"

"Miss Hammersmith says the dark blue merino, miss. The one with the long sleeves and the lace insert, or she won't go. She says it's dignified 'n won't draw unwanted attention."

Hammersmith sat as rigid as a ship's figurehead at the end of their row. Laughter, gasps, and applause parted like waves around her. Claibourne sat next to her, casually elegant in dark pantaloons and a fitted jacket. Jacelyn was next in the row, with Lady Rhodine on her other side. Overdressed for a dinner at Carlton House, Rhodine looked even more out of place next to Jacey in her conservative dark gown. At first Rhodine was noticeably uncomfortable with all the attention she was receiving from the rest of the audience, a very eclectic group indeed. There were rich merchants and their families, shopgirls and their beaux, a pickpocket and his decoy celebrating a good day's work. No one was dressed as richly as Rhodine, with four flounces to her pink gown and her hair prinked into ringlets. Jacey tried to set the other girl at ease by describing all the wonders she'd seen that day, even mentioning the ride planned for tomorrow.

"Why don't you come along? I'm sure Lord Farthingale won't mind."

Colouring up, which made her seem more like a strawberry meringue than ever, and lowering her eyes and her voice, Rhodine declined. "I'm not that good a rider. I would only slow you down."

Arthur, on Rhodine's other side, reassured her. "Quite all right, Lady Rhodine, not every woman can ride like a red Indian, and not every woman can sing as prettily as you did last night. Meant to tell you."

"That's true, Rhodine," Jacey told her, ignoring the gibe, "but no matter. You can still come. You can ride in the carriage with Lady Hockney, Farthingale's mother."

Now the blush fled from Miss Endicott's face, leaving her the colour of milk spilled on brick floors. "I lied," she gasped. "I'm not just a poor rider. I'm frightened of horses but . . . but the duchess scares me more!"

Luckily, the lights dimmed, shifting everyone's regard away from Rhodine to the center of the dirt enclosure. Jacelyn did consider how terrible things must be at Endicott House, for the horse-shy Rhodine to visit Astley's with them—to see the trick riding!

A tall man came out then, wearing a red coat and satin britches tucked into high white boots. He welcomed them, and Jacey forgot all about Rhodine and her problems.

There were tumblers and jugglers and groups who did both. There was a bear in a little skirt, which danced on two legs while the orchestra played a waltz. There was a lady whose gown was so covered with sequins she looked like silver-polishing day at Versailles. She had four little white dogs who danced and twirled and jumped through paper hoops. On their last turn around the enclosure and through the hoops, another performer entered the ring and joined the circuit: a tiny pink pig with a red collar. The audience whooped and whistled. Arthur stamped his feet. Farthest away from Miss Hammersmith, he was naturally the least inhibited. The others applauded.

Then there were the horses. Drill team horses, dancing horses, horses that could count—all with neither rein nor rider. The man in the scarlet coat directed them with only his whip and his voice.

The earl whispered to Jacelyn, "And here I was so proud that Baron would stay on command." She didn't answer, too intent on a trio of white horses moving in precise formations, long white manes and tails flowing as they cantered into figure eights, three across. From the sides you could see only one set of legs, so evenly matched were they.

The orchestra played a fanfare, and the man in red introduced the first rider, a man called Jesse. Wearing white sequined tights and an open-necked shirt, Jesse rode out on a black horse—but standing on the horse's back, not sitting at all! A few turns later, he jumped down, landing lightly on his feet. After that he was a blur of motion, as the black horse kept to its steady gait around the ring. Jesse somersaulted over the horse, did handsprings to its rump, tumbled under its pounding hooves, and came up astride without using his hands. For a finale, Jesse dismounted in a roll and bowed while the horse also lowered its head and right foreleg.

The lights came on, to a great gust of noisy appreciation. Clapping fiercely, Jacey felt like weeping because it was over.

"Don't worry, sweets, it's only the intermission."

Arthur eagerly chipped in: "The women riders come out in the next act," earning him a frown from Hammersmith. He turned to Rhodine to find out if she was enjoying the entertainment, despite her lack of affection for horses. She was, immensely, though her particularly favourite act was the little dogs. Before either Jacelyn or Arthur could comment on this heresy, she added, "That and the remarkable man on the black horse." Turning to Jacelyn, she asked, "Wasn't he handsome?" Arthur sucked in his stomach when he and Leigh went to find refreshments. Claibourne looked back and winked at Jacey.

The girls couldn't go much further with talk of the virile rider, not within the bounds of propriety and Hammersmith's hearing, so they turned to other topics.

"You're going to Almack's Wednesday, aren't you?

I suppose you've been before." Jacelyn chattered, not waiting for answers. "I'm going to wear the gold tissue gown I had made in Ryefield. Aunt Amabel doesn't know it yet, that I'm not wearing white or a pastel. She'll have the vapours, but it's the prettiest gown I've ever owned, and I'm sure to need it, facing all the owl eyes and raised lorgnettes. *Belle-tante* approved anyway, didn't she, Hammersmith? What are you wearing, Rhodine?"

It was the wrong question. Losing her cheerful animation, Rhodine became a limp rag.

"Oh." Jacey delivered a vast understatement: "You don't like it?"

It seemed that Miss Endicott not only disliked her dress for Almack's, a pink and white confection with every froth, furbelow and flower a berserk — or greedy — dressmaker could attach, she hated it. Moreover, she hated all her dresses, how they made her look childishly silly, how they made people stare. She hated having her stepmother Tina select them for her, and she hated all the money the gowns 'cost, when everyone knew they were only window dressing. The Endicotts' pockets were to let, but her father insisted she be gowned like a duke's granddaughter, lest anyone forget.

No one ever forgot her clothes, she wailed, but no one remembered the girl in them!

Another injured pigeon, and Jacey vowed to do her best to fix it. It wasn't long before she'd convinced Rhodine that between them — them being Jacey, Pinkie, and, with a slight nod, even Hammersmith — they could improve any gown. It would have to wait for Wednesday, since Jacelyn was committed to the daylong ride on Tuesday, but they

161

could work miracles. Pinkie was such a hand with the needle, and Hammersmith had a way with curls, and maybe Jacey wouldn't have time to get so nervous, if she was helping her friend.

The gentlemen, meanwhile, were making their way back through the crowds. Arthur couldn't believe the earl had spent the day sightseeing, much less taking in the cultural highlights.

"Zounds, you really went to the Parthenon exhibit and the Royal Academy in the same day? With all the attractions London has to offer, you chose those? Incredible. Why, I'd rather go to the tooth drawer. I can't believe it, Rake Claibourne bear-leading a brat in and out of museums!"

"Actually, old son, I can't recall enjoying a day more. You should try it."

"Now I know you're dicked in the nob."

The earl just smiled. "Your day will come, Arthur."

"Me a benedict? Not on your life."

As they reached their seats, however, the earl noticed his friend's face was red and his brow furrowed, from the concentrated deep breaths he took to flatten that paunch!

The second half began with four riders cantering into the ring: two women in silver tights and short sequined tunics on black horses, two men in black tights and black vests on white horses. The quartet proceeded to change horses in midair, sometimes doubling up on one mount, sometimes with the women being tossed back and forth, and all while they stood, barefooted and upright, on the horses' backs. It was like juggling with people!

Four different riders came out next and began to juggle in earnest: oranges, plates, top hats, hoops, still standing, not sitting astride. While their horses circled the ring, then changed direction, each kept his three or four items in the air. It was hard to count, they moved so fast. Two more turns and the men started throwing to each other. Colours blurred and objects flew, and the horses kept going 'round. Jacey clutched the earl's hand. The jugglers didn't drop even one orange, and each rider ended with his own matched set, and the thunder roared.

The lady with the dogs came back. This time the dogs rode the horses. The horses didn't seem to mind, but the dogs had their tails tucked firmly between their legs, so Jacelyn wasn't as impressed with this act. She whispered to Claibourne that she'd once tried to convince Pen to ride a horse. Jacelyn had been scolded for the claw marks on the saddle. Worse, Pen hadn't gone near the stable yard with her for days.

Six women in sequined stockings and barely decent dresses did some graceful ballet steps atop their mounts. Hammersmith snorted loudly. Arthur joined the whistlers.

Jesse came back, dressed as a red Indian this time, complete with war paint and feather headdress. He did the same routine as before, but with loud whoops and warbles.

The orchestra played a long, dramatic drumroll. This was the finale, the announcer intoned, the Magnificent, the Marvellous, the Mysterious Miss Moira herself.

The horse was an enormous grey, almost as tall as

163

Baron, and Miss Moira stood posed on its back like a Joshua Reynolds portrait. All draped in multicoloured layers of gauze, you'd never know she was standing on a moving animal. As the orchestra, then the horse, picked up tempo, Moira began to move. She tossed at least an el of gauze to the announcer, while Hammersmith clucked, to reveal white tights and a brief white top which resembled a corset. Jacey and Rhodine shared a scandalised giggle. Heaven knew what Hammersmith did. Jacey couldn't look over, too fascinated by the equestrienne's actions. Moira was standing on one foot, kneeling on one knee. She was twirling at the horse's side, only one hand on the bridle. She was spinning in the air, grasping the horse's tail! It was the most wonderful exhibition Jacey had ever seen; not just the woman but the horse also won her exuberant applause. The big grey seemed to anticipate the girl's every move, to increase or lessen the stride to be in the perfect place for her landings on its back. Of course it helped that the horse's back was wide and flat, like Baron's. . . .

She stopped clapping. It was as if the sun had just come out—the moon and the stars too! Eyes wide and shining, face lit up with near-religious inspiration, she turned to Claibourne.

"No." Lord why hadn't he thought of this! Why? Because it was a long time since he was ten and tried standing on his pony. Luckily, the pony had short little legs or he'd have broken his skull instead of just his arm. Jacelyn? If ever there was a stunt more calculated to appeal to the minx, he didn't know it. He cursed himself for being three kinds of a fool, bringing her to Astley's.

"No," he said again as they waited for the carriage.

Making certain that Hammersmith was with the others, she pleaded: "Not my gelding. He's too skittish. I wouldn't be that caper-witted. And the mare's too narrow. But Baron is broad, and well mannered, and he'd do anything you asked of him."

"No."

Nothing more was said about it in the carriage, of course, not in front of Hammersmith, and not until they had dropped Rhodine at her door and Arthur at his club.

His lordship escorted Jacelyn and the maid to the door of Parkhurst House. Hammersmith went in first, but stood in the open doorway next to Marcus, her arms crossed over her boney chest, daring Claibourne to dawdle over his good nights.

"I'll call for you at the regular time tomorrow, for our ride," Leigh said clearly, for the servants' benefit. "Unless you'd rather forgo it, since we'll be all day in the saddle out to Richmond?"

Jacelyn shook her head, not really paying attention.

Then: "No promises, scamp," he whispered, "but bring your britches. I'll see what I can do."

She gave him a quick peck on the cheek before scurrying inside. Claibourne could swear Hammersmith slammed the door on him. It couldn't be Marcus, not with all the *douceurs* Leigh'd been handing him for just such occasions.

"This is against my better judgement, pet, and I am only doing it to keep one jump ahead of you."

"I don't know what you mean."

"Don't you? Tell me you weren't figuring a way to

bribe the people at Astley's for a chance to ride! Maybe it would have been better. I understand they use ropes and pulleys to train."

"But Leigh, that would spoil all the fun!"

"Fun? Remind me how much fun we had when I have to explain your black-and-blue body to your aunt, my aunt, and more devoted servants than the heir to the throne has!"

The foursome — Claibourne, Jacelyn, Lem with a small satchel, and Pen loping alongside — were on their way to the stable where Baron had his stall, which happened to have an indoor schooling ring. Jacelyn was bubbling with excitement; the earl was grim. She had on two layers of clothes, Lem's outgrown britches under her heavy riding skirt; if she had as many layers as he had worries, they'd have to roll her to the stable.

Leigh's first concern, though not necessarily his greatest, was that she'd break her damnfool neck. If no one had done it for her yet, though, he decided, she must lead a charmed life. Besides, he had enough confidence in her natural grace, Baron's steady gait, and his own ability to catch her if she fell, to rest easier on that score. For insurance, he'd dickered with Lawrence, the stable owner, for a fresh load of sand to be put down.

There lay his next botheration, the expense of this venture. The money for the sand and silence wasn't important; his skill at cards held even when luck wasn't with him. If worse came to worst, there was always the challenge book at Jackson's Boxing Parlour, and side wagers. The cost Leigh regretted most was Baron's services for two days, Lawrence's fee for one half hour's private use of the indoor ring. The grizzled old veteran had justified such extortion of his ex-officer by pleading honesty. He could have used the stallion any night Claibourne wasn't watching, couldn't he? Not if he wanted papers on the foals, he couldn't, the earl had countered uselessly. Good thing he was better at sparring than at haggling, else he'd be under the hatches *and* horseless. The worst of it wasn't even having to ride one of Lawrence's hacks for two days; it was how surly Baron would be later, going on rocking-horse rides in the park.

Claibourne's main worry, however, was one he'd least expected when he woke at dawn this morning. He'd discounted Jacelyn's claims of being followed yesterday, and the garbled account of stray dogs and pigeons made no sense at all. Yet this morning, when he arrived at Parkhurst Mews early to give Lem his instructions — and bribe — the stable yard was abuzz with talk of a horse left there overnight. The poor brute was still tethered to a crosstie where, it was assumed, someone had tied it after the stablemen had gone to sleep. Obviously mistreated, with great weals and scars across its back, the horse was standing three-legged, head down.

"By Jupiter, man, what are you waiting for? Put the poor nag out of its misery — and do it before Miss Jacelyn gets here, for goodness' sake!" Claibourne felt his own stomach wrench at the horse's condition; he could only imagine Jacelyn's reaction.

"Yessir," Henesley answered, "we're waitin' on the knackers' cart. Misdoubt the beast could make it that far on's own."

They decided to get the wretched horse into a stall, as quickly as they could move it. Henesley brought a

167

bucket of grain. "Least we can do is let 'im go with a full belly, sorry bastard. I'd like to have my hands on the devil what done this."

"Have you any idea who it could have been, or why?"

"Talked to the night watch, just afore you came. He was goin' off. Says he saw a tall, skinny gent leadin' a horse, around three or so. Thought it was some nob whose horse'd cast a shoe."

"A gentleman, you say?"

Henesley spat. "No gentleman did this. The watch says the swell was all over jewelry. Noted it particular, he says, 'cause the toff was lookin' out for dark alleys 'n such."

"And tall?"

"Real tall, he says, 'n skinny as a fireplace poker."

Lem told Jacey that the shot she heard as they rode away was a rat in the hayloft Henesley'd been after. So big it was, it near ate the old tom.

Her floppy hat kept falling off. Lem would leave Baron's side and chase after it, until Pen decided this was a new game.

"Leave the blasted hat, and come back to your place," Claibourne called. "No one is going to come in anyway." He was riding a gelding on Baron's inner side, and he was exasperated.

Jacelyn didn't even notice, having such a grand time in her britches and stockinged feet. She could go from her seat to a kneeling position easily now; Leigh only had to steady her arm once. She could rise to a standing position without much trouble, with Baron at a walk. It was the canter that was eluding her. She sat down, hard, on Baron's bare back, doing neither of them much good. She did better the next time, standing for a few paces after Claibourne clucked Baron into the faster pace.

The earl caught her, grasping anything he could. For a second he had her feminine softness pressed all over him, till he could deposit her back on the stallion's withers. Lord, he thought, if she didn't manage to stand soon, he'd lay her down right there in the sand.

"Let's try the whole thing at a canter, instead of changing gaits while you're balancing," he suggested, and it worked. He paced Baron around the ring, saying, "On boy, steady there," keeping the gelding as even as he could.

Jacey soon got the rhythm. She rose slowly until she was finally erect, her arms spread out, and a huge grin on her face.

"I did it! Now you back away."

Claibourne pulled over a bit, so her glory was complete, until he called, "How are you going to get down?"

Disconcerted, she looked down, and found herself sailing over Baron's rear end. She landed in a whoosh of sand and dirt. The earl was beside her in an instant, gathering her into his arms, cradling her.

"Are you hurt? Did you twist anything?"

"Is our time up, or can I try again?" she asked, hugging him back, proving the ground hadn't knocked any sense into her.

That clinched it. Lifting her to her feet and brushing off the seat of her britches as delicately as he could, Leigh decided to forgo the ride to Richmond. He just didn't feel right about going without Baron, without finding out what Percy was up to, without a cold bath — or whatever it took to get Miss Trevaine's perfect little body off his mind.

11

"Nonsense, Jacelyn, of course you'll go. His lordship's note said he had urgent business. You have none. It's much too late to cancel; Lord Farthingale would be offended, to say nothing of his mother, Lady Hockney. Oh dear, Lady Hockney. You simply must go, Jacelyn, I insist."

Jacelyn did not want to ride out to Richmond, not without the earl. She couldn't even take Pen, not having asked Lady Hockney. There was no reason to take Lem, and Pinkie didn't ride. She would be all alone, just like on her first night in London, lonely in a crowd.

"What foolishness! Claibourne wrote that Arthur would take care of you."

"Arthur? Aunt Amabel, Arthur couldn't even take care of his toes, if they weren't attached." Jacey thought of asking Mr. Sprague, who was indoors so much he could use the ride. Except that he'd be tortured by Priscilla's flirting all day. No, it was just Arthur, till they met the others at Hyde Park, then she'd be the odd, extra female. Blast.

"Come, Jacelyn. This isn't like you. You'll go,

meet new friends. You don't want to sit in the earl's pocket, do you? He's older, you know, and . . . and used to certain freedoms. I'm sure you'll find it more convenient, after you're married." Lady Parkhurst blundered on: "If you don't make mice-feet out of it now."

Leigh would dislike a wispy, weak clinging vine above all things, Jacelyn silently agreed as she left her aunt's bedchamber and trudged to her own room for a much needed bath. Sitting in a hard saddle didn't seem like a pleasure right now, whatever the company, but yes, she would attend. She'd go to be polite, and to show the earl that she could manage without him, no matter how precious his companionship was becoming to her, whenever he tired of debutante do's. Urgent business, in a pig's eye! But, and it was a very big *but,* she'd thought they were friends. She wouldn't have let one of her friends down this way.

Pinkie wasn't any help. "At least you'll get to wear your pretty new habit," she said, lifting the heavy brown velvet over Jacey's head. "It's a pity his lordship won't be there to see it." The new outfit had baby-blue braid, and a full, shorter skirt instead of an awkward train. When she sat in the saddle a bit of her ankle would show, an ankle encased in a sturdy black leather riding boot. If that scandalised Lady Hockney, so be it. It would be better than tripping all over. The waist was tightly fitted, but the sleeves were loose, giving her freedom of movement. On her head she wore a brown hat shaped like a man's, with a brim to protect her face from the sun. Its masculine severity was broken by a wisp of a blue gauze veil, held on with a nosegay of silk forget-me-nots. Jacey agreed with her maid: the outfit was pretty. And it was wasted.

There were more people waiting at the park than she could remember the names and faces of, and more than a few she'd rather forget. As they rode out behind Lady Hockney and her companion in the carriage, the group split into twos and threes. When they left the city traffic and reached country roads, a strange quadrille began. Riders kept shifting positions, partners, even steps — in this case gaits. Some would gallop ahead in a private race, others would drop back to chat with stragglers, or jog up to reintroduce themselves to strangers. The rules of this dance seemed to include talking with every member of the party.

Lord Farthingale rode up to her and Arthur. He was enthusiastic about Jacelyn's mare, wanting to know her parentage, her times on the flat, if Miss Trevaine would care to try her paces against his gelding while they were still fresh. Arthur moved away to join Miss Chadwick and Captain Highet. He didn't stay there long, riding ahead to the next pairing. Priscilla Ponsonby, meanwhile, joined Farthingale and Jacelyn before they could determine the length of their gallop. Jacelyn had the pattern of the peculiar dance, but not the protocol. Was she supposed to ride off, or was Priscilla? Or even

Farthingale?

Priscilla hadn't improved with daylight, time, or closer acquaintance. In fact, Jacelyn reflected, Priscilla would only improve with distance, so Jacey set her mare to a gallop. As she rode she recalled her father's estimation of Napoleon: he was one of the few men of all time who could so benefit the world — by leaving it. Jacey wanted to let the mare out; Farthingale wanted to look good in her eyes, so met her challenge and took off after her; Priscilla wanted Farthingale and knew she'd never catch them. She therefore made a remark about how unbecoming hot, dusty females looked.

Happier after the race, which she graciously conceded to the viscount, since she had had a head start, Jacey decided to avoid his company if she could. She just wasn't comfortable with Farthingale's high-flown praise of everything she said or did, especially without Claibourne there to smile at the absurdity. She had no desire to speak with Priscilla, Chadwick/Highet, or — Lords, was that Humboldt from Squire's house party? It must be; he was staring at her all goggle-eyed. No, not him either.

Two blonde ladies, sisters or twins, she couldn't tell, rode with a blushing young man who wore yellow breeches, a green jacket, and a large red rose in his buttonhole. Lord Tayson, he stammered. The ladies were Miss Brynne and Miss Beryl Roth, but Tayson's nervous stutter did not make clear which was which. The sisters made no effort to help him. They did, however, ask if Jacelyn had been at the

174

last Devonshire House ball. Jacey moved on.

Oops, Lord Anton-Fredricks was part of the next couple. If Farthingale's compliments were effusive, at least they seemed sincere. Anton-Fredricks proceeded to declaim his joy at riding with two such heavenly examples of feminine grace. Jacelyn immediately decided she liked the older woman riding with him when that lady's first words were: "Poppycock, sir. Save your breath to cool your soup." In truth, the kindest thing one could say about the lady's looks was that her horse wasn't *much* prettier. Anton-Fredricks tipped his hat and rode away, affronted. The lady grinned, held out her hand for a firm grasp, and said, "Smarmy caper-merchant. I'm Riva Montmorency. We met earlier, in the crowd."

"I'm Jacelyn Trevaine, Miss Montmorency, and I *do* like your style!"

Farthingale interrupted. As usual in his presence, talk turned to horseflesh. Miss Montmorency was knowledgeable and interested. Jacey excused herself and galloped briefly toward Arthur, who was riding with the last unknown member of the group. She was a tall, handsome woman with a superb seat, and the two seemed engrossed in their conversation. Jacelyn hesitated about approaching them, and was even considering revising her plans for Arthur and Rhodine when she noticed that Arthur was doing no talking, only nodding his head. He looked relieved to see Jacey.

"Miss Kinbeck was telling me about a book you might find interesting, Jacelyn. Miss Trevaine's father is quite a scholar, Miss Kinbeck, I'm sure he's

175

heard of it: *Indication of the Rights of Women*."
He rode off as quickly as he could when both
women corrected him to *Vindication*.

"Were you really discussing Miss Wollstonecraft's
book with Lord Ponsonby, Miss Kinbeck?"

The other woman was indignant. "Why not? All
women should be well-informed and well-read."

"Of course. I meant *Arthur!*"

So it went until they finally reached the gardens
at Richmond, where servants in blue and gold
Hockney livery were waiting to take the horses and
lead the party to refreshments. Jacelyn's idea of a
picnic was what she'd experienced at Treverly: Cook
packed some bread and some fruit and whatever
was left from last night's dinner, you found a comfortable spot, put down a cloth, and opened the
hamper. The only thing similar here was the comfortable spot.

Tables, chairs, blankets, cushions were laid out
under some trees overlooking the ornamental lake.
Two tables held the huge buffet, and uniformed
footmen served. They also poured from a selection
of wines, fruit drinks, and even hot tea.

"What," Jacey asked Miss Montmorency, with
whom she was quickly on such terms, "no finger
bowls?"

The ride may have been merely an excuse to
overeat in pretty scenery, but Jacelyn had been
looking forward to seeing the topiary gardens and
the famous man-high yew-hedge maze. Most of the

party, though, seemed content to relax on the cushions after the heavy luncheon. The ladies fanned themselves, if they couldn't find a flunky like Highet to do it for them. Arthur had a cloth over his face and was wuffling into it. Miss Montmorency assured Jacey it was permissible to wander about, since this was a very informal party, but Jacey wasn't sure the other woman could be accounted a proper social arbiter, not with her outspoken views. She was relieved, therefore, some minutes later, when Farthingale asked to escort her to the maze. Other groups were taking his lead and bestirring themselves to stroll around the lake or through the formal gardens. Priscilla looked as if she'd eaten a bad oyster, hearing Farthingale's offer, and drafted Lord Humboldt to show her the rose gardens.

"Arthur," Jacelyn gently prodded, "I'm going to the maze with Lord Farthingale. I didn't want to leave without telling you."

"What's that? What in blazes do I care what— Oh." He remembered his sworn obligation, and Claibourne's handy fives. "Quite all right, I'll be there in a moment. Meet you at the centre." He nodded off again, confident it would take her awhile to find her way in. He, of course, would purchase a guide from the maze keeper.

"You needn't worry about getting lost, my dear Miss Trevaine," the viscount was saying as they approached the entrance. "I have the route by heart."

"But, my lord, one is supposed to get lost in a

maze! That's why they let the shrubbery get so high, to make it harder!"

The silly pup was so proud of his cleverness, Jacelyn couldn't give him the set-down he deserved. It was her own fault, she acknowledged, for forgetting her resolve to avoid him. He only wanted to coddle her, but, "I must insist on going in alone, my lord. You are much too downy, but I think I'll enjoy the challenge."

Crestfallen, he asked, "May I at least wait in the centre for you?"

"Oh no, the fun is trying to remember the way out, once you're in! Here come the Misses Roth. I'm sure they'd be delighted to find the heart of the maze without all the effort. I'll just wait here a moment so your voices don't give me any clues, and don't worry, if I get too lost, I can always call out."

The maze's interior was like tall green corridors, very hushed, cool, and shaded. Some of the blind alleys ended in pocket-sized flower gardens, or rose-bushes, or benches. Some other paths just wound back on themselves till Jacey had to giggle, passing the same birdbath the third time — unless the maze's designers were so diabolical as to repeat landmarks. She didn't think that was the case, just that she'd missed a turning. The next path had a lot of gaps leading to other alleys, whose ends she couldn't see. She decided to try the straight course first, then backtrack to each corridor in turn, if need be. Her way ended at a small dolphin fountain, just like the one at Treverly. She could hear Farthingale's proud voice on the other side of the hedge, so she must be

178

close to the centre, even if she couldn't get to it from here. She stayed at the fountain, listening to its quiet babble for a few moments till the voices faded, and she missed her father and her home all over again.

The second pathway back from the fountain brought her to the centre, after only one dead-end bluff. The heart of the maze was larger than she'd suspected, from all the outer rings. It had stone benches surrounding a garden where the sun could more fully penetrate, and in whose centre was a sundial. Jacelyn took off her gloves and sat on one of the benches, lifting her face to the warmth.

"Ah, like one of Nature's petalled beauties, lifting toward golden Sol's caress, and I, the wandering bee, to sip its nectar."

Phoo. Anton-Fredricks was taking a seat next to her on the bench. He was lifting her bare hand to his wet mouth—and what was that drivel about nectar, anyway? She stood up, ready to curtsey and leave, but Anton-Fredricks still held her hand.

"Please, sir, I must be going. The others . . ."

"Not so fast, lovely lady. I saw you delay until I approached the maze, and I know you were waiting here in the centre for me, clever puss. Now you shall have your reward."

Of all the idiocy! "I did not do any of those things, and I insist—"

He pulled her to him and was kissing her! This slicked-back shabster was actually drooling on her face, very much against her will. With one well-coordinated effort, necessary due to the disparity in

179

their sizes, she brought her hard, wooden-heeled riding boot into contact with his right shin, and her open palm into contact with his left cheek.

"How dare you!" she hissed, not wanting a raised voice to bring anyone to witness this. Lord, what this could do to her reputation! She wiped her mouth on her sleeve, in disgust.

"Very pretty act, ma'am, but I heard you weren't quite so clutch-fisted with your kisses." He reached for her again. She slapped him again.

"Oh God. I knew it. I take my eyes off the chit for ten minutes, and look what happens. Damn you, Jacey Trevaine, can't you ever stay out of trouble?"

"No trouble at all, Arthur, I was just leaving." She took his arm and hurried him out. He didn't even have time to consult his map. At the fountain, Jacey drew him to a halt.

"I didn't do anything, Arthur. Really I didn't. I was just sitting there when he came along."

"Cut line, Jacey. I know that. You don't even know how to flirt. You may be flighty, but you ain't a high flier. Still and all, Claibourne's not going to like it."

"But there's no reason to mention it, Arthur. I'm sure Lord Anton-Fredricks won't bother me again, and I'll certainly keep out of his vicinity."

"Tain't that so much, as Claibourne's the man to teach you. Here, look. You don't hit a bounder with your hand. Make a good tight fist and throw it from the shoulder. Leigh'll show you.

"Why, thank you, Arthur!"

Shoop had once tried to teach a very young Miss Trevaine about topiaries, how you have to train the shrub with wires, and trim it as it grew, for years and years. Years were bogey men to Missy, then: when you grow up; your next birthday; in two years. So she took a shears and a likely looking privet bush, and started clipping. At first it was going to be a rabbit, but one ear disappeared by mistake. Fine, a duck would be—oh-oh, a double globe. A small heart?

The result was that Miss Trevaine had great admiration for topiary and its sculptors. Richmond had some of the finest of both. Knights on horseback, jousting. Dragons and unicorns and griffins. A mother goose and three little goslings. All in thick green shrubbery. Jacelyn was enjoying the display with Miss Montmorency and Miss Kinbeck, and enjoying their company.

Miss Mary-Margaret Kinbeck had all manner of irrelevant information, which she cheerfully shared, and which Miss Riva Montmorency just as cheerfully called tomfoolery, pifile, and tommyrot. Soon the three women were happily using first names and making plans to meet again.

"Shall you be at Almack's tomorrow night?" Jacelyn asked.

Riva answered: "Mary-Margaret's too much of a bluestocking to enjoy the social chitchat, but I always attend. I love to dance." Jacelyn was surprised. She would have thought the graceful and

181

truly exquisite Mary-Margaret would be the party-goer, not the less-favoured, rough-tongued Riva. The world was a strange place.

"Drat! I must have left my gloves in the maze! Will you accompany me back there?" Jacelyn said.

As they walked, the conversation drifted into deeper waters: "I understand you're to make a match with Claibourne," Riva said.

"It's . . . it's not definite yet," was all Jacey could think of to answer. She didn't want to mention any of the circumstances around her problematic betrothal, nor did she want to sound evasive to such a straightforward individual.

"Good," Mary-Margaret put in. "Take your time, make sure. It's always a mistake, the way they rush young women into decisions, as if marriage were like a new bonnet."

"Listen to her, Jacelyn. She's had six years of offers to consider, and she hasn't accepted any."

"Don't you want to get married, Mary-Margaret?"

Miss Kinbeck reflected on the question as though she'd never heard it before. Refusing eligibles for six years, she'd heard it aplenty. "I am not certain," she finally admitted. "I have recently been considering Mr. Fabian Holmes's kind offer. He is in orders, you know. I feel I could be of great service as a prelate's wife. Alternatively, I have wondered if founding a school for indigent children wouldn't be more worthwhile than having just one or two of my own."

"Couldn't you do both? Start a school and marry

your cleric?"

"Capital!" Riva teased. "The best of both worlds."

"And what about you, Miss Montmorency, Riva? Have you plans for matrimony? That is, if I am not being impertinent?"

"Impertinent? How could you be when I've just asked about you and Claibourne? It's a question, incidentally, all London is itching to ask. My future doesn't merit the tiniest scratch, I've been so long on the shelf. But yes, Ferddie Milbrooke and I have decided we might as well have the banns read next spring. The music's good."

Mary-Margaret snorted. "About time." But Jacey asked about the music.

"Pianoforte, you know. We play together a great deal, even try composing some new material. We may not have stars and cymbals and the earth opening at our feet, but there are some very pretty duets."

"I met Lord Milbrooke at the Ponsonby musicale, but he didn't play. Why didn't you attend if you—"

"Do you think Priscilla Ponsonby would invite anyone to her affair who could play better than she can? Not half likely. The only reason she saw that I was invited today—and Mary-Margaret too—was that she knew we wouldn't steal any of her beaux. How you got invited is another matter."

Jacey giggled. "Lord Farthingale and his mama wanted me. If Priscilla's nose was any more out of joint, she'd be wearing it as an earmuff."

There were so many pictures of matrimony in

Jacey's mind — and none of them a masterpiece. She had Claibourne's description of the hunt for money and prestige, then her aunt's ill-concealed hints that a wife might find it convenient to ignore a husband's lapses in fidelity. Miss Chadwick and Captain Highet were engaged, inseparable, and insipid. Now Miss Montmorency would marry someone who shared her hobby, and Miss Kinbeck would wed to do good works! Whatever happened to true love?

When they were finally at the maze Jacelyn stopped her musings to concentrate on the proper pathways. This was no time to get lost, when the servants were starting to resaddle the horses. She'd been through last, even though she'd exited by instinct rather than memory, so the other women followed her lead, right to the little fountain.

"How foolish of me, but no matter. The centre is just two turns back. Here, through this gap and left. There! See, my gloves are right on the bench where I left them."

And right on the other side of the sundial, on another bench, were Priscilla Ponsonby and Lord Anton-Fredricks. Springing apart. Red-faced. Mussed.

Miss Kinbeck *tsk*ed; Miss Montmorency muttered something about dirty dishes and demireps, but Jacelyn simply said: "How nice for you, my lord. You found what you were looking for also!"

She rode home in the coach with Lady Hockney.

* * *

184

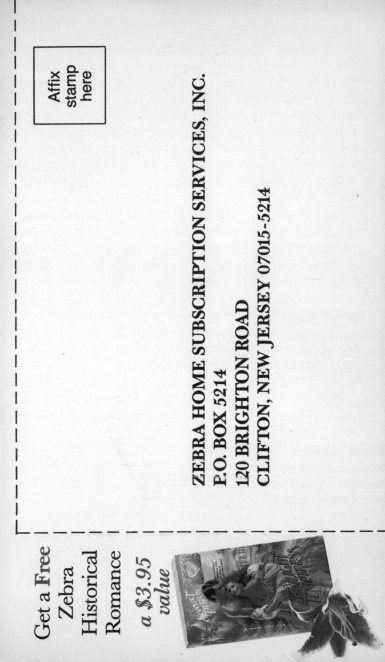

BOOK CERTIFICATE

FREE

ZEBRA HOME SUBSCRIPTION SERVICE, INC.

YES! Please start my subscription to Zebra Historical Romances and send me my free Zebra Novel along with my first month's Romances. I understand that I may preview these four new Zebra Historical Romances Free for 10 days. If I'm not satisfied with them I may return the four books within 10 days and owe nothing. Otherwise I will pay just $3.50 each; a total of $14.00 (a $15.80 value—I save $1.80). Then each month I will receive the 4 newest titles as soon as they come off the press for the same 10 day Free preview and low price. I may return any shipment and I may cancel this arrangement at any time. There is no minimum number of books to buy and there are no shipping, handling or postage charges. Regardless of what I do, the FREE book is mine to keep.

Name _____

Address _____ Apt. # _____

              (Please Print)

City _____ State _____ Zip _____

Telephone ( )_____

Signature _____

          (if under 18, parent or guardian must sign)

Terms and offer subject to change without notice.

12-89

MAIL IN THE COUPON
BELOW TODAY

GET FREE FREE GIFT

To get your Free ZEBRA HISTORICAL ROMANCE fill out the coupon below and send it in today. As soon as we receive the coupon, we'll send your first month's books to preview Free for 10 days along with your FREE NOVEL.

ACCEPT YOUR **FREE GIFT** AND EXPERIENCE MORE OF THE PASSION AND ADVENTURE YOU LIKE IN A HISTORICAL ROMANCE

Zebra Romances are the finest novels of their kind and are written with the adult woman in mind. All of our books are written by authors who really know how to weave tales of romantic adventure in the historical settings you love.

Because our readers tell us these books sell out very fast in the stores, Zebra has made arrangements for you to receive at home the four newest titles published each month. You'll never miss a title and home delivery is so convenient. With your first shipment we'll even send you a FREE Zebra Historical Romance as our gift just for trying our home subscription service. No obligation.

BIG SAVINGS AND **FREE** HOME DELIVERY

Each month, the Zebra Home Subscription Service will send you the four newest titles as soon as they are published. (We ship these books to our subscribers even before we send them to the stores.) You may preview them *Free* for 10 days. If you like them as much as we think you will, you'll pay just $3.50 each and *save $1.80 each month* off the cover price. *AND you'll also get FREE HOME DELIVERY.* There is never a charge for shipping, handling or postage and there is no minimum you must buy. If you decide not to keep any shipment, simply return it within 10 days, no questions asked, and owe nothing.

Zebra Historical Romances Make This Special Offer...

IF YOU ENJOYED READING THIS BOOK, WE'LL SEND YOU ANOTHER ONE

FREE

a $3.95 value

No Obligation!

—Zebra Historical Romances
Burn With The Fire Of History—

The Earl of Claibourne was hoping Jacelyn's day had gone better than his. He should have gone with her; he shouldn't have left her among strangers while he chased his tail around London all day. He'd been in every gaming hall he could think of, most of the taverns a well-heeled man could walk into — and safely out of — and a few bawdy houses. The afternoon was wasted, he'd thrown a small fortune to boys to hold a dumb horse, and more to butlers, barkeeps, and abesses, all for nothing. He'd found neither hide or hair of his cousin Percy, nor anyone who'd seen him in days. Nothing. Two places he didn't think to make enquiries: the house of his own one-time mistress La Fleur, née Flora Cobb, and Josiah Fenton's residence on Mount Street. His wildest imaginings couldn't have made any connexions to the first. His worst nightmares wouldn't have taken him one inch near the second, where, unfortunately, Percival was still retching from the horrid sights he'd encountered at the knackers, and all the Blue Ruin he'd drunk to erase them.

When Arthur returned with the tale of Anton-Fredricks's lechery, Claibourne wanted to rush to Jacelyn's side and beg her forgiveness for not being there to protect her. It was dinner time, though, Arthur reminded him, and he'd not been invited to Parkhurst House until nine. He settled on pulling the libertine's cork then, but Arthur didn't think much of that idea, either. There was no need, he said, since Jacelyn had handled the loose screw like a trooper.

"Not much science, but plenty of pluck. Besides, if you call him out or anything, it'll be all over Town. That would put paid to any hopes of keeping Jacey's name clear."

Claibourne sat down again. "I can't just ignore it, you know."

"Actually, since Miss Trevaine was in my care, it's my obligation. I'm thinking of having a few words with the rum touch anyway. I think he's trifling with m'sister too, though heaven knows she asks for it. Something else went on in that maze, but nobody's talking. Jacey and her friends came out giggling like schoolgirls. Priss left, like a storm cloud. So het up she was, she didn't watch her skirt. Tripped right into m'arms. Not like Priss. A few minutes later Anton-Fredricks came out. Going to talk to m'mother about it, if she'll listen to me."

"Very well, I won't do anything rash until we see who gets to flatten him first. Now tell me, who are Jacelyn's new friends? Do I have to worry they'll lead her into more scrapes?"

"That girl doesn't need *anyone* to find mischief! Do you remember a Miss Kinbeck? She's been out for ages, devilish handsome woman, but a real bluestocking. Couldn't understand three words in ten she said. The other's Riva Montmorency. You know, the platter-faced female who talks like an artillery gunner and dances like an angel? Nothing to worry about there. But young Farthingale . . ."

Leigh was at Parkhurst House at the ninth chime,

with a huge bouquet of flowers and a prayer that Lady Luck would be at the faro table later tonight. First, though, he and Jacelyn played piquet for bonbons, under the not-so-watchful eye of his great-aunt Simone. Mme. Aubonier had her book, but she'd much rather be abed and her throat clearing made her opinion plain: whatever damnfool *pas d'fous* he'd started now, he'd better end it soon.

"I'm sorry I couldn't go with you today, Jacelyn, especially when Arthur told me about —"

"My point again. You're not concentrating, my lord. I have all the bonbons."

"You've been eating some of mine, Captain Sharp. Seriously, I feel badly, when I promised you and your father."

"Was your business really urgent, or did you just not want to go?"

"Is that what you think? I wouldn't have accepted in that case. You should know by now I almost never do what I don't wish. Life is too short for that. I did think my business was important, although it turned out not to be."

"It . . . it wasn't to do with 'certain freedoms,' was it?"

"Freedoms? What maggot have you got in your head now?"

Jacelyn couldn't meet his searching blue eyes. "A woman?"

Leigh leaned back in his chair and laughed. "Cads, sweetheart, neither Baron nor I could handle another woman!"

Assuming he meant the bareback ride that morning, Jacelyn was convinced as much by his smile as by his words. "And we're friends?"

"Friends . . ." He turned the word over like a new taste. "Yes, I suppose we are. Good friends." He popped a bonbon into her mouth and said good night.

12

"Where's Baron? He wasn't hurt by my ride yesterday, was he?"

"Quite the contrary,. Ah, that is, he's back at the livery. I'm exercising this new hack for Lawrence, as a return favour. I'm thinking of purchasing him."

"Why would you? He has a surly disposition, and he doesn't like dogs."

"True. Shall we get down and walk? I'm enjoying this as little as the horse."

They left both horses tied to a tree, in Lem's care. Now the earl could relax, and Pen could race around without fear of being kicked if she came too near the bad-tempered gelding. Jacelyn was happy enough to dismount. What was tender yesterday was sore today, despite hot soaks. Not intending to gallop, she had worn the brown velvet habit again, only incidentally hoping for his lordship's warm approval. She only had to fluff out the skirt once or twice with her crop, and adjust the blue veil on her hat before he noticed.

Grinning, he said, "Very becoming outfit, by the way. I meant to tell you at the mews, but I was so

189

overcome I couldn't get the words out."

"Gammon! I suppose Spanish coin is my reward for fishing for compliments."

"Pet, you don't need to fish. Why, I'd be singing your praises right now, if I didn't fear it would turn your head." When she laughed he realized that one of her greatest charms lay in her not believing quite how beautiful she was. He doubted even the acclamations of the Polite World would turn her into a spoiled Diamond, thank goodness.

"Seriously," he went on, "aside from what's in it, the style is very attractive, and practical. Not all that ungainly yardage to be tossed over your arm like a dishcloth."

Since Jacelyn was now using both arms to tug a stick away from the dog, she agreed wholeheartedly. "Isn't it silly what some women will do for fashion's sake?"

"I'll wager more will be adopting this style. I, ah, understand Miss Ponsonby had a bit of difficulty with *her* train yesterday," he said, doing some fishing himself.

Jacey chuckled. "Miss Ponsonby was a tad overset. Would you believe Miss Perfection herself acting so unladylike? Tripping over her skirts and"—she looked back at Lem, in the distance—"being found in a compromising position. I wouldn't say anything to Arthur or anyone else, but I know you'll appreciate the jest."

"Anton-Fredricks?"

"Of course, though how she could—"

"And how compromising?"

"Not fatally, I suppose. It would be enough to

give Aunt Ambel kitten-fits if I did it, but they were only embracing in the center of Richmond Garden's maze."

"That's bad enough. Tell me something: Why didn't you tell Arthur or Lady Hockney or any of the others? You can be sure Priscilla would have been the town crier, if it were you."

"I know, and I thought of all the satisfaction it would have given me to tell. I even thought it wouldn't be a bad thing if she and Anton-Fredricks had to marry. They deserve each other. I couldn't do it though, and Miss Kinbeck and Miss Montmorency agreed: no woman should be forced to marry against her will."

"Miss Trevaine, I compliment you as that rarest of women. Not only beautiful, but kind and wise beyond your years—and your deuced ox of a dog has its muddy feet on my new Hessians!"

"If Cinderella's godmother could make a coach out of a pumpkin, I'm certain we can do *some*thing with this gown."

Pinkie wasn't so sure. "But Miss Jacey, ma'am, Cinderella's godmother had a magic wand!"

They were in Rhodine's bedchamber, where the drapes were threadbare and the ceilings had water stains, and where one of the ugliest dresses in creation hung from the wardrobe door. Pinkie just stared, dumbfounded, Hammersmith sniffed, and Jacelyn tried to keep Rhodine from weeping, though her own confidence was shaken at the task confronting them. If this gown were an infant, she

191

thought, its own mother would disown it. Getting some cheerful conviction into her voice took an effort, but she did it. "We'll have more of an idea when we see it on. It will look better, I'm sure. Do you want Pinkie to help you, or shall you call for your maid?"

Lady Rhodine did not have a maid of her own, sharing her stepmother's abigail. Tina did not stir until noon, and the dresser, taking her cue from her mistress, played least-in-sight for Rhodine's needs. The girl was pitifully grateful for Pinkie's help. All in black as usual, Hammersmith looked like a judge finding the whole ménage guilty of a severe breach of propriety. Such goings on in a gentleman's house!

The house, the maid, the selfish stepmama, nothing was to the point, only the Dress. Jacey was wrong. It didn't look better on. Now it looked as if a berserking tent had dragged itself across Araby, through an oasis of roses, to savagely attack poor Miss Endicott. There was a pale pink satin underdress, totally unstructured on top, except for a loose waist, puffed-out sleeves, and a neckline that did just that, with a stranglehold on Rhodine's throat. Fashion dictated a fitted bosom and no waist, tiny cap sleeves and, if not cleavage, at least a collarbone!

"Tina said I mustn't look fast."

"You don't even look human, much less fast."

On top of the underdress was a white tulle overskirt consisting of four tiers of gathered ruffles which stood out so stiffly Rhodine could have sailed to Calais in a strong breeze. More of the gauzy stuff was gathered at the collar, and trickled out of the sleeves, halfway down her arms. More? Roses. Pale pink satin roses made out of the underdress material, with green silk leaves and stems, with a white satin bow around each stem. The flowers were strewn haphazardly, so the white ribbon streamers dangled everywhere. The matching headpiece, a mixture of all of the above ingredients, was laid out on the dressing table like a casket wreath.

"Do you have a long cape? Oh Rhodine, I'm sorry. Don't cry! We'll fix it . . . won't we, Pinkie? Hammersmith?"

Pinkie was soon rummaging through her workbasket, while Hammersmith was poking and prodding, trying to find if Rhodine actually had some shape in there. She also pulled at the girl's prinked curls. Too bad it wasn't a wig, the maid's expression said.

Then they got to work. Gown off, hair washed. The entire overdress was soon in a pile on the floor; Rhodine's hair had a soft wave to its pale, streaky blonde. Underdress back on. Damp hair gathered up into a knot. Another conference.

The women, Jacey adding encouragement as well as creativity, decided it was better already. At least there was less of it. Now all they had to do was make it fit like a gown, not a sack. Pinkie pinned and basted and cut and sewed. There was no time for perfect edges with tiny little stitches, so the new neckline would have to be camouflaged. Jacey's job was cutting the roses off the netting, then undoing the white ribbons. She found a housemaid willing

193

to press them, for a coin. Hammersmith worked on Rhodine's hair, using ingredients from her tapestry satchel. They worked straight through the luncheon no one offered them. When the maid came back with the ribbons, Rhodine ordered her to fetch something from the kitchens. The girl stood staring wide-eyed at the room in chaos and at the stepdaughter who had never demanded anything, and was now requesting meals for servants.

"Go on, girl, get." Hammersmith flicked a towel at her. "You heard your mistress. Gawking like a bumpkin at a two-headed chicken won't get your work done. And mind your tongue in the kitchen."

"Yes'm." It was Hammersmith who received the curtsey. Pinkie giggled, but kept on sewing.

It was nearly four o'clock when they finished. Jacelyn would be late for tea with the dowager Lady Parkhurst if she didn't hurry. That, according to Aunt Amabel, would be enough to set the old girl off on her high horse. But it was worth it.

"Remember, don't go down to supper; have it in your room. And call for that other maid to help with the buttons, not Lady Endicott's dresser. And don't lie down, it'll muss your hair. Put your wrap on upstairs so by the time Lady Tina sees you it will be too late to change."

"Yes, yes, Aunti Jacelyn, I'll remember! Now you'd better go, or you won't be ready on time yourself. Pinkie, will you please help me out of the gown?"

Jacey took one last look at her friend's glowing smile and knew it would be worth it, even if she missed Almack's altogether. No, she amended, she had to get there early, to see Lady Tina's face—and Arthur's! Rhodine was lovely, the gown was superb. The slip dress was now gathered under the bust with long streaming white ribbons. The collar, cut down to a modest décolletage, was edged with a thin rolled layer of the white gauze, with one of the pink satin roses at the V. The gauze also formed tiny strap sleeves and small flounced insets at the sides of the swagged hemline, held by two more roses. The rest of the roses were twined together to make a caplet for Rhodine's hair, now a shining soft-wheat crown with loose curls at the back. Even her cheeks had a delicate blush, thanks to Hammersmith's satchel. The sparkle in her eyes, though, came from the heart, not a bottle.

Jacelyn burst through the rear entrance of Parkhurst House, Pen bouncing around her in welcome, and called a hallo down the long corridor to Marcus at the front door. Her hair was undone, her gown was creased and had threads and snippets of gauze clinging to it, and she was late. She made a turn for the stairs, and nearly bowled over a tiny, plump old lady just coming out of the west parlour. Aunt Amabel was behind her, shredding her handkerchief.

"Doesn't look much like a countess to me," the dowager grumbled. "Nor even like a lady."

Jacelyn was far from a Long Meg herself, but she looked down on the round little figure, not many inches over four feet, and said, "Good, we're even. You don't look much like Satan's stepsister either, but we'll both manage, won't we?" She curtsied, kissed her aunt's trembling cheek, and fled up the stairs.

She wasn't born a tall, willowy blonde with a peaches-and-cream complexion. She hadn't turned into one recently, and it didn't appear that she soon would. She didn't have Rhodine's pale, fragile prettiness, nor Priscilla Ponsonby's stately golden aura, nor even a magic wand. She'd done the best she could, though, with Pinkie and Miss Hammersmith's assistance. It wasn't half bad, she told herself, for a little brown wren. The gown from Ryefield was deceptively simple: a deep gold slip dress of sheerest silk, with four lighter gold, spiderweb-soft Valenciennes-lace panels falling straight to the floor from the underbust waistline. When she moved, the panels flared loosely around her, letting the underdress cling to her hips. The top was entirely unadorned, what there was of it. Not indecently low, it still managed a rounded softness and an expanse of honey-warm skin, broken only by a large topaz on a gold chain, one of her mother's jewels. She also wore a gold tiara from the Treverly vault, confining the thick coils of chestnut hair. The few tiny wavelets around her face, seeming to be there by artless chance, had taken Hammersmith forty-five minutes to accomplish. Tiny gold satin slippers with ribbon laces and long cream-coloured gloves completed the effort, with a light dusting of powder to conceal the last of the freckles. Not china-doll pretty, but regal, elegant, exquisite. Or so everyone said when she went down to dinner.

"Fine as fivepence, my dear," Lord Parkhurst declared. "I might be tempted to dance with you m'self."

His mother answered Jacey's demure curtsey with a muttered, "And I always thought you couldn't make a silk purse out of a sow's ear."

Aunt Amabel was still uncertain about the gown's colour. The whole evening was so fraught with tension, though, she ignored this minor issue and said, "Charming."

It was Leigh Claibourne whom Jacelyn looked to, however, not the smiling Mr. Sprague nor the "Bien" of Mme. Aubonier.

His lordship was looking bang up to the mark himself, Jacelyn noted, with muscle-contoured black satin knee-breeches, wellfitted midnight-blue coat, sparkling white linens, a small black pearl in his intricate neckcloth, and blond curls casually brushed. Right now his blue eyes were gleaming as he told her simply: "I'll be the proudest man there." It was enough. Then he handed her a tissue-wrapped parcel. "Here, little princess, for your first dance."

His gift was an ivory filigree fan in a gold holder, with a tiny pencil attached. He showed her how her dance partners' names could be written on the delicate spokes, by entering his own on the first and another toward the end.

"Only two?" she asked, disappointed.

"That's all the patronesses will approve, dewdrop, otherwise I'd be tempted to claim them all."

Mr. Sprague wrote his name, and then Marcus

197

was announcing the arrival of the dinner guests.

They were fourteen to table in all, with Jacelyn, Claibourne, and Sprague the only young people. After Aunt and Uncle Parkhurst, in fact, no one was much under sixty. These were the dowager's friends, the Old Guard of London Society, when men wore powdered wigs and high-heeled shoes and the ladies wore patches and paint. The dowager now sported purple bunting and a red turban with an enormous diamond in the front. The turban was nearly all you could see of the elder Lady Parkhurst as she sat to her son's right at the long mahogany table. Her chin barely crested the tabletop, and how she could reach her glass was a mystery to Jacelyn, who was trying not to embarrass herself by giggling.

Lord Parkhurst tapped his glass with his spoon, raised the glass, said, "Health," and they all drank, starting the meal—and giving Jacelyn an idea.

She caught Marcus's eye at the sideboard and, when he approached her, whispered her idea to him. Claibourne, at her side, raised that sardonic eyebrow but Jacelyn turned her attention back to her soup. Marcus disappeared. When he returned, concealing something behind his wide girth, he nodded to Jacey. As the soup bowls were removed and the wine was changed for the next course, Jacelyn tapped her own glass and stood up.

With a lady standing, every gentleman in the room had to rise also, but with this group, it took some time, and some canes and footmen's aid.

"I'd like to propose a toast to my aunt," Jacelyn said in a clear voice. "Will you all rise?"

Now this was unusual. Ladies rarely proposed

toasts, hardly ever stood to do it, and never demanded that other ladies rise, especially not white-haired matrons in turbans. She turned to Mme. Aubonier in silent appeal. Madame shrugged, but stood. The others followed, again with effort. When they were all erect except Aunt Amabel, Jacelyn turned in her direction, all attention on her, and said, "For all your kindnesses, ma'am, in being like a mother to me at this important time, I wish to thank you most sincerely. To my aunt."

Everyone sipped and sat down to the next course, prawns in drawn butter. Aunt Amabel was bewildered; she hadn't had two conversations with the pesky girl in the week she'd been here. The dowager, however, now perched on the sofa cushion Marcus had slipped onto her chair while she was standing, smiled and raised her own glass to Jacelyn.

Not much got past Claibourne, despite his casual air. "I wonder how many other hearts you'll win tonight, sweetheart," he said.

He would never see the inside of Almack's Assembly Rooms, not in this twisted lifetime, but Josiah Fenton spent the afternoon getting ready for it all the same.

His unfocussed eyes gazed on the future, and he didn't like it. The poison of his hatred writhed around him in smokey black tendrils. His right hand contracted, and his head fell forward on his scrawny neck, then jerked upright again.

"Percy!" he shouted.

199

The loud noise startled Percy, who was in the midst of his usual occupation: pouring fluid from one container to another, so it went more smoothly into the third. His hand twitched, and the liquid spilled, so he dispensed with the intermediary step, lifting the bottle of brandy straight to his mouth.

"Damn you for a simple-minded sot, Percy. How many have you had?"

"Bottles or glasses?"

"Oh God. Put it down and listen. What have you done about the Trevaine girl?"

Percy set the bottle on the table, but dabbled his fingers in the puddle there. "Trevaine? Oh, Claibourne's chit. I followed her around one day, like you said."

"Stop sucking your fingers, lumpkin. You're not a child, you only think like one. What was she like?"

"Small. Dark. Drab except for an orange dress so I could spot her easily in the crowds. Blue-nosed. Seemed to like the bookstores and the galleries. I couldn't see what Claibourne would want with her."

"Only wealth, a willing wife, and heirs, nothing you'd understand, you raw-boned rattlepate. So what have you done about getting rid of her?"

Percy did not want to remind himself of the whole terrible incident of the horse—or the dogs or the cats—so he searched for some cheerier information to relate. Beaming like a baby who's just found his toes, he uttered: "She smiled at me."

Fenton's glassy eyes grew round, his mouth dropped open. "It couldn't be. I cannot believe it's true. Percy, tell me, do you really think to end

Claibourne's engagement by stealing his bride's affections? *You?*"

"Miss Trevaine's got nothing to do with it, Da. Brown dab of a female. I told you I'd talk to La Fleur. Today she looked right at me . . . and smiled." Percy was in love.

"At least there is some limit to your stupidity. Do you know what today is?"

"Wednesday."

"See? And tonight?"

"Uh, Wednesday night?"

"It's Almack's, you cup-shot cabbage head! Where the aristocracy goes to play. The French may have had the right idea after all."

"Smart people, the French. They make damn good brandy." Percy eyed the bottle longingly. His father ignored him.

"They go to their private club to show each other how exclusive they are, as if they needed to be reminded of their social standing- once a week. You're not invited to Almack's, you're nobody. You get accepted there, you're Somebody. Claibourne's little nobody will be going tonight, and you've got to see she doesn't become a Somebody."

"Huh?"

Fenton pounded his fist on his wasted legs. "You see these, shrivelled and shrunk from lack of use? That's what your brain must look like! I'm telling you, you've got to stop that woman from being a success tonight. Once she's recognised by the social set, Claibourne can never back off; it wouldn't suit his notion of honour. Nor would having a bride who's a social outcast. Those Merrills and their

201

fancy family pride! You've got to stop it, Percy!"

"Me? I mean, how? You need somebody to go inside and make the girl look no-account, and you just said I'm a nobody, gov, I think."

"Don't think, boy, save your effort for breathing. I have a plan that may work."

"I ain't going back to the butcher."

"I pay a cook to do that, you fool. Besides, they don't serve meat at Almack's, only cake, tea, and orgeat."

"No liquor? I'm glad I'm a nobody. Now Fat Mona's place is kind of private, but *any*body can—"

"Shut up, Percy! From the *on dits* pages and what Jensen picks up, the girl's a high-strung hoyden. So far she's not gone in over her head, but a scene outside Almack's ought to put her beyond the pale. Here's my idea: You and Jensen will hire an old broken-down horse and cart. Buy it, if you have to; it'll be worth the price. You'll take it to Almack's, and when you tell Jensen the Trevaine chit is coming, he'll pretend to start whipping the horse and—"

"Hold on, governor. Those swells take their horses seriously. It could get real ugly. Now if Jensen was to beat an orphan . . ."

"The girl likes horses. She'll get hysterical and start an uproar, mark my words. They—that's the Somebodies inside—don't like mingle-mangles, especially if there are dirty, smelly peasants involved."

"What dirty, smelly peasants? I didn't hear you mention any."

"You and Jensen."

"I don't see why Jensen can't do it alone. Claibourne might recognise me."

"You have to identify the girl, you long-legged looby. That's why I sent you to follow her. You'll be in disguise, and you can disappear as soon as there's a crowd. Jensen can just act like the village idiot till it's over."

"He gets the easy part! Uh, gov, I think I'll pass on this one. Clever idea and all that, but Claibourne will be there. He'll kill me if I bother the girl."

"And Jensen will if you don't."

Five hours to prepare were four and a half too many for Percy's precarious hold on sobriety or sanity, especially as he switched from the bottle to his father's pipe as soon as Jensen had carried Fenton upstairs. By the time Jensen was ready with the ancient horse and cart, reality was like last month's weather to Percy, a vague memory. He must not be recognised, he knew, or someone would murder him, but gads, he wouldn't put such foul rags on his body! Not Percival Fenton. No, he had the brilliant notion of donning the costume he'd worn to the last rowdy masquerade at Vauxhall Gardens, half mask and all. Great night, that was, with those French girls. Exiled nobility, they said. Maybe they'd be at Almack's . . .

Jensen's horse made the one Percy bought at the knackers look like a Derby contender. To help it along, the giant-sized servant got out and walked. Then Percy got out. Then Percy led the horse while

Jensen pushed the cart. On King Street, though, one block from Almack's, there was a hill. Not a big hill, mind, just a slight incline. To this horse it might as well have been Mount Olympus. And time was passing. Carriages were starting to turn the corner; fancy coaches with crests on their doors drove past them. Jensen unhitched the cart and put the yoke over his own shoulders, then grunted for Percy to get the nag moving.

Soft words and coaxes got him a few steps. Going to the other end and pushing won him a few more, and a dry throat. He tipped up the flask he'd managed to conceal under his disguise, and remembered that afternoon's spill. He dipped his finger in the mouth of the flask and offered it to the horse. It was sloppy work, but effective, for a while. The horse followed Percy as far as it could, until its back legs gave out and it sat, doglike.

"Aw now, old sod, we've almost got it. A bit more now, you can do it."

But the horse slowly laid its front end down. Percy held up the head, pleading. "Here you go, old chap, you can make it. I have just the thing to set you back up."

That's when the Parkhurst entourage drove up to the red carpets at Almack's doors. Stepping down first, Claibourne looked back. What he saw stunned even him: a huge, ragged man pulling a cart and his cousin Percy, beak nose under a sequined half mask, hairy spindleshanks under a short Roman toga, pouring whiskey down the throat of a half-dead horse.

Claibourne shook his head. The vision was still there. Lord, he'd like a few words with Percy right now, but first he had to see about getting Jacelyn and the aunts, the dowager, and the other antiques into Almack's with the least fuss. He thought of declaiming the classic *"Ave, Caesar, morituri est,* etc., which would be wasted on Percy. Instead he just called out: "Chariots just aren't what they used to be, eh?"

13

Don't expect much, and you won't be disappointed. That's what everyone told Jacey about Almack's, and they were right. The place itself was dingy and dowdy—but oh, the people! Jewels, feathers, finery, she wanted to stare as she'd done at the gallery, but Claibourne tugged her ahead, following her chaperones. What an unlikely trio they made, these three Fates in charge of her introduction to Society.

Mme. Aubonier was in black as usual, tall, dignified, selfcontained. She greeted acquaintances with a nod, like an emir bestowing his favour. She made sure that Jacelyn's first curtsey was to the patroness who had secured her vouchers, Princess Esterhazy.

Aunt Amabel was in lavender chiffon. Her shawl kept slipping as she greeted everyone they passed with an embrace, as if she'd been out of the country for two years.

It was the dowager, though, in her glaring purple and red, short little legs trundling ahead, who kept them moving from introduction to introduction.

"Sooner we get the tomfoolery over, sooner I can find the card room. Chicken stakes only, but it's better than watching these silly geese trip over each other."

"I can see to Jacelyn's introductions, Mother Parkhurst, if you'd rather sit down," Amabel dithered, after Mme. Aubonier left them to sit beside Lady Drummond-Burrell behind the velvet rope marking the still-empty dance area.

"You can't even untangle your draperies, Amabel. The gel needs countenance. Let them all see I approve; that'll hold their clacking tongues. There's Countess Lieven. Not as bad a gabblemonger as Sally Jersey, but bad enough."

Jacelyn had her little how-do-you-do's down pat. "Yes, ma'am, I'm delighted to be here. Thank you for the invitation. The pleasure is all mine," etc. She even had a rote reply to enquiries concerning her London visit, and how much she was enjoying everything, when the matrons were kind enough to ask. She was taken aback, therefore, to meet with a cutting remark *à la* Priscilla from a total stranger.

The countess was coyly looking around Jacey and asking, "What, no livestock?"

While Jacey was wondering how this woman could be so rude and still be considered a judge of polite behaviour, the dowager was answering. Jerking her head first in Aunt Amabel's direction, then Claibourne's, she said, "The gal's got a peahen and a gamecock, she don't need any stringy old chickens clucking at her.

"Toughest is still to come," the dowager told a wide-smiled Jacelyn, when they paused to let Claibourne fan Aunt Amabel's flushed cheeks. "They call her Silence, 'cause she never is. Damned impertinent, because she can get away with it. I don't know why. Her own history isn't any lily-white. Mind your step, though, child."

Lady Jersey was holding court with some of the older members of the Beau Monde, Alvanley, Petersham, Byng, the Regent's cronies. Most of them raised their monocles to survey Jacelyn like a new species of water bug while Lady Jersey exchanged the usual pleasantries, giving an especially warm welcome to Leigh.

"So nice to see you among us again, Claibourne. I'm glad to see your rakehelling days are over. And here is your little Miss Trevaine," she purred, still addressing Leigh, whose lips were twitching. "I hope she realises what a fortunate girl she is, to have landed such an eligible *parti*. So many girls in this situation find themselves at sea in London. You know, Leigh, all those little country girls with fat dowries who find themselves the target of every flat and fortune hunter in Town."

Jacey looked at Lady Jersey's diamond-studded hand resting familiarly on the earl's arm, and the shy little country girl replied: "Better the devil you know."

Sally Jersey was poised like Julius Caesar about to give the thumbs-down signal. Impudent chit, implying Claibourne was a bounder or a basket scrambler, when she, Sally Jersey, had gone out of her way to congratulate the girl. Poor taste to refer to his financial embarrassment, and poor choice of audience to utter any kind of outré opinion, especially for a girl with a gamey reputation. Esterhazy would hear about this—and all of the ton. But Claibourne was laughing, and old Lady Parkhurst was cackling about the girl's spirit, and the Carlton House set behind her were all smiling and nodding, so obviously the girl was a witty charmer, not a coarse baggage after all. Small, but spunky. Obviously. She, Sally Jersey, decreed it so.

Luckily the music started then, and Leigh led Jacelyn off to the first set. It was the cotillion, with a lot of bowing and curtseying and smiling to complete strangers.

"Unless I miss my guess," Claibourne told her during a quiet interval, "you're about to take London by storm. Look at all the nods you're getting, and all the bucks hanging around your poor Aunt Amabel."

"Silly, that's just Arthur and Carter Sprague. Besides, I noticed how you were welcomed back to the fold with open arms.

"I told you I needed you to give me respectability."

"With *wide* open arms. Soft, clinging, jewel-encrusted arms."

Claibourne laughed out loud, drawing attention to them, and even more when he raised her hand and kissed it, still following the dance's movements.

209

Tongues ran on wheels. It was true, then, Claibourne was cotched at last. Whatever tales had been circulating about an honour-saving offer could not be disregarded, as well as rumours of a market marriage. It was enough that he was attending Almack's at all, but that he was enjoying it said a great deal about Miss Trevaine. She was certainly worth meeting, the talk went, and her name was added to those mental lists hostesses were forever compiling.

"This is our very first dance, Leigh."

"Why, so it is, my love. And you are as graceful a partner as a man could wish."

"You're much more accomplished."

"Only more practiced. I've been at it a deal longer."

"Leigh, are you . . . that is, did you, ah, find Lady Jersey attractive?"

Claibourne laughed again. "I'm not about to take a page from Prinny's book and admire women old enough to be my mother, if that's what you mean. What has you in a pother now?"

"Arthur said I don't know how to flirt, and she did it so well!"

"Did she? I didn't notice. Come, precious, look up at me with those twinkling eyes, and show your dimples. That's all the flirting you'll ever need."

When the dance ended, he led her to Aunt Amabel, sitting on a little gilded chair behind the velvet rope. Seated next to her was her bosom bow, Lady Ponsonby, so Priscilla was nearby, scowling. The

Ponsonbys had arrived too late for the first set, leaving Priscilla on the sidelines like a wallflower while everyone exclaimed over Miss Trevaine and her earl. Priscilla was waving her fan so vigorously Arthur complained of the draught. After all the insincere greetings, and before the next set was begun, Jacelyn nudged Arthur aside and asked if he was promised for the next dance.

"Only for watching out for Priscilla. I'm to stand by in case no one asks her to dance, you understand."

Jacey didn't. "All night? You have to dance with your sister all night?"

"Of course not. She's very popular, a real Diamond. The company's still a little thin, is all, and her arrival may have gone unnoticed. Quite the thing to do."

"If Priscilla can spare you, do you think you might dance with Miss Endicott, Lady Rhodine, that is? She was very nervous about this evening, and she's very shy, you know. I felt since you're already acquainted . . ."

"Of course, be delighted. Nice girl. I don't know why, but I forgot all about her. Where is she?"

"She just came in, over there by the door, with the stunning redhead. That must be Lady Tina, her stepmother."

"Where? I don't see—Good heavens, is *that* Lady Rhodine?"

Without consulting his mother or Priscilla, he excused himself to go welcome Miss Endicott.

"Doesn't know many people. Quiet girl, don't you know." He only stepped on one dowager's foot in his haste. Jacelyn made sure Claibourne was smiling too.

When the music started for the next selection, a country dance, Mr. Sprague ended his conversation with the earl and headed toward Priscilla. She slowed her fanning and turned her head away. The lady wasn't interested, not in some minor government functionary. He walked right by her and led Jacelyn out! They were headed toward Arthur and Rhodine Endicott's set, and no one had yet asked Priscilla to dance!

None of her other admirers seemed to be around. Damn Arthur. Claibourne was still nearby, though, talking with her mother and Lady Parkhurst. He seemed to be acceptable in polite company, suddenly, and he was certainly handsome, if one didn't mind his nonchalant, almost flippant manner. Those blue eyes and broad shoulders . . . No, it wouldn't hurt Priscilla's consequence in the least to be seen with the worldly earl. They would make quite an attractive pair, in fact, both fairhaired, tall, dignified. Not like the couple he made with that harum-scarum little gypsy. Priscilla paced the fan's rhythm to her eyelash fluttering. The earl didn't seem to notice. Priscilla mentioned, "Oh dear, the music is starting, and my partner hasn't arrived," and the infuriating man asked Lady Parkhurst if she was dancing that evening. After her tittered denials, Claibourne turned to Lady Ponsonby. Priscilla's own mother! One of the spokes of her fan snapped in two.

"How ungallant of your partner, Miss Ponsonby. Might I take his place?" Claibourne finally got around to asking.

"My pleasure," she answered through clenched teeth as he led her past dancing couples to the same set the others had joined. When the movements of the dance brought Arthur as her partner, Priscilla stomped on his foot, hard. He yelped and hopped about, however, instead of taking his punishment like a man, which made her look like a clumsy cow. The dance wasn't over soon enough for Priscilla, who accepted Mr. Sprague's offer to dance even before reaching her mother's seat, lest the shame of being partnerless repeat itself.

Jacelyn was to dance next with Arthur, and Claibourne with Rhodine, so they all stood near Lady Parkhurst, chatting amiably, while Priscilla seethed as she turned down four men she'd rather dance with than that prosy Sprague. At least her dance card was getting full! She absolutely refused to acknowledge that some of her gentlemen had also put their names on Jacelyn's and Rhodine's cards, and two had actually asked Jacey first!

The quadrille was a complicated dance, and both Jacelyn and Arthur had to mind their steps. He did manage to compliment her efforts on Rhodine's behalf, though.

"What, did she say I had anything to do with her new style?"

"She was telling everyone over by Lady Tina how much you'd done to help. Nice girl, appreciates kindness."

"Poo! No, I don't mean Rhodine isn't nice; she's the sweetest thing in nature. I just meant I didn't do anything. My maid and Aunt Simone's did all the work."

"It's more than m'sister would have done, help someone who's much pre—Um, ah . . ."

Jacelyn laughed, and almost missed a turn. "You can say it, Arthur, Rhodine is the image of the English beauty. She just needed a little push, that's all."

"Still, it was a deuced fine thing."

"Why, Arthur, I believe you may even grow to like me one of these years!"

His choking caused a button to pop off his straining waistcoat, causing the gentleman behind him to lose his footing. Skidding, that man grabbed his partner for balance, throwing her off the measure. She stepped back, and right onto the flounce of the lady next on the line, tearing it. It just wasn't Priscilla's night.

Jacelyn next danced the boulanger with Lord Farthingale. She'd hastily introduced Rhodine to Lord Tayson, who was to have partnered Priscilla, and sent them into the dance. Now she was too worried about how quiet Rhodine and the nervous, stammering Lord Tayson would manage a conversation to pay much attention to Farthingale's flattery.

"Come, my lord, there must be a more interesting

topic of conversation than my gown. How did you spend the day, for instance, or have you any fascinating plans, and have you seen any of the new plays? We're to go to Drury Lane next week."

Another contra dance followed, with Lord Tayson with his rose boutonniere. Luckily, the figures kept partners changing, so Jacey didn't have to sustain a long conversation. She did recall the questions she'd put to Farthingale, to stopper his high-flown compliments, and used them to good effect with the young nobleman, until he was finishing whole sentences before moving to the next lady in the figure. She also met three new gentlemen and found they were happy to speak of themselves and their interests, rather than just the usual gossip and polite inconsequentialities.

Jacelyn was becoming so popular with those who had met her, and so attractive to those who'd only seen or heard of her, that the spokes of her fan were nearly filled by the time the next set started. It was a waltz, which she had to sit out until approved for it by one of the patronesses, under some peculiar ruling. No matter, she was glad of the rest, and the cool drink Claibourne had waiting for her.

"Aren't you promised, my lord?"

"Only to you, pet. I'm here to beat off the hordes of admirers, remember?"

She told him, with a giggle, to leave enough of them for her to dance with. "I'm having a wonderful time! Are you? Are you very bored?"

"Not at all. I danced with Lady Rhodine and

heard you nearly recommended for sainthood; I listened to five dowagers tell your aunt what a delightful girl you appeared; and I had seven chaps tell me what a lucky dog I was while they waited in line to sign your programme. Delightful evening."

"You could go dance with Sally Jersey."

"Minx! Be quiet and drink that insipid stuff, or I'll tell all your admirers how you gallop in the park."

After that, Jacelyn danced straight through to the intermission. She danced with Lord Farthingale again, and all the new young men, and the Spanish count, de Silva, which raised Claibourne's brow, which in turn made it hard for Jacey to keep from laughing during de Silva's long, flowery speeches. She danced with her uncle, passing between the card room and the front vestibule where he could enjoy blowing a cloud. She danced with some of the older set, Miss Montmorency's Lord Milbrooke, for one, who found her refreshing, and whom she found charming and courtly. She did not dance with Anton-Fredricks. She couldn't believe the man had the gall to ask her, and took great pleasure in announcing that her card was filled. Arthur, nearby with Rhodine, crossed his arms over his chest and glowered.

"I see," said Anton-Fredricks, looking from one to the other.

"I thought you would, old boy," said Claibourne.

Arthur and Rhodine strolled off to find what refreshments were available. Ponsonby, like

Claibourne, had danced a few duty sets, and otherwise stood near the chaperones, waiting for the ladies to be returned. He wasn't there for his sister's sake, now, but for Miss Endicott's, whose own chaperone seemed to have disappeared, rather than stay to hear more about her stepdaughter's dewy beauty. Rhodine was dancing nearly every dance too, for the first time in her life, and not just with those who couldn't get near Jacelyn. But Arthur was always waiting there, with a cooling drink, or to wave her fan, or to receive her tremulous smiles.

"He's positively hovering over the girl," Claibourne told Jacelyn. "You were right, she's as helpless as a kitten, and he's a natural guard dog. I congratulate you on your foresight. Now what in hell are you going to do about that puppy Farthingale? He's been drooling over my shoulder all night."

"Now you're encouraging my matchmaking? What an aboutface!"

"I've seen it succeed. While you're at it, what about Sprague? The poor fellow had his dance with the Iceberg and went home."

"I know. Isn't it sad? But don't worry, I'm working on it. I haven't got it quite settled between them, but I think one or the other would be perfect for Sam. You know, Squire's daughter Samantha. She's to come for my ball next month. Can you see Squire with a future duke as son-in-law? And a sports-mad one at that? I don't know if Sam would like being a duchess though. She might prefer Mr.

217

Sprague's quiet gentility and good sense. Squire would be pleased with a man who earns his way in life too, instead of what he'd call a fribble. I'll have to let Sam decide."

"Kind of you, my dear."

After the intermission, Jacelyn had her second dance with Leigh, and another with Tayson, at ease with her now. All the young men were, in fact. The girl was cheerful and pleasant, without all those airs the Incomparables adopted. Furthermore, she was a beautiful little handful, a regular Pocket Venus. She was soon dubbed an Original, for her style and her outspoken views. Why, she'd argue the merits of crossbreeding as easily as discussing the weather. She was kind, too, didn't make a fellow feel no-account if he forgot the steps, and look what she'd done for the Endicott girl, the one who'd been all over frills and frizz, and no conversation. Miss Trevaine was safe, besides. Some of those other girls, you danced with them twice and their mamas were calling you son. Miss Jacelyn was as good as spoken for, with Claibourne at her side all night, looking as if he were just casually passing time, and giving all her partners a look that would freeze their livers if they had dishonourable thoughts. If they did, they got rid of them fast and simply enjoyed the young woman's unaffected charm. So relaxed were they in her pleasing company that they found themselves excitedly telling her about yesterday's races, and last week's mills, and tomorrow's cockfights in Little Dene.

"We have to stop it, Leigh, can't you see that? It's dreadful, what they do to the poor birds!" They were sitting out another waltz.

"Yes, it is dreadful, Jacelyn, but we cannot stop it. It's the way of the world, and nothing will change that."

"I won't accept that. It's wrong and shouldn't be allowed. We can notify the authorities."

"And what would that do? It might even be legal in that village, for all you know. The authorities don't care, if it keeps the people happy. You've heard of bread and circuses, haven't you? This is the same. The young bloods from London will go bet their blunt, but it'll mostly be country folk, poor farmers and down-at-the-heels workers. It's one of their few pleasures, and no one wants to be the one to take it away. The folks who live there? Think of all the traffic and trade for a little market town. Do you think the locals would be pleased to see their windfall outlawed?"

"But what about the birds, and how immoral it is to wager on another creature's life!"

"I'll tell Lady Ponsonby to pray for their souls. Listen, Jacelyn, whatever notion you're entertaining, get rid of it. This isn't like playing ducks and drakes with Squire. These are rough, violent men. It would be dangerous to interfere with them in any way. Do you understand?"

"I understand you won't help." She was disap-

219

pointed and disillusioned. As for Leigh, he wanted to shake her.

"Jacey, I am not a Farthingale to parrot every opinion you make, and I won't agree with you when you're wrong. I cannot think your thoughts, nor vice versa. And this time you are wrong. It's sad, sweetheart, I know it is, but you can't save every fallen sparrow, and you cannot change the world singlehandedly."

"Then why did you volunteer to fight Bonaparte, and stay so long? Did you think he wouldn't be defeated, else? Yet you were only one man!"

"I was only one man, but there was a whole army beside me. You are one woman. You cannot take on a whole cockpit!"

It was easy for Jacelyn to discover the location of the cockfight, some few miles outside of London along the Great North Road, and to watch for the crossroads signs at Upper Dene's Landing. The young Corinthians were speaking of nothing else, though once she had the information she needed, Jacelyn refused to discuss it further. One overeager enthusiast kept at it, till she told him to go find a like-thinking friend, put bladed spurs on, flap their arms up and down, and try to cut each other to shreds. It would be better sport! When the man laughed at her "wit" she walked off the dance floor, claiming a ripped flounce.

She didn't even have a flounce, but she went to

the ladies' retiring room anyway, to get away from the chatter and music, and think. She wasn't sure what she could do about the cockfight. That was for later. Right now she had to think about Leigh. They were friends — he'd said it just last night — although she felt so much more. Claibourne was almost a part of her, sharing all those silent jokes at the silliness around them, touching her hand gently when he sensed she needed reassurance. He was there, for her, this whole night that could have seen her disgraced. It was his stature that had lent her the credit to be a success. So why was she so hurt, so angry, that he couldn't support her in this? Maybe because they were so close, to her thinking, and she was beginning to dream of their being one. Which was foolish, she knew. Even if he loved her with his whole heart, they would still be separate people, with separate beliefs and separate feelings. Even if he loved her . . .

The last dance was another waltz. Leigh considerately asked if she would like to go home, rather than sit it out, but Aunt Amabel was still deep in conversation. Mme. Aubonier and the dowager had left ages ago with Lord Parkhurst, so there was no need to consult their wishes. Jaccy wanted to talk to Leigh. She glared at de Silva till he veered off, blowing a mock kiss, and then she turned to the earl.

"I owe you an apology, my lord, for not respecting your opinions. I know I must not expect you to agree with all of mine, yet I am sure you will grant me the right to hold them, no matter how cork-brained. As I must yours."

"I don't have cork-brained opinions, poppet, but thank you. I was afraid you were still angry with me. You know, I can't decide if you are more charming at your most sincere or at your silliest. Come." He took her hand.

"But . . . but, Leigh, I can't dance with you! I haven't been given the nod to waltz, and Aunt Amabel said I would be labelled fast if I did it without permission. And we've already danced twice. You know—"

"I thought we agreed on that at least, that all these silly conventions were so much manure to wade through. Do you want to waltz?"

"Oh yes!"

"With me?"

"Of course!"

"Then come."

A corner of heaven must be reserved for young lovers' first waltzes. It was almost like kissing to music, the way Leigh did it, holding her closer than customary. They were breaking so many rules, one more didn't matter. Nothing mattered to her now, except his warm hand around her, the brush of his thigh against hers, those blue, blue eyes staring into hers like eternity.

It wasn't till the dance was over that he told her he'd gotten approval from Sally Jersey. Sally hadn't even asked for a favour back, thank goodness. Some sacrifices he was willing to let Baron make for him, but there were limits to the others. He didn't discuss any of this with Jacelyn, who was still humming the last refrain. Nor did he mention that the third dance was as good as having the banns read. It was time to go home.

14

The window or the servants' door, that was the question. Coming back through the kitchen in britches would be hard to explain, when the staff might be at their own breakfasts. But the dog couldn't climb trees—up or down—so the rear exit it had to be. On second thought, Jacelyn turned back and opened the window for the return trip. She could always scramble up the tree and leave the dog in the courtyard, saying she'd let Pen out early.

Getting into the stable was no problem; the door facing the rear gardens was always unlatched. She didn't dare open the wide stable doors facing the mews, for the noise would surely wake the grooms asleep overhead, so she led the mare back through the courtyard and out by the small delivery gate. She couldn't latch it behind her, of course, but perhaps it would go unnoticed in the morning's bustle. As for getting the mare back, if the stablehands were awake—well, she'd worry about that later. Perhaps she should have taken

Lem, but he would have argued with her till it was too late to go. Besides, as she'd just written in a long letter to her papa, she had to fight her own battles.

Jacelyn had stayed awake for three hours after sharing her success with a rapturous Pinkie, rather than chance staying asleep past daylight. She filled in the time with writing home. She'd previously told her father about the bareback ride and Richmond, so now she related her experiences at Almack's, and the people she'd met, and how nice most of them were, just as he'd said they'd be. Lord Trevaine's last letter, in his fine angular script, had advised her to look for the best in people, and laugh at the worst, if she could. If she was unhappy, he'd written, she should come home immediately. She made sure he wasn't fretting himself that she was miserable, or that she was so enamoured of this new life that she didn't miss him and Treverly. She also explained to him — and herself — some of the lessons she was learning. She'd always been independent; it was easy in the country. Here in London, where she was never alone, other people had a much greater say in her life. The very trip to London itself wasn't her choice. Now there were so many telling her what she must and mustn't do, where she should and shouldn't go, even whom she should and shouldn't talk to. She felt she was losing part of herself, even more by trusting so fully in Claibourne. She must not let herself become a hollow shell filled

225

with social conventions, nor an empty extension of the earl's will. She'd managed by herself at Richmond; she would manage tonight. What she wrote to her father, without mentioning cockfights or solitary 4:00 a.m. rides, was something to the effect that a man — or woman — had to do what a man had to do, and stand on his own two feet to do it.

Or her mare's four feet, as the case may be.

The ride through London was quick. Her route bypassed the less savoury neighbourhoods she had been warned about countless times, thank goodness, and the Great North Road was wide and clear. There were even some travellers about, mostly draymen and farmers going to market. None paid any mind to the boy in the floppy hat, if they noticed him at all by the moon's uncertain light. She reached the crossing at Upper Dene without incident. A few times she thought she'd heard hoofbeats other than her mare's, but the imagination played tricks on dark nights, she knew. Pen never signalled anything untoward so she'd kept riding. Now here she was at the five-fingered crosstie, trying to stand on the mare's saddle to change the direction signs.

Pen was off in the bushes and the mare was fidgety and Jacelyn couldn't quite reach. Every time she got her hands on the Little Dene marker, the horse took a step ahead, or tried to put her head down, or whuffled nervously. Jacelyn then had to sit down and pull the horse back into position, all while she kept looking over her shoulder. It was spooky out here, alone, miles from home, in the dark. She stood in the saddle again, wishing it were Baron's back. His was rock-steady and a lot taller. That sign was high, she was short. "Drat."

"Need some help, sweetheart?" asked a voice from behind the bushes, followed quickly by Jacelyn's shriek, then Pen's barking.

"You . . . you bastard! What do you mean, sneaking up on me, scaring me half to death!" Jacelyn sputtered as the earl slowly, casually, walked over to her and her horse.

"What I'd meant to do, you widgeon, was throw the fear of God into you. What in bloody hell are you doing out here with only your overgrown rug rat for protection, when I specifically told you how dangerous it was?"

Avoiding the question, more than a little nervous at the harsh expression on his usually smiling face, to say nothing of his hand steadily tapping a riding crop against his leg, she countered: "What in . . . bloody hell are *you* doing here?"

"I am following my instincts, which right now tell me to use this"—the whip—"where it will do the most good."

She shivered. Lord, he meant it! This wasn't Squire's burning fury, nor her father's warm, sorrowful regard. This was cold, hard anger. She'd never seen anything like it in the easygoing earl, and she didn't want to see any more of it. She

227

pulled her horse back.

"Stay." She stayed. "Miss Trevaine, did you ever, I repeat, *ever*, stop to consider that you might be in danger, riding around the streets of London by yourself?"

"I did think of it, my lord. No one would bother a poor boy off on an errand."

"Not even a poor boy on a rich man's horse? You foolish little innocent. No one bothered you, my *lady,* because I was a block behind, with a pistol very visible in my waistband. Otherwise you would not have gotten past Portman Square."

"You . . . you followed me from Parkhurst House?"

"To my dismay, I find I am beginning to understand how that hare brain of yours works. Your charming apology didn't quite answer; it never said you'd give up, even if it was a hen-witted idea. Therefore, yes, I followed you, lest someone break your sweet little neck before I got a chance to!"

As he took two steps closer to her, Jacelyn began to speak, quickly: "My lord, I can see where you might be a trifle overset—"

"Hah!"

"—since you are responsible for me, and your aunt is sponsoring me, but you *must* understand that I couldn't *not* do something about the cockfight."

"I must?" He took another step, but the whip tapping was, at least, less frequent.

"Remember what you said about saving every

228

fallen sparrow? I know I cannot even come close, but what if I could save even *one* rooster? Wouldn't that be worth trying? And I did listen to you. I would have gone to Dene's Landing in the morning and demanded they call off the fight, but for what you said about all the rough folk."

"Thanks for small favours, puss."

Ah, he was back to the pet names. His "Miss Trevaine" was more chilling than the threats. "And I thought of going there tonight and freeing the birds . . . if I could find the place, and if the cocks were there yet, but I decided that would be too dangerous also. See, I'm not entirely foolhardy."

"Do you know about the simpleton who jumped off the bridge after the ha'penny he dropped? He was clever enough to remove his boots, but he still couldn't swim."

"It's nothing like! If I could just switch the signposts, I'd ride home and no one would be the wiser."

"Certainly not you," he muttered. Louder, he asked, "What, my sweet, did you hope to accomplish? I can see you mean to confound the London bucks, send them off to . . . where? Upper Dene? Bathny Willow?"

"Actually I was hoping they'd get halfway to Scotland before they realized the mix-up. Lord Forster said most of the men would stay up through the night, at their clubs, rather than have a few hours' sleep. I can only think they'll be somewhat worse for it, by seven or eight."

"Which is all the more reason why this was a chaw-bacon scheme!"

"I won't be here then. Besides, most will be driving too fast, racing their curricles as the sporting group seems to do all the time, so they won't be paying careful attention to the markers."

"That's not to the point. You send a few Town bucks to the rightabout, but you haven't ended the cockfight, or even delayed it."

"I know," Jacelyn admitted sadly, "but it was the best I could think of. I reasoned that the young gentlemen from London had the most money, and the most leisure time. If they weren't there to make their enormous wagers, perhaps it wouldn't be so profitable for the local men, who would then go back to their chores. If there wasn't so much betting, maybe, just maybe, one bird wouldn't have to die for their pleasure. Do you understand?"

"Get down . . . For heaven's sake, stop looking like a frightened rabbit. I'm not going to beat you. Yet. You can reach the signs from Baron's saddle." He whistled for the stallion while she dismounted, then lifted her up.

"This is another crime against the Crown, you know," he remarked casually from the ground as she tugged and twisted at the fingerposts. "I'm not sure where it ranks in relation to kidnapping, but you are certainly turning out to be the felonious sort, aren't you? You know, my dear," he added

230

just when she finished, "I think it's time you learned that crime doesn't pay."

Jacelyn thought of adding another misdemeanor: stealing the horse she was on and riding away as fast as she could. Baron would come to Leigh's whistle, though, even if she weren't standing upright. She stayed where she was, but Leigh walked around the horse and, reaching up, grasped her firmly around the knees.

"Yes," he said, "it's long past time you learned that your womanhood won't always protect you from the results of your follies."

He lifted her off the horse, then down the length of his own body to the ground, still in his arms. He brought his mouth down to hers in a fierce kiss, while his arms tightened around her till their bodies touched everywhere. The kiss went on and on, and where his hands or his lips didn't touch she ached for him.

At last he raised his head, but still held her cheek pressed against his chest. "Oh, Lord," she heard him groan, through the smooth fabric of his jacket, and over the blood thundering in her own ears. "What was the deuced lesson?"

"Listen to this, George. Jacelyn writes that they are calling her "Miss Trevaine, the Toast of the Town.' What do you think of that?" Lord Trevaine turned the sheets of his daughter's latest letter while Squire sipped his wine and studied the chessboard.

"To be honest, Elliot, I wouldn't believe a word of it, if m'sister hadn't written the same thing."

"I'm having difficulty crediting it myself! My Jacelyn, in her pigtails and boy's clothes, always in some bumblebath . . . curtseying to the Queen. My sister Amabel says she did it gracefully, too. Jacelyn writes that she had no time for her own spasms over the hooped skirts, she was so afraid Amabel would succumb to the vapours and swoon dead away."

"Damned foolishness, if you ask me," said Squire, capturing Trevaine's bishop.

"I agree, and so does Jacelyn. She says that she enjoyed the literary evening at Miss Kinbeck's much better, but that Amabel fell asleep."

"Shouldn't wonder. I always told you the girl didn't need all that fancy book learning you kept spoon-feeding her. Isn't she going to any balls and such? That's all Clothilda ever writes about. Who danced with Priscilla, who sent flowers. Mrs. Bottwick's interested in that piffle. Says it'll help next year when my Samantha makes her curtsey. Not looking forward to it, all that doing the pretty."

"Indeed, there seems to be a great deal of that. Listen: 'In the week since Almack's I've hardly spent two hours at home, except to change my clothes and sleep. There are so many invitations Mme. Aubonier and Aunt Amabel have long arguments over which should be accepted. Claibourne and I have had to delay our morning rides and

Pen's exercise until after ten, we get home so late. Friday we had tea at Miss Montmorency's, dinner at Lady Hockney's, attended the Royal Theatre (an undistinguished *Richard the Third*) and then went on to two different balls! I need more gowns, Papa, but Mr. Sprague assures me my account is still solvent.' "

"Hell and blast, they never have enough gowns. Be thankful you've only the one daughter, and that one discovered fripperies late in life. For a female, anything over the age of five is late! Lord, what it's cost me in India muslin already, I could have bought the whole deuced East India Company."

"You'll be interested in this, I'm sure: 'I've been helping my friend Rhodine alter her gowns also. You'll remember I wrote about her. She's the over-dressed girl with the sweet nature and the evil fairy-tale stepmother. Except Lady Tina is a real dasher! Anyway, I think dear Rhodine and Arthur will suit perfectly, and they seem to agree! He is very solicitous of her, and she doesn't mind!' Have you heard anything about this from your sister?"

"Yes, and she wasn't best pleased at first, I can tell you. No money there. Endicott's run aground, they say, gambling. The girl wasn't much either, though Clothilda says she's coming along, whatever that means. She wrote Mrs. Bottwick that rumour says Spenborough might come down heavy, if he likes the match. M'sister's reconciled to it, she says, if Arthur's set on having the girl."

"It sounds like it: 'Arthur now rides with us in

the mornings, along with half the Corinthian set, so there's no more riding astride' " — Squire snorted — " 'and he spars with Lord Claibourne at Cribb's or Jackson's, for the exercise. I can only hope this is to impress Rhodine, and is a good sign.' "

"Exercise, eh? That does sound serious. Does she say anything else about the girl? Part of the family, don't you know."

"Let me see . . . no. She did mention in her last letter that Lady Rhodine was coming out in the carriage most afternoons, and she was getting used to Penelope, but still had no liking for horses."

"Pah! Trust that coxcomb of a nephew of mine to find a shrinking violet. But a duke's grand-daughter . . . What else does she say?"

"Hm, she writes that her Aunt Amabel took to her bed for three days after the dowager left."

"Parkhurst's mother? That old curmudgeon still around? Cads, she was a tartar when I was a boy on the Town! How did your spitfire deal with her? Like fire and ice, I'll wager."

"Quite the contrary. Lady Parkhurst introduced Jacelyn all around as her granddaughter, or as near as she'd get since that 'twiddlepoop Parkhurst' never provided her with one."

"That sounds like the old bat. You have to give your girl credit. An old besom like that would eat my girls alive. That Frenchie aunt of Claibourne's didn't seem any too accommodating either. How is that working out?"

"Seems ideal. Jacelyn has the fondest regard for her, and even her maid. We didn't see the woman, but Jacey's first letter had her carved in granite. Now they all rub along nicely. Mme. Aubonier has taken Jacelyn to tea with some of the old French aristocrats living in London, and she said I'd be proud of her French now. One old *vicomte* had the girl in alt, last letter. Didn't I read that one to you? It's right here. He was one of the wealthiest men in France; now he's teaching music. Jacelyn was so impressed with his exquisite manners and his courage that she's determined to have her friend Miss Montmorency 'discover' him to her musical friends."

"So your girl seems to have found her feet. I'm glad, Elliot. Nasty business, that was."

"I was worried myself. It seems to be going smoothly and yet . . ."

"And yet there's still no betrothal notice."

"Nor does she mention Claibourne much except by name. 'We go to Covent Garden tonight with Claibourne,' or 'Today Claibourne and I saw the waxworks,' like that, nothing more."

"What do you think it means?"

"You're the one with three daughters, you tell me!"

"It wouldn't matter if I had twenty-three, I'd be danged if I'd understand a one of 'em. And that goes double for *your* daughter. Check."

From rout to ridotto and from balloon ascension to Venetian breakfast, London's newest star was busy every minute, mostly in Claibourne's company, but never solely in Claibourne's company. Mme. Aubonier or Aunt Amabel was always along, or Pinkie during the day, when a young lady was considered less vulnerable. Leigh and Jacey hadn't been alone together since that morning after Almack's, weeks before.

Neither mentioned that kiss, though both carried the memory like a bouquet. And neither mentioned the betrothal Lord Trevaine and Squire Bottwick were so troubled about. Aunt Amabel, Great-aunt Simone, Pinkie, Lem, and Arthur could be added to the concerned list—and all of London to the curious. Claibourne swore he would give Miss Trevaine what was left of her first Season, to be a belle, to enjoy herself, and to reconcile herself to the marriage. He wanted so much more than that, but he would woo her and wait. Even if it killed him. It had to be her choice.

As for Jacelyn, it had to be love. It had to be mutual. The affection was there, she knew, and the attraction. The last was obvious. So many tiny sparks were kindled by even the most casual touch between them, she was surprised no one else noticed. But there was no talk of love. She thought of asking him outright, but even her candid nature quailed at the idea of hearing his affected London drawl say, "What's that to the point, poppet?" or some such. There was no one else to consult, either. She resolved again, as she had almost every day, to accept what she had, his comfortable friendship and his charming company.

He spent so much time with her, doing the pretty as Squire would say, that one day she had to ask, "Leigh, haven't you anything better to do with your time than escort me all over London?"

"You wound me, Miss Trevaine. Are you tired of my company so soon?"

"Silly. I mean, are you bored, or am I keeping you from something important?"

"What could be more important, rosebud? No, you see a man of leisure, your typical London loiterer at your service. Unless you'd rather I filled my afternoons with lewd women, in addition to my late evenings."

"Gammon. Arthur says you go to your clubs with him at night."

"You mean I really am a reformed rake? Arthur would know. Now that he's *cap-à-pie* over Lady Rhodine, he's become even more fusty."

"If possible!"

"If possible. You know, kitten, I have been thinking of a worthwhile occupation for my time, now that I am become so upright. Not that Lady Cowper's amateur theatricals, et cetera, aren't worthwhile or anything, but I've been considering taking my seat in the House of Lords. Your uncle has mentioned it, and Sprague, of course. What would you think of going with me one afternoon

237

next week to see the great statesmen of our time in action, so I might see if it's too dull even to consider."

When they approached Sprague, he was delighted to be of assistance. A friend of his, in fact, was giving a speech next week which Sprague had helped draught, and he would be pleased if Claibourne and Miss Trevaine would be his guests in the visitor's gallery. Lord Medford Broome's speech was in favour of a bill protesting the plight of child labourers in the mills, and it stood almost no chance of passage. Lord Parkhurst hadn't felt he could sponsor such a doomed measure; therefore Sprague had worked with his friend Broome. Sprague mentioned to Jacelyn that he had been thinking of inviting Miss Ponsonby; what did Jacelyn think? She had to tell him, honestly, regretfully, that she didn't think Priscilla would be interested, at all. He nodded in resignation. He didn't think so either, unfortunately.

The gallery was almost empty when the two men, Jacelyn, and her maid attended. So was the floor of the chamber. The few members who'd bothered to appear wore robes and wigs. A few were asleep. Most were chatting among themselves like ladies at tea, or reading the newspapers, or writing notes. No one seemed to be listening as the earnest young man stood to address the assembly. Jacelyn, for one, was not impressed with Parliamentary procedure. She was, however, thoroughly impressed by what Lord Broome was saying, and soon forgot the rest of the audience.

Broome spoke of children working ten-hour shifts. Of tiny girls set to bobbins, because their hands were small. Of little boys sent to work underground, because the shafts needn't be so large, then. He spoke of huge, deafening factories, where six-year-olds spent their short lives, without breathing any but poisoned air, without seeing the sun. The money they traded their childhoods for? It wouldn't even buy them a piece of the fine linen they wove, much less decent, nourishing meals.

Pinkie was quietly weeping, thinking of her little brothers, who might have been forced to the mills too, if not for her wages. A muscle in Claibourne's jaw twitched as Broome declared the situation a national disgrace, perpetuated by greed and indifference. Think of your own boys and girls, Broome said, for you are the fathers of all the nation's children.

He bowed his head and took his seat. There were coughs and shuffled papers as the Upper House prepared for the next speaker, and the same undercurrents of muffled conversations. Then there was applause: a steady, determined clapping by a pair of small hands in tan York kid gloves. After a startled moment, Claibourne joined her, then Sprague and a tear-stained Pinkie. Some of the members on Broome's side of the aisle took up the acclaim, and then those who hadn't even heard the speech. The opposition even added to the ovation, and Lord Broome, red-faced, was being patted on the back and having his hand shaken.

Jacelyn turned to Mr. Sprague and congratulated him. "The speech was marvellous. I'm sure the bill will pass, if not today then soon." She impulsively planted a kiss on his cheek.

As they turned to leave, the earl whispered for Jacey's hearing only: "Were you just putting your mark on him for Samantha's sake, or do I have to worry?"

"You have to see about taking your seat here," she told him. "There's so much to be done."

15

Miss Trevaine was enjoying London to its fullest, and London was enjoying her. Her refreshing candour, her innovative styles, her seeming to do what no other woman had ever done—bring Rake Claibourne to heel—all were chewed over with the morning's chocolate. Except in one house on Mount Street, where the new day began past noon, and where anything as sweet as chocolate was as foreign as a Hottentot. Here Jacelyn wasn't considered delightful, effervescent as champagne, or an exquisite wild rose among London's hothouse beauties, as reported in the papers. Here she was that damned interfering nobody, or Claibourne's cream-pot connexion, or his two-bit tumble. Once she was established and accepted, it was worse. Claibourne would never throw her over now.

"You botched it, you bandy-legged boob. You could have shown the girl for an hysterical hoyden. Now we'll have to go the other route, dis-

241

credit Claibourne. And the demned cub's been acting the saint, from what I hear."

Percy was sprawled on the sofa as usual, dreamily contemplating the wine in his glass. "La Fleur."

"Stop flogging a dead horse, boy!" Fenton didn't even notice when Percy's wince caused the wine to overflow down his shirtfront. "Claibourne hasn't been next or nigh that jade in months."

Percy was busy mopping at himself with his loosened cravat. When he finished, his hands automatically retied the now-splotched neckcloth into its usual crooked, droopy knot.

His father looked on in disgust. "Well," he said, "what are you going to do about it?"

"I'm going to see they meet again, Claibourne and La Fleur."

"You slack-jawed jackanapes, it'll take more than a meeting between the cub and his old doxy to get the Trevaine tart up in the boughs."

"I know that, governor, I ain't as stupid as you think."

"You couldn't be, boy, you couldn't be."

Percy ignored this. He smiled and went on: "They'll meet at the theatre 'n everyone will see."

"So what if they are seen together? You've got to show he's a womanizer, a rakeshame, not that he's polite enough to greet his ex-mistress. Besides, how do you know they're going to meet at the theatre?"

"That fellow Kean's doing Shakespeare Friday. You know, the one the toffs make such a fuss

242

about. *Macbeth? Hamlet?* One of those, no matter. Claibourne will be going, mark my words. That chit's bookish, remember. And Miss La Fleur has box tickets. I made sure of that."

"Well, well. I didn't think you had it in you. You mean you're actually on terms with the woman, to know her engagements? Maybe we'll come about after all, if she cooperates."

"Not exactly. I've been standing her doorman a few rounds now and then, so I know what's what." Percy swallowed what was left in his glass, then undid the neckcloth again to use its ends as a napkin. He belched, then grinned. "She said good day yesterday, though. It's a start."

"Percy, your nursemaids didn't just drop you on your head; they must have played Albert-Had-an-Apple, with you as the ball."

Jacelyn was already disturbed on the afternoon of the theatre party, and it had nothing to do with Percy's machinations, or even Claibourne. Strangely enough, it was concern for Priscilla Ponsonby that was discomfitting Miss Trevaine.

The afternoon's carriage ride had seen Jacelyn and Rhodine riding with Mme. Aubonier and Monsieur Blanc, as the *vicomte* turned music teacher now called himself. Arthur and Claibourne rode alongside for awhile, until the flow of traffic forced them apart. Jacelyn saw Claibourne ride to pay his respects to Lady Tina, Rhodine's stepmother, where that elegant auburn beauty was posed artistically in her pink-satin-lined coach under a stand of trees. Arthur had joined a group around a showy phaeton, where Priscilla was perched on the high seat next to the driver, Lord Anton-Fredricks. Priscilla was tittering shrilly, although whether her nervousness was real or put on for the effect, Jacelyn didn't know. The phaeton was a spindly, fragile thing, no doubt fast, and assuredly dangerous. If Priscilla wanted to risk her neck in such a perilous contraption so the sporting gentlemen would admire her, well, that was Priscilla's choice, wasn't it?

Then Monsieur Blanc held up his looking glass. "That is Lord Malcolm Anton-Fredricks, from Lancashire, *non?*"

"Yes it is," Rhodine answered, "and the beautiful lady with him is Arthur's sister, Miss Priscilla Ponsonby."

"This Miss Ponsonby, she is very wealthy?"

Mme. Aubonier told him in rapid French, to save Rhodine's blushes, that the family was respectable, the girl had a decent portion, but there was more pride than substance.

"If Miss Ponsonby is not very, very wealthy, she has more to worry about than that so precarious equipage," the old gentleman told them.

There was a man in Lancashire, it seemed, Chater by name, was a wealthy mine owner. Monsieur related this, not to carry tales out of school, they must know, but for family. Chater was of the bourgeoisie, better than most. His mines did not collapse as often as others'. Chater wished to better himself, and his family status. To this end he hired a music teacher for his talented daughter, the best instructor he could find, Blanc. The girl had a pleasing touch, but her hands were too small. *Enfin.*

While Monsieur Blanc resided under Chater's roof, the wealthy capitalist contracted a marriage for his daughter with the son of a minor nobleman in the vicinity . . . Lord Malcolm Anton-Fredricks. Blanc had played the organ at the wedding in the local church, at Miss Chater's fond request. In the last letter the new Lady Anton-Fredricks had written, she was practicing her scales diligently, while awaiting the birth of her first child, next spring. Perhaps, she'd added, Monsieur would see her husband in London; Anton-Fredricks was attending Parliament to look after Mr. Chater's interests in labour laws or such.

Rhodine had her hand to her mouth, so it was left to Jacelyn to exclaim, "That swine! That scum! I feel like going right over and telling Priscilla and the others."

"You mustn't, Jacelyn! Oh, please don't! Arthur will have to call him out, you know he will. And Arthur could get hurt, or arrested, or . . . or killed."

"Sh, Rhodine, we won't let Arthur challenge him. But Priscilla has to be warned. She—"

"Pah!" Aunt Simone put in. "That one would

not thank you, *petite*. She likes playing with the fire. *Tiens*, I think a small lesson might do her some good. The Season has only a few weeks left to it, then we all go home, no? And Anton-Fredricks goes to be a papa, and Miss Ponsonby polishes her beauty for the spring Season. Maybe no longer too proud to consider a man of true values, no?"

"Carter Sprague? But the humiliation, *Belletante*, if anyone finds out! I just don't know what's right to do!"

Jacelyn was still undecided by the first curtain that evening at Drury Lane. She wondered if she should discuss it with Leigh during the farce, which no one listened to, or even sat down for. There were so many people coming and going in the box the Parkhursts and the Ponsonbys shared, however, that there was no opportunity for privacy. Farthingale stopped by, acting as if he'd never seen a pink gown before. Jacey's deep rose velvet from Ryefield was regal, perfectly fitted, but utterly unadorned. She wore only her mother's pearls, and a single white rose in the shining coils of her chestnut hair, for contrast. Claibourne wore his relaxed, amused expression, but Jacelyn noticed that he put his arm across the back of her seat while Farthingale rhapsodised about her celestial beauty. "Fustian" was all he said, though, when the viscount left. Lord Tayson silently handed Jacelyn a pink rose, which quite ruined the effect of her gown, but she tucked it into her hair next to the white one, anyway. Tayson blushed, bowed, and left, obviously too overcome by the full box. The *Conde* de Silva visited, weighted with gold braid, diamonds, and compliments so grandiose they could all laugh. Even the young politician, Lord Broome, came to pay his respects, and ended up losing his heart to the lovely young woman who was so enthusiastic over his cause.

Lady Endicott stopped by, to check on her "dearest Rhodine," who was totally ignored as Lady Tina usurped the chair next to Leigh.

"We're old friends, you know," she told Jacelyn, who was staring at that lady's bare arm resting on Claibourne's satin-covered thigh. A lot of the rest of the lady was equally bare. When she left, Jacelyn whispered to the earl, "How come you almost outdid the grandee in your flattery of Lady Tina, and you only told me I looked charming?"

"Because she is nothing without her outward appearance. You would still be your exquisite self no matter what you wore. And stop pouting, or I'll put you to the blush by telling you exactly how I'd like to see you dressed . . . or not."

At least she didn't have to worry about Leigh, not tonight, thank goodness, because through all of this, all the mock courtships and friendly banter, Priscilla was flirting with Anton-Fredricks.

It almost turned Jacelyn's stomach to hear Priscilla's lisp and "La, sirs," and to watch her flutter

247

her fan and her eyelashes at him. The more gentlemen who came to the box to greet Jacelyn, the
shriller Priscilla's voice seemed to get; the more
heady the compliments to Miss Trevaine, the more
coquettish Priscilla's behaviour. Jacelyn could *not*
let her make such a cake of herself over such a
libertine. As the lights were dimmed before the
first act of the major play, Anton-Fredricks was
sucking each of Priscilla's fingers in farewell. Ugh.
Jacelyn had to warn the other girl. After that,
Priscilla could make her own choice.

The play was *Othello,* and the great Edmund
Kean was playing the evil Iago. Last month, Jacelyn understood, he'd played the title role. The man
was amazing, but she kept seeing Anton-Fredricks
as the double-speaking standard-bearer. Watching
poor Othello's unravelling, she was glad she wasn't
the suspicious type. Jealousy was such a terrible
thing.

When the curtain came down the applause rose
like a wave, a uniformed footman brought a four-
folded note to the box on a silver tray. It was for
Claibourne, who unfolded it while the others
watched curiously.

"Nothing wrong, I trust," Arthur commented.

"No, not at all," Leigh replied, refolding the
note and placing it in his inside coat pocket. "Just
an old friend who asks me to visit during the
interval. Will you excuse me, my dear?" he asked
Jacelyn, and left.

When Arthur and Rhodine also went out, to get

refreshments for the ladies Parkhurst and Ponsonby, Jacelyn was too concerned with her planned conversation with Priscilla to wonder why Leigh hadn't taken her along. If she could only speak to Priscilla before all the chitter-chatter began again and — Speak of the devil.

"Lord Anton-Fredricks, I hate to impose, but could I trouble you to procure me a lemonade? Claibourne was called away, and I have a terrible thirst. You'd like one too, wouldn't you, Priscilla? Oh no, you mustn't go off with Lord Malcolm and leave me alone. Besides, it's been such a long time since we've had a comfortable coze."

Priscilla was glaring. As soon as the gentleman unctuously bowed himself out, she snapped: "What are you trying to do, Miss Hobbledehoy, steal this beau of mine too? You have nearly every man in London at your feet. Isn't that enough?"

"Be still, Priscilla, I have something to tell you. I feel I have to give you warning, as a friend. It's . . . it's about Anton-Fredricks. He's only trifling with you, Priss. His . . . his affections are already committed elsewhere. I felt it best to tell you, rather than—"

"Why, you jealous little cat," Priscilla hissed, her eyes narrowing. "How dare you! You're only telling these nasty lies so I'll stop throwing him lures and you can step in. You spiteful brat, how would you like to hear some home truths, hm? Just look over there at the 'old friend' your precious earl had to visit."

249

She directed Jacelyn's view across the horseshoe-shaped theatre. Jacelyn could recognize Leigh's broad back, narrow waist and tousled blond curls anywhere. The lady alone in the box with him she'd never seen before. Full-figured, raven-haired, red-mouthed, she had a diamond the size of an ostrich egg nesting between her breasts. If the fullness of the woman's bosom was any indication, the blasted thing would hatch soon!

"*Who is she?*" she squawked. "Surely Leigh knows many women."

"He knows them all, Miss Greenhead! This one has always been one of his favourite bits of muslin. La Fleur, she's called. The flower's a bit past bloom, I'd say, but there's no accounting for a man's taste. The *on dit* is that he's always welcome at her house in Islington, no matter that she's another man's mistress. He used to stay there sometimes when he was in London on leave, before he and Arthur took lodgings together. They even say La Fleur purchased his army commission for him." Priscilla gave the dart a moment to sink in, then she rammed it home: "So you don't have to worry about his pride, Jacey, he's used to living off his women's money. Even if they earn it on their backs."

Jacelyn was too stunned to move. She wasn't sure what she was thinking about Leigh and this . . . this Cyprian, for she could now tell that the woman was no lady. The way the two were laughing, and touching, they were far more than friends. Her mind refused to focus, though, only backing to the beginning. "But Priscilla, Anton-Fredricks is—"

"Mine, and you better remember that. Look to your own, Jacelyn Trevaine, before you start making accusations. Here's another 'friendly warning,' all in the family. Watch out for your earl and Lady Tina. Dear little Rhodine's stepmama has been his flirt for the last six months. You knew he was a rake, didn't you? Or didn't anyone tell you what that meant? I'm sure you can figure it out for yourself now." She got up to leave. "One more thing: If you tell your Banbury tales about Malcolm to my mother or Arthur or *anyone,* I'll tell all of London how you spent the night alone in the gardener's cottage with Claibourne. They've overlooked the whispers because of your connexions, but they'll listen if I shout it loudly enough, you can wager on that. See how popular you are then, Miss Trevaine."

Jacey sat, turned to stone. It surely was a good thing she wasn't the jealous type.

There was a bit of confusion in that other box when Leigh walked in and Mr. Farley Unger discreetly left on an errand.

"You mean you didn't send this note, Flo?"

"Lord love a duck, pet," answered La Fleur, Flora Cobb. "My writing's better than that. And I wouldn't put any silly little flower by the name, neither, not to you, Leigh. 'Sides, you should have known I'd never send for you like that, not with your pretty little miss sitting over there, nor Mr. Unger sitting here." She fingered the boulder on her chest. "He's a diamond importer, is Mr. Unger."

"I'm sorry, Flo, truly I am. I did think it must have been urgent for you to ask for me here, so of course I came. I'll explain to Mr. Unger, if you wish, that we seem to be the victims of a hoax."

"No need to worry about Unger. If I can't handle a middle-aged merchant, my name's not La Fleur."

"It's not!"

"So there!"

They both laughed at this foolishness, then Claibourne said, "Since I'm here anyway, Flo, it's good to see you. You're looking as ravishing as ever, but is everything well with you?"

"Nothing's wrong that a little more money and a few less birthdays wouldn't cure."

"Are you in trouble? I don't have much of the ready, but I could—"

"Go on, Leigh. You save your guineas to buy that girl something pretty. If you want me to talk to Mr. Unger for you, just let me know. No? Well, I hear she's a real charmer, and I wish you happy, indeed I do."

"Thank you, Flo. I think I will be. You take care of yourself now, and if you ever do need anything . . ."

252

"You always were the sweetest, even when you didn't have two coppers to rub together. Oh, Leigh, before you go, you know that cousin of yours?"

"Percy? Don't tell me you know Percy Fenton? I've been looking for him for weeks."

"Have you? If he's the queer nabs I think he is, I know where you can find him."

"Really tall, skeleton-thin, slept-in fancy clothes, a nose like a turkey vulture's, and more money than brains. With Percy, it would only take a shilling. And he's always in his cups."

"That's him, all right. He's been weaving up and down my street for weeks now, days and nights. Sometimes he sits on the bench across the way for hours; sometimes he just passes out in the street. He's been giving my man Remington money, so I make Rem pay for the hackney to get the poor cawker home. He'd catch his death of cold out there, castaway, if the pickpockets or press gangs didn't get him, or the watch. 'Sides, it's off-putting for my guests."

"I'm sure. What does he pay your man *for*, though, Flo? I can't figure what he's about."

"No more can I. At first he wanted to come up, but I'm not currently receiving gentleman callers. Except for a few dear friends, of course. Then he wanted to know if you'd been around. That's why I thought he might be that cousin. Remington knows not to tell any more than he has to, to cover the hackney fare. I pay him plenty enough as it is. This week he told the poor bastard I'd be coming to the theater." She waved a hand around expansively. "Everyone in London is here, so it was no secret. . . . I bet the nodcock's the one what sent the note getting you here. And I just thought he was a harmless mooncalf on the go."

"He is, for the most part. He used to be, anyway. I think he's up to some devilishly queer business now, though. If he shows up again, you might mention that I'm looking for him. That should chase him away. Otherwise you can always send for me if he's a problem."

"If I can't handle a cup-shot cawker, my name's not La Fleur!"

"Flo, it's no wonder I love you. I'll stop by soon to see what Percy's up to."

Claibourne returned to the box just as the curtain was going up for the second act. At the next intermission he noticed that Jacelyn was pale and quiet.

"Do you feel all right, dear heart? Would you like to walk in the corridor where it's cooler? Shall I send for the carriage?"

She waved away his concern. "It's only the play and Mr. Kean. So affecting, don't you know."

The play was finally over. Instead of applauding madly like everyone else, Jacelyn just kept weep-

ing, for poor mad Othello and sweet Desdemona—
and herself. Jealousy was such a terrible thing!

16

"Aunt Amabel, I have to talk to you." It was the next morning. Jacelyn had sent a message down to the stables for Claibourne, saying she was too fatigued to ride. Of course she was tired; she hadn't slept at all last night. Now she was trying to get her aunt to listen to her, never an easy thing before noon. Poor Lady Parkhurst was doing her best to look alert, peering owlishly up from the bedclothes through the frills of her lace cap.

"Yes, dear, what is it? Um, what time is it?"

"That doesn't matter. Aunt, you have to tell me something. Are all men unfaithful to their wives? And if a man is unfaithful *before* she's his wife, does that mean he doesn't care for her at all? Aunt Amabel? Aunt Amabel!"

Jacelyn rushed to the door, calling for Davis, milady's dresser, to come quickly, with the smelling salts. The second footman Eugene, he of the easy morals and roving eye, was carrying the first of the day's floral tributes upstairs, so he ran to help.

Jacelyn slammed her aunt's door in his face. "Not you!"

Next Jacelyn approached Mme. Aubonier, who placed a finger, not a marker, in her book, to show the interruption would be brief. This was between Jacelyn and Leigh, she told the girl.

"You knew he was a man for the ladies; you know he is a man of his word. Take your anguish to him to resolve, *chère,* and stop bothering old ladies. Such romantic hobbles are for the young."

Leigh returned to Portman Square at eleven, with his curricle and a small nosegay of violets. He was not best pleased to see all the other bouquets on the hall table, awaiting dispersal. Nor was he happy to be told by Marcus that miss was not receiving that morning.

"Damn it, man, this is me, not some jumped-up Johnny Raw. Where is she?"

"I'm sorry, milord. That was Miss Trevaine's message."

"Is she in bed? Is she ill?"

"I couldn't say, milord."

"Well, has the doctor been called?"

"Not to my knowledge, milord."

"You're being damned helpful, Marcus."

"Yes, milord."

Claibourne was undecided. His horses couldn't be kept standing, yet if something was wrong, he had to know.

Marcus was undecided. His employers' interests and the generous earl's interests did not coincide, but where were his own best interests? "If I may suggest, milord, perhaps you would step into the yellow parlour. I believe Mme. Aubonier writes letters there. . . ."

Claibourne strode down the hall, calling back over his shoulder, "Have Lem walk the horses, they're fresh." When he came back out to the hallway a few minutes later, his brow was lowered and his mouth was set in a firm line. "Will you please tell Miss Trevaine that I wish to see her, *at once*."

"Yes, milord."

Marcus turned to Eugene, rigid at attention next to him. Eugene went up the stairs at a suitably dignified pace and scratched on Jacelyn's door. Pinkie answered, correctly, listened to the message, and shut the door behind Pen, who went downstairs to greet the visitor. The dog, at least, was happy to see Claibourne.

Pinkie repeated Claibourne's request to her mistress.

"He does, does he? You can tell my Lord Claibourne that . . ."

Pinkie opened the door, quickly erased the grin from her face, and whispered to Eugene. He went down the stairs and spoke into Marcus's ear.

Marcus gathered all of his butlerish dignity, as much as he could muster, considering his portly figure, less than adequate hair-covering, and reddish nose, from ensuring the quality of Lord Parkhurst's private stock. Shoulders back, looking past the earl's left ear, Marcus announced: "Miss Trevaine, my lord, says your lordship can go hang."

"Does she? Why, that little—" Claibourne headed toward the stairs, Pen happily circling around him. Marcus blanched; Eugene stepped aside, smartly. Then the earl thought better of it, as his hand closed on the dog's collar. "You may tell your mistress that I shall wait in the parlour for ten minutes while she puts on her bonnet. After that, her dog and I are going for a ride. I am not quite sure when we'll return, possibly this evening, possibly tomorrow."

He led the dog to another parlour, where his aunt was not, and proceeded to feed Pen macaroons from the claw-footed end table, so she would stay with him. "London's no good for females," Leigh told the big dog. "Your mistress is putting on airs, and you are getting fat as a flawn."

The ormolu mantel clock with its silly amorettos didn't seem to be working. Claibourne picked it up and gave it a good shake. It was ticking. Ten minutes to the second, he got up and herded Pen out the parlour door. Marcus silently handed over Claibourne's beaver hat and just as silently opened the front door for his lordship, who marched out, to see Miss Trevaine prettily seated on his curricle's bench, staring straight ahead. She, of course, had

259

gone out the back door and walked around the side of the house, rather than give Claibourne the round.

"Witch," was what Leigh said as he climbed up after Pen and took the reins, signalling for Lem to release the pair's heads.

"Kidnapper," was what Jacelyn said, pulling the dog closer to her side, without turning her face a whit.

Jumping up behind, Lem grinned. Nothing more was said until they reached the park and Lem had charge of the horses again. Jacelyn scrambled down from the high seat as best she was able in her gown's narrow skirt, rather than wait for the earl to lift her down. He ran a hand through his already windblown curls. Where to start?

"Jacelyn, listen. I'm sorry if you were disturbed about my visit with Miss La—deuce take it, her name is Flora Cobb. She is one of my oldest friends, just as I said last night. It would have been discourteous not to answer her invitation, even if she didn't—that's beside the point. She has been very kind to me. She even helped me get my army commission."

"So I heard, my lord, and how she helped you."

"That old story, eh? Let me tell you, my girl, sarcasm and snide remarks aren't becoming."

"How about bare bosoms and dampened skirts and arms that wrapped around you like ivy creepers? You seemed to find that becoming! How do you think I felt when my . . . my escort was fondling some . . ."

"Don't say it."

"Woman."

"I told you she was a friend, Jacelyn. I shouldn't have to listen to this."

"What about Lady Tina? Another *friend?* You slobbered over her a good half hour!"

"Lady Endicott too? Good grief, Jacelyn, if I seem familiar with these females, it's just out of habit. I'm used to holding a lovely woman, that's all. It doesn't mean anything. It's only among the debutante set where men and women can't touch except to dance. A man's used to these easy affections."

"You're what? You . . . you lecher!"

This was too much for the earl, who'd been valiantly trying to maintain his composure. He felt badly about Flora, but wouldn't have acted any differently. As for Tina Endicott, he'd thought her obvious lures amusing; Jacelyn obviously hadn't. But to be called a lecher when he'd been living like a monk for two months—and not enjoying the experience—was past his limit.

"Listen, you little shrew, I won't be subject to the Inquisition every time a woman smiles at me, nor vice versa. I told you I would honour you, and that had dashed well better be the end of it! I won't live my life as a Cheltenham tragedy, and I won't answer to you!"

He was really angry now, surprising even himself with his raised voice. Unlike the mercurial Jacelyn,

261

who was always in the boughs over something, then just as quickly all sunshine and smiles, it took a great deal to upset the earl enough to lose his temper. Like that whole table filled with bouquets from Jacelyn's admirers. He wanted to shake her!

"While we're at it, Miss Trevaine, what about your own behaviour? How do you think I feel watching every fribble in Town fawn at your feet?"

"What do you mean?"

"I mean that herd of wet-eared calves you don't wean away. For a girl who didn't know how to flirt just last month, you've done admirably, and I don't like it above half."

"How dare you!" She was rigid, hands clenched at her sides. With the fist, Arthur'd said, not the open palm. Claibourne stomped out of her reach.

"Poor Tayson's bad enough; that Bartholomew Babe won't go beyond the line, though, nor that Broome speechifier. And de Silva knows it's a game, but that Farthingale fop! It's disgusting how you encourage the man-milliner to dangle on your chain when you are just leading him on."

Words dripping ice, Jacelyn said, "Perhaps I'm not."

"What in hell is that supposed to mean?" he shouted. "Perhaps you're not what?"

"Perhaps I'm not leading him on, you bonehead," she yelled back. "You always said I might find a better man than you."

"Well, you haven't, damn you!"

Well, she hadn't. She took a step back and took a look at him. Even with his arms folded across his chest, his jaw outthrust, his hair all mussed, and his blue eyes glaring at her, he was still devastatingly handsome, even if he reminded her of a terrier picking a fight with the kitchen cat. She supposed she must be the angry feline then, hackles up and hissing. What a pair! She had to laugh at them.

It took a moment before the earl could laugh too, but soon they were smiling sheepishly at each other and what gudgeons they'd been. Leigh gathered her in his arms for a quick hug, and kissed the top of her head before he stepped back.

"Come, precious," he told her, tucking her arm in his and starting to amble about the pathways. It wasn't a fashionable hour to be in the park, thank goodness, he thought, though they did receive one or two curious glances. Had they been shouting that loudly? He laughed again at two of London's luminaries putting on a Punch and Judy show for passersby. "We can do better than this, rosebud. Let's start over, shall we?"

He began with Flora. Yes, she was his lover once, his friend still. When he was sent home to convalesce, she was the one who had taken him in. She'd taken him out of the hotel where he'd lain feverish for days, without anyone having sense enough to send for a physician, and no one else in all of London caring enough to investigate. When the man who was then paying Flora's bills objected, she showed him the door. It was her house, after all. She'd worked hard enough for such independence, for just such occasions. She did not have to "entertain" anyone she didn't wish. As for buying his colours, the rumour was totally unfounded. He'd managed the funds by selling off a hunting box he couldn't afford to maintain anyway. Flo's protector at *that* time, however, was an Austrian baron, an officer with the Allied Forces, and a comrade of then General Wellesley. As a favour to Flo, he put in word enough to get the new officer appointed to the general's own staff. "He was a fine gentleman. I named my horse after him, in appreciation.

"As for Tina Endicott," he went on, "the woman is a born flirt. She'll never be any different. If I once accepted what she was offering . . ." He shrugged. "I cannot apologise. I can only repeat that it was before I met you. I shall never disgrace you, and you'll have to trust me for that. I can see where it will take time to convince you, with all the gabblemongers, but we can see our way clear, I know."

It was Jacey's turn. "I really did think Farthingale was just paying me court because I'm the fashion this week. You know how he likes to keep up with the styles. If you think he is really forming a *tendre* for me, though, I'll discourage him from the notion as soon as possible. He's a nice boy; I wouldn't want to see his feelings hurt."

"Boy? The jackanapes is three years older than

264

you, Miss Maturity. Besides, how are you going to dislodge him without wounding his pride? You make it sound so easy."

"It is, with people who only care about outward appearances, like Farthingale. You'll see."

"Looking forward to it, my dear. There is, ah, one other thing, just to clear the air." He pulled her behind a row of bushes and held her close. "I do love to have a woman in my arms, and that will never change!"

"Just any old woman?" she asked, turning her face up for his kiss.

"Only ones about so high"—kissing the top of her head—"with freckles here . . . and here . . . and here. And lips that taste like . . ."

A short, but not too short, while later the two headed back to the carriage, holding hands.

"You know, puss, how we've had to cancel the trip to Vauxhall Gardens twice because of the rain? What would you think of going tonight? There won't be many more evenings warm enough."

"But we're promised to Lady Manderby's rout tonight."

"There will be five hundred people there, in room enough for fifty. Lady Manderby won't miss us. Wouldn't you rather see Vauxhall's famous Dark Walks, hm, sweetings?"

"Aunt Amabel says I mustn't. Dire things happen to girls who stray down just such primrose paths. What time shall you call?"

The Dark Walks, with their lovers' bowers, the shaved ham and arrack punch, the stupendous fireworks displays, the fairy lights strung from the trees. These were some of the reasons Vauxhall was called London's Pleasure Gardens, and why so many people came. Another reason many of the *belle monde* attended Vauxhall that evening was to escape the crush at Lady Manderby's.

The box Claibourne had rented for their small party was filling up. Lady Parkhurst thought it would be impolite to the Manderbys to renege on her acceptance, so she and her deputised escort, the ever-agreeable Mr. Sprague, waited in the carriage row for half an hour outside the party, inched up the stairwell for another twenty minutes, and shook four hands on the receiving line. When Arthur asked who was on the line besides Lord and Lady Manderby, Aunt Amabel asked back, Who cared? It took another hour to get back down the stairs, have their carriage brought around, and navigate the traffic on Curzon Street. Aunt Amabel was wilted, but had energy enough to describe her travails to all the callers at the box, Jacelyn's usual retinue. An equally exhausted Lady Parkhurst was thankful when Arthur offered her a seat and some punch. Priscilla and her friends would be up shortly, she announced, after they greeted everyone on the esplanade.

It was as good an excuse as any for Claibourne,

266

eyes twinkling as much as the hanging lanterns, to suggest that he and Jacelyn, Arthur and Rhodine, take a stroll around, before the fireworks. Mme. Aubonier, deep in conversation with Monsieur Blanc, waved them on. Sprague declined playing dogsberry to the two couples, with a laugh, and with Claibourne's permission ordered another supper.

"I didn't think this place would be so large, this close to the city," Jacelyn said, looking around.

"We haven't even seen half," Rhodine told her. "The last time I came we walked the other way, near the boats, where there are all kinds of little tents and booths. You can see a puppet show or have your fortune read or have your eye painted—"

"Ugh! Why would anyone want their eyeball painted?" Arthur exclaimed.

"To give to their lover. I think it's very romantic. Don't you, Jacelyn?"

"I'd rather have my fortune told."

Claibourne laughed. He lowered his voice and solemnly intoned: "Cross my palm, O beauteous maiden, and I will read the leaves. Ah, I see a man . . . tall, dark—oops, fair—and very handsome. He will give you your heart's desire, unless you wish your eyeball painted."

They went merrily on, through the crowds.

"I don't see how these Dark Walks can be very private, with so many people around."

"You should see it on Masquerade Night if you

think this is crowded." A cough and a frown from Claibourne hurried Arthur on: "Of course, Masquerade Night's no place for ladies. Very rough trade here then, you know. Anyone with a shilling can get in, and disguises seem to bring out the worst sorts. You never know if that fellow in the domino is a member of White's or a pickpocket. The, ah, lower orders get rowdy at their revels. No place for a lady. Not at all. Not the thing, you know."

Jacelyn's eyes were shining. "It sounds wonderful! When may we go?"

"Arthur," Leigh informed his friend in disgust, "you are the greatest fool in nature. How could you even think to mention something dangerous, foolhardy, and improper to Miss Trevaine? Haven't you known her long enough?"

"Dashed sorry, Leigh. I forgot."

Jacelyn was pulling on Claibourne's arm. "Oh, don't be so fusty! Say we can go, do! You know the gypsy said you'd give me my heart's desire."

"You cannot believe anything a gypsy tells you! You, madam, with your deuced curiosity, are the perfect illustration of why we got evicted from Eden! Of course I never agreed with that concept. If the Creator was so almighty, He had to be omniscient, so must have known what would happen if He gave Eve the chance. According to Milton, however—"

"I am not going to discuss free will at Vauxhall Gardens! You're just trying to avoid talking about the masquerade. Will you take me, or shall I find someone else to do so?"

"You see that pretty little bench under the tree over there? Why don't we sit and talk about forbidden fruit, hm? Arthur, why don't you and Lady Rhodine find a bench of your own to discuss original sin?"

It didn't take ten minutes. Claibourne promised to get Jacey to the masquerade, if she could slip out of the house, since there was no way either of the aunts would countenance the expedition.

In that same ten minutes Arthur stunned himself by proposing marriage. He was accepted eagerly.

"How wonderful! Let me be the first to congratulate you, old man!"

Jacelyn and Rhodine were already embracing and laughing and weeping. Then Leigh kissed Rhodine's hand, but Jacelyn threw her arms around Arthur in delight. She had to hug Claibourne too, to make things even. "I'm so happy for you both! Can we tell the others? Shall we order champagne to celebrate?"

There were rivers of champagne. Everyone in their box, the surrounding boxes, passing below on the walkway even, was invited to share in the couple's joy. Even Lady Ponsonby unbent enough to permit Rhodine to kiss her cheek.

"You can wipe that cat-in-the-cream look off your face, minx." Leigh smiled softly to Jacelyn. "You didn't do it *all* by yourself, you know."

"Of course not, silly. It's just that they really

love each other, and they'll be so happy. I mean, it's not the marriage of convenience everyone talks about. It's not for money or status or honour, or anything but that they're perfect for each other. *That's* the way it should be." In her excitement, she didn't notice his querying look.

There were at least two people in the box who were not happy to be there, and who didn't care tuppence about the newly affianced pair's happiness. One of these was Malcolm Anton-Fredricks. He didn't like what he read in Claibourne's face, for one thing, and he finally remembered where he'd seen the old man in the back of the box with Claibourne's aunt, for another. There hadn't been a formal introduction, with so many people talking at once, but there was no doubt. Worst luck! He had to get away from here.

The other person who was almost as desperate was Priscilla Ponsonby. She looked around her and saw, not joyous, loving couples, but plainer girls, with less distinguished families and smaller dowries, getting engaged before her, to better catches than she had. That hoyden Jacey, mousy Rhodine, even her friend Marcella Chadwick, who was a simpering ninnyhammer if Priscilla'd ever seen one. They were all nearly settled, whilst she, the Diamond, was still on the shelf. Next Season they'd call her an ape leader . . . if she didn't do something about it tonight. Too bad Farthingale wasn't hanging around Jacelyn as usual; it would have to be Anton-Fredricks. At least he seemed to have a large fortune at his disposal, despite being a mere baronet. Carter Sprague was dismissed instantly. He was a nobody, and too much of a high stickler to fall in with her plans anyway. But what providence! Here was Malcolm asking if Priscilla would like to take a walk, almost as if he could read her mind. Perfect.

"I would be delighted. We can be sure to get good spaces for viewing the fireworks. I *do* enjoy the spectacle so." She addressed the rest of the box: "You'll all be coming along shortly, won't you? It wouldn't do for us to be alone for too long, now would it? Lord Claibourne, do be sure to bring Jacelyn. She won't have seen such a display in Ryefield, or even in her fertile imagination."

"What was that about, my love?" Claibourne asked when Priscilla was gone.

"Nothing much. I tried to warn Priscilla about Anton-Fredricks, that he was,"—she caught Rhodine's unspoken plea—"not worthy of her, but she wouldn't listen."

"You know what they say, Love is blind."

"In this instance it would have to be deaf and dumb as well. I don't think this one is a love match though; I don't think Priscilla is capable of loving anyone but herself. Still, she hadn't ought to be alone in the mawworm's company. Shall we go too? I'm looking forward to the fireworks, no matter what Priscilla said, just like a provincial tourist."

271

Three or four couples eventually followed Priscilla and Anton-Fredricks down the path toward the cascading fountain, beyond which the fireworks were held. Jacelyn made certain Mr. Sprague came too, simply by tucking her arm in his and pulling. They were going to an entertainment, she teased, not a tryst. They were all laughing and talking loudly enough to be heard over the fountain's noise, when a shrill scream pierced the night.

"By Jove, that sounds like Priss!" shouted Arthur, running down a less well lighted side path. They all hurried after, especially when they could, indeed, recognise Miss Ponsonby's strident: "Unhand me, you brute!"

At the small clearing, Arthur was already Squire-like: redfaced, short of breath, and bellowing. "What in bloody hell is going on here?"

Priscilla was sobbing on the bench, her hands fluttering between the torn lace of her bodice and her disordered curls. Anton-Fredricks, however, was simply dumbfounded. His slicked-back hair was as well oiled as ever, his neckcloth barely crushed.

"What the deuce are you shrieking about, Priscilla? You were enjoying it as much as I was."

Priscilla's sobs grew louder; her shoulders shook. Rhodine ran to put her arms around the other girl, but no one else seemed to know what to do, where to look, though Jacelyn noted that Claibourne appeared more amused than upset as

272

he said, "Your play after all, Arthur."

Arthur was outraged. "The scurvy swine! It's obvious what happened, isn't it? What kind of man would force an innocent girl—"

"I didn't force anything on her, Ponsonby! She led me here and she—"

"That's enough! You cannot get away with this kind of behaviour, not while I've got breath in me to defend my womenfolk! You'll meet me, Anton-hyphen-Fredricks, if you're not too lily-livered to face someone your own size. Leigh, will you second me?"

Rhodine was now sobbing as loudly as Priscilla, on the stone bench. Captain Highet led Miss Chadwick away, commenting, "Disagreeable scene, what? We shouldn't be privy to it at all. Not suitable."

Claibourne put his arm on Arthur's and calmly explained, "It needn't come to pistols for two and breakfast for one, old friend. I think there is a less strenuous method of retrieving Miss Ponsonby's honour than that. You wouldn't want to have to flee the country for killing him, would you? No, I believe Lord Malcolm will be quite content to do the honourable thing. Miss Ponsonby, would a proposal counterbalance the offense?" She sniffed her assent. "You see, Arthur, all right and tight. No need to exert yourself at five in the morning. Anton-Fredricks? You *do* see your way clear?"

His way was clear as mud, but Anton-Fredricks

grunted. He'd be out of London before daybreak one way or another.

Claibourne took the grunt for agreement. "See? No problem. What a night for betrothals. Shall we—yes, my love?"

Jacelyn stopped pulling at his sleeve. "There *is* a problem, Leigh. In Lancashire, with another coming in spring." She glared at the now-furious Lord Malcolm. "Or weren't you going to mention your wife?"

"*Wife?*" Arthur roared. Priscilla pretended to swoon, right into Carter Sprague's arms.

"Is it true?" Leigh demanded of the greasy baronet and received the smallest of nods. "That does change things a bit. Hold, Arthur. Not with the ladies present. Sprague, would you be so kind as to escort the women back to our box while Lord Ponsonby and I tidy up the grounds here? I'm sure Miss Priscilla would like to go home. . . ." He didn't look back to see that Rhodine and Mr. Sprague supported Priscilla between them, but Jacelyn stayed put. "A moment more, Arthur. You wouldn't want to muss your coat, would you?"

"But, but," Anton-Fredricks spluttered as Claibourne helped Arthur remove his tight jacket and loosen the fitted cuffs of his shirtsleeves. "But what about the duel, pistols, seconds?"

"My, my," Claibourne drawled. "You *do* have a misunderstanding of the social niceties. Duels, old chap, are only for gentlemen."

While the sound of fireworks filled the air, another type of pyrotechnics took place behind the bushes. When Jacelyn couldn't watch any longer, she called out: "Arthur, don't kill him! Think of that poor girl and her baby!" Arthur did, and hit the other man once more for each of them.

Claibourne turned around. "What, you still here, pet? I should have guessed." He faced her in the other direction while Arthur wiped his knuckles. "It's a strange choice, actually, for someone who denounces blood sports."

"I never said vermin shouldn't be eliminated, Leigh. Besides, now you *have* to bring me back for the masquerade. I've missed the fireworks!"

"How is your sister, Arthur?" They were riding in the park late the next morning, and Jacelyn wanted to know how Priscilla was weathering the storm.

"Not as bad as m'mother. She's prostrate, refuses to talk to Priss. She says she'll have to rusticate till next year, at least, before she'll dare show her face in Town. I don't know. Lady Tina's talking of throwing a ball for Rhodine. M'mother would have to come. Maybe not Priss."

"Stuff and nonsense! Another scandal will occur next week, and everyone will forget," Jacey reassured him, which had Claibourne only half jokingly asking what she was planning. "Not funny, my lord. You know, Arthur, if her friends would stand by her . . . Well, I can see that Miss

275

Chadwick won't be a help, but perhaps one of her other admirers will come forward. For a moment I thought Mr. Sprague might . . ."

He mightn't, it seemed. Priscilla had thrown herself at him till the carriage arrived, according to Aunt Amabel, and he had simply bowed and shut the door on her and her mama, saying he was committed to seeing Lady Parkhurst home. Quite correct, and quite like a man who has finally recognised his idol for what she was: selfish, spoiled, and manipulative. *Vraiment,* Mme. Aubonier had added, Priscilla'd gotten no more than she deserved. Sprague was too nice a young man for her.

". . . But I can see that Priscilla and Carter wouldn't suit anyway. Carter needs a quiet girl who will help him with his career. Priscilla needs a rich, social, shallow — 'faith, there's Lord Farthingale! Let's ride over, shall we?"

"Now what was that faradiddle all about, my lady? Since when am I too busy to help you exercise your dog in the park?" Claibourne demanded.

"Since I don't need Farthingale, and Priscilla does!"

"Jacey, men aren't like spigots you can turn on and off, you know. I'm happy to see you hint Farthingale off, and I do think he and Priscilla are well suited. They would spend their days being

276

beautiful together, and save two other unfortunates from being bored to death. I'll even grant you that your motives are admirable, but, my sweet pea-goose, Farthingale is thoroughly smitten with you, and La Ponsonby is currently Priscilla *non grata* in polite circles."

"Minor impediments only. You'll see. No, you won't. You're too busy to ride this afternoon, remember?"

"Of course. Perhaps you ought to remind your fellow conspirator of her role also. For a beast needing so much exercise, Penelope seems quite content to lie by Lem's horse, awaiting our return. That last squirrel almost mistook her for a log and nearly hid a nut under her tail."

"I think she grew bored with the squirrels when she realised she'd never catch one. Leigh, isn't that your friend Miss La Fleur in that barouche over by the fountain?"

He turned in the saddle. "Yes, and her Mr. Unger, the jewel merchant. Very handy occupation, that. Flo thought that he would give me a bargain, but I'd like you to see the Claibourne diamonds first. We could have them reset or—"

"Leigh, will you introduce me?"

"To Mr. Unger? I'm sure Rundell and Briggs is handier for your shopping, pet."

"No, to Miss La Fleur, Miss Cobb. She sounds like such a generous, kind-hearted person, I'd like to know her."

"Of all your strange and varied whimsies, dear

277

heart, this is one of your most hare-brained. A man don't introduce his fiancée to his mistress!"

"I'm not your fiancée yet, and she's not your mistress, still," she persisted.

"Cut line, baggage. A lady isn't even supposed to talk *about* such women as Flo, much less talk *to* them. As much as I like Flora, there's no denying what she is, and what she is just isn't suitable for you."

"Why? Do you think she'll encourage me to take up the life of sin?"

"Jacey," he finally said in exasperation, "it doesn't matter what I think, or what the social arbiters decree. Flo wouldn't want to meet you. It would only embarrass her and make her feel ashamed of her . . . her profession."

Jacelyn thought about it awhile. "Leigh, does Flora like what she does?"

"Lord, Jay-bird, I don't know! I surely wouldn't ask her!"

"And what about when she's older and not so attractive? What happens to women like her then?"

"With luck, she'll have put some money away. If she's been lucky and her gentlemen have been generous, she can sell off the baubles she's accumulated, like the king's ransom Flo wore the other evening. Why?"

"Just curiosity, I suppose. I never knew any . . . any *demimondaines*. Only Sal, down at the Speckled Pony, but that was different. She was barmaid, so everyone could pretend she didn't do the other."

"In London, gentlewomen pretend that other doesn't even exist."

"Here they come. Can I at least smile?" She did anyway, before he could answer. Leigh raised his whip in greeting, and Flora tilted her head, slightly. Mr. Unger searched his sleeve for specks of lint.

"What a hubble-bubble convention! Leigh, do you think Mr. Unger will marry her? Or maybe one of her other gentlemen will?"

"A man doesn't marry his mistress, primrose. He doesn't need to. Gads, I hope you don't tell anyone about this conversation! You know, the only reason I said I'd take you to the masquerade at Vauxhall was that I feared you'd go by yourself. And the only reason I had this discussion with you was to keep you from accosting some poor girl waiting for business outside the theater or somewhere. I've never been so glad to see. Lem. Squire was right: you *do* have an odd kick to your gallop."

Leigh parted from her at the stables, reminding Jacey that he wished to hear all about her dealings with Farthingale, that evening at Wrenthe House. "And if that puppy is still trailing after you, you owe me a kiss!"

"And if he's not?"

"Then I owe you a kiss!"

Consider the man who thinks so much of his appearance that he'd wear the latest fashion, no matter if it were war paint and feathers. In Farthingale's case, he wore his starched shirt collars so high he could blind himself with a quick denial. His waistcoat was nipped in so tightly he couldn't eat in public, and tying his neckcloth in the delicate *trône d'amour* took one valet, seven snow-white linens, and forty minutes. All this was for a walk in the park with Jacelyn and her dog.

Farthingale cared inordinately for what he looked like, but more for what he looked like to others. Perhaps it was because the viscount had such a high position to live up to, or that his mother was so disapproving, or just that the other boys hadn't let him play knights and dragons. Jacelyn didn't know what made a man—or a woman—wear such a social façade with so much pride, but she knew how to handle him gracefully, without injuring that same *amour propre*. With a dog, of course.

That same dog who is such a friendly topic of conversation among strangers, its antics and ancestry, is not quite as comfortable up close. A person-to-canine meeting, among strangers, is a hound of another colour. The lovable star of all the anecdotes is liable to embarrass its companion worse than a split seam to sternward. The darling pet will happily relieve itself as near to the stranger's boot as possible, in full view of passersby, of course, and then indulge in a loud, vulgar display of personal hygiene. If two of the little dears get together, their introductory rituals could send a gently reared female into palpitations. As for four-footed romance . . .

That's why no one ever brought any but the tiniest lapdogs to the park, and rarely put them down.

That's why Jacelyn fed Pen a large meal at noontime, and a whole bowl of broth, and did not have Lem walk her near the house as usual, before getting into Farthingale's carriage. And that's why she insisted they get out to walk right at the entrance to the park, where all the fashionables were gathered to see and be seen.

Jacey had to hold her parasol; could Lord Farthingale please hold the leash?

Pen was your typical dog, only more so, since she was larger. Farthingale was used to hunting-hounds in the woods, not this. He was mortified. People were turning their backs, snickering, lifting their noses and their skirts to step around them, and Miss Trevaine was twirling her parasol! He prayed the ground would open up and swallow him—or the unconventional girl and her impossible pet! No such luck, as Jacelyn just kept chattering, walking onward slowly, behind two ladies whose skirts the dog was sniffing! Death couldn't undo this blow to his self-esteem. The shame was bound to haunt him throughout eternity.

Jacelyn finally took pity on him when she saw the tears start to form in his eyes. "Shall we go,

281

my lord? I think Pen has had enough exercise now, don't you? You have such a way with dogs, we have to do this again soon. Perhaps tomorrow. No? I'll see you this evening at Lady Wrenthe's, shan't I? You have other plans? That's too bad."

As Jacelyn told Claibourne later, making herself and Pen into Scylla and Charybdis was the easy part. Getting Priscilla to look like safe harbour was a little more difficult.

"Did you hear about Arthur and Lady Rhodine? Lady Tina is throwing them a ball on Friday. It will be one of the premiere entertainments of the Season, I'm sure. Everyone will be there."

Farthingale was having a little smoother sailing, now that they were in the carriage and out of the park. His colour changed from green back to its usual baby pink. The chance to gossip enheartened him further, especially the word "everyone."

"I wonder if Miss Ponsonby will attend? Shocking thing, that, everyone's talking of it."

"Poo. Anton-Fredricks was a cad, that's all. We were all right there; no harm was done, except to him, of course. Priscilla will naturally attend her own brother's betrothal ball, and I'm sure she'll be all the rage. She was so brave, fighting off that madman and calling out for help. I'm sure everyone will want to hear her story. I'll wager there won't be any getting near her. And dear Priscilla will be looking as beautiful as ever, despite such a harrowing experience. I don't know how she does it, never a hair out of place, never a spot on her glove. What do you think?"

"Mother thinks Priscilla's no better than she should be, but the way you tell it . . ."

"You couldn't think *Priscilla* was at fault, could you? Why, everyone knows Miss Ponsonby is the most *proper* girl who ever lived. My own aunt is forever holding her up as an example to me. I may have acted a trifle impulsively at times, which everyone has so kindly overlooked, but Priscilla? Never!"

"Deuced fine looking woman."

"A real Diamond." Jacelyn sighed. "I'll never be like her. At least you won't have to worry about not having a dance with me at the Endicotts'; my card is never as full as Priscilla's."

"I might just pop over there this afternoon and ask her to save me a couple. Quite the thing to do, you know. Show the dear girl all men aren't bounders."

"How kind of you, Lord Farthingale. You won't come in for tea, then? Oh, and I so wanted to show you how Pen drinks from the saucer."

"So now you and Arthur have to see that Priscilla comes to the ball and acts noble," Jacey told Leigh.

"She's way ahead of you, sweetheart. Arthur says that after Farthingale's visit Priscilla actually started to believe she was a heroine. By the night of the ball she'll have vanquished Anton-Fredricks

283

herself, in single-handed defense of British morality. If no one else dances with her besides Farthingale, Arthur and I will, and I suppose we could ask Sprague, now that his eyes are open. That will be enough, with her pride. I salute you again, ma'am, for successfully completing another difficult mission in enemy territory. I only wish we'd had you in Spain for the Peninsular Campaign! Shall we proceed to the balcony where I might give you the decoration for valour?"

17

Sniff . . . sniff? "What's that smell, boy? What are you doing over there?" Fenton put down his newspaper.

"Roses, gov. I'm writing a note to go with them."

Fenton rolled his Bath chair down the long room to where Percy sat at the desk. On the desk, the floor, his lap, were piles of little calling cards. Some had ink splotches, some had spatters. Others had messages: *fondly, Claibourne,* or *with affection, Leigh. Yours truly, Merrill,* etc. Close by was a large parcel, two dozen red roses tied in tissue with a silver ribbon. The roses were already browning at the edges from being out of water so long.

Fenton looked at the roses, flipped over a few of the cards. "Your mind doesn't work fast, Percy, when it works at all. I assume you're still trying to get Claibourne and his straw damsel together; I just can't understand why. He saw her at the theater, in front of the girl and the whole ton. So what? The *Gazette*'s still full of their doings, Claibourne and the chit, together."

"He called at her house."

"Did you see him there?"

"No, thanks be. Miss La Fleur had her man tell me Leigh was there looking for me."

"You brandy-based bubblehead, that means he suspects you're involved with the theater contretemps, not that he's interested in the woman! Besides, even if he does call there, he'll be discreet. It won't have any damned effect on the Trevaine twit. The only way your cork-brained scheme could work is if the doxy is on our side. That's like hoping the Tower of London falls on Claibourne's head. Have you even talked to her yet?"

"She likes me. She wouldn't have her man warn me, else. You're right though, Da, I should be trying to win her affections to m'self, not my cousin Leigh."

"Percy, your attics are to let! You could rent your brainbox to a couple of starlings—and still have room for a squirrel!"

Percy wasn't listening. He was torturing a new set of cards. *Fondly, Fenton? With affection, an Admirer? Hopefully, Percy?*

Fenton read two of the blotched efforts, shook his head. "At least I won't be going to hell. I've already done my penance. . . . I have a new idea, boy, lucky one of us does. Percy, put down that

286

damn pen and listen to me!"

Percy blotted the nib on the penwipe, then naturally tucked the blackened cloth into his waistcoat pocket, like a handkerchief. "Listening, governor."

"Aargh." Fenton backed away. "There's a ball tonight, according to the *Gazette*, and Claibourne's sure to be there. It's for his friend Ponsonby and Endicott's daughter. The girl is friends with Claibourne's chit, so it's the perfect time."

"Perfect time for what? You know La Fleur won't be at any fancy nob's ball."

"Use what little wit you have, Percy. It's the perfect time to show the gel Claibourne's character, make him out a libertine and worse, a debaucher of women."

"Is a debaucher anything like an accoucheur?"

"You skitter-witted slowtop, it's a man who would seduce a virgin, get her with child, then just walk away."

"Oh, a bounder. Whyn't you just say so? It won't fadge, though. Claibourne ain't one. Everyone knows he don't go near the innocents, except for Miss Trevaine, of course."

"Exactly, but she *doesn't* know it. She'll believe the worst, if she sees proof right outside Endicott's door."

"Huh?"

"You stage a show for her, Percy, before the party, one to give her a disgust of Claibourne for once and all. They'll all see it. He'll be cut dead, tossed out of his clubs, finished in polite circles, just like they did to me."

"Uh, gov, what kind of show is that? That horse bit outside Almack's wasn't any great success, you know."

"Did you think I wouldn't know, you gnag-nosed nodcock? This plan is so simple even you can do it. All you need to do is find a woman who's breeding. A young, pretty one. You point Claibourne out to her, and you pay her to stand outside Endicott's yelling the brat is his. That should settle his account, by Jupiter!"

"But, gov, where am I going to find a pregnant woman? You know I ain't in the petticoat line."

"You ain't in the petticoat line, you ain't in the banking line. You ain't in the shipping line, and you damn well weren't in line when they were handing out brains!" He wheeled his chair to the doorway, calling for his man Jensen. He shouted back toward Percy: "You'd better do it, boy, if you want to stay in line for my fortune."

Percy sat thinking for a minute. You could tell: his mouth was open. Then he took the pen, dipped it in the ink, and painstakingly inscribed a fresh card: *Please let me love you. Percy.*

"You want a pretty young woman who's breedin', for one night? I don't know, Mister Percy." Cook was eyeing him as if he was some kind of pervert. She was backing toward the meat cleaver. "There's my sister's girl Fanny, but I can't say as how she'd oblige. Her man's a mail driver, so they don't need the ready. I'll ask for you, if you just get along now, so I can do up these nice trotters your father likes."

But it had to be tonight, and Percy had to have a pregnant woman, guaranteed. The only women besides Cook he ever dealt with made sure they never found themselves in an interesting condition, so that option was out. Down by the East End, Seven Dials, or the Docks, though, there were always half-naked urchins begging in the streets. That seemed as likely a place as any to search.

Percy was lucky. It only took three dingy taverns, and a few rounds of cheap gin in each, to find a pregnant woman. But she wasn't very pretty, with her scarred face and stringy hair, and she wasn't even very far gone. He gave her the time, address, instructions, and half the fee, in case he couldn't find a more suitable increasing actress. He secured the deal with another drink, and a bottle to carry with him. What do you know? His luck was getting better. There were two big-bellied women at the next grogshop, sitting sideways at the table. One of them was almost pretty, too. Sure, she'd claim King George was the babe's dad, for a half crown and a few drinks. Only thing was, she was very close to her time and didn't like being out alone, so far from home. Could her friend come too?

If one unwed mother was a disgrace, two really ought to put Claibourne in the basket, so they drank to their success.

The barkeep couldn't watch those half crowns being tucked into bodices without wanting a share for himself. "What about m'wife upstairs?" he volunteered. "We got a tyke and a infant at suck. Your swell can't have all his buns in t'oven at oncet, can he?" Furthermore, the barkeep had a cart; he could see all the "delicate" lasses got to the right place on time. That had to be worth an extra crown or two, but the next round was on the house.

A cat can look at a king. But why would one want to, Jacelyn wondered, seeing the larger than usual crowds on the sidewalk in front of Endicott House. Whenever there was to be a huge ball, hordes of the uninvited gathered to watch the nobility. They oohed and ogled, and in general acted as vocal theater critics for the aristocratic play. Jacelyn would never get used to it, nor the way the invited guests had to queue up on the red carpet outside the house, waiting to have some stiff butler intone their names and titles.

Tonight was no different, except there were more women than men and — gracious, nearly every one of them was breeding or had a babe in arms. Aunt Amabel was asking if the lower orders held conventions for that sort of thing, while Lord Parkhurst facetiously wondered aloud if the Regent was expected. All these women were here, he surmised, to hold the infants up and the babe-filled bellies out, for the future king's blessing—so he wouldn't beggar the country before they were weaned.

The women weren't holding those children for Prinny, however, they were just waiting for Claibourne to step out of the coach.

"There he is! There's the man what ruined me!"

"Here, Claibourne, see what your wicked ways have brought!"

"Hey, yer lordship, how'm I to feed the brat you left me?"

"He done me wrong—twice!"

The situation was absurd, of course: every *enceinte* woman from the East End accusing Leigh Claibourne of siring her child. Soon the ladies on line were atwitter, and the men were laughing outright. The crowd on the pavement was delighted, calling uproariously vulgar comments and ribald suggestions. Lord Parkhurst and Mme. Aubonier had to lead Amabel back to the carriage so she could faint without dirtying her gown, leaving Leigh and Jacelyn on center stage, without a script.

After the first moment's shock, Leigh began to chuckle, and then trade jokes with the bystanders, most of which Jacelyn could not understand, luckily. "Come ladies," he was saying good-naturedly, while she was wishing someone would shake her and tell her to wake up, it's only a nightmare. "I have only been home from Belgium for five months. Wellington himself couldn't have done the job from there."

"Them British musketeers have good aim, Major."

"Not that good, friend, so I'm thankful to all you lads at home for standing in for us so nobly."

They were finally at the door. Before entering the house, Leigh told the women to meet him around back in ten minutes, he'd buy the babies their first pairs of shoes.

"What are you doing, Leigh? You're going to go talk to those women—and leave me here all alone to face *this?*"

This was everyone in the room laughing and pointing and holding fans over their mouths. Even Arthur, on the receiving line, had heard about it.

"Great show, Leigh. Here we were all wondering how Priscilla would be received, and you go set them all on their ears. No one will have a spare tongue-wag for her. Thanks."

"You'll find this hard to believe, Arthur, but I really wouldn't have subjected myself and my friends to such a spectacle, not even for Priscilla. Lady Endicott, may I please trouble you for the use of a back room to interview some of the mamas-to-be? I've got to find out who has the quirky sense of humour. Would you also look after Miss Trevaine? Her aunt didn't appreciate the jest much either."

292

"Leigh, you can't!"

"I'm sorry, pet, you have to stay here and look amused."

Amused? She hadn't been so amused since she'd caught her hand in the barn door. Now she felt like Farthingale must have with the dog—only worse. Farthingale merely looked less elegant than he wished; Jacelyn looked like a red-faced fool. She didn't want to become an outraged fishwife, and she didn't want to marry a man who could even be suspected of such behaviour. She didn't believe any of it, needless to say, but if not these women, then others. And he'd said he'd never disgrace her. Hah! What did he think tonight's display was? A schoolroom tea party?

A farce, that's what Leigh thought, in the small pantry behind Tina Endicott's kitchen. He was surrounded there by seven, no eight, women who looked like a pod of beached whales. It was a comedy and they were all laughing at the hoax. The real disgrace was the women's condition. He left them a moment so he could bribe, threaten, and otherwise coerce the horrified cook into serving them cake and ale. He swore to make it right with Lady Endicott's household account, for the wheels of cheese and fresh apples and oranges he brought back to the pantry.

His lordship was a real fine gent, the ladies decided. Kindhearted, generous, polite even to the likes of them—and so devilishly handsome with his easy pearly smile, they wouldn't mind if the babes wore his butter stamp after all. Asides, he'd laughed right along with them, not run off like that queer nabs who'd hired them. The women were happy to oblige Claibourne with anything he wanted to know, even if they were disloyal to their employer. He wasn't there with the other half of their pay; Claibourne was.

Fifteen minutes later, the earl sent his latest conquests home in the barkeep's wagon, having emptied his pockets and the cook's larder. He now owed his life's savings to Endicott's servants, if his life was worth saving, after Jacelyn got through with it, for here was Lady Tina herself. She had come to thank Claibourne for enlivening Rhodine's dull little gathering, and to lead him back to the party. Tina's gratitude was almost as deep as her neckline, but not quite, and she guided him to the ballroom with all the sinuous grace of a tigress stalking her prey. Since he'd been using her house as a home for unwed mothers, common courtesy required him to ask her to dance. Bad luck made the orchestra choose a waltz.

Jacelyn was dancing with the Spanish count, barely listening to his ornate compliments, when Claibourne danced by with their hostess nearly wallpapered to his shirtfront. If Jacelyn's looks were daggers, both of them would be skewered like ducks on a spit.

Her next dance was promised to Lord Tayson, but Claibourne persuaded the young lordling that Miss Trevaine needed to catch her breath and would be sitting out—with him.

Jacey ignored the earl as he took a seat next to her. She couldn't ignore the smell of cheap perfume, or the lip rouge on his neckcloth. She glared at him. "I see you were as friendly to your back-room brood mares as you were to Lady Endicott."

Laughing, he wiped at his cheek where she was staring, and said, "Don't be shrewish, darling, and don't worry. If you're breeding, I'll marry you."

The wound wasn't like a clean cut that bled, hurt, then healed. This was more like the pain of a deep splinter, which festered and throbbed.

All those women, all those Lady Tinas. The world was full of them, Jacelyn knew, and the only thing presently keeping Leigh away from them—if he was, indeed, keeping his distance—was herself, her reputation, her money. It wasn't enough.

If he loved her, she could laugh at the silly prank last night, and she could shrug off Lady Tina's clinging with simple pride in his attractiveness. If he loved her, she could even disregard all the thinly veiled hints about what an ideal match theirs would be, for both of them.

She knew, had always known, how much he needed her money, and she really didn't care. She would be glad her fortune could ease his way, if that wasn't the only reason for this continued parody of a near betrothal. Everyone, even Leigh, she thought, assumed they would make it official soon, at her ball, perhaps, or over Christmas. It wouldn't happen, not if it killed her, for he didn't love her. They—her father, Squire, Aunt Amabel, Leigh himself—could no longer argue that her good repute and social well-being depended on Leigh's name. Just look at Priscilla; it only took a bit of courage and a fresh scandal. As for Jacey's future happiness . . . that did depend on Leigh. She didn't quite see how she would live without him, but she'd have to, rather than slowly being nibbled to death anyway, by all the doubts and uncertainties. Just a few more weeks, and she and Pen could go home, alone.

Claibourne was relieved to see that Jacelyn wasn't angry when he met her at the stable for their ride. He'd been prepared for fireworks, vowing to hold his own temper in check this time, for last night *had* been an awful experience for the young girl. It hadn't been any picnic for him, either, so he was pleased there wouldn't be any brangling now. If Jacelyn seemed quieter than usual, it matched the overcast, dank morning. The dog wasn't interested in chasing sticks, and even Baron took exception to the bare branches clicking in the raw wind. Claibourne's mood was all of a piece.

His lordship had a lot on his mind, not least of

which was figuring out what in Hades Percy was trying to do with these skipbrained schemes to humiliate his cousin. To find out would mean finding Percy, most likely at Flora's place in Islington. Claibourne's presence there was sure to get back to Jacelyn, and cause her still more upset. Unless he was to tell her beforehand. Deuces, just when he was glad there were no storm clouds. He decided to take the cowardly path, mentioning Flora only as he left Jacelyn at Parkhurst House later, so they could keep on with the quiet, reflective ride now.

Percy could wait. Claibourne's finances couldn't. Mr. Pettigrew hadn't had any good news lately, and he couldn't take any more money out of the estate. Applying to Trevaine was out of the question, as was visiting the cent-per-centers. Leigh had no intention of paying twice for what he used once. There were no calls for Baron's services, and the cards just weren't falling right. Leigh was too astute to wager where the chances of winning were so poor, and no one would bet against him in other contests, like culping wafers or three-round sparring matches, where the odds were so heavily in his favour.

It was dashed expensive, this London living, if you added the price of courtship to clothes, lodging, and horses, besides incidentals like last night's unexpected debts. With all the gratuities he was handing out, he felt like Golden Ball on Boxing Day.

He was thinking of selling the curricle and pair, but he'd only have to rent job horses and rigs to take Jacelyn driving. He could ask Arthur for a loan until the dibs were in tune, but with his own marriage to plan, Arthur mightn't have as much of the ready, and Claibourne hated to ask his friends, anyway; he'd had more than enough teasing about his coming change of fortune. There might be a position for him at the War Office, but not necessarily in London. Then again, he might take himself and his pistols somewhere away from Town, to Bath or Brighton, perhaps, where his skill wasn't as well known. He only had to hold out a few weeks more, until the end of the Season, when he could ask Jacelyn to marry him. It would be the shortest engagement in history if he had anything to say. If she said no . . . It didn't bear thinking of, and the money had nothing to do with it at all. He could live on very little at the Abbey, and without Jacey's laughing eyes, that's all it would be, barely existing.

"Will you come in for breakfast?"

"Thank you, pet, no. I have some errands to run. One of them is tracking down my cousin Percy. Ah, he may be at Flora's house, so I'll have to stop there this afternoon."

"Will you take me with you, Leigh?"

"Don't be a widgeon. Flo isn't suitable company for you, but she's a Sunday-school teacher compared to Percy."

"That's all right, I forgot I'm promised to Rhodine after luncheon anyway. We're to select a pattern for her wedding dress."

Jacelyn half-expected him to question plans for her *own* bridal gown, and it was almost on the tip of his tongue to do so, but he'd vowed not to pressure her, and he wouldn't. Instead he asked: "Incidentally, Jacey, are we promised anywhere for the next few days?"

"I don't think there is anything very grand until the ball at Lady Hockney's country home next week, except you did promise to take me to the Vauxhall masquerade Saturday. Why?"

"I didn't forget the promise, dear heart, I already hired the closed carriage. I just might have to be out of town before then."

She looked at him like he'd crawled out of the kitchen tiles. "Tell me again. You are going to visit your mistress, and be out of town for two days?"

He blinked, then grinned. "Ah. She's not my mistress, remember? And one trip has nothing to do with the other, you adorable peagoose." He quickly kissed the tip of her nose, then said he would see her at tea.

Trust him, he said. Don't listen to the gabblemongers, he said. He'd be there for tea, he said. That was easy for him. He wasn't at the dressmaker's where even the fitters giggled about how Claibourne was raising his own army. He wasn't at the silk warehouse where Lady Tina teased about his lordship's taste in women: warm and willing. And he wasn't on time for tea. Of course not, he was visiting his mistress! Fortunately for the Sèvres tea service, there were other callers in and out all afternoon.

Leigh's luck was still gone begging. Percy hadn't shown at Flora's, it being earlier than his usual time, but Unger had. Rather than cause Flora any embarrassment, Claibourne had left by the kitchen door. Gads, creeping out of a noted courtesan's door like some guilty, henpecked husband! Then Arthur had reminded him that no one but crones, consumptives, and caper merchants were in the resort areas at this time of year, so that notion was discarded. He hadn't wanted to be out of town anyway, not without seeing Percy.

All in all, his lordship was in a foul mood. Seeing Jacelyn entertaining some mushroom in yellow pantaloons did not improve his temper.

"Lord Claibourne, how nice of you to join us." Jacelyn managed to get anger, resentment, and nagging at his tardiness into the one sarcastic statement. She hadn't gotten up from the Queen Anne desk where, Claibourne could see, she was writing a cheque. The cit had stood, though, so she introduced him.

"Lord Claibourne, I would like you to meet Mr. Godfrey Durbin. Mr. Durbin is the founder of a new group, the Benevolent Protectors of Innocent Creatures. Its goal is to provide food and shelter for all the homeless dogs and cats of London. Remember last month when Aunt's people were having all those difficulties with strays? I'm to be a charter member. Oh, Mr. Durbin, this is Leigh Merrill, Earl of Claibourne."

Durbin didn't know whether to bow or put out his hand. Neither would have mattered, as his lordship pointed to the door.

"Get out, you charlatan," he ordered, "and don't ever let me see your ugly phiz in the neighbourhood." Then Claibourne took the cheque from Jacey's fingers and ripped it in two. "Still too green by half, my girl," he drawled.

Jacelyn jumped up in furious indignation, hands on hips, and shouted the first hateful thing that came to mind: "How dare you! I'm not your girl and it's not your money yet!"

All the colour left Leigh's face, then returned in a quick bloom of red. He turned on his heel and left.

Percival Fenton was not your average fool, nor even your average drunk. He had to be the un-luckiest inebriate idiot on earth. He was so stupid, he thought he was lucky to have missed his cousin Leigh earlier. He was so drunk, he didn't even duck. Of all the times and places to be where he was, Percy'd picked the worst.

301

Claibourne had been wanting to talk to Percy for weeks, ever since the Roman scene outside Almack's. That is, he felt he should, whether he wanted to see the muckworm or not, to find out what all the tomfoolery was about and put a stop to it. With one thing and another, he'd never run him to ground, until today. Leigh wasn't a vicious, violent maniac, either, until today. Today, however, he didn't want to talk, he wanted to murder anyone in his way — who just happened to be Percival Fenton.

Maybe being hit on the side of the head knocked some sense into the clunch, because he did the only intelligent thing possible: he stayed where he was, flat on the ground.

"Get up and fight, you bastard!"

"Oh, do you think so, too? M'father swears I'm none of his but I — "

"I don't give a damn about your ancestry. I only wish you were no relative of mine." Leigh had him up, willy-nilly, by the neckcloth, and was roaring at him. "What I want to know is what the bloody hell is going on?"

Percy dangled there, thinking, then he said, "I could be wrong about this, mind, but I think you're going to beat me to a pulp. Knew it would happen, told the governor so."

Claibourne shook him like a sandy rug. "Why, Percy? No, blast you, not why am I going to pop your cork. Why have you been bothering me and my friends?"

302

"It's the governor. He don't like you. I never had anything against you m'self."

"Thanks," Leigh said dryly. "Why did you do all those crazy things then?"

"He said he'd have his man Jensen kill me, else."

"Well, I'll kill you now if you don't tell me the rest. I don't like your father any more than he likes me, but I don't go near him. What does he want?"

"It's your marriage. He don't want you leg-shackled and starting your nursery. He says I'm to be your heir."

"*You!*" Claibourne shook Percy so hard his previously loosened teeth rattled. "You cannot be my heir," Leigh raged, "because you're not going to outlive me." And he hit him again. Picked him up and shook him again.

"Uh, Leigh?"

Claibourne paused, right arm way back.

"I never hurt that horse, that time. The one I left at Parkhurst's stables. Found him that way at the knackers. I wouldn't have done that to a horse, honest."

So Leigh didn't kill him.

Even if he didn't love her, even if he only wanted her for her money, even if there really had been a Benevolent Protectors Society, which Mr. Sprague confirmed there wasn't, she should not have said it. Even if he was high-handed, arrogant, and smelled of patchouli when her own scent was lavender, she should have bitten off her tongue before uttering those words. But she hadn't, and he was gone, most likely back to La Fleur's house, where he'd be welcomed with kind words and satin sheets. Fallen women always had satin sheets in the novels she read, and they never yelled like fishwives. He would stay there and help La Fleur count her diamonds, and never, ever know how sorry Jacelyn was.

In a pig's eye, he would.

She put on her dark blue merino dress with the long sleeves, grabbed a shawl, told Marcus she was going to the stable, turned the corner, and kept going. The hackney driver took her to Islington, but baulked when she ordered him to find Miss La Fleur's direction.

"I knows where the Flower lives, I does, 'n I knows it's no place for the likes a'you, miss."

"Don't be impertinent, sir. We are having a meeting of the Benevolent Protectors of Innocent Creatures Society, and Miss La Fleur and I are charter members. She is a great champion of the downtrodden."

"That right? 'N here I allays thought she were a rich man's whore. Beggin' your pardon, miss."

He set her down at a pleasant little whitewashed house with a brick wall, and hedges all around. She paid the fare, the jarvey took off, and she wondered what on earth she was going to do now.

304

What if Claibourne wasn't here? Worse, now that she considered it further, what if he *was* here?

She was standing in the roadway, debating with herself, when she heard terrible noises coming from the hedges. She ran to the moan's direction, and found what had to be Percival Fenton, from Claibourne's description of him: an elongated scarecrow, losing its stuffing. He was also losing a lot of blood from above his right eye, which was quickly swelling shut. His jaw was already empurpled, and he held one of his teeth in his hand. Jacelyn hurried to his side and started to mop at the blood with her handkerchief.

"Percy? Percy, it's Jacelyn Trevaine. Can you understand me?"

He looked up and nodded. Then at the same time, they both asked, "Is Leigh still here?"

"Gads, I hope not," swore Percy, and Jacelyn *amen*ed it, then asked, "Was it Leigh who did this to you, because of the pregnant women?"

"Yes'm, but I didn't hurt the horse."

"I should hope not. If you touched Baron he would kill you for sure."

"He's an earl, not a baron. You should know that, if you're going to marry him. M'cousin's a downy one. He won't like a widgeon-wife."

Jacelyn had Percy's neckcloth off and was making a pad for the cut, while trying to make sense of his conversation. He must be concussed, she decided, leaning over to press the bandage in place. His breath nearly made her eyes water.

"You're foxed!"

"Yes'm, usually am."

"You mean you're never sober?"

"Not if I can help it."

"Oh dear. I think you'd better get inside. Can you stand?"

He couldn't, so she wadded up her woolen shawl and put it under his head. "Wait here," she told him unnecessarily, and went to pull the door knocker. Miss La Fleur herself answered the door, in a pink satin negligee—in the daytime! Jacey didn't have time to consider the implications as she tried to explain who she was, why she'd come, and what Percy was doing groaning in the grass.

"That bag of bones? I had my man warn him to stay away, but he wouldn't listen. It's Remington's day off, or I'd have him put your friend in a hackney, like usual."

"But he's hurt badly, and Leigh said how kind you are. Couldn't he come in? We could clean him up and—"

"What's this *we?* Leigh would kill all of us if he found you here! I'm sorry, miss, about Percy, but I've got a, ah, gentleman caller due soon, and it would be awkward-like having the cawker bleeding in the parlour."

"It can't be any worse than having your guest trip over him in the walkway. He really needs someone to take care of him. Will you at least come look at him?"

The next time Percy opened his eyes, two thinly

covered breasts dangled right above him. He thought Claibourne must have killed him after all. His horizon filled with satin tits, he must have gone to heaven. Wouldn't the governor be surprised! It was better than heaven, by Jupiter; it was La Fleur herself, come to wipe his brow!

"I love you."

"I know you do, you poor sod. Here, let's have a look at you."

"He loves you?" Jacey asked, incredulous. "Then you *have* to take him in."

"He says he loves me, he writes me notes and sends flowers. I never met him before today, though. He sure don't look like much."

"Leigh did this to him!"

"He's got no chin," Flo pointed out, as if Percy were an inanimate statue—sculpted by a Bedlamite. "Leigh didn't have anything to do with that."

"True, his chin is a bit weak, but his nose is strong enough to compensate."

"It's a shame Leigh didn't break it for him, could only be an improvement. He sure is skinny, too."

"He only needs fattening up, some healthy food, regular meals, you know. If it's a matter of money . . ." Jacelyn was fumbling to untie her reticule.

"It would be another mouth to feed, now that you mention it."

Percy, who'd been lying on the grass worshipping, now put his hand to his waistcoat and pulled out a bulging wallet. "I've got plenty of blunt," he said, handing it to Flora, his one good eye never leaving her face.

Flora glanced through the wallet quickly. "He's getting prettier by the minute."

"You know, Miss La Fleur, Leigh says he is very wealthy, and he really seems quite fond of you. His name isn't such that he has to worry over what connexions he makes, if you understand me. Who knows where it might lead?"

It led right upstairs to the bedroom, Jacelyn under one shoulder, Flora under the other, Percy grinning like a roast pig with an apple in its mouth.

"I'll let him set a bit, I suppose, if only to keep an eye on him for Leigh's sake."

"I'm sure he won't trouble Leigh anymore, will you, Percy?" Jacey asked, giving his arm a jerk.

"Oh no, ma'am, Miss La Fleur. I wouldn't do anything you didn't like, ever."

"Pitiful. Sweet, but pitiful. All right, you stay. And it's Flora, to my friends. Flora Cobb."

They had him on the bed now, his boots off. "Flora . . . Flora Fenton," he whispered before he passed out.

"He'll keep till Remington gets back to help. You better leave, miss, before Mr. Unger gets here. This is going to be hard enough to explain as is."

When they reached downstairs again, Flora couldn't resist asking, "What were you doing here anyway, miss, if you don't mind my prying? I mean, it's not every day grand young ladies drop in to tea, if you ken my drift."

"Well, I did want to meet you, but Leigh said I mustn't — "

"So you did anyway."

"I wouldn't have, but he said he was coming here, after Percy, and . . . and I wanted to apologise to him for something terrible I said."

"Here? You were going to apologise to him here, in my house? I don't know who is more addlepated, you or the tosspot upstairs! I can see where you'll lead Leigh a merry chase. Good. He needs that."

"You're not mad, then? And you'll tell him I'm sorry, if you see him?"

"I won't be seeing him, dearie, if that's what's on your mind, and no, I'm not mad. If that rummy sobers up decent, you may have done me a good turn. Now I'll do you one and get you a hackney. And, miss, take my advice, don't ever mention to Claibourne that you were here, or you'll be sorrier still."

"Thank you, Flora, and thank you for being kind to Leigh when he was ill, and for taking in Percy. It's been a pleasure meeting you."

"And you, miss. You're a real lady, and I don't mean titles and such. Leigh'll be proud. There's no question either; he'll make you real happy."

* * *

"Ar . . . Ar . . . Ar-choo. Choo. Archoo."

"Typical, you twit. Other men come home from two days of raking with the pox. You come home with a head cold!"

"Not a cold, Da, it's snuff." Percy was practicing opening the small enamelled box with one hand. So far there was a damp layer of brown powder all over him.

"*Snuff!* You're shoving tobacco up your nose so you can sneeze? Only a simple-minded sop would get pleasure from that!"

"Gave it up, gov. No more Blue Ruin."

"Gave up gin, did you? That only leaves brandy, wine, port —"

"All of it. Am doing snuff instead. It's more manly. *Ar-choo.*"

Fenton rolled his wheelchair away, out of range, and dabbed at his sleeve in repugnance. "Manly? Boy, you're as manly as the sultan's soprano. Just look at you!"

It took a strong stomach to do so: one totally shut blackened eye that shaded off to bilious yellow; a huge purple bruise on the jaw; swollen, split lip; missing tooth — and lace ruffles.

"That bastard Claibourne did this to you?"

"Told you he would. He didn't like your idea about the pregnant women."

"My idea? *My idea?* You paper-skulled popinjay, I told you to get a female who was increasing. *One.* What do you bring? Ten! If you can count to twenty-one with your pants on I'll be amazed!

310

Besides, I'm surprised Claibourne didn't kill you, hanging around his mistress like that."

"You were right: she ain't his mistress anymore." He grinned proudly. "She's mine. I'll be staying there. Just came 'round to tell you."

"Gads, that woman will do *any*thing for money."

"Not so. She likes me."

Fenton shook his head. "You poor deluded dunderhead. Will she help us queer Claibourne's marriage plans?"

"No, she likes him too. She doesn't want me messing with him neither."

Fenton slammed his fist into the armrest. "And you call yourself manly! Look what he's done to you! Look what those bastards have done to me! You'd let him get away with it all; you'd throw rice at his demn wedding!"

"Doubt I'd be invited, gov. Leigh ain't too keen on our branch of the—"

"Shut up! *I* won't sit still and watch it happen, boy, I won't. If I can't get rid of the wedding, I'll get rid of Claibourne. It's what I should have done from the first. Yes, once and for all."

"Uh, I'll just be toddling off now, before you get another of your ideas."

Fenton sneered. "Did you think I'd send you against Claibourne? As well send an ant to itch an elephant's arse."

"Well, I don't want anything to do with it. Don't want the title, don't want any draughty old castle in Durham."

"Percy, somewhere, somewhere on this earth, I say, there's got to be a greater fool than you. But when that man dies . . ."

18

Two days had gone by with no word from Leigh. Two very long days. Jacey wondered what the rest of her life would be like, if he never came back. Her restless sleep left her more exhausted, and she couldn't eat, not with the lump of granite in her throat. The dog might have cheered her, but Pen had grown fat and lazy in her London life, and was content just to lie by the fire. Shopping held no attraction either, not if he wasn't around to dress for.

It was Saturday, the night of the Vauxhall masquerade, and she didn't know what to do. She'd begged off accompanying her aunt to Lady Richardson's rout, and she'd told her watchdogs Pinkie and Lem that she wouldn't need either of them that evening. She was going to read a book and retire early, she'd claimed. The book never got opened.

What should she do? They had talked about meeting at the corner by the stables, but no time was given. She couldn't very well go stand on the street corner in her evening gown and wait to see if he remembered. On the other hand, if he did come and she wasn't there, he'd think she was still angry.

The best solution she could devise was her usual one for these situations: the boy's clothes. She could get out by the tree and over the garden wall, and no one would think anything odd about a lad out at night. She'd be safer from recognition at Vauxhall too, in Lem's castoffs.

"The only problem," she told the dog sprawled at the hearth, "is that I want him to see me looking pretty." The dog thumped her tail twice and went back to sleep. "You're no help," Jacey complained from the bottom of the clothespress, where she'd stowed the outfit.

She was stuffing her hair up under the floppy hat when someone scratched at her door. Good grief, what if it was her aunt home early, or Aunt Simone? She mustn't be seen in britches! She went to the door, but didn't open it. "Yes, what is it?"

"It's Eugene, ma'am. A parcel just came for you."

"Would you put it down by the door, please. I am not, ah, presentable. Thank you."

She cracked the door an inch and peered out. It would be just like that libertine to lurk in the hall to catch a glimpse of her *en déshabille*. Why Aunt Amabel kept such a creature was a mystery. She scooped up the paper-wrapped bundle and scurried

314

back inside her room.

It was a scarlet domino, a long, hooded cape that would conceal nearly every inch of her! He didn't forget! The note read *Ten o'clock*. It was already nine-thirty, drat the man, and she would *not* go in britches! Off they came and back to the closet. Out came one of her new gowns, a low-cut pink crêpe. She chose it because of its fuller skirts, besides its daring neckline, in case the side door was locked later and she had to climb up the tree to get back inside. She was pleased at how the gown swirled around her feet and clung to her hips when she moved, but she couldn't do up three of the tiny buttons at the top of the back! There was no time to change, and she still had to do something with her hair. She brushed it so fiercely it crackled, then hurriedly plaited it into one long braid she could pin into a circlet atop her head. She tied a matching pink bow around the knot, laced pink sandals on her feet, and donned a dark wool pelisse to cover the gown's gaping back—and therefore sagging front. She refolded the domino and held it against her body, under the pelisse.

"Come on, Pen. I know you'd rather spend the night here, but I need you as an excuse to leave the house. Don't worry, old girl, I won't be out all night."

Marcus and Eugene were both at the front door. To avoid having the footman delegated to accompany her, Jacelyn headed for the library, whose glass door opened to the courtyard.

"I'm just taking Pen out to the stable, Marcus. You can lock up the library when you wish. I'll come back through the kitchen to get some warm milk, and I'll most likely use the back stairwell. Good night."

"Good night, Miss Jacelyn. I hope you're feeling more the thing by morning."

"Thank you, Marcus. I know I shall. I'm feeling much better already."

Leigh's reasons for staying away were twofold. First, they both needed time to calm down after those angry words. He shouldn't have been so high-handed with her, and she shouldn't have said what she did. Second, his face didn't bear looking at. Not as gruesome as Percy's, Leigh's black eye gave him a raffish look, but it still declared he'd been in a fight. Leigh had chosen not to make explanations to the ton or to Jacey. In the closed carriage, with a black domino pulled low over his brow, the bruise was hardly noticeable. He wouldn't have to lie that his ragtag cousin had landed a lucky punch, nor tell the truth, that he'd been in a prizefight for the money.

When he was finished with Percy, two days ago, he still wasn't quit of his anger, so he visited Jackson's Boxing Parlour. Everyone there was talking of a promising young pugilist they'd seen working out that day. Even Jackson was impressed. Lord Alvanley was so confident, he wrote an open wager in the betting book, offering five-to-one odds to anyone challenging Treadway for a three-round match, Jackson to judge. Claibourne took the bet.

"Arthur, can you lend me a hundred pounds?"

"Are you sure, Leigh? You're good, but, fiend take it, man, Treadway's twenty-two. He's got ten years on you!"

"Ten years of practice, Arthur. The money?"

"Of course. No need to borrow it, in fact, it's yours. Remember that night at the Cocoa Tree, after the Victory Celebrations? I borrowed five hundred from you. Forgot all about it till now."

"Lord, I don't even remember going to the Cocoa Tree that night! Arthur, you're a prince. A little late, now that I've entered my name in the book, but a prince nonetheless. Give me two and hold the rest for me, will you?"

The fight had taken place Friday morning. The first and the second rounds were Claibourne's. His skill and finesse left the younger man dazed, punching air, and losing his footing. In the third round Treadway found his tempo and landed a few solid, punishing blows, but it was too late, as long as the earl could stand. A fourth round would have finished Claibourne, but the match was his. Now he had a black eye, a bandage holding his ribs together, and enough money to last a good long while, if he didn't make any more foolish desperation bets. He wouldn't. He'd much rather

317

spend the blunt on Jacelyn, making sure she enjoyed herself.

Like tonight, at Vauxhall, if she came. She shouldn't be there at all, certainly not alone with him, so Leigh had made plans for her safety, and more, which was why he was so late. He just couldn't move as fast as usual. Those ten years felt like twenty, today.

The hackney driver slid the call box open. " 'Ow much longer we goin' to wait, then, gov?"

"A few minutes more. She has to come."

"Its your silver, mister. 'Avey-cavey business though." He slid the little door shut with a snap.

Then she was there. He helped her into the seat opposite him and tapped on the coach roof with his cane for the driver to start.

Jacelyn was staring at him, her face filled with joy. "You came."

"I promised, sweetheart."

"I'm so sorry about that other day, Leigh. I didn't mean what I said. I don't care about—"

"Shh. I'm sorry too, kitten. I missed you."

"Oh, Leigh." She threw herself across the carriage into his arms. He almost fainted from the pain. A good soldier never complains though, so he just held her close while he caught his breath. In a minute she sat back, withdrew the domino, shaking it out onto the other seat. She started to undo the bow holding her pelisse closed, and made a silvery little laughing noise. "I had to let Pinkie have the evening off, Leigh, and I couldn't

318

do up all the buttons. Would you . . . ?"

"I recall volunteering to be your dresser once, didn't I? Come here, my wanton, so I can reach."

She took off the pelisse and made an effort to hold up her bodice while turning around, but even in the dim light from the lanterns on the coach doors, Leigh could see the creamy glow of her skin above the fabric. He had to catch his breath again. His ribs be damned. With her back to him, he folded her in his arms, his cheek against the softness of her neck. Then his lips moved to caress her shoulders, her ear, and his hands moved slowly over the material of her gown. Instead of doing up the top three buttons, he undid three more, until he could cup her breast in his hand and slowly stroke the nipple. Jacelyn moaned softly, calling his name. She turned to face him, and then she was lying in his arms, the gown at her waist, and he was kissing her heart while she grasped his neck and combed her fingers through his curls.

"Oh, Leigh," she whispered again, until his mouth was on hers and there was no more bumpy carriage or flickering street lights, only his kiss and his hands, waking her like Sleeping Beauty to his passion.

His hand was caressing her thigh, through the silky crêpe, and down her leg, drawing the skirt and petticoat up till he was touching bare skin and their breaths were more like gasps.

Snick. The sliding door opened. "By Jupiter, I knowed it! We're at Vauxhall, governor. D'you want me to pull up or should I just drive 'round a few times?"

Vauxhall was vastly different on Masquerade Night, from when the ton attended. There were more soldiers, and more girls in low white blouses with rouged cheeks. There were Pierrots and Elizabeths and Henrys. Cats and devils and nuns and nymphs. And a lot of hooded capes and half masks, like theirs. Not just the outfits differed; the outlook was more relaxed, noisier, jollier. These people didn't have every night of the week to eat, drink, and be merry. They had to do it all at once. At first Jacelyn was enjoying herself. The people seemed so happy, dancing with enthusiasm never seen at Almack's, cheering and singing, laughing out loud. Then, as she and Leigh meandered along the paths, she realized that most of the crowd was on the go. They all, men and women alike, had bottles and flasks and full glasses waving in their hands. Those who looked so companionable were often holding each other upright, and beneath the laughter and the music she could hear angry shouts, an occasional scream.

"I can see that you and Arthur were right, Leigh. This is no place for a lady." She moved closer to his side.

"Have you seen enough then? Shall we go?"

"After the fireworks, all right? I'd really like to see them."

320

"Of course, my sweet."

But not tonight. Just past the cascading fountain, near a huge oak tree, a roughly dressed man staggered out of an unlighted alley. He bumped into Jacey, and his hands were groping at her body. She pushed him away and turned to Leigh, but he was grappling with another man! The first, a thickset man with long, bristly sidewhiskers, saw her attention turned and grabbed for her reticule. Jacelyn pulled back, shouting, "Thief! Thief!" to which no one paid the least heed. The strings broke in her hand, and the man was headed down the alley. "Leigh! He's getting away."

Claibourne had dispatched his assailant while Jacey was diverted, and now raced after the thief. "Stop, you!" he shouted, and caught the man by the shoulder. He swung him around and connected his fist with the man's chin, it appeared to Jacey, from where she stood next to the tree. The man went down, and Claibourne retrieved her reticule. He hurried back to her, while the thief scuttled under the hedges.

"Oh, Leigh, how terrible! Are you all right? How can things like this happen?"

"It's all over, my dear, nothing to concern yourself about."

"How can you say that? You might have been killed! And if you weren't so quick and strong and brave, I might have . . . have been . . ."

"There, there," he told her, gathering her against his chest, patting her back, and smiling. His plan

321

was a success! His man Haggerty and Haggerty's friend Jack had played their parts just as they'd rehearsed. In one easy lesson he'd taught his madcap love never to come here on a lark, to listen when he warned her of danger, and that he'd lay his life on the line for her. Impressing her with his prowess was a bonus. He hadn't intended to dally in the Dark Walks, but she was clinging so trustingly, tightly—blast Treadway's right cross—and temptingly.

Someone pushed him from behind. "Haggerty, what the hell are you—" It wasn't Haggerty. Possibly it wasn't even a man. It had a little head with piggy eyes all red and squinty, and a huge body with oxlike muscles bulging under its clothes. In a hand the size of a coal scuttle, the creature held a knife. Oh Lord. "Haggerty!"

Leigh got in a quick jab. The attacker hardly felt it, but at least it showed Leigh he wasn't fast with the blade. He didn't have to be. Leigh couldn't disarm him, not without the cane he'd dropped for the first act. He surely couldn't overpower the beast, even if his ribs weren't broken, and he couldn't run—not leaving Jacelyn there.

"Jacey," he shouted, circling, crouching, never taking his eyes off the giant. "My cane!"

His cane? Jacelyn found it, but how to get it to him? Then those other men came running out of the bushes toward Leigh, the ones who'd assaulted them first. Attack the earl three-to-one, would they? That bear-man had a dagger too, so it was even more unfair! Jacelyn stepped into the fray, beating Haggerty and Jack with the cane before they could get to Leigh.

"Hold, miss, we're on your side," Haggerty yelled, shielding his head. "His lordship needs his cane!"

The other man, Jack, was indeed pounding on the giant's back. Not Leigh's, and not to any effect, but he was definitely coming to Claibourne's aid. She let the man Haggerty take the cane from her and toss it to the earl, still keeping his distance from that deadly blade. Now Leigh could act: feint, parry, thrust, counter. *Whack* with the cane and the dagger was in the leaves under the tree. The cane snapping was the last Jacey could see clearly, as the four men made one blurry pile of moving arms and legs.

Jack went down first, flying over the bushes to land with a thud. Haggerty was straddling the giant's back, whomping on his head like a berserk piggyback rider, while Claibourne was bruising his knuckles on the behemoth's midsection. Leigh didn't want to get in close, knowing that one jab to the ribs by the tree-trunk arm, and he'd be out for the count. Then Polyphemus growled and whirled, flinging Haggerty off his shoulders like a sack of cornmeal. Haggerty stayed down.

By now Jacelyn had found the dagger, again with no way to get it to Leigh, so she kicked it farther into the leaves. She also found a big branch fallen from the oak. She managed to give the man-mountain a good wallop on his arm, getting his attention, which finally allowed Leigh to connect with a scientific right that would have floored Mendosa. The colossus shook his head. He looked at Jacey with her stick, Claibourne with his right, and Haggerty on his feet again and coming, and shook his head once more. He gave Claibourne a shove, not even a punch, but a push in the chest that flattened Leigh, and then he took off into the alleys.

"Should I follow him, Major?"

"Not without reinforcements, Haggerty, like the entire Fifth Cavalry. Are you hurt? What about Jack?" The earl managed to drag himself to the tree where he could sit, propped up by the trunk and Jacey's arms. "You were valiant, my lady," he told her, gasping.

Jacey looked around: the dagger, the broken cane, the two thugs standing by on guard. "Leigh, I don't understand what's going on."

"Not surprising, dear heart. I haven't the foggiest idea myself."

"Can we please go home?"

"You didn't get to see the fireworks."

"They'll have to hold them in Portman Square. I'm never, ever coming back to Vauxhall!"

"Incompetents! I'm surrounded by idiotic, imbecilic incompetents!" Fenton raged. "Jensen, you mammoth mole-mind, you've been hanging around that fool Percy too long."

He scrawled a message on a piece of paper and shoved it into Jensen's hand. "Here, take this to the Red Lion in Cheapside. Ask for Newgate. That's what I should have done months ago, hire a professional. . . ."

"If this is another of your freakish schemes, Leigh Merrill, I am not amused!"

"Shut up, you peagoose, and get down! Those were real shots!"

He had a pistol in hand and was looking for something to aim at. There was no need to tell Lady Parkhurst to duck; she'd collapsed unconscious to the carriage floor at the first cry of "Stand and deliver." Luckily *Tante* Simone had decided she needn't come.

They were about a half hour outside of London, halfway to Hockney Hall, the duchess's country residence. Not the Farthingale family seat, it was just a huge pile where the duchess liked to entertain. They were already late when the message came from Lord Parkhurst, telling them to go ahead, he and Sprague might be hours more at their meeting. Because of the delay, there were few other carriages on the road this dark, moon-clouded night.

The carriage came to a lurching halt. Jacey could hear shouting, from Lem up on the box with the coachman, then another shot! The door was wrenched open, and a voice growled, "Out, all of ya, or yer coachie gets killed. Girl first."

Leigh nodded and Jacelyn got out, stepping over her aunt's limp body. A gun was pointed at her by a mounted man in a brown frieze coat, cagily positioned behind the door, out of Leigh's line of fire. The highwayman leaned down, grabbed her arm, and pulled her next to him. When Leigh came out, he had no chance to act. The one bandit held a gun to Jacelyn; the second, shorter, man was covering the servants on the box, having taken their weapons. The Parkhurst outrider was on the ground, but alive, moaning. His horse was halfway back to London.

"A'right, yer lordship, drop the popper, or I glom the skirt."

Leigh tossed the pistol and raised his hands. "There's no need for anyone to get hurt. You're welcome to whatever we have."

"Oh yeah? What if we wants the mort?"

Leigh charged him, Jacey screamed, the horse reared, a shot was fired and went wide. Leigh was grappling with the frieze-coated rider, trying to unseat him, when the other highwayman rode over and smashed the earl on the head with his pistol. Claibourne went down, hard, and didn't move.

"Leigh!" Jacelyn was on her knees beside him.

"Whyn't ya shoot him?" Frieze-coat demanded.

"The skirt was in the way. 'Sides, I got a better idea. 'Is Royal Navy'll pay pretty good for a able-bodied seaman, willin' or no. We kill him, we get

326

paid oncet. We dope him 'n ship him off, we gets it twice, and the old coot's none the wiser. Here, gimme a hand gettin' him up."

Frieze-coat dismounted, and together the bandits dragged Leigh across Shorty's horse's withers, face down, despite Jacey's screams, kicks, and flails.

"Should we see if the flash mort's got any baubles?"

"Nah, we got what we come for. Let's ride 'fore someone comes. You there"—to the coachman—"you keep your dubber's mum till we're out a'sight or yer fine gent gets it. Understand?" The two men took off, Leigh's head and feet bumping against the horse's sides. There was nothing for Jacelyn and the others to do but watch the bandits ride away through the dense forest along the side of the road.

"Oh, God, we've got to save him! Lem, cut the horses loose! Zack, go see to the outrider. Oh, Leigh!"

"We can't follow them through *that,* miss," Lem told her, "not in the dark, on carriage horses. And they took all of our weapons with them."

"I know, I know! Zack, how is he?"

"Bleedin', but it's just his shoulder, miss. His pistol's still here."

"Good. Listen, here's what we'll do: Lem, you take one horse and ride ahead to Lady Hockney's and tell them what happened. Get a search party, men, lanterns, guns. Zack, you'll stay here with the coach and the pistol. You guard the postillion

327

and my aunt, but don't try to wake her. She's better off in her faint! A coach should come along soon, I hope. I'll take the other horse and ride back to Town for help."

"But, miss, we can't even begin to track them until daybreak."

"*We* can't, but Pen can! Are you done with the knife?"

Lem was through cutting the traces of the lead coach horses. He finished and handed over the knife. Jacelyn gathered the hem of her gown in one hand and slashed it up the middle with the other. She repeated this with the back, then snatched his lordship's greatcoat off the coach seat and drew it around her. Lem led one of the horses to her, gave her a leg, and she was up, and away. "Hurry!" she yelled back.

"Get up, you lazy good-for-nothing mutt! Get up, Pen!" Jacey was pulling on her britches. The house was in an uproar around her. *Belle-tante* was for once *not* placid. She was wringing her hands and sending Marcus off to the Watch, to Bow Street, to the Magistrate, and the War Office!

"There's no time, Aunt! I've got to go now! Marcus, get a message to Lord Parkhurst. Tell him to get people to watch the ports and the press gangs. Tell him Henesley will follow me with the dog cart, but I can go faster on my gelding, and get through the woods, too. A pistol! Marcus, find my uncle's pistols—and load them!"

"Run, Pen, run. We're almost there, you can keep up!" The coach was up ahead; she could see its lanterns. She spurred the gelding on. "Zack, have they come?"

"No, miss. A carriage came by and took up milady and the outrider, on to Hockney with them. Help should be getting back here soon."

"I cannot wait! Henesley's behind me with fresh horses, but Pen will do better while the scent is fresh. I wish she weren't so out of shape! Here, girl, smell this. It's Leigh's greatcoat, Pen. Leigh. Here, his cane is still in the carriage. Leigh, Pen, find Leigh!"

The big dog was panting, her sides heaving, but she gamely followed Jacelyn's horse to the woods where Jacey thought the men had entered the forest. Yes, the branches were broken. "Here, Pen, please!"

The dog put her nose down and wuffled. She wagged her tail and whined—and she set off! "Good girl! Not so fast, it's dark. We have to watch out for low branches, Pen. We're coming. Good girl!"

Jacey lost her hat to the next trailing vine, and a twig scratched her face and caught in her hair, undoing all of Pinkie's efforts to send her to Hockney House an elegant lady. After five more minutes of this mad rush, all the pins were out, and Jacey had to keep brushing the hair away from her eyes just so she could see. Pen was slowing down, thank goodness. Unless, it suddenly, horribly, occurred to Jacey, the dog was tracking a rabbit all along!

No, there was a glow up ahead.

"Pen," she whispered, "to me, girl. Let's scout around first." Jacelyn dismounted and tied the horse to a bush. She could hear the dog's almost wheezing breaths, and patted her on the head. "You did fine, Pen. Shh, just a little closer." Her intentions, as she crept closer to the light from a small cottage's window, were to get a good look at the place, see where the horses were, count if there were more than the two highwaymen's mounts, etc. Then—and she wasn't decided yet—she could either try to find her way to the carriage and lead the rescuers back, if she didn't get lost and if the bandits didn't ride on, or she could stay where she was, waiting. The men had to move Leigh, if they were going to take him to a ship or something, and when they came outside for the horses, she could shoot. The shortcomings of this plan were that her aim wasn't terrific at this range, and she wasn't entirely sure she could pull the trigger on a real person. Both of her choices had a common drawback: the men could decide to kill Leigh at any time.

Jacey stopped while she was still in the trees' cover, about twenty yards from the house. She couldn't see any horses or hear any voices. There might be two men or twenty; she had no way of knowing. Five yards more and she let go of Pen's collar to take out the pistols. One was in her waistband, uncomfortably; the other was in the pocket of Claibourne's caped greatcoat, still buttoned around her. The pistols were not the light duelling weapons her father owned, but were heavy, double-barrelled guns. At least she had two shots to each, which ought to be enough for Frieze-coat and Shorty. She *had* to know if there were others. Maybe she could follow the forest line around back, where the horses must be. She moved slowly, stealthily, trying not to step on fallen branches—then Pen barked. The dog headed right for the front door, following orders to find Leigh.

Immediate tactical revision: attack!

Jacelyn started howling like a banshee, zigzagging, calling out to Arthur and Lem and Zack. Pen kept barking. Jacey fired a shot and called, "Over here, men. The dogs have them." Another shot. "Surround them, boys!" *Boom*. "Let's go in!" She was at the door with one shot left, and her army of rescuers was one loud, tired dog. Oh dear!

The kidnappers didn't know that, however. Frieze-coat and Shorty dived out the back door for their horses as Jacey crashed through the front and fired at a retreating figure. "Yeow!" came back to her, and she was satisfied. So much for scruples.

Pen was racing around the room, licking Leigh's face, coming back to Jacelyn, panting and whining. "Down, Pen, let me see."

Leigh was on a faded sofa, his head hanging over the back. "Leigh! Leigh, darling, wake up! Oh, Leigh, please!"

Her voice roused him. With an effort, he opened his eyes and smiled that sweet, lopsided grin. "Changed your hair style, did you, pet?"

"Leigh, you have to get up! We have to reload the guns in case they come back. Can you walk? Oh, Lord, don't go back to sleep! I know your head hurts, but help will come soon. Here!" She spotted a bottle of wine and a glass on the mantle and brought the glass to him. "Just the thing."

"No, Jacey, not that." He weakly brushed the glass away.

"Yes, Leigh, it'll set you right back up. Please, we have to leave. Oh God, what now?" Pen was howling. Was she hurt? Had one of the pistol balls ricocheted and hit her? Jacelyn hurriedly pushed Leigh's limp head back against the sofa and tipped the contents of the glass into his mouth.

"Thanks, sweetheart, I needed that," he told her, slurring the words. She was already on the floor near the fire, though, where Pen was whimpering and writhing. Leigh managed to pull himself up to see. "Pup . . . puppies."

"Puppies! *Now?* Pen, how could you? And I made you run so hard, poor baby. Leigh, what do

332

we do?"

"Do? You keep her in . . . inside during her season. Now . . . nothing to do but wait. The guns . . . I'll reload. Not much . . . not much time left for me."

"What do you mean? You're not going anywhere!"

"To sleep, Jay-bird. . . . You just poured half a bottle of lau . . . laudanum down my throat, remember?"

A few hours later Jacey was holding a pistol in one hand and a tiny brown and white puppy in the other. "You lightskirt, Pen. This could only be Jasper's get. Won't Squire be pleased?" There were six others nesting in the only quilt the place had, next to an exhausted Pen. The earl was draped across the sofa as comfortably as Jacey had been able to manoeuvre him, his greatcoat covering him. Jacelyn put more wood on the fire, and tried to stay awake.

The highwaymen hadn't come back; help mightn't locate them until morning. She couldn't go in search of the rescue party, not with the earl unable to defend himself or Pen. Even if she could lift or drag Claibourne to her gelding, Pen and her babies couldn't travel, so there was nothing for it but to wait. The cottage was dusty and smelled of mildew, and had no foodstuffs whatsoever. She was tired, hungry, dishevelled—but her

333

two best friends were safe!

Leigh woke up at first light, cramped and headachey and with a throat so dry he could barely swallow. Jacelyn was curled up in a chair, fast asleep, a pistol in her lap. He got up slowly and tucked the gun in his waistband. He sniffed the bottle on the mantel, then drank some of the wine. Poor quality, but not drugged, at least.

"Good morning, mama," he whispered to the dog. "I forgot all about you and your pups. Can I see them?" Pen wagged her tail, so he picked up a soft little wriggler making piggy noises. "Foxhound, eh? Well, they always say that where there's a will, there's a way. Good girl."

He made up the fire again, then lifted Jacelyn in his arms and carried her to the sofa. She stirred and mumbled "Leigh?"

"No, its Simple Simon. Go back to sleep." He cradled her in his lap, wrapping them both in his coat, and went back to sleep himself.

That was the way the rescuers, all twenty-odd of them, found them two hours later. Some of the saviours were liveried servants with ancient muskets. Some who had been searching the woods all night were still in their evening clothes. There were two soldiers and a few yeoman farmers, draughted, presumably, because they knew the countryside. There were Lem and Arthur and Farthingale and de Silva, all the other young men Jacelyn usually danced with. They were standing around in varying degrees and combinations of

334

astonishment, aggravation, and embarrassment at the cozy little scene. Jacelyn, in britches, hair tumbled down her back, was wiping her eyes in confusion while Leigh stood and drawled, "Congratulate me, gentlemen. Not only am I still alive, but I am already a proud papa." He held a puppy in each hand. "Oh, yes, Miss Trevaine and I will be announcing our betrothal next week at her aunt's ball."

19

"Damn your luck, you blue-blooded bastard."

20

"Jacelyn had dinner with the Regent last week," Lord Trevaine told his friend, over the chessboard.

"Did she, b'gad. What did she think of our Prince Florizel?" Squire asked, making his move.

"Not much. More to the point is what he thought of her. She took him to task for the opulence of Carlton House, when so many of the people are hungry, to say nothing of the condition of the animals in the Royal Menagerie."

"She didn't! On second thought, I'm sure she did just that. Lord, I'd like to have seen Prinny's face! What did he say?"

"According to Jacelyn's letter, he is going to visit the Menagerie with her, to see for himself."

"Claibourne better keep an eagle eye out. Our Prinny's been known for his appreciation of the, ah, finer things in life."

"Jacelyn didn't mention Claibourne. She wrote about seeing *Othello* and a new opera, and a picnic. Not a word about Claibourne. I received a letter from my sister today also. Hers was dated Saturday, three days after Jacelyn's."

"Can't trust the mails these days. What did Lady Parkhurst say?"

"She recrossed her lines so often I had trouble deciphering. As far as I can tell, she's in a swivet. Her servants said Jacelyn and Claibourne had some kind of row, and he hadn't been seen nor heard from since."

"I knew it was too good to last. That gal's too hot at hand. You should have — "

"Wait. I got another letter this afternoon, an express from Claibourne. That's why I asked you over. Where is it? Here, listen: 'Informing you I shall announce the betrothal at Lady Parkhurst's ball Saturday. Yours, Claibourne.' That's all. What do you think?"

"I think Miss Jacey's up to her usual bobbery! That girl's never done what anyone expected."

"I don't want to see her make a mistake and have to live with it for the rest of her life."

"Course not, but who's to say what's the right thing? Look at my nevvy, Arthur. Getting betrothed before talking to Spenborough. What if the Duke don't take to Arthur, and he cuts the girl out of his will? Arthur says he'll have her either way. These young people go around making life hard on themselves."

"Still, I wish I could go to London. This curst cough of mine, though . . ."

"We'll be going down, come Friday, the wife and

I and Samantha, for the party. There was no peace in the house till I agreed. I'll take a look-see for you, find what the rumgumtion is this time. You don't want to move there, man, leaves your queen open."

"Oh, sorry. My mind's just not on the game. Friday will be too late, George. By the time you get to London, you won't be able to stop the announcement."

"Stop it? It'll be the best thing for the gal! What she needs is someone to shake some sense into her!"

"The doctor says I mustn't travel, at least not until it is warm again."

"Quite right, you might take a chill. You know, Elliot, the fox season's nearly over. . . ."

"Is it? You know I don't pay attention to those things."

"The ground gets too hard. Dogs can't pick up the scent. The hunt wasn't so fine this year anyway."

"That's strange. I would have thought with Jacelyn gone . . ."

"I know. I thought so too, but, oddly enough, it wasn't the same. I'd ride out *knowing* nothing untoward would occur. Oh, Vicar might take a toss, or a horse might refuse at the wall at Kraft's farm, but it was dull! I even pulled the dogs back, when I could, letting Reynard go, by damn."

"Jacelyn would be happy to hear that."

"She would, wouldn't she? It's been quiet without her. Too quiet. Maybe I'll toddle off to Town early. Give m'womenfolk a treat, extra shopping and all that. It'll cost me, but dang, it's been dull here."

A treat? When their gowns weren't ready, the house wasn't in order, Lady Ponsonby couldn't be warned to expect her relatives three days early? Samantha was *aux anges,* but Squire's wife was not pleased, until Bottwick told her about Trevaine's three letters. They managed to reach London on Thursday, only one day early.

They were to call at Parkhurst House at eleven Friday morning, having heard conflicting reports from the Ponsonbys about kidnappings and such. Priscilla was in her usual high dudgeon, having decided that Farthingale would finally have come up to scratch at his mother's ball last Saturday, if not for Jacelyn's latest hobble.

Another imbroglio, eh? Squire thought along the way. Well, look how neatly he'd tied up the last. There was plenty of time to set Miss Trevaine right and reassure her father. See? There was Claibourne, standing right beside the girl to greet them. This should be easy as pie.

Five minutes later Squire was lost, heart, mind, and body. He forgot all about Jacelyn and her questionable engagement, all about his ailing friend's concerns, all about his waiting wife and daughter. No amount of pleading could pry him out of the kitchen, where Pen and her brood were star attractions.

"Settle your own hash," he told Jacelyn when she brought him tea at the servant's table. "You never listened to me anyhow. What do you think? The one with the white spot on his tail or this fellow here?"

It was up to Mrs. Bottwick and Samantha to make sense of Jacelyn's explanations.

"So you're going through with the betrothal because of the night at the cottage?"

"Yes, I see where we must, but Leigh says we still needn't marry."

"Don't you want to marry him, Jacey? He's *so* attractive," Samantha enthused.

"I know, you peagoose. I'm not blind, you know. And I do want to marry him, more than anything. But it wouldn't be right."

"But if you love him, dear, the other reasons, the cottage and all, are nothing to the point."

"I know that too, Mrs. Bottwick, but it's so confused. He never said he *wants* to marry me, only that we should be engaged. Now he doesn't even want me near him. He says we cannot ride in the park or go for carriage drives or anything, until he decides it's safe."

"Safe?"

"He thinks someone is trying to harm him, and the fool tells me not to worry! As though his telling me not to worry takes away the danger! How can I not worry when men attack him in the park with daggers and kidnap him on the King's highway? What kind of unthinking, uncaring, unloving man would tell me not to worry?"

"None, dearest. I think you'd better have him anyway, when all this is over."

"I think I intended to from the first. I just wanted to make the gudgeon love me!"

It was her ball and it was beautiful. Her friends were all enjoying themselves, even the guests Squire dragged one by one into the kitchen, giving the chef palpitations. Arthur and Leigh had managed to pry Squire away to White's for the afternoon, leaving Chef to his creative concentration. The resultant dinner had been a masterpiece.

Aunt Amabel was so relieved that her mother-in-law had decided not to attend that she relaxed and enjoyed the meal too, especially since Jacey had done all the work of organising the ball.

Jacey was proud of all her efforts, not just the superb dinner she and Chef had consulted over for days. The seating chart had taken almost as long, with equally satisfying results. Monsieur Blanc had been deep in conversation, between Aunt Simone and the musical Miss Montmorency; Squire was pleased to find Arthur's intended a gentle, quiet sort of girl who let a man eat in peace; Samantha had charmed both Mr. Sprague, who found her an intelligent listener, and Lord Tayson, who found her full of bubbly chatter, so he didn't have to strain to make conversation. Jacey couldn't imagine Squire complacent about the dandified Lord Tayson as son-in-law, but he was a likeable enough sort, and well connected. Carter Sprague was still Jacey's first choice for Samantha. They made a handsome couple, she noted, as they passed by together on the way to the ballroom.

Jacelyn was standing in the hallway, greeting the rest of the evening's guests with her aunt and uncle — and Claibourne. This made it official, then, even before the announcement Uncle would make at the first dance. Leigh looked so handsome she wanted to sit down and stare at him! What she didn't want was him kissing the hands of all those women whose mouths said congratulations, but whose eyes said they were still available, what was a little engagement, between sophisticated friends? She caught his eye and he winked at her. That was all right, then.

The last guests having arrived, Aunt Amabel led the way to the ballroom, which was decorated with the usual swagged greenery and pots of flowers. When Jacey decided to wear the cream gown from Ryefield, with its bodice embroidered with butterflies, she also thought of adding silk butterflies to the decor, as a novelty. Now the multicoloured creatures seemed to hover over the flowers, on gold threads, and flit among the greens. With all their airy shimmer they seemed to epitomise the evening for Jacey: bright, insubstantial beings dancing their courtship rituals till the end of their short seasons. Don't let her love be as ephemeral, she prayed, as hard to hold and to keep. She squeezed Leigh's hand, and he brought hers to his lips, just as Lord Parkhurst made the announcement. Everyone applauded. She and Leigh walked to the centre of the room to begin the first waltz while they all watched.

Butterflies on the walls, butterflies on her gown, and butterflies in her stomach. Tonight she was going to ask Leigh, once and for all, if he could love her, if not now, then some day. Otherwise . . .

"Smile, dear heart, these are all your friends."

"I know, Leigh, it's just that—"

"Shh, pet, we'll talk later, when there aren't two hundred people watching. Just think, now that we are officially engaged, we'll be permitted ten minutes or so alone. Perhaps we could disappear after supper without causing an uproar. I still haven't presented the Claibourne diamond to you."

"I don't know where we could find any privacy! There are card tables in the east parlour, Monsieur will be playing pianoforte in the west, with Lord Milbrooke, if I'm not mistaken, and Squire Bottwick has decided Pen would do better in the library."

"I'll wager the petty despot in the kitchen tossed him out. Don't I see lanterns in the courtyard?"

"Yes, but it's cool out there."

He swung her in a twirling flourish to end the

dance. "Don't worry," he whispered in her ear, "I'll keep you warm."

After the waltz came the congratulations and well-wishes, Aunt Amabel's tears, and *Tante* Simone's contented *bien,* before she left for the music room. Arthur and Rhodine teased about who would be wed first, and Samantha just hugged her. Even Priscilla was magnanimous, now that Jacelyn was no longer a threat.

Squire's words, though, affected Jacelyn the most. He led her aside, on a stroll to the library, in fact, and took a small suede pouch from his pocket.

"Your father asked me to give you this tonight, but it, ah, slipped my mind until now. It was your mother's. He sent a message too, said to tell you he hopes you'll be as happy as he and your mother were, but that your joy should last forever."

There were tears in Jacey's eyes as she opened the drawstring. Inside was a simple gold heart on a chain. The inscription read *With all my heart, for all time.*

Jacelyn undid the topaz necklace she was wearing and slipped it into her uncle's desk drawer. She asked Squire to clasp the locket for her, which he did with trembling hands.

"We haven't always seen eye to eye, Jacey, and you're not what I'd want my girls to be, but damn, I'm as proud of you as if you were my own, as proud as your father would be, if he saw

345

you here. I had my doubts, I'll admit it now, that you could play the lady or fix Claibourne's interests. You proved me wrong, lass, and I'm glad. He's a fine man, Claibourne is, and . . . and if he doesn't make you happy, you tell him he's got me to answer to."

Squire patted her back awkwardly while she wept on his shoulder.

"There, girl, you don't want to go all splotchy for your own ball," he said, sniffling himself. "Come see, I think the lads have grown an inch since noontime."

By supper, Jacey's hand ached from being shaken, her face hurt from smiling. It was a relief to sit down to lobster patties and champagne, even more of a pleasure to leave all the music and laughter behind as she followed Leigh into the library. Squire was helping Farthingale choose a pup while Priscilla tapped her foot in impatient aggravation. Farthingale should be out under the stars proposing to her, not picking names for dogs! Leigh and Jacey smiled at each other as they walked out the open library doors to the courtyard.

Leigh took off his jacket and draped it over her shoulders.

"Now you'll be cold," she protested.

"So come warm me." So she did, walking into his embrace as naturally as breathing.

346

"But, Leigh, we have to talk," she told him a few minutes later.

"Indeed, it's not proper to kiss a woman without putting a ring on her finger." He fumbled in the inside chest pockets, next to *her* chest, longer than strictly necessary, but Jacey wasn't complaining. He finally retrieved a tiny box. They walked until they were directly beneath one of the lanterns, before he opened the lid.

"Oh Leigh, it's beautiful. It really is. I was afraid it would look like one of Flora's investments, from what you said."

"Will you wear it for me, then? Not just for tonight, or for appearance's sake?"

"You mean forever? And really get married?"

"Don't sound so surprised, dewdrop. That's what an engagement ring is for, isn't it?"

"Of course it is, but we have to talk more about this."

"Talk, precious, I'm listening." But he wasn't, really. He was leading her away from the lantern's light and nuzzling at her neck.

"This is serious, Leigh. I have to know if you—"

"*Boom!* Something flared between them, and it wasn't any spark of desire. It hit the wall and sprayed concrete shards. Leigh yelled "Down!" and pushed her flat to the ground, covering her body with his. There was another explosion, then pandemonium. Priscilla shrieked, and Farthingale shouted for help. People were running outside with

347

candles, others were panicking in the ballroom. Pen was barking. The grooms were pouring out of the stable, shouting, "We're under attack! They're trying to assassinate the Prince!"

Arthur came running, yelling, "Leigh? Are you all right? Is Jacey with you? Was it another attempt on your life?"

And Squire roared, "Are the pups safe?"

The earl was helping Jacelyn to her feet. Her face was smudged and her skirt was torn, and she was trembling.

"Don't you *dare* tell me not to worry, Leigh Merrill!" She stood there, shaking her fist at him.

"Damn, woman, at least get inside where it's safe to do your fussing!"

"Don't you talk to me that way! I told you to go to the magistrate's. I said hire a Bow Street Runner, and you said you'd handle it! *This* is how you handled it?" She swept her arm out, now they were back inside. The guests were frantically taking their leave; even the orchestra was packing. Whistles were blowing up and down the street as the Watch was called. Aunt Amabel was being carried upstairs, and Aunt Simone had streams of tears down her wrinkled cheeks. The chef was running after the departees, crying in French about his dessert *extraordinaire*. Arthur was trying to direct the carriages, getting in Marcus's way, and Lord Parkhurst and Mr. Sprague were in conversation with two men in uniform, discussing round-the-clock guards.

Squire stopped by Jacelyn and Leigh on his way out, herding his wife and a white-faced Samantha. "I knew it," he said. "I knew you wouldn't get through a whole night as a lady without at least one ruckus, riot, or rowdydow."

21

"What do you mean, you know Percy's not involved with the attacks?"

It was late afternoon of the next day, Sunday, and the first Jacelyn had seen of Claibourne since the shooting incident. He'd been holding his own investigation, while she'd been to church, then tea at the Ponsonbys' with Mrs. Bottwick and Samantha. She'd also made a few other calls. Leigh now adjusted the tassel on his Hessians. "I, ah, was not aware you knew my cousin."

Oops. "I happened to make his acquaintance one day. So when all of this happened"—she waved her hand—"I thought he might have knowledge of the matter. He didn't. You know, he's not half as awful as you said; he's just a trifle peculiar."

"If Percy's just a trifle peculiar, Prinny's just a trifle overweight. Jacelyn, pet, I am not sure I wish to know, but it does occur to me that Percy's been deuced few places recently. You mightn't have spoken to him—by chance, of course—at Flora Cobb's?"

"Now that you mention it, wasn't that a strange coincidence? There I was, visiting my old nurse in Islington and who should live next door—"

"Jacelyn!"

"It doesn't matter! Flora's very nice, and her looking out for Percy is precisely what he needs. He wasn't the least on the go, I don't think."

"It's hard to tell with Percy, isn't it?"

"Leigh, be kind. They're both concerned over you, and want to help. So do I!"

"No. I told you I don't want you anywhere near me, except here, of course, in my arms."

She pulled away. "What, for an hour? Then you are going back on the street by yourself? That's the most chuckle-headed notion of all."

"I explained, puss, I'm not alone. Arthur will meet me here, and my man Haggerty is right outside. He'll walk ahead of us, scouting. His friend Jack from Vauxhall will trail after, to see if anyone follows."

"But that still leaves you exposed to whatever madman is hiding in an alley or doorway. Why can't you just have Fenton arrested?"

"Because there is no proof that he's done anything. You cannot charge a man with hating you. This is the only way, baiting the hired killer into a trap, then snabbling him. He'll name his employer, rather than hang, and there, it's all over. Otherwise we'll never be safe."

"I don't like it." She stamped her foot.

"I'm not thrilled myself, dear heart, but it's the only way. Let me tell you something else that wouldn't thrill me: finding your perfect little nose in the business. You didn't listen to me about Percy, and you didn't listen to me about Flo. You *shall* listen to me now. If I find you out there in your britches, or tagging along with your uncle's pistols, or putting yourself in any kind of danger, you'll wish that bullet last night hadn't missed. Understand?"

"Yes, Leigh, but how am I to know you are all right? You cannot expect me to sit with my knitting while you're providing target practice for a paid assassin!"

"Can you knit?" He kissed her and stepped back quickly, before he was tempted to stay. "Don't worry, I'll send messages."

The messages came regularly, a boy with a rose at six, a book of poetry at seven. Leigh, looking like he was actually enjoying himself, and Arthur, just looking weary, arrived in person at nine, to share tea and reassure the family. They were going back to Half Moon Street, in case anyone was waiting for Leigh at his lodgings, and then onto the clubs. Squire was going along with them, and Lord Parkhurst and Mr. Sprague thought they too might pop into White's, Watier's, or Crockford's. Claibourne smiled but told them he was trying to look vulnerable, which was hard to do amid a phalanx of armed defenders.

"I'll wait up till I know you are home safe," Jacelyn warned as she walked him to the door. Marcus pretended he was another piece of furniture as they shared a hurried embrace.

"It won't be much past one or two. We cannot stay inside; that would be a waste of time. I think the attack, if there's to be one today at all, will be waiting outside Half Moon Street when we get home. I'll send a messenger over, when we're all tucked in bed. Just think," he teased, "if we were married you could be waiting there for me, in something soft and lacy. I'd come home at eleven."

"If we were married, my lord, you wouldn't be going out without me!"

"Oh-ho, is that the way it's to be, under the cat's paw? We'll have to see about that."

"We haven't even seen if there's to be a wedding!"

"We never did finish that conversation, did we?" Arthur coughed, over by the door. "Right. It will all be academic anyway, if there's no bridegroom. Rest easy, rosebud, everything will work for the best."

The message didn't come at eleven, or twelve, or one. Jacelyn was in bed, reading, when it finally came at two. *Home safe,* it read. *Sweet dreams, sweetheart.* She tucked the note in the book and blew out the candle. Now she could unclench her muscles and relax. If that message hadn't come soon she was all prepared to climb down the tree and go to the earl's lodgings herself, no matter what he'd threatened.

The tree. Were there trees at Half Moon Street? Leigh and Arthur rented the second floor. What was to stop someone from climbing up and shooting Claibourne through the window while he slept? He thought he'd be safe in his bed, and most likely had no guards outside the house. Someone could even break in and strangle him, without waking Arthur. Or they could put poison mushrooms in the pantry. Anything could happen!

This time she took Lem. She knew he was awake; he'd brought the message up from the stable. She needed him to help watch the back entrance while she took the front. Besides, if his lordship found her, he'd be less likely to beat her in front of witnesses. Leigh's warnings didn't give her pause, beyond that. If she was willing to risk her life for his, it was her own decision to make, not Leigh's. Of course, he still didn't know how little her life meant to her, without him. . . .

Jacey and Lem separated at the house, each taking one of the pistols and tiptoeing to a sheltered hiding place, to watch. There *was* a tree, and no one keeping lookout. Good thing she came! She pulled herself into the shrubs to the right of the doorway and crouched down, trying to make herself comfortable, but not enough to fall asleep. The Watch went by, then nothing. No bird sounds, no carriage wheels, nothing. And then a sneeze.

354

The noise came from the opposite row of hedges. A cat? No cat sneezed so loudly. It had to be the attacker, or a guard Leigh had set out after all. There was only one way to find out. Jacey stood, pointed her pistol, and called, "Halt. Who goes there?"

Instead of calling back that he was a lookout, the lurker panicked and bolted for the street, so Jacey shot him. She heard the man cry out—then yell for Flo! Oh God, she'd shot Percy!

Jacey ran over. "Percy, it's me, Jacelyn! Did I hurt you? What were you doing here? I thought you were the gunman!"

Percy was holding his arm. Jacelyn undid her loose neckcloth to wrap around it. "I knew they'd hang me if anything happened to Claibourne," he said, "so I came to protect him." Jacey threw her arms around him.

Claibourne, meanwhile, came flying down the stairs while lights went on all over. He was barefooted and bare-chested, but had a pistol in his hand. He saw Jacelyn struggling with a man, so he hit the assailant over the head with the gun barrel. The man folded like a house of cards. Jacey screamed.

"Whatsit? Whatsit?" Arthur was yelling, in his long white nightshirt and tasselled bedcap. He was waving a sabre around.

"It's Percy! He came to save Claibourne, and I shot him, then Leigh bashed in his head. Poor Percy!"

355

"Haggerty," Claibourne shouted. "Come help get this cawker inside, and send someone for the surgeon. I suppose I'd better send for Flora too."

"Lem can go. Where is he? He should be right here, with all the yelling and shooting. Lem?"

Then they all heard what they'd missed over the other confusion, the sounds of a scuffle at the rear of the house.

They all ran back, Arthur flapping like a ghost, Leigh, Haggerty, Jack, and Jacelyn with her one remaining shot—leaving poor Percy flat on the sidewalk.

Lem was struggling with a man who was a lot larger than himself, but the second man, Shorty, had already emptied two cans of alcohol and was setting the house on fire!

Haggerty tackled the torchbearer, and the earl came to Lem's aid, shouting, "Don't kill him, Haggerty. Someone run for the fire brigade!" He pounded his fist into Frieze-coat's face, then again for good measure. He pushed the now-limp figure toward Arthur. "Find some rope and keep them safe. I'm going to make sure Mrs. Dawe from upstairs is out. She's hard of hearing." He went into the house, through the flames.

Jacey was in the way of Lem and Jack with the well buckets, so she raced around to the front of the house to make sure Percy didn't get stepped on by all the people running around. An old woman with a shawl over her nightgown grabbed her arm. "My kitty's in there, lad. My poor, poor kitty."

356

"Where?" Jacey asked, but the woman just kept crying about her poor kitty.

Leigh wouldn't even know to look for a cat! The front of the house wasn't touched by flames so, without hesitating, Jacelyn tore up the stairs, and up to the third floor. It was smokey here. She couldn't see well, and was coughing, but she got down on her hands and knees to look under the sofa. No cat. She scrambled along till she found the bedroom—and Leigh's boots.

"What the hell?" He tugged her upright. "By all that's holy, girl, don't you have any sense?"

"Mrs. Dawe's cat!" she gasped, from the smoke and her arm being yanked nearly from its socket.

"Damn!" He let go of her and looked around. "We'll never find a blasted cat!"

"Stop yelling and help me. He's under your side of the bed." Jacey couldn't quite reach. Claibourne got down on the floor and grabbed the animal—and got bitten for thanks.

"Is Mrs. Dawe outside?" he asked, shoving the cat at Jacey who at least had on a jacket. There were claw marks across Leigh's bare chest. "Then you and the deuced cat get the hell out of here. I'll see about the fire downstairs." He gave her a not so gentle swat. "And listen to me for once!"

Jacelyn waited till the fire was out, and Flora'd come in a hackney to take Percy home, and Leigh was talking to the magistrates. When it appeared that the earl, dressed now, might have time to remember her presence, she called to Lem.

357

"We're not needed any longer, Lem. We better go home."

"That is the only clever thing you've done all night," Leigh called out, his arms crossed over his open jacket. "I'll be finished with these men in five minutes. If I see hide or hair of you when I'm done . . ."

"Good night, my lord!"

"You mean you're just going to let him go free?" Jacelyn wanted to know the next morning, walking in the courtyard.

"What would you have me do? Plant him a facer or have him sent to Botany Bay? He's a sick old man in a wheelchair."

"But all those terrible things he did! It doesn't seem right he shouldn't be punished."

"Whatever happened to that sweet little girl who wanted to save every fallen sparrow? You've shot at least two men this week, that I know of."

"At least I didn't brain my own cousin twice."

"Only because you don't have a cousin. Fenton will be punished enough, knowing he failed. He's lost Percy, besides, for what that's worth. Percy and Flo are emigrating to the colonies."

"I know. Percy wants to go into government."

"Good grief! And how do you know that, miss?"

"Flora sent 'round a note, telling me that Percy was doing fine, and wasn't mad at us for what happened to him."

Claibourne started to exclaim, "Mad at *us?*" but Jacey hurriedly put in: "Percy is better off abroad, but I still think Fenton is getting off too easily. What about Mrs. Dawe's cat? Fenton didn't care how many people he hurt, besides you."

"Thank you, my dear," Claibourne said dryly, "for considering my life as valuable as the cat's. The actual criminals, the ones Fenton was paying, will go to prison. They have confessed, and named Fenton, so he is just as guilty. The magistrates and I have offered to keep him on parole, since he never leaves his house anyway. He knows, however, that if there is the slightest hint of trouble, his gargantuan Jensen goes to gaol too. He'd be lost without the man. Beyond that, if anything whatsoever *ever* happens to you, or me, or our families, Fenton hangs, wheelchair or no. He's sworn *pax*, and I am tempted to believe him."

He led Jacey to a stone bench. "Enough of Fenton and Percy and the magistrates. It's time for another reckoning, Miss Trevaine. What the devil were you doing there last night?"

"Saving your life. Again."

"Oh." Claibourne abruptly sat down next to her. "Did I thank you?"

"No, you didn't. You threatened and yelled and sent me home like a schoolboy caught putting worms in teacher's desk."

"You know, I hadn't quite seen it from that perspective. From where I was standing, it looked a great deal as if you were endangering your life and your reputation, despite my orders to the contrary. You don't make a good soldier, pet."

Jacey giggled. "Too bad, now you can't have me court-martialled."

Claibourne was serious. "Indeed. So what am I supposed to do with you?"

Jacelyn took a deep breath and spouted: "You could tell me you love me, for a start." There, she'd said it!

Claibourne raised an eyebrow. "I could? I've been thinking about this a lot, Jacelyn"—and about time, she thought, but didn't say it—"and I think perhaps you were right all along, we don't really need to marry."

"*What?*"

"I know it's an about-face, but it's for the best. You should have someone younger, not an old officer like me who'll be forever telling you what to do, and getting angry when you do the opposite. You should have lots of Seasons, beaux, and balls. You deserve someone who doesn't drag around a parcel of dirty-dish relations like the clanking chains on a castle haunt. And you need someone you can trust, not someone with such a spotted past that you'll always wonder."

"What do you need, my lord?" Jacey asked quietly.

"I need to return to Durham. I should have been there ages ago, to see to the land myself. And I need to know I can support my wife, without living off her income. The money would always come between us, Jacelyn."

"No, Leigh—"

"Shh, let me finish. You say it doesn't matter, but it does. You wouldn't respect me, and I would resent being in your debt."

Jacey's eyes were wet. Leigh couldn't see because his back was turned. "It's because of my distempered freaks and silly scrapes," she decided.

"Never, Jacey," he said, turning and taking her limp hands in his. "All of that is just part of your bright honesty, your goodheartedness. You mustn't ever change. You're like a rose. The thorns are there, certainly, but oh, how sweet the blossom." His voice was breaking. He stood and walked away.

"I . . . I'll be leaving after dinner, I think. It will be easier all around. I've spoken with my aunt. She'll stay on in London with her French friends for a while.

"You should send a retraction to the newspapers when you return to Treverly. By spring everyone will have forgotten all about the engagement. Will you make my farewells to Lady Parkhurst?"

Jacey couldn't talk, for the lump in her throat. She just nodded, eyes down. He came closer and kissed the top of her head. "I only want what's best for you, Jacelyn. I'm not it."

And he walked away.

Jacey cried for an hour, out in the courtyard, then she got mad. The concrete benches fought back so she went inside and attacked a row of china shepherdesses on Aunt's mantel. Then she found Pen and cried some more, hugging each of the pups in turn.

There wasn't a soul, from the scullery maid to the Squire, playing three-handed whist with Lord Parkhurst and Mr. Sprague in the parlour, who didn't know that Lord Claibourne was gone, and Miss wasn't half pleased. Aunt Amabel locked herself in her bedroom. Lord Parkhurst and Mr. Sprague shrugged helplessly. Squire waited until he could hear Jacelyn's footsteps trail up the stairs before he went into the library to help Pen wipe her sodden puppies.

Jacelyn was spread-eagled on her bed, damp, drained, devastated.

Tante Simone passed Pinkie, weeping on a chair in the hall outside, and scratched on Jacey's door. *"Petite,* may I enter?"

"Entrez-vous, madame."

The old woman, dressed in black as always, sat at the foot of Jacelyn's bed. "He is gone?"

"Yes."

"And he told you why?"

"He gave me a barrelful of reasons. The sense of it would fit in a thimble. He doesn't love me."

"Non, cherie, he loves you a great deal."

362

"Aunt Simone, he wouldn't leave if he loved me."

"He leaves *because* he loves you."

"I don't understand."

"How could you? He is only a foolish man, trying to be noble. Logic and reason have nothing to do with a man's pride, child."

"Then you think he really does love me?"

"I know it. He told me."

One half hour later Jacey was in the library, wearing Lem's britches and jacket, her uncle's pistol in the waistband, unloaded, her streaming hair held back with a ribbon. She'd never replaced the hat, and she didn't care. Lord Parkhurst had turned craven and disappeared to his club. "Private affair, I'm sure," Sprague had mumbled, bowing himself out. Squire appeared not to notice her odd ensemble as he continued his hand of solitaire.

"I'm not going to let him just ride off without a by-your-leave! It's my life he's ruining too, for the most hare-brained reasons I've ever heard. Arthur could reason better than that. Pen could reason better than that!"

Squire turned over a red three. He needed a black three or a red four. "Damn."

"And I am going to ride through the streets of London just like this so he sees I don't care what anybody else thinks of me. It makes no difference if I'm ruined, if he won't come back with me."

The red four. "Ah!"

"Did you hear me? I'm going after him."

"What's that you say, m'dear? I wasn't attending."

"I said I'm going after him!" she shouted.

"Of course you are. I'd be shocked if you weren't."

"You would? But . . . but . . . ?"

"You're still Jacelyn Trevaine, ain't you? Never did the conventional thing in your life, nor let anyone hold the bridle for you. I don't figure you to start now."

"Then you approve?"

"You never paid that any mind before, either. There's just one thing you should know, missy. If you go off like that, you better be prepared to marry him. I sent your uncle out for a special license and a vicar. There's been enough of this harum-scarum engagement. You understand?"

"Stand and deliver," came the command from the bandit up ahead.

"What the blazes?" Haggerty was on the box; his lordship was inside, sleeping after being up all night. Baron trotted along behind.

Haggerty peered and pondered. This was the strangest holdup he'd ever seen. Broad daylight, the gun wasn't even drawn, and the highwayman's face mask was a paisley scarf. He grinned and pulled up.

Jacey rode over and dismounted, taking the pistol out of her waistband. She entered the coach and aimed it directly at the earl, who had woken at the carriage's change of tempo.

Claibourne was not amused. "You little fool! I suppose you rode through Town like that, too, after all we've done to protect your deuced reputation. We settled it all this afternoon, Jacelyn. Your dramatics won't change anything, so what the hell is this about? And if that damned pistol is loaded, I'll put you over my knee right now. If it isn't, and you rode out here alone and unprotected, I'll use the carriage whip!"

Jacey ignored the last, saying, "This, my lord, is a kidnapping. We settled nothing this afternoon, and now we are reopening negotiations. I am holding you for ransom."

Claibourne laughed bitterly. "Wasn't this where I came in? Jacey, that's the whole point. I haven't enough money to buy farm seed, much less my freedom. You've made a bad bargain, my dear. There *is* no ransom money."

"Then I'll just have to keep you."

He took her firmly by the shoulders. "Listen, dearest, I'll try to explain again."

"No, Leigh, I only want you to answer one question. Do you love me?"

"More than I've ever loved anything in this world. That's why—"

"Shush. Here, take this." She put the gun in his hand, pointed it at herself, and whispered, "Help!

365

Help! I am being held prisoner!" She took a cheque out of her pocket and handed it to him, as he sat there, grinning foolishly.

"It's blank," he said, putting the gun down and drawing her onto his lap.

"Of course it is," she told him. "You've just captured me, my lord, for all time, and you can demand everything I own." As she turned her face up for his kiss, she added, "You already own my heart."

For all time.

REGENCIES BY JANICE BENNETT

TANGLED WEB   (2281, $3.95)

Miss Celia Marcombe's dark eyes flashed with righteous indignation. She was not a commodity to be traded or bartered to a man
as insufferably arrogant as Trevor Ryde, despite what her high-
handed grandfather decreed! If Lord Ryde thought she would let
herself be married for any reason other than true love, he was
sadly mistaken. He'd never get his hands on her fortune—let
alone her person—no matter how disturbingly handsome he
was . . .

MIDNIGHT MASQUE   (2512, $3.95)

It was nothing unusual for Lady Ashton to transport government
documents to her father from the Home Office. But on this particular afternoon a gust of wind scattered the papers, and suddenly an important page was lost. A document desperately
wanted by more than one determined gentleman—one of whom
would murder to get his way . . .

AN INTRIGUING DESIRE   (2579, $3.95)

The British secret agent, Charles Marcombe, had done his bit
against that blasted Bonaparte. Now it was time to nurse his
wounds and come to terms with the fact that that part of his life
was over. He certainly did not need the likes of Mademoiselle
Therese de Bourgerre darkening his door, warning of dire emer-
gencies and dread consequences, forcing him to remember things
best forgotten. She was a delightful minx, to be sure, but it would
take more than a pair of pleading emerald eyes and a woebegone
smile to drag him back into the fray!

GOTHICS A LA MOOR — FROM ZEBRA

ISLAND OF LOST RUBIES
by Patricia Werner   (2603, $3.95)
Heartbroken by her father's death and the loss of her great love, Eileen
returns to her island home to claim her inheritance. But eerie things begin
happening the minute she steps off the boat, and it isn't long before
Eileen realizes that there's no escape from *THE ISLAND OF LOST RU-
BIES.*

DARK CRIES OF GRAY OAKS
by Lee Karr   (2736, $3.95)
When orphaned Brianna Anderson was offered a job as companion to the
mentally ill seventeen-year-old girl, Cassie, she was grateful for the non-
troublesome employment. Soon she began to wonder why the girl's family
insisted that Cassie be given hydro-electrical therapy and increased doses
of laudanum. What was the shocking secret that Cassie held in her dark
tormented mind? And was she herself in danger?

CRYSTAL SHADOWS
by Michele Y. Thomas   (2819, $3.95)
When Teresa Hawthorne accepted a post as tutor to the wealthy Curtis
family, she didn't believe the scandal surrounding them would be any concern of hers. However, it soon began to seem as if someone was trying to
ruin the Curtises and Theresa was becoming the unwitting target of a
deadly conspiracy . . .

CASTLE OF CRUSHED SHAMROCKS
by Lee Carr   (2843, $3.95)
Penniless and alone, eighteen-year-old Aileen O'Conner traveled to the
coast of Ireland to be recognized as daughter and heir to Lord Edwin
Lynhurst. Upon her arrival, she was horrified to find her long lost father
had been murdered. And slowly, the extent of the danger dawned upon
her: her father's killer was still at large. And her name was next on the
list.

BRIDE OF HATFIELD CASTLE
by Beverly G. Warren   (2517, $3.95)
Left a widow on her wedding night and the sole inheritor of Hatfield's
fortune, Eden Lane was convinced that someone wanted her out of the
castle, preferably dead. Her failing health, the whispering voices of death,
and the phantoms who roamed the keep were driving her mad. And although she came to the castle as a bride, she needed to discover who was
trying to kill her, or leave as a corpse!

*Available wherever paperbacks are sold, or order direct from the
Publisher. Send cover price plus 50¢ per copy for mailing and
handling to Zebra Books, Dept. 2850, 475 Park Avenue South,
New York, N.Y. 10016. Residents of New York, New Jersey and
Pennsylvania must include sales tax. DO NOT SEND CASH.*